MAISON LEGACY:

Cari Chesterfield
& 3X the Charm
BOOK III

SHARON
ELIZABETH
SARKISIAN

Maison Legacy:
Cari Chesterfield and 3X the Charm BOOK III
All Rights Reserved.
Copyright © 2013 Sharon Elizabeth Sarkisian
v4.0

ISBN: 978-0-9860202-0-9

PRINTED IN THE UNITED STATES OF AMERICA

*X*X*X*DEDICATION*X*X*X*

TO   Hagop and Nuver Kasakian, my grandparents:

WHO   took us in and gave us a home when we needed one,

WHO   supported us,

WHO   loved us,

AND,

WHO   did not deprive us of our LEGACY.

--ALSO--

TO   Hagop Kasakian and Dr. Stephen G. Svajian, my great-uncle, who were instrumental in various matters pertaining to the early funding and administration of the St. Vartan Armenian Cathedral at 630 Second Avenue in New York City. Dr. Stephen G. Svajian was associated with locating the site for the St. Vartan Armenian Cathedral and for the St. Gregory the Illuminator Church, the sale of which he tried to prevent.

--ALSO--

TO   Jack Skylark Castle, my own Charmer, who my mother wished to name Scaramuche, but I just called ♫ ♪My Sweetheart From Him-a-lay-a♪♫.

Cari Chesterfield's invitation to a mundane housewarming yields more than she bargained for in terms of excitement. Kidnapping, a hunt for gold - soon turning into a hunt for diamonds, arson.... They are all interwoven throughout this maze of a pair of secretive, old historical mansions. Past discoveries coalesce with present ones to culminate in the resolution of a past mystery regarding an attempted murder. A healthy dose of zesty competition for Cari's affections factors into this web of intrigue to salt and pepper the ongoing tale.

NIGHTMARE

How dare he displace the murky curtain of my somnolence -
somber robes and frilly collar, lace cascading down his
vest,

His zealous flights and bloodshot, crimson lights affording
me no rest,

Sowing seeds of doubt which make me shout and cringe in
fits of fright,

To bolt upright, and stare outright - out, into the night?

PREFACE

Twirling downward. Swirling down a tunnel of whirling oblivion. A bottomless pit. WHAT HO! Impact with a thump! Crowded into a dark enclosure. Jostling for position with many, many - a multitude of - others.

It was a long journey. A lot of twists and turns and involuntary pushes in various directions until finally reaching a destination preordained the harbinger missive delivers its screaming message of finality.

Longing for blissful release. Shouts of elucidating announcements and pronouncements are unnecessary where a quiet release is all that is needed.

Separation from the clump of a clamoring group, singled out from the multitude yet seldom appreciated wisdom emanates. Ripping liberation is all that is needed to relieve the illuminating and enlightening message pressure. A quest. The QUEST!!!

It begs the question: Who am I? Ultimately, secrets are revealed.

CHAPTER 1

"I won't go. I won't go. I will not go! Je refuse. There is absolument no way, ne façon, you can make me!" Pierre Dûçot insisted adamantly.

"Oh, darling, be reasonable. They are our friends, for goodness sake!" his wife exclaimed with exasperated fervor.

"<u>Vos</u> amis, peut-être, Edi. <u>NOT</u> mine!" he declared with an air of finality folding his arms stubbornly, thrusting forth his chin and assuming a more erect stance.

Carina and Randmore McKinley exchanged looks of frustration mingled with semi-distaste as what had begun merely as a friendly visit to her Aunt Edith Chesterfield Norden Dûçot's ('Try saying that name three times fast!' Cari had often joked to Randy) home, Chesterhollow, turned into a tug-of-war. Lying abandoned and forlornly unfolded upon the coffee table occupying the center of the room was the letter proving to be the bone of contention causing the current state of unrest among the occupants present and most assuredly was at the core of Pierre's distress. The envelope's return address was that of Mr. and Mrs. Calvin Mason.

"Elvie's invitation is very gracious and including us in her good fortune is very considerate of her."

"I have no problèmes avec her <u>or</u> Dudley - he made the extremely wise choice of saving the life of Pierre Dûçot! But...the wilderness?" he expostulated with obvious reluctance.

"Laureltown is NOT a wilderness. It is an established community. It is just a little bit...out in the country!" justified his wife,

Edith, with lukewarm enthusiasm as she wrestled with her words to convey a positive sentiment which she did not exactly feel or was entirely sure about.

"Un peu out in the country?! And their residence.... There is not even running water. Et la salle de bains - c'est dedans la forêt!" he objected.

"Well, the newlyweds are making improvements to their new property as we speak. Give them time. LaurelsHeath will soon be in possession of all the comforts and amenities that we enjoy here as soon as all of the additions to the house have been completed." she parried in defense of her position. "How thrilling it must be to have a piece of history handed down to them from their Father. And to think that Jan LaFitte was holding on to it all this time just waiting on the chance to hand it down to a Maison. It is so heartwarming that now Elvie and Calvin can start their new married life in their very own home! Just think. Calvin and Dudley might have lived their whole lives through deprived of heritage and inheritance had Jan not discovered that Cal's Uncle and Father had shortened their last name from Maison to Mason on coming to America."

"Pah!" spat Pierre pessimistically before continuing. "And that Cal!" he exclaimed and began to kiss the air smacking his lips to-gether noisily. Puckering his lips in an exaggerated fashion and bestowing a liberal round of smooches to no one in particular Pierre paused momentarily to speak: "Buttering up the sides of Jan comme ça. How disgusting! Just intolérable. It would make one ill to see him fawning all over him SI it were not so très amusant. Je ris: HA, HA! Oui. Such a display. Très tragique. Mais la plus drôle." he concluded judiciously with self-righteous dignity intact.

"Pierre! Cal is NOT kissing up to him." his nephew-in-law, Randmore McKinley, interrupted him long enough to laughingly point out. "He just found out that he and Jan are related!"

"That is what he says. But who is he really? Vraiment? How

do we know this for certain? Where are his papers, eh? What is his proof? J'ai besoin de voir des détails. I need the documents. I need the WITNESSES."

Pierre hammered each of these points home as if they were nails being pounded into Calvin Mason's coffin not only with his expressive tones but by pounding his fist on the coffee table before him where the poor delicate, fragile china teacups clattered their unwilling affirmations of his statements as well with each solid thump almost spilling their liquid contents.

"I do not know presque you mais I need cette vérification. Où did he attend l'école? WHO were his teachers? WHAT," Pierre asserted with damning finality, "are his political leanings?" he stopped speaking suddenly and stared at Randmore piercingly. "LAUGH, if you must, Randy, but THESE are legitimate questions." he sniffed disdainfully with the kind of knowing hauteur which indulged the ignorant as another small, stifled chuckle escaped Rand's lips. "You are being very naïve, Randy. C'est certain. Bien sûr. Quelqu'un as influential as Jan is will always attract, comment dit-on, the Glory Seekers!"

He turned his face to one side in profile to them while picking up an old antique pipe Edith kept on display as a knickknack in an ashtray on the coffee table and putting it in his mouth with authority bit down hard on the bit of the pipe stem striking an austere pose.

Cari began to chuckle outright at these theatrics and covered her mouth with her hand to smother the sound of mirth while a slight smile began to tug at the corners of her Aunt Edith's lips.

"Don't forget to ask him what he knows about American baseball!" interrupted Alex Caine breezing into the room as well as into the conversation of which he had only heard the latter portion of.

"Tu vois! Il a raison!" Pierre asserted eagerly relaxing his stance to agree heartily with the newcomer.

"I always make good sense. Now, who are we talking about?"

Alex inquired with lighthearted ignorance.

Randmore pulled his cousin aside to explain while Cari spoke logically to the Frenchman.

"But Pierre," ventured Cari in a placating manner "Jan LaFitte SAVED Cal from being arrested and going to prison. Of course he was grateful!"

"Détails. Détails. Toujours the détails with you two." he addressed her demurrer and then nodded in Randmore's direction to include him in the rebuff. "These petit détails do not conceal his true intentions from moi."

"Dearest Heart. Speaking of concealing things - Jan LaFitte may not even be the man's real name." Edith noted sedately in stride. "LeLoup told me-"

Rushing to her side Pierre clapped a hand over his wife's mouth before she could continue speaking, betray LeLoup's confidences and perhaps reveal further information regarding his elusive friend with the admittedly sketchy background by the name of Jan LaFitte. Pierre idolized Jan and jealously guarded the gentleman's privacy. At the same time, he feared the swashbuckler's wrath. In addition, LeLoup might be held culpable for revealing such privileged and confidential matter to an "outsider".

"Be careful what you say - he may be listening…." Pierre whispered. "Do not risque offending Jan's generous nature. A KINDER MORE GENEROUS FRIEND WE DO NOT KNOW!" he finished speaking in a booming voice which was obviously much too loud for their private conversation.

"Oh, rubbish! No one is listening-" she scoffed, removing his hand.

"Kind nature! GOOD nature!" Pierre shouted cutting off his wife in mid-sentence. "His spies are everywhere." he counseled her hoarsely in a low whisper as he regarded Rand sharply with guarded suspicion. "Are you truly Randy McKinley - vraiment?" he quizzed

Randmore suddenly, whipping out the question with damning accusation.

Pierre's swift, pointed speech was calculated to catch the suspect Randmore unawares, unprepared and by surprise attack, confuse him and trip him up, thereby, eliciting an honest response from a possible agent of Jan's who might well be in disguise or possibly be wearing a realistically lifelike mask.

"Oh, stop the utter nonsense!!!" cried Edith throwing up her hands in patent exasperation as Pierre, on receiving no reply from the astounded younger man, stepped up to pinch Randy's cheek in order to verify his identity and she astutely gauged that both Randmore's and her niece's successful struggles at suppressing their overt expressions of mirth were becoming rapidly ineffectual. "And as for Calvin," she asserted, attempting to divert Pierre's attention to the more pertinent topic at hand, "he was merely being POLITE to Jan. Nothing more. Nothing less!"

"Mais, chérie!" protested the Frenchman.

"NOTHING MORE!" she reasserted vehemently and stubbornly lest her tenuous newly found control over the situation be impugned and thus evaporate. "Calvin was merely catching up with a long, lost relative." finished Edith soundly with a quelling glance.

"Pah!" scoffed Pierre. "He was bragging of his très unselfish behavior in relinquishing the treasure to him. Treasure, I might add, which he STOLE." he pointed out with continued persistence.

"It was very unselfish because when he understood that it did belong to Jan, Cal summarily returned it all back to him. After all, at that time he was unaware of Jan's true identity and took it on PURE faith that he was the rightful owner. This sort of act speaks to his moral behavior and character and sense of fairness and justice!"

"Je vois. I see. I see." he stiffly acknowledged abruptly, pacing back and forth and slightly miffed. He then sniffed with superiority: "Cette situation est très grave. Quelle tromperie! I can see that this

Calvin has fooled you, my <u>own</u> wife, aussi."

Edith was taken aback and appeared flustered by this statement. After recovering her equilibrium and poise, however, she began laughing breaking the tension among the room's other occupants.

"Oh, Pumpkin Eater...you are so cute when you are jealous!" she exclaimed indulgently. "You are jealous of Cal and Jan's friendship."

"Pumpkin Eater...?" Randmore and Alex both articulated quizzically in unison with gleeful surprise and zest coloring their voices.

"As in Pierre, Pierre, Pumpkin Eater...?" Cari sputtered in disbelief while she speedily rose from her seated position on an armchair and ran hurriedly from the cozy sitting room gasping and giggling with the utterance. "Wait until I tell the others!" she teased Pierre her laughing words now emanating from the hallway and echoing down the corridor.

"I am with Cari!" Rand teased Edith and Pierre mischievously. "I am sure we won't hear you kidding Alex about <u>his</u> snacks anymore!"

"Yeah." enjoined Alex scoffingly. "Would you like some 'milk and cookies' with that, Pumpkin Eater?"

CHAPTER 2

The hills of the countryside rolled out before them, whistling by and swiftly past to lie behind the passengers, as they flew forward toward their destination. Rotating carriage wheels protesting, clickety-clack, and horses' hooves thundering, the sights blended into a softly changing and moving scenic picture that once seen was destined to be soon forgotten as the next colorful topographic display presented itself for momentary perusal. Among those enduring scrutinizing inspection were innumerable majestic oaks, birches and maple trees standing tall. Their welcoming stalwart branches were weighed down by the array of colorful leaves that they each unabashedly sported boastfully proclaiming a lasting, prolonged, steadfast period of Indian summer. Shades of crimson, ochre and orange gracefully adorned the leaves on their boughs and appeared to the casual observer as the bold, artful brushstrokes of Mother Nature's paintbrush. Birds and squirrels inhabited the peaceful, green acres stretching out before them. The occasional deer bowed his head to touch his lips to the cool, crisp water of a babbling brook whose forking branches formed a pattern of interlacing channels among the tree trunks resembling latticework. Groups of cows congregated together on nearby farms softly mooed in the clover-spotted meadows and the lowing voices wafted to the travelers in various muted degrees almost as if they were tones on a musical scale of notes. Another voice, this one petulant and demanding, disturbed this peaceful scenario. Sounds of woeful distress combined with a strident whining.

"I have to go to the lavatory!" cried little Megan Flanderly as she fidgeted in her seat.

"Now, ye see tha', Ellie. We shouldna come - we have to go back!" the doctor stated firmly and abruptly in a mock exhibition of artificial concern, skillfully mingled with forced regretfulness, coloring his statements.

"Oh, stop yer nonsense, Matthew! Ye should feel ashamed. Use'n yer own daughter as an excuse fer yer puir behavior an' yer inhospitable attitude!" chided his wife.

"But, ye heard the little lassie. Now let us turn around and go home. They can christen their new home without us. An' we would be crowdin' the newlyweds in any event." he justified reasonably.

"I know ye dunna quite trust Cal or Dudley, either." she quickly interjected before Matthew could speak another word. "But, they did save the lives o' our friends-"

"After try'n' te KILL me." he countered.

"Now, ye know that was not their intention. 'Twas merely an accident - ye KNOW tha'. AN' ye know, as well, tha' once we drop the bairns off at camp there will be plenty o' rest rooms at the wee ones' disposal!"

"Bah! Who ever heard of an' upstandin' camp worth its salt bein' open fer business durin' the autumn season? And, I still say tha' we should ha' stayed home." maintained Matthew stubbornly.

"'Twill only be for a short visit. Then, on the way back te home we can pick up the wee ones from camp-school with no trouble a'tall!" Eleanor pointed out.

"I still ha' to go to the lavatory!" pouted little Megan beginning to cry as she lost the solicitous attentiveness of her parents - she had to regain it somehow!

"Ahhh…. She's just a big baby!" observed Matthew Alexander feeling very superior and mature at all of 10 years of age.

"Dunna tease yer little sister now, M.A.!" scolded his mother sternly as she glared in Matthew's direction. "Do ye see what ye started now? Now, tell the coachman te stop o'er te the side there, Matthew. Then, M.A., take Megan's hand and walk her te the bushes in the corner te do her business - and dunna ye peek at her whilst she goes about doin' it, either!"

"Ah, Ma - do I have to?" he complained.

"Yes, ye ha' te do it - dunna ye spake back te yer Mum. An' give te her these disinfectant towelettes te use." she directed him handing them over with aplomb. "Cleanliness is next te Godliness!" she informed him piously.

Once Matt bid the driver to stop and the conveyance that they were riding in slowly came to a halt his son, M.A., and daughter, Megan, one after the other exited the vehicle onto the rocky terrain outside. Matthew Alexander then obediently took Megan by the hand and led her to the secluded group of bushes in the corner of the field beyond.

"Here we are alone, now, Matthew, so you can tell me true. What is it exactly tha' ticks ye off 'bout Calvin and Dudley. They couldna be more apologetic about their scurvy, underhanded dealin's with regard te the treasure an' the explosion on tha' mountain ridge. An' they did save everybody from the fiendish plans o' that horrible Hank Colden. I canna approve of how they carried on in certain situations but I be the first one te admit te ye that nobody is perfect - we all have our faults. An' from time te time, te be sure, our feelin's and our pride undoubtedly will be hurt. But there comes a time fer all of us te bury our hatchets and set aside our differences. Te let sleepin' dogs lie, if ye will. Though, perhaps, that is a puir choice o' words, te be sure, considerin' the sleepin' potion that dastardly heathen fed te those innocent hounds!" she said shuddering at the thought as the gruesome picture of their lifeless bodies sprung to her mind.

"It is not tha' I wish te perpetuate a feud, Ellie. I know tha' they are repentant fer what they did. But...."

"But?" coaxed Eleanor cajolingly.

"But - me treasure!" cried Matthew slapping his thighs with the folded local newspaper in his lap.

"Are ye <u>still</u> goin' on about tha' foolish treasure, fer lands sake?!"

"But it was <u>my</u> treasure. They had NO claim te it and yet they connived and conjured te spirit it away from me grasp!" he declared peevishly.

"Matthew! I'm surprised at ye. Ye know they believed it te be rightfully theirs in the first place and as it turned out it wasna belongin' t'either of ye. Now. When we get there try te be civil an' wish them well. Remember, Elvira is a dear, sweet girl an' Callie is a dear friend. They are married to those two Mason brothers an' we should be polite." she concluded reasonably.

"'Maison', those two are callin' themselves, now! La-di-da!" he articulated petulantly in a disparaging tone of voice.

"Ye know 'tis only fittin' an' proper te go by 'Maison' now tha' they discovered their true heritage!" she asserted.

"Just because their original name was 'Maison' they inherit an old-world style mansion with all o' the trimmin's and with no strings attached te it - with no trouble at all mind ye - an' are set te enjoy a life of leisure!" bellowed Matthew in frustration. "The injustice of it all!"

"I see tha' there is na any use te talkin' te ye so at least <u>try</u> te be cordial te our hosts when we arrive. Now, WHAT is keepin' those children o' ours?" she said changing the subject.

She was at the end of her rope - her patience with Matt was exhausted.

"Takin' their own sweet time, they are, an' we ha' a schedule te keep."

Eleanor spoke in exasperation at her errant children's tardiness. She poked her head through the window of the carriage door and strained her eyes to ascertain a glimpse of her little ones. However, they were nowhere to be seen. She turned to face her husband with much concern in her eyes and he appeared to be dumbfounded as to their whereabouts as well.

"You're gonna get us inte trouble!" shouted M.A. as he chased after his little sister who in turn was chasing after a fluffy white cat with a jingling collar from which dangled various ornaments of different shapes and sizes about her neck.

The tinkling sound created by the jouncing adornments encircling the feline wearer's neck was all the siren song needed to entice an inquisitive young girl who had been cooped up for an interminably long time in a close vehicle riding over bumpy roads and wanted to stretch her legs and play.

"But she's so cute!" Megan cried breathlessly stealing a backward glance at her pursuer.

However, on turning back the cat was...gone! She screeched to an abrupt halt, put a finger to her little rosebud of a mouth and tears began to well up in her eyes.

"Here, kitty, kitty. Here, kitty, kitty!" she called out in a broken, half-sobbing voice. "She's gone!"

"We gotta get back - c'mon!" directed M.A. as he caught up with her, huffing and puffing and bending over to his knees to catch his breath before continuing. "I'm probably the one they're gonna yell at, not you - I'm supposed to be watching you. Just because you need a baby-sitter I'm gonna get it! BABY!"

"You're mean. You take that back! I don't need - LOOK!" cried Megan joyously and started to run toward a tree from behind which a furry, white face with blue eyes peeped out, yawned revealing the interior of a pink mouth with its dancing pink tongue, and winked coyly.

Turning puffy tail to flee in the opposite direction the perky animal shimmied her hindquarters flirtatiously. As the captivating feline pied piper scampered nimbly off she eluded the two children and disappeared beneath a plethora of tangled shrubbery. They followed after and pushed aside the clingy vines in their path only to stop abruptly. Open-mouthed and wide-eyed the youngsters gasped in unison as they were met by a pair of legs, taller than trees and as thick as tree trunks, too, encased in dusty, black pants which appeared as wide as tents to the little wayward imps whose own immature limbs and slight forms were dwarfed in comparison. They slowly gazed upwards in frightened, undisguised awe at the behemoth dressed totally in black garb examining every inch of the imposing giant before them. His barrel-chested upper body appeared to be made of iron. His craggy, bearded face and hooded black eyes bespoke of gruesome intention as his two brawny arms with their overlarge hands reached downward toward them.

CHAPTER 3

"Where is the baby?" queried a disappointed Elvira Maison at the absence of the two-year-old.

She looked about seeking the toddler.

"Randy and I decided that it might not be wise to bring her seeing as how at her age she gets into just everything - you've heard of the "Terrible Twos"! You're trying to fix up this place not tear it down! Not that the house is not in beautiful condition already." Cari added hastily not wishing to offend her hostess yet at the same time noting the room's state of disrepair and wincing at her little white lie.

"Well. You know, Cari. I can't tell you that I <u>am</u> <u>not</u> disappointed little Jeanette Josephine didn't come with you...but maybe it's for the best this way." Elvie said nervously while shooting Cari a mysterious look and darting apprehensive, fearful glances at the crumbling drywall around her. "The walls have <u>EARS</u>." finished the spooked girl grimly in a solemn whisper while tapping her head knowledgeably with her index finger.

"Whatever do you mean, Elvie?" Cari inquired, approaching the young woman who, again, glanced once more about her fearfully before responding.

"I seen strange goings-on out here an' no one believes me!" she articulated confidingly, whispering from behind her hand.

Cari chuckled inwardly. Her Aunt had advised her of Elvie's penchant for the dramatic. "Give me an example." she prompted.

"People appear and disappear. An'-"

"Don't be frightening our guest with tall tales about this creaky old place, Elvie." interrupted a cold, morose voice in rebuke, its owner seeming to materialize out of nowhere. "Hello. I am Trudy. I have been taking care of this gloomy old house for years. And I know it from its groaning floorboards and its drafty halls to its moth-eaten draperies." rasped Trudy gruffly.

'My, this Trudy painted quite a glowing picture of the house.' Cari thought. She wondered if the woman had ever considered going into the sales profession, she quipped to herself sarcastically. Trudy was an extremely tall, gaunt woman of an indeterminable age. Her sunken cheeks and thin, pointed nose emphasized her facial structure with its deep set, vapid eyes and bony body frame.

"Yes." she continued. "These damp corners over there and there," Trudy pointed fore and aft "have seen many an 'apparition', I am sure, but you will all get used to the bleak interior and shady passages in due time. Your imagination can go wild here if you don't." she finished blandly in a secretive timbre.

"I am definitely pleased to meet you Trudy, but you must not scare Elvie so! The task of renovating this old house must be daunting enough for her and Cal without you pointing out all of its faults to her-"

"Well someone should." she immediately snapped fiercely, cutting off the surprised Cari Chesterfield McKinley before she could finish her thoughts on her chosen topic. "The roof needs to be retiled, the ceiling's leaking, the faucets are dripping - the place is a mess! If you ask me-"

"We are not asking you, Trudy," she put her arm around Elvie to underscore their closeness and unity as she spoke "and as we all know: "Actions speak louder than words.", so they say. I do not mean to offend you." Cari spoke staunchly. "I just think that we should all do our best to be positive and help the newlyweds out. After all, this clean-up is a project which will require all our help and support and goodness knows - it will take some time to get organized!"

"What are you doing in this unkempt area, of all areas, of the house! We have been looking all over for you two!" Edith exclaimed cheerfully peering around the half-open door.

"Edith!" cried Elvie running to her side. "I'm so glad you came. I was showing Cari around here and I was telling her it was better off that Jenny Jo didn't come 'cause there are some mighty strange things going on around here. Why, just the other day I was talking to the cat an'-"

"Excuse me, dear. Did I hear you correctly? You were talking to the cat...?" she asked dubiously, squinting deeply in thought while attempting to understand and wrap her brain around what Elvie had just imparted.

"Exactly. And then...she weren't there!" Elvie affirmed querulously as wide-eyed and panicky she established eye contact with first Edith and then with Cari.

"What were you and the cat talking about?" Trudy interjected the question while smothering a grin with the back of her fist.

Elvira cast her gaze downward in embarrassed shame at being scoffed at with the insincere question to ostensibly observe the floorboards and a tear sprang to her eye in the process. She understood Trudy's implication. She had feelings, too. She had not failed to notice Trudy's masked laughing grin or her skeptical taunt. Her implied barb had met its mark and she felt its sting. No one ever took her seriously it seemed!

"Aunt Edith, this is Trudy. Trudy, this is my Aunt Edith Dûçot." Cari interposed smoothly into the awkward breach, created by the older woman, on noting Elvie's hurt expression.

Cari had been the new mistress of an established manor house once, too, and knew what it felt like to be treated as an outsider. By acquainting her aunt with the house's caretaker Cari sought to provide sufficient distraction to afford Elvie adequate opportunity to swallow her tears and compose herself. Therefore, she continued speaking.

"Trudy has looked after LaurelsHeath until Elvie, Calvin, Callie and Dudley came to take possession of it!"

"Pleased to meet you." Trudy said perfunctorily in an abrasive tone of voice as Edith smiled and acknowledged their new acquaintanceship in a warmer timbre.

"It is so wonderful to meet you, Trudy." Edith graciously acceded. "However," she proclaimed taking hold of a broom in a storage closet against the wall, "I can see that there is much work still to be done! Now, where to begin first-"

Trudy angrily snatched the broom from her hand before she could finish her thought. She replaced it in the closet, closed its yawning doors firmly shut and favored Edith with an intimidating, glowering stare.

"Don't you touch that!" she berated bitingly. "Don't you go pokin' your nose into places where it don't belong in the first place. I've been doing this longer than you have, Missy! I, well...."

On remarking Edith's stupefied regard Trudy's acerbic tirade suddenly ran out of steam and, like a chugging locomotive on a railway, eventually slowed to a full stop.

"I just meant you shouldn't go soil your hands - you're a guest." she amended, suddenly projecting a cordial demeanor. "And it's a good thing you didn't bring that Jeanette an' Jenny Jo with you. We've got enough problems to look after - I mean, the <u>house</u> has enough problems to it - the little darlings might hurt themselves and we would not want that, would we, now?" she ended sweetly on a note of concern which resonated hollow in its insincerity.

The astonished gazes the three other females in the room wore bore various degrees of dumbfounded surprise and they were all rendered speechless by this semi-threatening tirade of implication issuing from Trudy's mouth. Cari, for one, could not imagine that Trudy had any motherly concern at all for her baby's well-being. Now, the <u>house's</u> well-being...that was a horse of a very different color, altogether! Trudy seemed almost obsessed when it came to the house. Or, was it just that particular room that they were in?

"No. No. We would not." Edith spoke up stutteringly on regaining her composure. "And, Jeanette and Jenny Jo are just one baby. You see, her full name is Jeanette Josephine, and sometimes we shorten her name to Jenny Jo."

"Jeanette is my mother's name and Josephine is part of my best friend's name." Cari elucidated with cordial candor. "And there she is - my best friend in the WHOLE world! We're in here, Mary Jo!" called Cari while walking to where her aunt stood near the room entrance and poking out her head into the hall to better view Mary Josephine's approach and to intercept her friend who had been roaming through the abode in search of her. "Where are the guys?" Cari asked Mary Jo Caine as she joined her and the other ladies.

"They're just being men!" Mary Jo responded impatiently. "Oh…! They make me so crazy. They're just like a bunch of children. As soon as we got here and they saw Cal and Dudley it was like they were in some secret SOCIETY of their own. It was: 'who has the better fishing gear' and 'who has the fancier boots' and 'who can make a stone skip the most times on the pond'. Then, they all went off together to examine these stocks that are in the center of the property."

"Stocks?" said Elvira quizzically. "What are they?"

"The stocks." Mary Jo jogged her memory of history. "You know the stocks." she prompted exasperatedly. "We learned about it in school. That's where they used to chain people if they did something against the law to make a public example of them. Anyway, they were taking turns putting their arms and heads in the openings and playing 'cops and robbers' when I saw them last."

"COPS AND ROBBERS?!" exclaimed a disbelieving Edith. "At their ages - that's a child's game!"

"Well, you know what I mean." said Mary Jo. "They were imagining what it was like in the old days."

"They should be careful down there - they might hurt themselves." warned Trudy with ominous undertone. "Or BE hurt." she added superciliously.

Mary Jo cast a curious glance at the poker-faced woman from whom the utterance had emanated and politely waited for her further commentary. As Trudy's tongue seemed to have gone dry and she spoke no more Mary Jo continued her dialogue.

"There is even a moat and drawbridge out there - can you believe it? Anyway, I left them to do their little explorations on their own. Men will be men. Live and let live is what I always say-"

"Really?" Trudy interjected morosely with a sour face.

Mary Jo looked expectantly at the woman who yet again had interrupted her, directly this time, but it again appeared that she had nothing to contribute to the conversation beyond this one word comment and so she resumed speaking.

"Anyway."

She abruptly ceased speaking. She stared at the woman standing opposite her once more, and then satisfied that she was finally holding her peace, recommenced speaking.

"I picked this up along the way. It was lying near a cluster of some majestic oaks. It looked like some litterbug must have dropped it so I picked it up to throw it out..." stated Mary Jo as she paused briefly to remove a square of cotton-like material from her pocket and unfolding it showed it to the group, "but it looks like it was just left by some prankster."

She pointed to the center of the unwrapped square of cloth.

"See? Right there." she declared.

"It appears to be some kind of moist towellette." Cari noted as they all gathered around Mary Jo and viewed the flattened-out fabric on which was written in blue crayon, in uppercase letters, the word: "HELP".

CHAPTER 4

Pierre shifted his weight from one haunch to the other as he squatted and attempted to garner a better view down the shaft of the cannon. He squirmed and strained with his efforts. The back of his protruding head abruptly drew backward from the cannon's mouth as he raised his face to the sunlight squinting against the glare. Gunpowder residue from the rim of the cannon's mouth clung to where the lips of the tubular vessel (sans cannonball) had formerly been pressed against Pierre's skin, framing his face with a circular ring of thick , dark soot.

"I see ne rien chose dedans ici - what are you jokers laughing presque?"

"Here." offered Cal innocently, gratuitously thrusting a pair of binoculars into his hands quickly to distract him in lieu of responding to his question. "Try these." he suggested helpfully to his selected mark while simultaneously turning his body halfway around to fix his brother with the evil eye of warning to cow him into silence and quell his lighthearted antics and chuckles.

Taking heed of this wordless reprimand and not wishing to give up the ghost, Dudley grabbed at the shoulders of both Rand and Alex to maintain his balance and support himself as he began to double over on his way to collapsing to the ground into the fits of unbridled laughter that he wished to conceal - at least until the completion of Calvin's prank. Meanwhile, Pierre obediently complied with Calvin's request and peered intently through the handheld ocular device he had supplied him with into the shaft again only to throw his arms up in negative truculence when his search bore no more fruit than before.

"Pah! I see nothing down there. I told you - it is too dark!" complained Pierre whipping the ocular instrument away from his eyes only to reveal two additional black, circular, 360° round smudges which had not been present prior to its introduction. Freshly transferred and still moist, the rings surrounded each of his individual visual orbs where the rubber optic cups of the magnifier's viewfinder gauges had pressed against his skin and deposited the dark, smoky-colored, soiling leavings on being pulled away.

"Il faut le nécessaire à - <u>what</u> is wrong avec you people!?" he shrilly exclaimed loudly in mid-sentence stridently bellowing with the intensity of sheer frustration coloring his high voice.

Pierre looked on as, unable to support Dudley any longer, Randy and Alex, both, buckled under the pressure of his weight and collapsed in gaggles of laughter along with him and then Cal - the "Mason Brothers". On finally falling hard - or more accurately being unceremoniously dumped - to the ground Dudley could only point at Pierre's face and then clap the earth beneath him several times as he dissolved into hilarity's wordless pantomime. Gesticulating and pointing at Pierre they, one and all, seemed incapable of forming coherent sentences and this infuriated the Frenchman to no end.

"Finally, un peu de raison. Callie - where have you been? Would you tell me what has gotten into these foolish children?" Pierre demanded of her querulously as she approached.

"Let me guess..." pondered the young woman, slightly taken aback by his unorthodox appearance "you are a...raccoon - right?" she hazarded while studying on his appearance and awaiting a response. 'Was this some kind of a parlor game?' she wondered.

As Pierre opened his mouth to object and redirect Callie realized her mistake, revised her opinion and cut off his critique.

"No. No. Wait! You're a ghost and those dark circles-"

"Stop yer playin' at Cowboys an' Indians an' wipe off tha' warpaint! Can ye not never be normal!?Ye should be ashamed o' yerself. A grown man o' yer age - or whatever ye be. What kinda' example are ye settin' fer the younger generation?" blustered Matthew Flanderly argumentatively - yet piously - as with a purposeful gait he made his way toward the group.

Appearing out of nowhere Matt's quick, firm strides bespoke of a determined, unrelenting urgency.

"En premier lieu, I was aiding Calvin à trouver une chose qui tombe dedans the cannon-là. Après de ça..." Pierre indicated the still madcap bunch of men who continued hooting and hollering with glee "ils deviennent fous." he explained defensively to the pre-occupied man. "Ce n'est pas ma faute que je suis surrounded par tous ces incompétents." he continued acerbically after rubbing at his visage with his handkerchief and viewing the mixture of soot co-mingled with mud and old gunpowder staining its former pristine, white folds. Gazing disparagingly at Alex, Calvin and Dudley who still engaged in various stages and throes of comedic bliss, which included Dudley not only laughing hysterically with the others but rolling around on the ground as well, he turned on his heel abruptly aloofly presenting them with his back and spoke to Matt, Callie and Randy exclusively: "It appears that those three" he nodded his head backwards haughtily indicating the boisterous trio behind him "manque severely dans la maturité department!"

"Oh, come on, Pierre! Cal and Dudley were only joking. It could easily have been me or Alex with ashes on our faces if you hadn't pushed us both aside and volunteered to look inside the cannon first and waved at us to stay back saying that you were an expert when it came to finding 'des choses'." Randy pointed out reasonably. "Let's see.... What was the phrase that you used when you passed us by? Ah, yes. 'Separating the gentilshommes from the puppy dogs'. Get into the spirit of things - we're all just having fun."

"Yeah, if you can't stand the heat, get out of the kitchen!" Alex piped-up agreeably wiping the tears of mirth from his cheeks.

"Actually, I really wanted Alex to look in the cannon. I thought that the soot was just his color!" interjected Calvin playfully, intent on goading Alex to indignation as he placed a cupped hand behind his head under the hair at the base of his scalp pumping it up and down coquettishly as if to pat the hair into place while winking coyly in his direction.

In his other hand Calvin still held onto some extra burnt remains which were left over after he had finished setting up his previous pranks and hefted them meaningfully as he made direct eye contact with Pierre.

"I'll give you some color. How about a shiner!?" cried Alex almost immediately roused to action and waving his fist in the air with resolute ardor yet totally oblivious was he of Calvin's signal to the Frenchman who was now eager to make someone else the butt of the joke.

"Alors! Je pense que Calvin a raison." concurred Pierre thoughtfully nonchalantly approaching the pile of moist, black soot in a clump near the heavy artillery, scooping up a handful and approaching Alex from one side while Calvin approached him from the other.

"I ha' somethin' te say o' the utmost importance so will ye quit yer foolish shenanigans and leave the puir lad be!" Matt expostulated stepping between them to stand staunchly in front of Alex, sheltering him, when first Calvin and then Pierre rubbed their handfuls of decaying debris against each cheek on either side of the Irishman's face. "Enough!" he bellowed. "This is WAR!" shouted the irate man hefting a portion of the freshly derived incidental ashy muck he had just picked up from the ground and hurling it...at Randmore.

Shocked out of his role as a passive, innocent bystander when the soft ball of mud made contact with and splattered all over the front of his shirt Randy ducked as another clump soared through the air in his direction. Exercising his own pitching skills he began to pelt Matt, Calvin and Pierre with the slimy soot two at a time using both hands. They retaliated in kind and just like carefree children engaged in a snowball fight. The end result was a free for all. Randmore bent over to scoop up some more debris which he packed with his hands into a ball-like shape at the same moment that Pierre threw his own compressed projectile of bundled matter at Matthew who stood right behind his hunched-over form. As the projectile flew toward its desired target, Matthew, Randmore straightened up to stand erect and the slimy, sloppy mess struck him square in the face disintegrating on its impact into a pasty ooze spreading outward to cover his entire visage and drip down his countenance. All activity at that moment ceased and was accompanied by ensuing silence. Certainly, no one had meant for anybody to get hurt.

As Randy wiped the mud off of his eyelids with two simultaneous swipes of the fingers of both of his hands he looked straight at Pierre and queried:

"Why did you do that?"

Mortified at the carnage he had inflicted unintentionally to Rand's face Pierre uttered the only answer that first came to his mind:

"I was trying to 'get into the spirit of things'."

Covered with soot, soiled and breathless the group of previously merry men now became tired of catapulting one another with gunk. They felt deflated and glum. The accident with Randmore had been a sobering experience and had taken the wind out of their sails. But, this was only until all at once Alex was struck with an epiphany and voiced his sudden inspiration aloud:

"Why should we be the only ones to have spirit?!"

Randy looked quizzically at Matthew; Matthew looked

thoughtfully at Pierre; Pierre looked hesitantly at Calvin; Calvin looked inquisitively at Alex and Alex looked at all four of them with a wicked, mischievous glint in his eyes. The quintet nodded in agreement. Abruptly, they all turned and simultaneously began to descend upon Callie and Dudley menacingly waving their ammunition filled mitts. However, a new wrinkle introduced herself in the person of Eleanor Flanderly weeping profusely and blowing her nose intermittently between sobs. The five marchers halted their progress and all eyes turned toward the obviously aggrieved woman.

"The children!" Eleanor eked out wringing her hands. "Matthew. Ha' ye found the children?"

"Ellie!" exclaimed her husband who had been momentarily distracted from his anxiety regarding his missing son and daughter by engaging in the playful antics with his friends. "Ye're cryin'. So, the children - ye didna find them either?" he asked guiltily.

Eleanor regarded the chaotic scene about her suspiciously. It did not appear that he had even begun searching for their bairns.

"No. I didna find them." she responded querulously. "And yet here ye are playin' at yer foolish games when ye should be lookin' fer them yerself!" scolded the worried lady at her wits end.

"The kids are lost - why didn't you tell us, Matt?" Alex asked. "We would have helped you look for them!"

"I tried te'-" Matthew began only to be interrupted by Rand.

"You should have told us, Matt - what are we wasting time here for standing around like this? Let's canvass the area!" proposed Randmore.

"When did you see them last?" asked Dudley coming to his feet, dusting off the twigs and dirt which had accumulated on his clothes from rolling around on the ground and walking toward Eleanor with sincere concern etching his facial features.

"'Twere back there awhile - near some bushes-" she began to elucidate when her husband picked up the explanation and ran with it.

"Our wee one, Megan, ha' te, ye see...she ha' te...handle her...ladylike affairs-" explained Matthew awkwardly, blushing in embarrassment while attempting to approach the feminine issue delicately.

"Oh, quiet, ye oafish buffoon!" exclaimed Eleanor lashing out in nervous fear at Matthew with the only weapon she had at her disposal - her voice.

"That is just la chose que I have been saying." began Pierre.

"Hush, yerself, now!" she proclaimed boldly with uncharacteristic firmness to Pierre who she had always been more than a little bit timid of. "Now, I say tha' we all go te the bushes where we saw them prior. Then we must split ourselves up an' seek the wee ones out!" she commanded sounding just like a drill sergeant.

"The bushes near the path to the clearing?" Dudley asked hesitantly.

"Are ye speakin' te me again, Dudley?" Eleanor asked distractedly with half a mind while at the same time mentally formulating combinations of search groups and imagining the appropriate areas a child's curiosity might prompt him and/or her to investigate.

Eleanor bit down on a fingernail and worriedly considered the options while Dudley shared a fearful glance with Callie and Cal. More interested in juggling her own tumultuous thoughts than in noticing their body language their expressions of unease were lost on her.

"The bushes -" he prompted her "you know - near the stream?"

"Yer right. Some water be nearby. WHY DE YE ASK?" she suddenly demanded anxiously with suspicious fear creeping into her voice.

Eleanor's eyes had opened wide, her pupils dilated and her mouth had fallen partially agape.

CHAPTER 5

"I told you not to let anyone in here and now look what a commotion you have caused!" Simon scolded as he regarded the upended coffee table; various chairs which lay toppled over onto their sides; rugs askew and books and magazines decorating the previously clean floor. "Now, give me a reason - just one good reason - why I should let you loose. Anyone who would allow a boy and girl to tie him up deserves what he gets - and you don't even know them. What would your Mother say?"

"We were just playin'." said the large, hulking man defensively gazing innocently at his stepfather with wide eyes.

"Elroy, I do not know what I am going to do with you." Simon declared in dismay. "Just <u>HOW LONG</u> have you been like this!?" he demanded rhetorically.

Tied to a pole, the rope securing Elroy encircled him multiple times around and around and rather than appearing alarmed at his predicament he appeared to be quite complacent and calm.

"They'll come back to untie me." he said trustingly. "You're spoiling our game!"

Again contemplating the disheveled condition of the room that they currently occupied Simon could not help but think that it looked more like the scene of a struggle rather than the scene of a game. Shaking his head from side to side he untied the knot which was an unexpectedly stubborn, intricate fishing knot - impressive that a little boy would know how to twist rope together into that particular shape. He hadn't seen a knot like that since his old friend had invented one similar a long time ago. Simon paused as he re-membered the good old days of his youth. He had been very proud of that knot. Said that it should be patented. He chuckled at the fond memory. Old Wily Fingers. He had almost forgotten....

"What's so funny?" asked Elroy indignantly. "They will come back - they will! We was playing Cops and Robbers an' - you're ru-inin' everything!" he cried with the disappointment of a young child as Simon unwound the last circle of heavy twine binding him to the post setting him free. "Now when they come back to untie me-" Elroy began to whine only to be interrupted by Simon.

"Cops and Robbers? Was the game their idea?"

"How did you know that?" he gasped awestruck at the correct assumption.

"Just a wild guess." Simon allowed with a grim smile. "How long were they 'playing' over here before they tied you up." he asked casually again reassessing the disorganized state of the house.

One of the lamps lay on its side. Its porcelain body was bro-ken into three large pieces. Knickknacks, writing paper and a letter opener were among other objects which littered the floor. Curtains were pulled down off the rods while others were half askew. He wondered how long it would take him to clean up this mess.

"Just a few days.... Maybe a week." Elroy amended when Simon looked at him sharply with undisguised skepticism. "But now you have spoiled everything! Now when they come back to untie me-" he continued to pout bitterly before being cut short by Simon in mid-sentence.

"They are not coming back to untie you, son." he asserted to the ingenuous younger man. "They have likely gone home by now."

"But, it was my turn to tie <u>them up</u> next-"

"That is just why they left." Simon sighed and pulled up a chair for Elroy and one for himself. "Sit down, son." he articulated calm-ly and when Elroy complied with the request he, himself, did the same. "You see, son. No one wants to be forced to play with anybody. This is especially true when they do not know the person. And you are likely much older than them, too. You should know better. They are just little kids - you are a young man. You can't just go around literally picking up people and bringing them home with you. Especially children. They were probably terrified. Now, which way did they go - it is getting dark and I have to make sure that they get home safely if they have not gotten there already." he asked reasonably putting his coat and hat back on and preparing to leave via the front entrance of the house. Suddenly, he hesitated: "Did they exit through the front or the back door?"

"But I didn't scare them - I didn't." Elroy maintained stamping his foot in an infantile fashion and then holding his breath.

"WHERE - DID - THEY - GO, Roy." Simon articulated slowly accenting each word until Elroy responded.

"They went that way." responded the gentle giant sheepishly.

"The basement?" Simon asked in surprised shock.

"I guess they lost their way." stammered the younger man guiltily.

"But you know what is in the basement - you should have warned them!"

CHAPTER 6

"It's creepy down here!" M.A. whispered as he pulled away from a stray cobweb he had stumbled into.

As he picked off the strands of spun silk clinging to his face and hair Megan began to cry.

"It's dark and I'm cold!" the little girl whined clutching at her brother's arm for comfort.

"Would you keep your voice down! I hear people upstairs - you'll give us away. An' watch where you're stepping!" he warned sharply trying to keep the timbre of his voice low when he delivered the serious, scolding remonstrance as she tripped over some sports equipment. "We'll find someplace to hide and then when it gets dark-"

"It's already dark in here!" Megan pointed out in confusion.

"I mean outside, genius. Now, as I was saying, when it gets dark OUTSIDE an' they go to sleep we'll escape out the front door. WHAT IS IT NOW!" he asked in frustration his patience wearing thin.

Just as his Father would become short and querulous M.A. was also becoming short of temper and ready to explode in anger when interacting with others. A chip off of the old block? Was this his true nature or was this a response which he had learned after observing the reaction many times before from his significant role model? The stricken look on his little sister's face caused him to suffer a good deal of chagrin. Shaking off his impetuous burst of unfounded emotion he apologized to Megan.

"I'm sorry, Meg. Don't hold it against me. I am afraid, too." he admitted a bit shamefacedly. "Now, what can I do you for?" Matthew Alexander asked remorsefully.

"Well…." replied Megan thoughtfully and slowly with index finger supporting her chin now that she had M.A.'s sympathies right where she wanted them. "I'm cold and hungry."

"There we go." he proclaimed removing his jacket and wrapping it closely about her. "Is that better?" he inquired solicitously.

"I am <u>not</u> sure…." she said fidgeting undecidedly.

"Well, let's fix that then." answered M.A. regarding her a tad suspiciously.

Removing the jacket from her shoulders he slipped each of her arms through its sleeves; adjusted the plackets of the jacket so that they hung straight and were flush; aligned the zipper's teeth and pulled the tab interlocking them up to her chin.

"That's better - am I right?" he exclaimed proudly.

"Yes. It is but…." she said hesitantly drawing out the sentence to allow supposition to enter the mind of her older sibling and regarding his face consideringly, wondering how far she could play upon his guilt in order to get what she wanted.

She knew that he was keeping a chocolate bar in his shirt pocket.

"But?" he prompted her.

"I'm still HUNGRY." she ventured cautiously eyeing his pocket every now and again suggestively as she spoke to ensure that her hint was well taken.

M.A. screwed up his mouth with distaste at relinquishing the prized snack in his pocket, but give it up he did. He withdrew it from his shirt pocket and selflessly handed it over to his sister. As she took it from him without hesitating a beat and he watched her rip off the wrapper and then greedily scarf it down hungrily he wondered if she had been angling for the candy bar all along. With her energy renewed by the added calories of the chocolate, Megan took charge.

"This way!" she commandingly ordered M.A. directing him toward where she perceived was the ideal hiding place. "We can hide behind this old fence!" she proposed the idea to him proud of herself for contributing some positive input.

Filled with a newly found, independent zeal she rushed on ahead of him elated, shucking his supervisory yoke, toward the sheltering structure of vertical, wooden slats lashed together with rusty metal wire which was propped up against some artifacts in one corner of the dank room. This was a good plan and M.A. opened his mouth to say so when he heard his sister's high-pitched scream coming from behind the screen. Forging rashly ahead of him as she had done in her impromptu game of Follow the Leader her haste had indeed made waste as she had disappeared entirely, and was completely hidden, behind the fencing unintentionally preventing M.A. from viewing her degree of physical injury and emotional distress. It was from this location that her pitiable pleas for help echoed hollowly and reverberated eerily.

"Meg!" yelled the concerned boy as he ran to the area from where the plaintive cries were emanating to find an open trapdoor with steps leading down to a passageway below them.

Megan lay at the bottom of the staircase crying her heart out and M.A. descended to help her. Badly bruised and shaken, M.A. pulled her to her feet and together they stared down the seemingly endless corridor before them which branched out at various junctures. Dark and gloomy though it was luminosity shone from somewhere and illuminated what at first glance could be interpreted as an elaborate maze or a network of catacombs.

"Are you okay, sis?" M.A. queried in concern.

Before she had a chance to respond they both heard a pair of footsteps treading heavily on the floorboards above them and advancing in the direction of the trapdoor. Brother and sister both exchanged alarmed glances with one another. Young Matthew

Alexander grabbed hold of Megan's hand and together they raced down the corridor ahead of them as the dreaded sound of the ominous footfalls drew closer and spelled out their impending doom. At this point M.A. and Megan, both, had forgotten about her pain. Headlong down the passageway they flew with the wind at their backs and fear in their hearts until sudden movement distracted Megan and arrested the little girl's attention.

"Look!" Megan whispered loudly as she perceived the fluffy, white feline with the jingling collar materialize from around a corner further down the corridor and sidle back and forth as if to indicate "follow me" to the frantically fleeing duo.

Megan immediately gravitated toward the cat only to have M.A. stop her short and then release her hand. Placing one hand on each of her shoulders he spun her around to face him.

"Are you BONKERS?" he harangued staring piercingly into her eyes. "We've gotten into enough trouble by following that cat!"

Undecided as to what to do Megan looked up into the angry eyes of her brother and then at the wide blue eyes of the white cat that almost seemed to be grinning as she raised her paw in a silent "come hither" plea. She again began to sashay backwards and forwards. The little girl was torn between following the cat and staying the course with M.A.. She gazed once more at her brother seeking his guidance with a pathetic, pleading aspect but could find no understanding of her dilemma in his stony visage. She once more heard the sound of the footsteps beginning to draw closer and glanced with alarm obliquely in the direction of the portentous sound. Megan had made up her mind. With an apologetic look in her brother's direction she followed the cat leaving M.A. standing alone in her dust as she rounded a corner in hot pursuit of the fluffy, white feline. Feeling defeated and disregarded, the boy threw up his hands in resigned exasperation and then followed in her wake, pursuing his errant charge. Soon they were running together neck

and neck chasing the white feline who turned another corner and...
disappeared. The children had reached a dead end, literally. The
wall in front of them forbade twisting or turning of any kind. There
was hardly enough breadth of space for them to stand shoulder to
shoulder.

"Now what do we do?" asked Megan in unveiled astonishment.
"Where did the pussycat go?" she pondered in amazement with
wide-eyed curiosity and her mouth partially agape in her awe at the
phenomena.

"It doesn't make sense...." puzzled M.A. aloud. "I told you NOT
to follow that troublemaking ball of fur but you didn't listen to me!"

The footsteps behind them pounded more loudly.

"And now we're gonna get caught by that crazy giant who'll
probably eat us for lunch!" he scolded reprovingly gnashing his
teeth. "He's got us cornered." M.A. added hammering the point
home.

Megan began to sob and tears welled up in her eyes to spill over
staining her cheeks.

"Aw...you'll cry at anything!" he rebuked her and then nervously glanced quickly over his shoulder toward the loud, striking
claps of sloshing footsteps making contact with wet stone and then
producing a slow, lazy sucking noise on pulling back and away.

For no apparent reason M.A. was all at once aware of the trick-
les of water slowly gliding down the walls of the stone prison. He
all at once turned on his heel to face the problem at hand.

"There must be a trapdoor around here somewhere that the cat
went through. That cat didn't just evaporate." M.A. asserted authoritatively proud of the new vocabulary word that he had just learned
in Science Class at school.

He began pushing against the lower areas of the stone wall
searching for any kind of give in the barrier that a cat might be able
to push through while desperation set in and beads of perspiration

popped out of his every pore. As he felt across the apparently resistant wall in front of him he was obviously successful in triggering a latch-like mechanism because finally a large part of the side wall gave way - quite easily, in fact - and he fell through the swiveling barrier onto the other side of a broom closet. Little gentleman that he was, he held the swinging door open for Megan to pass through releasing it to fall silently closed shut on its own. As they both heaved simultaneous sighs of relief at their escape from captivity and recapture on turning they were confronted by a stern, older woman.

CHAPTER 7

"I told you I saw a giant over there, but you didn't believe me, Calvin!" Elvira said accusingly.

"There are no such things as giants!" Calvin corrected her vehemently giving Elvie a meaningful stare and motioning with his eyes to where Eleanor sat trying very hard to control her bitter tears of anguish which had suddenly begun to pour forth uncontrollably on hearing her careless 'I told you so' remark.

"I am not avec peur de this giant. Pierre Dûçot is not afraid of the n'importe quoi." Pierre said imperiously haughtily sniffing the air loudly for theatrical emphasis of his declaratory statement and, for additional effect, turning aloofly to one side to examine his fingernails.

"Pierre!" Rand cried with exasperation. "There are no such things as sea monsters. There are NO SUCH THINGS AS GIANTS!"

"Randy!" the Frenchman reprimanded him excitedly, dropping his feigned pose. "Do not be avec naïveté! I know this and you know this, but do they know this?" Pierre pointed out tapping his temple with his index finger in order to indicate and stress his superior, innovative, cognitive thought processes.

Rafe Cordell stared impatiently at the people before him. Crack pots. Why did he get all the crack pots coming to his door? Was he some kind of a crack pot magnet? Was he wearing some kind of invisible sign that read "All Crack Pots Welcome"? And this time they had brought reinforcements: an Inspector from outside the county to interfere with his investigation.

"I told you before," said Rafe "I have my top men looking for your children, Mrs. Flanderly, and they <u>will</u> be found. Now-"

"Excusez-moi." proclaimed Pierre vigorously interrupting him purposefully. "You may need these." he said dropping two heads of garlic, one at a time, to strike resoundingly and unequivocally onto Detective Cordell's desk.

"What is this?" Detective Cordell asked raising his voice, as well as his eyebrows, in shocked, unbelieving surprise.

"Ummm…. Garlic is for warding off vampires, Pierre." Alex corrected him. "And I thought you didn't believe in GIANTS!" he noted suspiciously. "What changed?"

"This is a legitimate question. Mais souviens-toi! Une personne <u>cannot</u> be too sûr. One must always be prepared!"

Inspector Jim Lahy suppressed a chuckle. 'Finally,' he thought to himself, 'someone else was experiencing these frustrating, mismatched personalities for a change!' Although, there was no doubt that you had to feel deep sympathy for Eleanor Flanderly. She adored those kids. It was the least he could do when she and her husband contacted him to rush over and help with the search. Whatever influence he could exert to get the investigation more seriously underway he was happy to provide and the extra officers he had requested be put on the case had already discovered a trail of clues - a small ring, a baseball cap, a child's vest, etcetera - leading to a group of summer cabins on the other side of a stream.

"Et en le cas that we need the, comment dit-on, insurance…" Pierre continued triumphantly delving a hand into his lower coat pocket, "<u>this</u>, as you Américains say, is 'the icing sûr le gâteau'." he boasted adeptly withdrawing a large metal cross which he proudly held up victoriously for display.

Inspector Lahy, who had held his piece up until this point, spontaneously let forth a hearty laugh.

"I don't suppose that you've got anything in there for me, do you?" Jim Lahy inquired facetiously indicating Pierre's pocket while attempting to quell his mirth so as not to offend anybody.

"Mais, bien sûr." replied Pierre quite seriously regarding Jim oddly while suavely removing a silver bullet from the breast pocket of his shirt with one deft motion to hold it above his shoulder and display it in the light between his forefinger and thumb as he regarded it admiringly. "I do not oublie mes amis." he steadfastly proclaimed tossing the projectile to Jim who caught it in stride with a surprised, yet comical, look on his face at receiving the unexpected gift.

Rafe regarded the bewildered Lahy and the others in their various stages of mirth who occupied the office. 'Were they seriously considering a fictitious giant as a suspect?' he wondered. What was this? Was this a bona fide, official investigation or a circus?

"Are you some kind of a comedian?" Rafe asked Pierre directly.

"I am Pierre Dûçot, World Renowned dance instructor - peut-être you have heard of me...."

Clyde Barnett listened outside Detective Cordell's office with his ear pressed up against the closed door. It seemed that a group of squatters had moved into LaurelsHeath mansion and were planning on setting up housekeeping. Not only were they asserting a claim ta the house, but the surrounding land as well and they had even invited some friends and a fancy-dancy police feller over from another county ta help cement the deal. Clyde gnashed his teeth together. It was just gonna be that much harder ta acquire the property. But by hook or by crook that was what he was gonna have ta do! From what he could hear, the group inside were a bunch of superstitious nitwits. Two children, Matthew Alexander, who they called 'M.A.' for short, and his sister, Megan, had been kidnapped, supposedly by this evil giant who just scooped them up and ran off with them. They had been missing for a few days already and this guy with a foreign accent - probably their mystical advisor - was suggesting these old wives tale methods to get them back safe. Whooo-ee, these city folk were odd! And they had the gall to call them backwoods hicks! 'Well,' Clyde machinated screwing up his face so nastily that the action accentuated his beady, little brown eyes, 'I am sure as shootin' gonna show those snooty newcomers a thing or two!' Upon hearing footsteps approaching the office door he was leaning up against he fell back from it just in time so that when it opened he did not stumble inside of the room.

"Clyde! What are you doing here?" Rafe asked in bewilderment on seeing the longtime local.

"Don't look so out of sorts, Cordell. I just saw two big, mangy mountain lions hangin' abouts on the south ridge out there." he fabricated the story quickly. "They looked mighty hungry, too." 'Maybe that would scare them newbies into pullin' up stakes and headin' back where they came from!' Clyde thought evilly as he wet his lips, pulling his tongue across them, with satisfaction. "I just thought I'd tell you about it out of precaution and all." he continued innocently. "I'm only tryin' ta be a good citizen. I wouldn't want them slaughterin' any of my cattle with their big, ferocious teeth. You know how downright mean they can get when their bellies aren't full." Clyde further elaborated for Eleanor's benefit as she collapsed with horror and fell into a dead faint.

CHAPTER 8

Matthew was heartsick as he entered the front door of LaurelsHeath, hat in hand and fingering its brim, muttering beneath his breath. He had failed. He had not found the children and his wife was lying down on a daybed in the drawing room with a cold compress on her forehead, grieving. He could not avoid it any longer. He had to face her. 'It was best to get this over with quickly - no need te leave her in suspense.' Matthew thought. False hope was just as cruel as no hope a'tall. As he made his way across the wide, expansive, square entryway emblazoned in the center with the inset of a lion's head surrounded by foliage of the Mountain Laurel, a wreath of Laurel set atop the head of the mighty beast resting as a crown, he pondered upon how different it would have been - how all of this terrible trouble and travail never would have transpired - if Eleanor had minded her husband and not come to this place. Wherever that balmy French fellow be trouble was sure te follow! As he shook off the unbidden, sour thought regarding Pierre Dûçot, Matt halted abruptly to contemplate the situation at hand while gazing thoughtfully at the crest of the lion insignia decorating the floor.

"The crown bespeaks of honor and distinction."

A feminine voice he was unfamiliar with filled the hall resonating with the deep, unshakable tenor of faith and certainty. Its rich timbre was almost regal and he raised his head to regard a striking, mature woman with an upright carriage and noble bearing wearing a long, grey dress who appeared to be floating toward him on a cloud of air. Along with her, though lagging farther behind, as if Matt's brooding meditations had unconsciously summoned him advanced Pierre and....

"Me bairns! Me darlin's! Where on the face o' the bonny, green earth ha' ye been?" cried Matt in jubilant throes of ecstasy as he ran toward the two AWOL absentees.

"We had an adventure and I was scared!" cried Megan racing to meet him and then throwing herself into her father's arms.

Trudy sent Pierre a look of warning and so he stepped-up to where M.A. had just joined Matthew and the three of them were locked in a three way hug.

"Des enfants ont des imaginations très forte n'est-ce pas?" observed the Frenchman calmly.

"I saw a giant!" Megan insisted stamping her small foot stubbornly. "We were captured!" she persisted, pursing her lips and jutting forth her little chin.

"She has been listening to Elvie - tu sais que la femme est folle!" interjected Pierre dismissively discounting Megan's statements out of hand nervously.

"Oh, be quiet ye blitherin' idiot. If my daughter says tha' she saw a giant, she saw a GIANT!" Matt stated emphatically humoring the little girl. "Were he a mean giant, darlin'?" he asked Megan gently in a lower tone attempting to ascertain the root of the issue.

"No...." she responded slowly suddenly unsure of herself - giants should be bad, shouldn't they?

"What was he? Was he terrible with big fangs an' a hump on his back?" Matthew inquired bending low and snarling as he stamped about growling.

"No!" she asserted in spontaneous outburst as she giggled at his tomfoolery. "Not like that. He was a nice giant. But all he wanted to do was play and I missed you and Mum and he wouldn't let me and M.A. go."

"Aw..." M.A. interrupted her skeptically, "she doesn't know

what she's talking about. There was <u>no</u> giant." he asserted adamantly sending Megan a look that said 'BE SILENT'.

"What be all the commotion transpiring...?" Eleanor, who had just poked her head out of the drawing room and around the mahogany door at the ruckus, complained querulously about all the noise. "Children! Me lost babes in the woods! Where'd ye come from?" she asked loudly without expecting an answer while she ran to hug Megan and M.A. close to her bosom. "Saints be praised yer both safe. I ha' figured tha' the mountain lions ha' gotten hold o' ye!" she blubbered weeping profusely.

"Mountain lions, ye say, Ellie?" Matthew repeated in bewilderment as he stared at her sympathetically.

"Some insensitive resident came into Detective Cordell's office and told us, right in front of Eleanor, that hungry mountain lions were roaming around eating cattle." related Alex indignantly in response entering the house in time to hear Matthew's question to Eleanor. "He should have known better than to say those things - he saw that she was crying!"

"In all fairness, Alex," Rand said reasonably "the man didn't know Megan and M.A. were out there missing with no way to protect themselves <u>OR</u> that Eleanor was their mother who was grieving for them." asserted his cousin following closely on Alex's heels.

"Where be this scurrilous blackguard who frightened me Ellie senseless?" demanded Matthew bellicosely, unbuttoning the cuffs of his shirtsleeves and methodically rolling each one up to his elbow, preparing to do battle with the nameless, loathsome foe.

"Randy be right, Matthew. The man couldna ha' known why I was spakin' te the Detective. Me only solace durin' the whole terrible situation was tha' ye were still out there lookin' fer our young ones." she flattered him soothingly to calm him down and distract his purpose - which, by the bye, she was successful in doing.

"Pierre?" asked Matt suddenly turning to face him. "Just what de ye ha' te do with this kettle o' fish?"

"What? I have done nothing." answered the Frenchman guiltily.

"Now <u>there's</u> a fine taradiddle if I've ever heard a one. Ye <u>always</u> ha' done somethin'. Ye <u>always</u> ha' yer finger in every pie. Stirrin' up every pot an' causin' some kind o' confusion. I <u>saw</u> ye with me bairns. What were ye doin' te them!?" he inquired precipitously, suddenly alarmed, checking the girl and boy for bruises or other telltale marks.

"I did nothing to them!" he said excitedly. "I merely took them out for ice cream after their harrowing ordeal with the giant...." Pierre cupped his hand over his own mouth mortified at his indiscreet slip-up.

Trudy became all at once alarmed and clutched at her grey sunbonnet agitatedly at Pierre's careless remark.

"Now, I <u>know</u> there canna be no giant - because <u>YOU</u> say tha' there <u>BE</u> a giant." Matthew stated decisively, his voice raised an octave higher than normal.

"I <u>TOLD</u> you there was a giant." Elvie stated emphatically to her husband on hearing Pierre's blundering admission as the front door opened a fourth time to admit her along with Calvin, Dudley and Callie in tow. "<u>NOW</u> do you believe me everybody? I <u>TOLD</u> you."

"There is no giant." M.A. confessed apologetically as he glanced fleetingly at Trudy and Pierre. "There is-" he began as Trudy held her breath; Pierre looked on helplessly and they both waited for the other shoe to drop.

"Oh, M.A., there you are!" Cari addressed him eagerly intruding upon his guilty confession as she entered the room quite unexpectedly to the varying degrees of surprise and/or relief of its occupants. "Where did you and Megan come from before?" she asked as Trudy and Pierre both visibly relaxed.

"Outside. Uncle Pierre took us for ice cream-" M.A. started to explain deliberately misinterpreting her question in order to avoid a telling response.

"No, I mean <u>BEFORE</u>. When Trudy and I were in the kitchen? I turned from the sink and you and Megan were there talking with Trudy."

"Oh." he answered while thinking fast. "Well, we came in through the backdoor." M.A. explained calmly.

"That is not possible. The back door is on the opposite side of the house." Cari noted. "You definitely could <u>not</u> have come in that way. I would have seen you! It was almost as if you guys had appeared from nowhere - out of thin air!" she assessed the past circumstance logically.

"I knew it. I kept telling you. People are appearing and disappearing around here. I'm not imagining things" Elvie cast a look of defiance in Trudy's direction "and I'm not making this stuff up. I <u>saw</u> it with <u>MY</u> <u>OWN</u> <u>TWO</u> <u>EYES</u>. And now, I have a witness!" Elvie asserted affirmatively to Calvin only to be distracted by another source - a new entrant stumbling into the helter-skelter conversation.

Elvira's head turned along with those assembled who were also caught unawares by this new, human wrinkle.

"Pierre!" gasped Edith as the door opened a fifth time and she hung on the knob of the open door, panting. "You ran off with Trudy and the children so quickly that I did not know what to think. Were you trying to 'ditch' me? Are you keeping secrets from me? Every time I came close to catching up with you four, you were whispering together. And then, when I turned around, after turning away for only a moment, you all were...GONE!"

"LOOK!!!"

All at once the clustered groups congregated in the entryway of LaurelsHeath stopped speculating on their own individual, various pet peeves and focused their attentions on Megan from whom the exclamation had arisen and who was pointing with arm outstretched at a fluffy, white cat with twinkling blue eyes wearing a collar from which hung many jingling ornaments.

"DON'T YOU FOLLOW THAT CAT!" M.A. yelled following his sister lickety-split racing after her as she raced after the cat.

"That is just Charmer." clarified Trudy to the stupefied assemblage who had suddenly fallen silent. "She is our house mouser."

CHAPTER 9

"I don't understand why we're still out here. If the kids are safe we should head on back." complained Alex to Mary Jo while slapping at another mosquito on his forearm.

Alex had so many mosquito bites on his neck and arms that he had lost count of them all - and that was just for today. The past three days had been more of the same. It had been a feeding frenzy for those stinging insects. He felt like a pin cushion. His skin was very sensitive and the pinprick-sized stings had swollen transforming themselves into a pattern of raised, little bumps adorning his tender derma in scattered clusters. He also had contracted a bad case of sunburn turning his already fair skin to a light shade of orange reminiscent of some of the boiled shellfish in the window of Laureltown's only fishery.

"My skin is peeling!" he also noted querulously.

"As soon as we find Jim Lahy and let him know the kids have come home and that they're safe, we'll head on back." soothed Mary Jo placatingly. "Then, the Inspector can call off the police search."

"When did they come home anyway?" he asked.

"That's the kicker. They just...appeared. It was so funny. Edith, Cari and I were speaking with Trudy - we were all gathered in the kitchen. Trudy went into the butler's pantry - it was almost as if she heard something or had a sixth sense because when we followed her.... There were M.A. and Megan. It was as if they had appeared out of nowhere. They were standing between her and the wall where all the cleaning equipment was hanging shaking with cold or fear or both. And when we asked them where they came from they looked terrified and wouldn't answer. Then, Trudy took them for ice cream. After they returned with Pierre, I told Cari that me and you would go out and find Jim Lahy to let him know we found the 'bairns'." she explained.

"You just <u>had</u> to 'rope' me into this - didn't you Mary Jo?" said Alex smiling crookedly at his wife as she gazed at him with tolerant impatience. "Don't you get it - 'rope' - it's a cowboy joke!"

"I am not amused, Mr. Caine." she observed semi-glibly as she spun on her heel playfully and pretended to walk away in a huff.

"Oh, come on, Mary Jo! Look at me - I'm a wreck!" shouted Alex following in her wake to catch up with her, upset that he might have irked Mary Jo and perhaps had gotten on her bad side. "Who's that?" he asked suddenly, halting abruptly, squinting into the distance and scratching his neck.

"He must be a stranger in town who's lost his way." Mary Jo surmised. "This is private property, after all." she reasoned.

"Looks like he's lost more than his way." judged Alex as he watched the tall, dark haired gentleman who was bent over pushing aside brambles and sifting through blades of grass - raking them with his fingers.

As Mary Jo and Alex advanced toward him the gentleman intuitively raised his head and straightened up on their approach. He held a grey western-style hat in one hand by its floppy brim and pulled his arm from elbow to wrist across his forehead wiping off the perspiration accumulated on the surface of his furrowed brow as he watched them and waited on them in anticipation of their imminent arrival.

"What you looking for?" asked Alex once he was within earshot of the fellow.

"My kid lost his lucky charm and 'dear old dad', that's me, has been elected to find it." responded the man resignedly.

"Ugh! I know how that goes." said Mary Jo. "A friend of ours has a little boy who just cannot hold on to his stuff - and they always turn up in the most outlandish places you could ever imagine. You know, the places you would least expect them to be. But the really disgusting part of it is <u>what</u> he loses. Frogs and lizards....YUK!" she exhorted with a shudder.

"She's just squeamish - WOMEN!" exclaimed Alex deprecatingly. "By the way. Please excuse my manners. I'm Alex Caine and this is Mary Jo, my wife. We're visiting some friends of ours at LaurelsHeath. I don't know if you've heard of the place." he stated casually deliberately ignoring the angry look on Mary Jo's face while kneeling to the ground and searching for the aforementioned object of contention between some rocks despite the fact that he did not even know what it was beyond the fact that it was a lucky charm or what it looked like. "Well, of course you've heard of the place. You live around here...don't you?"

"Over there, Alex. I think you've found something." Mary Jo exclaimed excitedly her recent anger forgotten.

Mary Jo joined her husband, bending down by his side, to pick up a rusty key which lay amongst some newly cast aside stones which, after being upturned by Alex, had been summarily thrown to one side, neglected and discarded.

"Is this what you're looking for?" she inquired, crowing proudly, holding up her find and regarding it in the sharp light of day.

"Thank you, Mary Jo. You've found it. My son will be very happy to have that back. He puts quite a store by that old skate key." the stranger elucidated reaching toward it to pluck it from Mary Jo's fingers.

"Hey, wait a minute!" cried Alex snatching it from Mary Jo's fingers before the man could reach the trinket. "This looks like <u>my</u> key. The one with the map they wanted to throw out because it didn't do anything - but I kept it! You remember, Mary Jo." he continued attempting to jog her memory. "This key."

Alex pulled a chain hanging about his neck out from beneath his shirt to display a key of his own dangling from it.

"And would you look at that! They're both broken in the same places, too. Though…. On second thought…" Alex conceded while analyzing the two keys "THIS one has more jagged, metal pieces sticking out on this side, here, and mine has less." he ended by pointing out the distinguishable discrepancy.

"If you think about it," ventured Mary Jo as she studied both keys together, now, where previously she had only been considering the one recovered from the ground, "separately, they appear to be two halves of one WHOLE key that might match if fit together…."

Mary Jo, as well as the man who had all at once become an avid, interested spectator, watched with bated breath as Alex put the half of the key hanging from his neck together with the "skate" key and the two came together seamlessly with no evidence of transition. They were a perfect match. The lines of the joining were indiscernible and it was a shame when the formation of this perfect union was broken apart without warning or prior indication when the nameless stranger hastily reached in to take his half of the key away from Alex and put it in his own pocket.

"Why did you take it away?" she demanded of the man. "They fit together perfectly. Maybe they're a clue to something!"

"Do not be upset with me, Miss. - Mary Jo. I am sure it is only a coincidence that the pieces fit. An intriguing coincidence, of course, but one that is likely of no consequence."

"You'll have to forgive my wife. Mary Jo gets carried away sometimes. You know women. Always romanticizing things and looking for mysterious secrets!" said Alex apologetically making light of his wife's concern and attempting to bond with the stranger.

"Oh, so when you and the others went and followed that crazy treasure map a few years back, that was nothing out of the ordinary - nothing to think twice about. But, when I say that maybe that key might be a clue to something I'm being fantastical and don't get the benefit of the doubt." retorted Mary Jo, miffed.

The stranger's eyebrows shot up in surprise and remained raised with interest as Mary Jo made her unrestrained declaration.

"Emmy! Don't be mad." cajoled Alex soothingly.

"It appears, son, that your young lady has a point. You found a... treasure map?" he asked curiously.

"Yeah. And it was a real one, too. It was even endorsed by a real pirate! And we did find a treasure." he asserted firmly and defiantly, particularly for Mary Jo's benefit.

"Where does one go about finding a real treasure map?" the man wondered aloud.

"I don't know, but this one was in an old tackle box - along with the key, or half key, around my neck."

"So. You do a lot of fishing, do you?" he asked conversationally.

"Me? Oh, well I don't. But a friend of mine does. And the tackle box was a birthday gift to his son."

"I see. So, he just dabbles in the sport. I get it."

"No. Actually, he's an expert." Alex boasted. "And he calls it a sport, too. Anything you want to know about fishing, he's your man. His wife isn't too happy about it, though, because he's always taking their son on fishing trips when she says that he should be doing his schoolwork and studying for exams. You see, she was a housekeeper - and there's nothing wrong with that occupation, it's an honorable one - but she wants a better life for him than she had. She wants him to become a doctor like his father. Anyway, we won't keep you. Mary Jo and I, we're just glad we were able to help you find your son's good luck charm. And, by the way, may I say, 'GOOD LUCK WITH THAT'!" he chuckled, the lighthearted sound trailing off as no one else picked it up and joined in. "Just a small pun there.... Good luck charm - 'GOOD LUCK WITH

THAT'.... Well, I thought it was funny." admitted Alex clearing his throat uncomfortably with the admission and shifting his weight from one foot to the other. "I apologize." he said abruptly changing the topic of conversation. "What is your name?"

"Simon." replied the stranger. "My name is Simon."

CHAPTER 10

Manual labor! Was <u>this</u> all that he was good for, MANUAL LABOR? At the realization that he was being under-appreciated and that his talents were being sorely overlooked Pierre Dûçot gazed with aversion at the sludge in the pails he was emptying from the overflowing sewer behind the house. He felt positively ill at the sight. 'In France this never would have happened.' he brooded darkly. Splashes of the concoction of wet dirt mixed with…other things soiled his garments as the grimy contents sloshed out of the buckets precipitately when he set them down for refuse removal later. 'Oh, la, la!' he thought distastefully with a sigh and a grimace. He would just have to burn his vêtements afterwards. They were so filthy and muddied as were his hands. He turned them palms-up and considered their condition. He would just have to scrub them with a strong solvent when he returned to the house. Pierre cocked his head as he considered the efficaciousness versus the adverse effects of boiling water quickly dismissing the idea as he briefly dwelled on the 'post-pruniness'. 'It would not do to have dishpan hands, after all!' he reflected silently as he regarded his hands critically and the possibility horrified him. He was not a plumber! However, he had agreed to aid them, or as ces Américains say, "Pitch In", and so he would not renege on his word. It was the Dûçot Code, after all. Honor came first above all. However, now only one salle de bains was usable now that the one in the west wing of the house had ceased functioning. This would make scheduling time for its occupation dicey. Fortunately, the children were being sent to camp and so they would not be there to compete with him for its coveted use. Bien sûr! His grooming routine was le plus qu'important partie of the day for him, after all, and could not be rushed merely to accommodate two young children no matter how adorable and endearing they were. And as for the <u>OTHERS</u> - they did not font de conséquence. Surely, they realized the requisite impératif absolu that Pierre Dûçot must look his best at all times. After all, what would his loyal fans and admirers think if he were to appear in the any least way shabby? Such a breach he would not ask them to tolerate. Pierre suddenly stiffened his posture, glanced quickly about him both to the left and then to the right, and then relaxed. Only Randmore McKinley and his cousin, Alex Caine, were visible in the vicinity. Pierre sighed with relief letting out a deep breath which he did not realize that he had sucked in out of nervousness and had been holding. Nonetheless, to be on the safe side, he pulled up the collar of his shirt to cover his neck along with the lower part of his jaw and pulled down the brim of his cap to conceal his eyes and shield his facial features from direct scrutiny. Pierre was fairly sure that these adjustments would suffice until he was able to reach the security of the house and cleanup. He frowned remembering the way that Matthew Alexander and Megan had appeared before he and Trudy had cleaned them up. The state of their apparel had been deplorable. They, themselves, had been so grimy! Their clothes had been torn in places and, oh, so dusty! Mais, bien sûr the tears in leurs vêtements could not be mended immédiatement, but once the dust had been rubbed off of them and their faces and hands were washed the average eye was not able to detect la différence. Cette sorte de la tricherie was assez à tromper l'oeil des autres mais it was not enough to rendre <u>him</u> the fool! Oui, he saw through the disguise! He was very discerning. Pierre mulled over his superior level of prowess while simultaneously raising and lowering each eyebrow and, with added hauteur, swiping at an imaginary mustache beneath his nose on his upper lip with his forefinger. Hurriedly he withdrew his hand as far away from his nostrils as possible coughing and gagging at the stench of the dark, grainy substance accumulated thereon. Undaunted by this small irritation, he then attempted to adopt a more unique, erect stance to set him apart from folk in general and convey the connotation of his obviously superior intellect. However, the noxious fumes emanating pungently from the pails of sludge combined with the smell in his nostrils and that lingering in the air of the dried sludge which was caked upon his forefinger, his hand and was crusted underneath his fingernails and, in one powerful blast of concentrated, vile odor, assailed his senses making this an impossibility. The fumes stung his eyes causing tears to erupt from them unbidden to roll down his cheeks in a creeping locomotion. The cavalcade of stench interfered with his concentration so that he could not effectively maintain his contrived posture and he lost his perspective as he reflexively bent over, nauseated. After his stomach had finished contracting, completing somersaults and performing various other gymnastics, he again considered M.A. and Megan. The children were to be taken to a camp in the vicinity. He decided that he would miss them. In fact, ce serait certain that he would miss them. However, their endearing, ingenuous natures were a danger to the confidentiality of Trudy's son, Elroy. They were so open and honest that they might unintentionally, comment dit-on, "spill the beans". Bien sûr, he hardly knew the woman - he had only recently made Trudy's acquaintance - mais her impassioned pleas on Elroy's behalf struck a sympathetic cord in his heart. He had always felt protective of the fairer, and more helpless, female sex. She had pleaded for his help to convince the children to keep Elroy's hiding place a secret and impressed upon him the injustice of the public outcry against her son by those who considered him a freak of nature because he was overly tall and a bit slow mentally. She told him how people were afraid of Elroy because he was big

and strong yet despite this liked to play with their children and might hurt them because he did not know his own strength or that he was much older than they were. She had broken down and sobbed pathetically as she related how unfair it was that such a kind, gentle boy had to deal with being ostracized by a society that not only looked on him with trepidation and fear but considered him such a threat and danger that they actually had a sworn order written out against him by a mental asylum to lock him up in an institution if ever he could be found and served with the edict. Of course, how could he refuse to aid her? Honor was his middle name and justice must be upheld at all costs! Trudy had assured him plusieurs temps that Elroy was harmless. He had argued vehemently with her about telling Edi of their agreement concerning Elroy - he could not keep secrets from his wife! Although, if she knew of the new alliance with Trudy she would be jealous, bien sûr! But he was willing to take the risque. However, Trudy was adamant that the confidentiality de cette affaire must be maintained at all costs and so they had spoken with M.A. and Megan to this effect. They were immediately receptive et en complete d'accord avec l'idée. They agreed to keep silent until the injustice of Elroy's plight could be exposed and set aright. Little Megan, however, was just a capricious little jeune fille and could not help but let small clues of Elroy's existence slip de temps en temps - she craved the adult attention that she garnered by revealing these snippets of half-truths. Pierre briefly cogitated on the question of why Trudy had chosen him to confide in. Of every person here she had known Calvin, Elvie, Dudley and Callie the longest so why did she not select one of them? He did not ruminate upon this for long, however. It seemed quite obvious to him that she recognized that he, and he alone, showed the subtle veneer of sophistication of a man of the world who was used to discretion in all matters no matter how...sticky....
An unflappable rock of strength that one might lean on in the times

of difficulté or consult with when seeking advice sûr des problèmes. It was certainly clear that his strong shoulders were the only ones that were broad enough to unload her troubles onto. Women were drawn to him, as the Américains said, comme the moth to the fire. His brow furrowed momentarily. She <u>DID</u> look at him strangely at times, though. He supposed that she must harbor feelings of...admiration for him. His mind cleared with the realization. Oui, c'est ça. He would not lead her into believing that there was any chance of a romantic alliance between them - he loved Edi, after all! He would just have to "let her down easy", as the colloquialism said. He would let her know that he was sorry but that he was a one woman homme.

CHAPTER 11

"Ya newlyweds! God bless yer hearts, ya always need some extra pocket money. I got it!" exclaimed Clyde Barnett with impromptu inspiration while clapping one palm against the other and then pushing off of it with a sliding motion. "Let me do ya a favor, gratis. How's about I buy a piece of yer land - just a small'un - so's I can build maself a place ta live onta. I'm a-gonna buy <u>some</u> piece-a land anyways so it might as well be yers. How's that sound ta ye? Rememba. I is only try'n' ta help a fellow neighbor out!" he finished enthusiastically and without guile while backing away with open palms raised to imply honesty and to indicate that there was no pressure for Dudley and Callie to accept his offer and that surely there was no benefit for him or personal advantage for him to gain if they agreed to his proposal.

'These city folk were so easy to fool!' Clyde thought gleefully as he watched Dudley help a squeamish Callie over some puddles of muddied, brown water to approach him in greeting with her. Calvin followed after the two as Elvie just looked about her haplessly at the devastation to their new property. It seemed that Mother Nature was on Clyde's side supporting his cause to oust these interlopers from the area. Clyde looked about him taking in the entire expansive view before him from the uprooted oak tree in one corner of the field to the water damaged barn that was still partially submerged despite the toiling, tireless efforts of the newlyweds bailing bucketsful of the standing water in their attempt to free it of the high surrounding water from the overflowing nearby lake which did not have the capacity required to contain the torrential rains which had literally assaulted and battered the area for the past three days. This kind of downfall had been a freak occurrence and was unprecedented. 'It did not often happen that the area flooded in this manner, but these interlopers had no way of knowing that! And what they didn't know wouldn't hurt them none neither!' he mused wickedly. The sweeping gusts of wind in the area had not only uprooted the historic oak tree which had stood mightily on the property ever since Clyde was a small boy, but had flattened adjacent bushes as well as other flora in the area. 'All of this combined dee-struction should make those newbies think twice and triplicate-time about setting down roots hereabouts.' meditated Clyde with fixated determinedness. He felt like swaggering about joyfully. As he quickly turned from the "newbies" the satisfaction which contorted Clyde's facial features was evident. 'Of course, this was only a small piece of the land.' he conceded inwardly. Only a small piece of the larger jigsaw puzzle, but he had to operate slowly and avoid their suspicion. Gain their confidence and garner their trust. 'Yeah, that was the ticket!' His eyes gleamed with anticipation as he plotted. Yes, he decided that step by step was the way to go. Bit by bit he would insert himself into LaurelsHeath and before the newcomers were aware of it - he would own all of the land. YOU HAD TO START SOMEWHERE, he reasoned. He turned to face the newlyweds masking his grimly resolved visage by pasting onto it a false smile of ingratiating jocularity.

"That there's too bad about yer barn - looks like ye'd just painted it, too!"

Clyde minutely regarded the woebegone structure closely as if seeing it for the first time. Elvie knew the truth of his statement and hung her head regretfully while pondering upon the many wasted weeks that they had spent - her, Calvin, Dudley and Callie - beautifying the barn as the man from the detective's office continued speaking.

"Looks ta me like ye'd got it all 'duded' up, too. Newfangled tiles on the roof..." he observed, regarding the obviously new, now sadly cracked, material covering the roof and the shingles dangling from nails on one of its corners, "fancy-lookin' winda's put in." Clyde noted stepping closer to examine the recently shattered window panes and flick at their broken edges. "Pretty penny...pretty penny.... Wheww-ee!" he concluded his estimation of the damage with a whistle. "An' now ya gots ta start all over. PITY." Clyde openly commiserated as he inwardly counted his chickens - 'Maybe this would make them amenable ta selling right quicker!' he plotted.

At Clyde's declaration of sympathy and his evaluation of the damages Elvira broke down dissolving into tears and clutched at Calvin in abject defeat.

"Hey. You know mister? You are making my wife upset!" shouted Calvin irately, not to mention threateningly, with his fist raised.

Clyde backed away innocently with one hand over his heart, and the other palm was open and upraised with arm stretched out toward Calvin.

"I sure didn't mean no disrespect, sir.... Calvin, is it? I heard Detective Cordell call ya Calvin - may I call ya, Calvin?" he asked apologetically.

"NO!" responded Calvin barking emphatically in a loud voice. "You can't just go around upsetting people, you know!" stated the irate young man who was hugging and softly cooing comfortingly to his tearful wife.

"Yeah!" cried Dudley as leading Callie by the hand over displaced rocks and piles of broken branches lying on the ground he joined Calvin and Elvie. "You just can't come around and talk to people like that! Can't you see we've got enough stress to deal with around here? Talk about INSENSITIVE.... Gee Whiz!"

"What is going on over there?" Rand yelled down to them from the hill, the question falling to their ears as he plodded purposefully in their direction.

"I didn't mean ta be rude ta ya's all. I was just makin' friendly conversation, is all - tryin' ta be neighborly. Welcome ya's ta the community. An' this is the howdy do I get!" said Clyde acknowledging Dudley and Calvin's criticisms with a sniff.

Clyde pulled his camouflage green raincoat more closely about him; raised his collar and then spat on the ground managing to appear slightly offended throughout the whole process.

"Now, I's a-figurin' we got ourselves off on the wrong doggy. So...." he acceded judiciously. "Here's what I'll do you fer. We'll let bygones be begat and fergit the whole shebang - how's that? Now. My offer still stands ta buy this poor, drowned out and scraggly plot of land. I can always use it fer a swimming pool! HA, HA!" he chuckled after speaking what in his own opinion was a witticism. "Clever, huh? Swimming pool - the puddles.... No one is smiling? Give me a break. I'm not what ya would call a comedian fer freakin' sake. Well, I came ta see if I could help ya cleanup the place." fibbed Clyde glibly - he had no intention of helping them, at least not in the way the newlyweds would want. "But, I can tell that ya got plenty of help." he continued and pointed at Rand, Alex and Matthew who were coming to reconnoiter with the newlyweds to ascertain what the ongoing commotion was all about and what the stranger had to do with it all. "So's I'll be hearin' from ya I hope soon - bye." he concluded curtly as he turned tail and jogged toward town quickly to avoid the approaching threesome.

"What was that all about?" Randmore asked his hosts as he watched Clyde's retreating back. "That's the man from Detective Cordell's office, isn't it?"

"I don't know who he thought he was, but he had a lot of nerve. Now, I wouldn't normally say anything, but I didn't like his attitude. He was just emphasizing all the NEGATIVE things and had nothing positive to say at all! He seemed...SLIMY. It's not fair to

say, because I don't know him well at all, but.... I didn't like him."
Callie finally blurted out with a shudder of distaste on remembering Clyde's overall demeanor.

"He said he was willing to take this…mess…off our hands."
Dudley elucidated, more to the point of Rand's query, while looking around him at the outdoor disarray which Mother Nature had wrought. "At this point, I'd tell him that he can have the land for free!" he exclaimed. "What a catastrophe!"

They all gazed at the exposed half of the burst apart water pipe jutting out of the earth; the water damage on the barn with its misshapen roof and the puddles all about. One could not help but concur wholeheartedly with Dudley's impetuous, impassioned sentiment. Until Calvin spoke up shrewdly:

"But does this Barnett guy have an agenda?" Calvin said tapping his noggin sagely with his index finger.

"An' yer all about AGENDAS - aren't ye?" Matthew jibed at him in a sour tone remembering how he and Dudley had conspired to 'steal his treasure'.

"I agree with Calvin, médecin." asserted Pierre authoritatively, ignoring Matt's bitter comment to Calvin as he flicked an imaginary speck of dust from his jacket.

The Frenchman had, quite surprisingly, seemed to materialize out of thin air.

"An' wherever did you come from? Sneakin' out o' yer natural home environment, were ye?" Matthew noted sarcastically as he pointedly gazed with much affectation down one of the deep holes created when some large oak trees had been uprooted from their Mother Earth and blown aside by the previously hurricane-like gusts of wind.

"Tu es très drôle, médecin. You are so plus funny, as you Américains say, que j'ai oublié à rire."

"Canna ye not ever be straightforward!?" Matthew argued in

frustration as he attempted to mentally translate Pierre's response.

"Moi?" Pierre proclaimed artlessly. "Je suis comme, how do you say, an 'open book'. I am la personne who told you - NON, NON, NON - who <u>begged</u> you, to allow me to guard our treasure. But you-"

"Be careful what it is ye say, mon ami. <u>GRAND-MÈRE</u> might be listenin' te ye!"

Matthew smiled broadly with satisfaction at the stricken look of fear which appeared on Pierre's face at the mention of his dead Grandmother's ghost. Calvin and Dudley just looked at each other guiltily. They had never told anybody of Calvin's part in 'resurrecting' Grand-mère Dûçot from the dead. It was not that they were deliberately <u>concealing</u> it. But they had merely forgotten about it. It was old news to them and they had never given it a second thought.

"Matt." Rand interceded in order to change the subject for if he did not, if the existence of 'Grand-mère' ever again became an issue, Pierre would be impossible to live with. "I thought that you, Eleanor and the kids were leaving for Charlottesville after all the jumbled up problems that have transpired since your arrival with the kids and all."

"Ellie and I were amenable te leavin', especially Ellie, an' I dunna believe Matthew Alexander was opposed te the suggestion. But it's me wee one, Megan, tha' put up a fuss. She canna get past tha' cat tha's roamin' the house. She luvs it so. She won't leave it an', fer the life o' me, I canna help but indulge her in her flight o' fancy. Yer only young once, ye know.... Tho' with some cases," he amended casting a cold, disparaging glance at Pierre "it be takin' a wee bit longer."

Matt watched in unbounded fascination as Pierre removed a necklace of strung garlic heads from within the folds of his jacket and hung it around his neck. Matt drew the tip of his tongue across the roof of his mouth to produce a clucking sound and shook his head from side to side in disbelief, continuing:

"An' <u>sometimes</u> even longer than <u>THAT</u>, te be sure!" he finished dramatically as he turned away with a flourish.

Pierre was not about to let those barbs of Matthew's, his galling suggestions that he - Pierre Dûçot - was in any way infantile, go by unaddressed. He opened his mouth to respond sharply only to be interrupted abruptly by Alex, his words quelling the Frenchman's potentially acerbic tongue-lashing.

"People! Look what I found!" cried Alex clamoring for everyone's undivided attention as he ran over from the site of the erstwhile functioning sewer.

"That's funny," observed Elvie who was still engaged in dabbing at her eyes and blowing her nose, "I cleared that place up and that weren't there before." she noted as she came to stand at Alex's shoulder and reached over to rub some of the mud off of the large, asymmetrical chunk of material in his hand to reveal a dark, yellowish, ochre surface beneath.

CHAPTER 12

"Ye've done it again, laddie - this boy is me good luck charm!" shouted Matthew vigorously clapping Alex on the back with so much unrestrained force that the young man fell forward.

As he lost his footing, Alex toppled onto Pierre and steadied himself by grabbing onto the said gentleman's arm erratically.

"Watch where you are going, Alex!" snapped Pierre peevishly and with much irritation shaking off the grasping hands of the stumbling fellow impatiently. "I say that this is nothing more than an ordinary rock." he continued with authority picking up the contested yellowish lump from the coffee table; holding it up to the light of day streaming in through the window and regarding it critically.

"An' I say," contested Matthew yanking the rock from his upheld hand lest he taint its credibility any further with his comments or actions, "that it be the genuine article!"

"I tell you it is faux, comment dit-on, "fool's gold"!"

"It be the real article I tell ye! It be me pot o' gold at the end o' the rainbow an' yer too thickheaded a goon not te realize it!"

Trudy looked on with amusement as Pierre stepped up to where, taking a bellicose stance, Matthew stood with feet spread apart and touched his nose to his.

"I say this rock ce n'est pas vrai!" Pierre rejoined scornfully as he forcefully regained possession of said object by grabbing it from Matthew's grasp; produced a monocle from his vest pocket and commenced his minute scrutiny of its every surface and edge.

Trudy, who was completing her dusting of the farthermost

corner of the room, could not conceal her ever-widening smile.

"Look, guys. Don't fight. All I said is that it <u>looked</u> like gold. I didn't say that it <u>was</u> gold." Alex said placatingly.

"Ye hit the nail right on the head, laddie. Yer simple phraseology has stated the obvious." Matthew assured him.

"I only made a comment - I don't know anything about mineralogy." he demurred.

"It not be scientific te know gold when ye see it - ye dunna need te be possessed of some high calibered degree te know what yer eyes are tellin' is before ye!" Matthew began to lecture.

All at once they both noticed it…. The silence. Pierre had ceased speaking. He was gazing dumbfounded at the "stone" in his hands and muttering to himself. When he did speak coherently it was not in his previously loud, blustering fashion. Instead, he spoke in more of a murmur to himself.

"C'est impossible…incroyable. Mais ici est l'évidence. Bien sûr, it was HIS maison…non, non, non. <u>But</u>. Si-"

"What are ye mumblin' about now?" Matthew suddenly asked Pierre curiously - yet gruffly (he did not want to appear TOO interested in his opinion after flouting it, after all) - interrupting his one-sided conversation.

"<u>This</u> symbol…. NON. NON. It is not possible. What would he be doing here? NON."

"I thought we had him for a moment there but we lost him, laddie." Matt said in exasperation to Alex in an attempt at wry humour.

"'NON' what, Pierre?" Alex timidly interjected, ignoring Matthew.

"I cannot tell for certain…. C'est très difficile à traduire ça. Peut-être-"

"Answer the lad ye cockamamie bag o' bones! Can ye never stop spakin' in yer riddles!?" cried Matthew in frustration as he stomped around Pierre grasping at sections of the hair on his own scalp in clumps.

"I am merely saying that cette marque, here," he explained pointing to the corner of the lump of compacted, hard material as Matt and Alex crowded around him eagerly to view the engraving thereon, "is <u>NOT</u> the marque of Jan LaFitte." he proclaimed quite pleased with himself at solving the mystery.

Crestfallen, Matthew - whose attention he had previously captured and interest he had piqued - looked fit to explode at the new revelation. Mouth partially open, he was ready to call Pierre out for raising his hopes with his highfalutin airs and caged meanings only to dash them in one sweeping, final blow with his last statement. However, Pierre's next comment forestalled the voicing of his grievances.

"<u>But</u>!" continued Pierre unaware of Matt's ire; Alex's angst and Trudy's flustered demeanor as she leaned in closer. "It is definitely in his handwriting."

"How can you tell that?" demanded Alex innocently. "It's just a bunch of uppercase and lowercase letters."

"The discerning eye can tell." Pierre voiced the belief with sage assurance nodding his head confidently and tapping his temple knowledgeably.

A small snicker was heard from the corner of the room. All eyes turned briefly toward Trudy who took great pains to conceal a blossoming smile and appear totally disinterested in their conversation and otherwise completely enthralled with every aspect of her dusting and associated housekeeping duties.

"As <u>I</u> was saying." continued Pierre finally after a pregnant pause during which time he had fixed Trudy with a curious stare and then dismissed the distraction she presented in order that he might recapture the attention of the other two. "These letters definitely display the characteristics of my <u>dear</u>, old friend, Jan LaFitte. And wherever nous trouvons Jan LaFitte's marque, we find…."

"Me gold! GOLD." cried Matthew ecstatically presumptuously finishing Pierre's thought for him. "I <u>knew</u> it, Alexander, me boy. You and I are goin' te be RICH! Just you and I."

"And just <u>how</u> do you make this calculation?" Pierre quickly interjected. "Alex - who is comme a <u>son</u> to me - found that gold. Therefore, it is his claim." he asserted with finality.

"But I want to <u>share</u> my good fortune." Alex said interrupting them both. "What good is having all that gold if I can't share it with my friends? And anyway, how do we know there are any more gold nuggets like this? This may be the only one."

"Ye hear <u>that</u> ye graspin' scalawag? Alex be wantin' te <u>share</u> his newfound wealth. Yer tryin' te corrupt the laddie with the avarice called GREED!" Matthew spat out as he placed an arm around the young man's shoulders and pulled Alex close to his side. "An' what, pray tell us, makes ye so sure all o' a sudden tha' this be gold?" he asked Pierre pointedly regarding him suspiciously.

"I <u>told</u> you médecin. Jan's handwriting guarantees this as fact." asserted Pierre impatiently.

The Doctor had fallen silent and bowed his head tapping the fingers of each of his hands against the other meditatively as he brooded, deep in thought. Finally, he raised his eyes and spoke:

"We are goin' te ha' te keep this little discovery o' the symbol a secret. Just amongst us three. On the Q.T.. If that money stealin' Calvin an' his brother ha' any say te it, they be claimin' the gold as their own!" he avowed affirmatively.

"What or who is this Q.T., médecin?" asked Pierre fearing that there might be another person with a supposed claim to the gold of whom they should be wary.

However, this question hung heavily on the air unanswered and ignored when Alex spoke up fervently.

"But Matt, I found the nugget on <u>their</u> land so it rightfully be-longs to them. And if there is more gold, then that belongs to them, too - or whoever has their initials written on the back of this chunk." argued Alex with forthright ardor.

"Let us not be quibblin' with the details o' the situation, dear boy."

"Matt. Who is this Q.T.?" Pierre again asked peevishly, puzzling on the identity of this new, potential rival.

"I see a 'L' - presumably for 'LaFitte'." Alex noted being more concerned with the mystery attached to the squarish nugget rather than to its monetary value or to Pierre's imaginary competitive claimants. "The only thing is…the other letters don't make sense. There's a small 'e'; an uppercase 'R'; a lowercase 'o' and an 'i'. That does not spell 'LaFitte'." he proclaimed stumped by the paradox and scratching his head as he pondered upon the engraved letters.

"WHO IS Q.T.?" Pierre demanded for the third time in a loud voice.

"Sure'n it dunna make sense te me either." stated Matthew, addressing Alex while at the same time ignoring the petulant Frenchman. "Let us work the cryptic message through, laddie. Ye've got yer 'L', 'e', 'R', 'o', 'i'. Now tha' dunna make much o' a clue."

"It spells, 'LeRoi'!" Pierre blurted out bombastically, frustrated that his question was not being answered.

CHAPTER 13

Clyde winced in frustration as he searched through his pockets one more time. Gone. It was gone. Doggone it! An' now that inspector feller got the city in on it, too, they were crawlin' all over the place. City employees.... What if they found somethin' over there. What if there were more of them nuggets lyin' around? With those hard hats crawlin' all over the place it were as sure as shootin' they'd find somethin'. Clyde was hot under the collar as he watched the city workers commissioned by Jim Lahy replacing the damaged sewer pipe with a new one; vacuuming puddles of standing water; clearing away fallen tree trunks and filling in the large depressions left by their upheaval. In the midst of all this activity was Pierre Dûçot. He appeared to be in his element as he directed the hubbub of operations. He wore the same denim overalls and sun visor acquired from Mr. Hines that he had worn when he had previously supervised the construction of Eleanor and Matthew Flanderly's house. Clyde could hear him barking out orders. He could not hear exactly what they were saying, but he could see those hard hats jumping as Pierre snapped his fingers and followed directly on their heels. Several times he repeated "Vite!" in a sharp haranguing litany.

"That was awfully nice of Jimmy to get those people to help us," said Callie, "especially after I broke his heart and all. I don't think we could've kept it together if we had to start all over after all that work - especially Elvie."

"Well, you can thank Aunt Edith on that score." Cari conceded. "Having run Chesterhollow she's learned a trick or two about getting things done. When she investigated the problem and saw that the broken sewer pipe extended into the town she figured it was the town's responsibility to repair or replace it and clean up the ensuing damage that it had caused. All that was needed was to light a fire under Inspector Lahy to commission the construction company. And, as for your relationship that's all water under the bridge! You two called it quits quite a long time ago. It was a mutual decision, for goodness sake! He's moved on with his life!"

"Well." Edith began speaking, seeking to pursue the former topic of conversation and thus avoid the uncomfortable subject of Callie's erstwhile entanglement with Jim Lahy. "For my part, I really did not do all that much. It was Pierre who threatened to sue the city for compensation otherwise Detective Cordell was set firmly against rendering any aid to us whatsoever! He is so forceful in situations of crisis! My Pierre, that is!" Edith amended tittering as she contemplated Pierre's manliness.

"Inspector Lahy looked like he was enjoying Detective Cordell's discomfiture when Pierre threatened to contact his superiors and expose his inept efforts at tracking down the children when they were lost and of shirking his sworn duty to rebuild the area ruined as a result of his supreme incompetence." Mary Jo offered with a giggle.

"I especially liked the part where Pierre said he would expose Cordell for the fraud of a law enforcement officer that he was. And said he would have him boiled in oil!" Cari added to Mary Jo's commentary.

"My Pierre DOES have a way with words!" Edith said happily. "Of course, that is just an expression that he used to express his frustration at the Detective's inability to get things done. And to get them done properly!" she added quickly.

"All I know is that he's in his element now helping with all the construction." Callie added. "He's supervising the work and-"

"And generally throwing his weight around!" Cari inserted into Callie's sentence finishing it for her.

"Assuring that the construction flows along smoothly and is completed correctly is the paramount consideration - is it not?" asked Trudy demurely.

"Where did you come from, Trudy?" Edith queried startled, almost jumping out of her own skin as she jerked her body around to face her.

"She walked through the wall." Megan giggled as she imparted the news and then waited silently for everyone's reaction.

"Oh, dear. Megan, your mother is looking all over for you!" exclaimed Edith flustered turning in the opposite direction toward the sound of the little girl's voice with a flutter of her skirt and an unladylike dual clunk of her boot's heels against the wooden floorboards of the kitchen at LaurelsHeath.

"I walked through the wall, too!" she piped up proudly. "I was playing with kitty!" elucidated Megan as she shifted her arms to better support Charmer who purred loudly in appreciation of her attentions.

"Now dunna ye be tellin' us yer tall tales, child!" admonished her Mother bustling in when she heard the sound of her errant child's voice. "'Tis no time nor place fer flights o' fancy!" she berated her offspring as she extended her arms toward Charmer, who seemed to be getting a bit too comfortable in her daughter's arms, to pull the cat away from her. "An'," Eleanor ordered with finality as her hands drew ever-closer to her curled up target, "put down tha' <u>dirty</u> cat. Full o' germs it likely be and likely te be givin' ye the mange betimes!"

Eleanor was within inches of grasping Charmer about the middle - wherever that was if she could find it amongst all of the cotton candy-like fur - when a huge hiss emanated from the feline. Startled, her confidence ruffled, Eleanor quickly drew back to a safe distance. She assessed the feline from all angles. It seemed to have calmed down once she had retreated. Heartened by this, with renewed courage she tried again, barely touching the fur of the animal before it drew back seeking further shelter in her little girl's embrace and with a growl of warning spat several times in her direction to dissuade her encroaching presence. So. The beast wanted to do this the hard way...did she now. But it didna know tha' Eleanor Cartwright Flanderly was <u>not</u> te be intimidated by a surly little spawn o' evil takin' on a pleasin' shape! Again, with a firmer resolve she reached out to grab the cat only to be swiped at in a warning pass by an extended paw.

"She <u>likes</u> me Mummy - don't be mean!" begged Megan as she hugged Charmer closer and drew back cringing to protect the feline from her mother.

"Would ye look at <u>that</u>!" she exclaimed flabbergasted to all who could hear her. "Yer actually protectin' the vile creature!"

"Kitty loves me!" Megan cried in response burying her face in Charmer's fluff of white fur.

Purring noisily at a rapid cadence, Charmer looked to be in a state of sheer, unbridled ecstasy and shook the collar of tinkling charms buckled about her neck several times and again.

"Harrumph." Eleanor scolded, clearing her throat, as she observed what she considered to be evidence of uncleanliness. "Who knows what <u>unwholesome</u> <u>vermin</u> be lurkin' about under all tha' fur!"

On hearing Eleanor's comment, Charmer ceased licking her paw to glare at her detractor triumphantly, and in an exaggeratedly slow, prolonged motion shook her head once more while the charms about her neck tinkled reproachfully.

CHAPTER 14

"These people are driving me crazy!" complained Rafe Cordell to Inspector Jim Lahy. "First, they demand a construction crew and then they threaten to go over my head if they don't get it! And now that I've got the city construction workers fixing up their place on the taxpayers' dime, they want to get the Laureltown Parks Department involved! When is this 'gimme this, gimme that' stuff going to end? How am I going to justify this to the Board - and election time is right around the corner. If the constituents think I'm wasting their money...."

Jim Lahy could be nothing but sympathetic to the Detective's plight and so he listened politely and attempted to appear attentive as he droned on and on. After all, those people had done similar things to him. Maybe they had not MEANT to have made him appear foolish to his superiors, but they had! It was a wonder that he had not been kicked off of the police force! For example, there was that time when Cari came all frantic to his office in Charlottesville when he worked there in the capacity of constable. She had claimed that a big shoot-out was in the offing and that it had to be stopped. On the strength of her word he had sent a deputy out to trail after and keep tabs on Matthew Flanderly and Randmore McKinley. He had justified this action, and the accompanied expense associated with it, to the higher-ups as necessary police business only to be embarrassed royally when the whole shebang turned out to be a hoax. He had only been trying to protect the public.... Then, when he had given them a light, slap-on-the-wrist punishment - even though they deserved more time in the hoosegow than he'd actually given them - merely as a courtesy to Edith Chesterfield Norden, now Edith Dûçot, who was revered for her and her family's good works in town - they created an uproar in the courthouse when Officer Clancy sought to escort them from the premises at the end of their sentence. There was also the time when the Flanderly guy had him petition the Mayor for a public ceremony to posthumously honor Brandon Chesterfield for his direct involvement in building the Charlottesville library. Now THAT one was a doozy. He had stuck his neck out and used his position and influence as constable to pull strings to make the event happen only to end up with egg on his face when everything escalated into a public media circus with the Mayor's knowledgeability of his constituents being put into contention when the whole thing went awry and blew up in their faces. No matter that everything turned out okay in the end - the damage had been done. It was a miracle that they had promoted him to Inspector, let alone kept him on the payroll. Although, they had shipped him off to a backwoods location where he couldn't get into any more trouble. At least that is what his professional colleagues thought because even that didn't thwart those people. It was as if they'd followed him there because they appeared out of nowhere. And do not get him started about the firecracker incident with M.A. when Mary Jo ruined his perfectly good, airtight arrest warrant with her amateur courtroom theatrics and drama. Not to forget the explosion on the ridge.... What a mess. Pierre had almost gotten himself killed during that one. Inspector Jim Lahy shook his head grimly. Yes. He could indeed relate to the emotions Rafe was feeling and the frustrations that he was experiencing. But, on the other hand, Rafe was only experiencing the agitation arising from just one disruptive brush with the bunch which he had come to think of as 'The Charlottesville Eight': Randmore McKinley - World Traveler; Alex Caine - English Scholar; Pierre

Louis Dûçot - French Dance Instructor/Mogul; Matthew Flanderly - Charlottesville M.D. and their respective wives, Cari Chesterfield McKinley - Spoiled Heiress; Mary Jo Wilson Caine - Farmer'ess'; Edith Chesterfield Norden Dûçot - Matriarch; Eleanor Cartwright Flanderly - Mother/Former Head Housekeeper.

CHAPTER 15

"**H**i there!"

With a friendly wave and brimming over with the spirit of helpfulness Cari strode enthusiastically with purposeful alacrity over tufts of mud-fringed grass and uneven sod as she worked her way over to the spot where an overly tall young man scanned the grass immediately before him.

"Can I help you with something?" she queried curiously addressing the bowed head meticulously perusing the patch of earth before him.

Craning her neck and tilting her head Cari sought to establish eye contact with the youth and capture his undivided attention. 'What beautiful curly, dark-red hair he has.' Cari considered in passing mindlessly gazing at the thick mass atop his scalp. Her mind dreamily cast back to a different time, a different era, a different place…. She shook her head several times in order to shake off a half-forgotten memory of yore in which she was raised up higher and yet even higher still in someone's arms as childlike laughter issued forth from her then infantile lips. It bubbled forth and spilled out into the air as if so much spilt milk and as she reminisced Cari raised her hand to her face in an unthinking motion to discover an unexpected tear on her cheek. Capturing the unbidden drop of moisture between her fingers she rubbed them together until the salty liquid was totally absorbed by her skin and then brushed away the remainder on her cheek with the back of her hand. The past should best remain in the past, she resolved firmly setting her emotions aside.

"Could I perhaps be of assistance...?" Cari persistently prodded the unresponsive youth before her whose eyes continued to wander in search of a mysterious something he was not yet willing to articulate and share with her. "Young man? Are you alright? Can I be of service-"

"Service." he echoed the word suddenly. "Service?" Elroy asked her as he raised his head to turn and look down at her after straightening up to stand at his full height.

He looked down at her because he was so tall. He was at least a foot or more taller than Randy, observed Cari in awe of his size. And he was so strikingly handsome from his wide, deep-green eyes to his thin, straight nose to his aristocratic chin.

"My uncle always talks about 'service'. Do you know my uncle?"

"I hardly believe that I do." admitted Cari with a grin. "But I am pleased to make YOUR acquaintance. I'm Cari and you are...?"

"Everyone calls me Elroy - though my uncle calls me LeR-"

"There you are, Cari!" Mary Jo exclaimed as she huffed and puffed her way hurriedly to where Cari stood conversing with a young man who, she perceived, wore quite a smitten look on his face as he gazed down upon her visage adoringly. "I've been looking for you everywhere!" she imparted with exhilarated exasperation as she glanced from Cari to Elroy curiously. "You know that we are supposed to choose the wallpaper pattern for the hallway today!"

Cari groaned inwardly. Choosing the wallpaper would be fun but once it was chosen she and Mary Jo also had been commissioned by the powers that be, aka the newlyweds, to hang it and she dreaded the chore. All that reaching up and down to adjust prepasted, wet paper sheets to the ceiling and floor moldings; easing and pressing the wallpaper into corners of the room and matching the patterned sheets of paper from side to side to maintain pattern flow and sequence accurately.... The sheer thought of it all made her balk. What a job! Cari shuddered with distaste as her friend regarded her behavior with dismay.

"Don't be such a lazy bones, Cari!" snapped Mary Jo as she noted Cari's displeasure impatiently. "It'll be fun being a decorator for one day."

"Mary Jo. You <u>know</u> that it is going to take more than just one day to pick out a wallpaper pattern and then paste it to the wall."

"That sounds like fun. I like to paste things in my scrapbook." interjected Elroy boisterously anxious to be part of the conversation.

He wanted to be included and accepted, too. And Cari was so pretty. Elroy tilted his head to one side and studied the planes of her face enraptured.

"And just <u>who</u> do we have here?" Mary Jo asked of Cari mischievously all the while gazing pointedly at Elroy. "Does Randy know about this one, Cari…hmmm?"

Cari blushed at the insinuation although she knew that her friend was only teasing her.

"<u>No</u>, he does not." she retorted. "And for your information I am helping Elroy look for something!"

"Elroy, is it, eh? Well, then what are you looking for?"

"Uh. Hmmm…. What am I looking for…."

"<u>Yes</u>, Cari, what are you looking for!?"

Conflicted as to how she should respond Cari stood shame-facedly before her friend and fidgeted searching for an answer. Failing to find one she turned to face Elroy whispering guiltily:

"You tell her, Elroy."

"Tell her what?" queried the perplexed young man dumbfounded as he studied upon the clear blue, cloudless sky above him seemingly stupefied.

Seeing Elroy's distracted state and realizing that no help would be immediately forthcoming from that quarter Cari gave up and decided to take matters into her own hands:

"What are we looking for, Elroy?" Cari asked resignedly out loud.

"Cari, I am shocked." Mary Jo reproved her. "You don't even know what you're looking for? Tsk, tsk, <u>tsk</u>!" she scolded while brushing her index finger against the back of the opposing one on her opposite hand. "You've just <u>got</u> to come up with a better story than <u>that</u> if you're going to fool anybody!"

"Oh, you...you are impossible!" complained Cari as Mary Jo giggled in delight at her friend's discomfiture.

"My rabbit's foot." asserted Elroy stridently seeking to recapture Cari's attention with his intense zeal.

"What!?" asked both women in surprise simultaneously being somewhat taken aback by the outburst as they had all but dismissed Elroy's presence.

"I lost my Rabbit's Foot." he explained. "I keep losing it - I dropped it somewhere around here."

"Oh! You must be the son of that nice man Alex and I met here a couple of weeks ago. But don't you mean that you're looking for a <u>key</u>?"

"No. I found my key. Now I lost my Rabbit's Foot."

"How gruesome!" Cari spouted vehemently without thinking. "Do you mean to tell us that you actually carry around the dried-out, severed-foot of a poor little rabbit with you?"

Elroy fell silent as he seriously considered the critical question and then suddenly became teary-eyed. His eyes became large.

"You mean it was <u>alive</u> once? I didn't know it was a live rabbit once - I promise I didn't know! I'll never carry it again." he blurted out tragically repentant of his crime.

"Oh, no Elroy - I...I was only meaning that-" Cari started to explain.

"I don't want it anymore!" Elroy asserted firmly attempting to distance himself from his prior habit which had now become horrific and shameful to his way of thinking.

"Well." Mary Jo exclaimed nervously seeking to change the subject and dispel the awkward mood of the moment with her impromptu interjection. "Cari, we'd better go anyway. We've got wallpaper to hang!" she improvised.

Cari was penitent nonetheless. She had not intended to hurt Elroy's feelings or cause him anxiety. Following Mary Jo's lead Cari strove to play along with Mary Jo and change the subject but could not think of a good topic to introduce into the conversation. Then a slight spark of inspiration shown in her eyes. She considered Elroy's height looking him over from head to toe and then pulled Mary Jo aside.

"He could help us hang the wallpaper! Elroy's the perfect size. He's tall enough to do it for us so that we won't have to strain ourselves stretching and climbing ladders to reach the ceiling!" Cari whispered excitedly.

"You mean <u>trick</u> him into working for us by making believe that the work is fun? Con him?" Mary Jo asked in surprise. "We <u>can't</u> do that Cari - it's not right."

"I didn't think of it that way, Mary Jo. You are right." she admitted, ashamed of herself.

"<u>BUT</u>." Mary Jo declared. "We <u>CAN</u> ask him. There's no harm in that - is there?"

"Mary Jo Wilson Caine! I am surprised at you!" chided Cari.

"Elroy?" Mary Jo asked meekly in a syrupy, wheedling tone as she slowly approached him in an overly casual manner. "How would you like to help us hang some wallpaper?"

CHAPTER 16

"If I have said it <u>once</u>, j'ai dit ça mille fois. Get off <u>my</u> property!" Pierre roared enraged at Clyde when he discovered him nosing about the grounds.

Pressed up against a tree trunk and nose to nose with the Frenchman, Clyde carefully and cautiously considered the outraged features of the kooky fellow he had come to think of as that "crazy mystic". Just how far could he push the envelope with this guy? What were his options?

"First off, <u>MR. SWAMI</u>." Clyde spoke up defensively with a sneer. "This ain't ya "property"!"

"It is obvious to <u>me</u> that you must be stupid. That is elementary. Ce terrain may not belong <u>directly</u> to me. However." Pierre lashed out at him acerbically while waving the machete with which he had been cutting overgrown foliage back and forth swiftly and adroitly as if it was a rapier and he was engaged in a fencing match. "As votre amis who are aussi sans intelligence would say - any way you "slice it" you are treading on private property!" he asserted backing up and away from Clyde's body only long enough to yank out a makeshift sign on a stick from where it was stuck into the ground with two violent tugs, advance toward him and then wave it back and forth before his face spastically like a pendulum gone haywire. "Can you read this?" he challenged triumphantly, and then quickly continued speaking nonstop without affording Clyde the opportunity to respond. "It says "<u>NO TRESPASSING</u>" and <u>YOU</u> are the trespasser. I advise you to leave this premises immédiatement before I clean your clock. Do not seek to tempt the fate mon scrawny little ami. Leave <u>NOW</u> and I <u>SHALL</u> forget about this <u>SMALL</u>," Pierre articulated and paused to raise his right hand and lower his index finger so that it almost touched his thumb, "incident."

He finished his statement hesitantly pronouncing the final word with drawn-out distaste as if it left an unsavory and unpleasant taste in his mouth. Pierre hoped that his intimidating demeanor was forbidding enough to dissuade Clyde from lingering in this area further and deter him from ever returning - especially to this spot. This was where Alex had discovered the gold block and it would never do if Clyde were to find a similar gold object and perhaps demand a portion of their claim. Alex was already threatening to <u>share</u> any gold bricks found on the property with Matt and the newlyweds! How <u>SELFISH</u>! Sharing.... Pah! Where did Alex come up with these crazy ideas from? C'est ridicule! After all he had done for him he was the obvious choix for partner if any loot were found, bien sûr! Why, he had practically been like a Father to the aimless fils. SUCH ingratitude! Pierre became exceedingly more indignant at the thought and sniffed loudly while fixing Clyde with a more intense glare.

"Look. I don't know who ya think ya are but Clyde Barnett ain't nobody's doormat! <u>THAT</u> is fer doggone sure. So don't ya go givin' me none of yer evil eyes or yer Hocus-Pocus! Now, that sign don't mean nothin' 'cause I happen to know from the time I was a little fella that this back piece of land has <u>never</u> <u>had</u> <u>no</u> <u>owner</u>. Ya an' yer friends are just <u>SQUATTERS</u>!" Clyde spat out nastily as he yanked the "NO TRESPASSING" sign from Pierre's rigid hand. "Ya people are the trespassers!" he replied smugly.

"Vous êtes tort! Cette maison is their legacy! It was left to them by their relative." Pierre began to enlighten him.

"PROVE IT." interrupted Clyde sharply cutting short Pierre's forthright explanations fervently with unrestrained ardor as he threw down the dagger-like challenge.

Now jutting forth his face forward to lie directly in the path of Pierre's face so that they were flush with one another it was a story of the shoe being on the other foot as Clyde in a snide voice now brought to light a question which Pierre had heretofore never thought to entertain:

"Where's the <u>WILL</u>? Huh? Can't answer that - can ya? That's because there <u>is</u> no will."

Pierre's mouth remained open in tentative reply but only his silence issued forth and was ensuing. He was for once in all of his life rendered speechless. He was at a total loss for words. A WILL? A WILL. This was an obstacle which he had never considered. What of Jan's word? What of his decree? Was it possible that this...<u>coarse</u> Clyde person had bested his friend? This idea was incomprehensible, but, weighing the facts of the situation before him, this was a legitimate question.

"That's right. That's right!" crowed Clyde confidently into the perplexed visage of the dismayed man before him on noting that Pierre had been summarily rendered speechless by his statement. "Ya never thought of <u>that</u> one, did ya?" remarked the erstwhile defensive man - now turned braggart and seeming to read Pierre's puzzled mind accurately - with an added spunk that seemed to mount, increase, and snowball with his every un-rebuffed and un-contested comment.

Pierre's lack of response to his contentions constituted a confirmation and an acceptance egging Clyde on.

CHAPTER 17

"I'll tell you, Callie. That key of Elroy's fit into Alex's exactly. They were a perfect match! Alone, both of them looked like separate keys. But. When you put them next to each other and interconnected them together they fit into each other perfectly into just one flawless piece. You'd never be able to tell that you could break it into two distinct pieces."

"Are you talking about that rusty old skeleton key that was in M.A.'s tackle box, Mary Jo?"

"Precisely. Remember how we were all perplexed because we couldn't figure out what it had to do with the treasure map? And then when we actually <u>found</u> the treasure the key became a non-issue. And then we found out that Cari was expecting and when the whole horrible episode with Hank Colden went down...." Mary Jo reminisced aloud brooding contemplatively with a pensive air about her. "And then-" she resumed only to be interrupted.

"We forgot about it." Callie concluded thoughtfully.

"That's right. We never gave it a second thought after that." concurred Mary Jo in unequivocal agreement.

"No one except Alex." observed Callie proudly in admiration of her relation's stick-to-itiveness.

"Now, <u>THAT</u> is an understatement! He's insisted on wearing that old key on a chain around his neck religiously as if it were a crucifix or a medal or something. You can't get him to take it off. He wears it when he takes a shower. He even wears it to bed!" complained Mary Jo, miffed.

"If I did not know better, I would think you were jealous of a key!" her cousin joshed with a crooked smile.

"Oh, stop being silly Callie. Of course I'm not jealous of a KEY. How can you be jealous of a key for Heaven's Sake?! It's just that he's worn it for going on three years now and I think that's kind of odd. Also, now that we find out it links-up perfectly to Elroy's key there just <u>has</u> to be some connection there, but for the life of me I can't figure out what it is. And now Pierre is saying that the writing on that gold-colored brick Alex found is in Jan LaFitte's handwriting." she concluded in agitation as she paused to gaze out of the living room window of LaurelsHeath mansion at her husband, Randmore, Pierre and Matthew searching the ground before them for additional gold pieces.

"So you're thinking that because M.A.'s tackle box the key was found in all those years back once belonged to Jan LaFitte, and the gold nugget Alex found has Jan LaFitte's handwriting on it that the two things are connected to one another and so Jan must be involved in this situation somehow." Callie said slowly and pensively as with creased brow she sought to piece the situation together logically and solve this elaborate puzzle.

"Well, why not? Pierre always thinks that Jan is watching him anyway. Who's to say that this whole tapestry isn't his handiwork? That he's not here now?" argued Mary Jo.

At a small shriek from the vestibule their conversation halted abruptly drawing the attention of the two girls to its source of emanation. They rushed from the living room window posthaste to find Cari backed up against the wall by an inquisitive Charmer rubbing her furred body against her ankles and purring loudly. As the cat wove in and out between her legs Callie bent over to capture the feline within her embrace and picked her up to cradle her within her arms as she stood upright. As Callie massaged Charmer's neck the furry white feline purred wildly and the trinkets dangling from her pet collar had cause to jingle as they clashed against one another. The shiny little bell in particular tinkled out repetitively.

"Are you afraid of cats, Cari?" Callie inquired as she continued to rub the feline's neck and shoulders.

"No. I was just startled. She came out of nowhere." Cari explained as she hung up her cape in the coat closet. "I didn't expect to have her brushing up against my legs like that - I almost stepped on her! I had to sort of dance around her to maintain my balance as I tried to avoid squashing her!" laughed the semi-flustered young woman as she put forth her defensive explanations. "Aunt Edith is right behind me." she enlightened Callie and Mary Jo, changing the topic of discourse. "I want to show her the room we finished wallpapering with Elroy's help. I am very pleased at the way that it came out. It came out just beautifully and I know that she will appreciate its fresh, new look. Now, there are just two more rooms to go and then we're done! The place has really shaped up! Elroy has been just an enormous help with things. I don't know how we could have done it without him." she stated as they all entered the newly wall-papered living room and she admired its freshly papered walls.

"Elroy was a great help." conceded Mary Jo. "He practically did the whole job for us. But..." she spoke thoughtfully and paused for a moment, "wasn't it odd the way that he was so protective of this room?"

"He did act sort of strangely when it came to this particular room. There were just certain corners of it that he would just not let us touch!" Cari agreed reflectively. "Every time I went to that wall, for example," Cari clarified as she turned to indicate the bookshelf wall next to the fireplace, "and every time I advanced with a sheet of wallpaper to hang in that area he quickly came over and took the wet sheet of paper from my hands and shooed me away while he hung the paper."

"That's because he has a huge CRUSH on you, Cari!" Callie

laughed as she imparted the intelligence. "Can't you SEE it?" she inquired as if Elroy's emotion of adoration was unmistakable and as plain as the light of day. "You can see it in his eyes!" she continued to the dumbfounded Cari who was at a loss for words. "He lights up like a Christmas tree when you're around or like one of those flying bugs that come out at night and periodically illuminate the darkness." she concluded forthrightly.

"He <u>does</u> hang on your every word." Mary Jo agreed nodding her head up and down as she concurred adamantly with Callie's comments in a stoically diplomatic fashion.

CHAPTER 18

"Hey, Simon!" called Alex to the man who was intent on rounding the corner of the barn unnoticed. "Come on over and meet the guys!" Alex extended the invitation with wholehearted enthusiasm.

Pulling his wide brimmed hat down low over his eyes, after gazing apprehensively and a bit fearfully in the direction of Matthew Flanderly, Simon disengaged himself from Alex's clingy hands seeking to drag him forward to meet his three advancing friends.

"Don't be SHY!" Alex coaxed him. "We are all friends here and the more is the merrier."

"Alex, how nice it is to see you again!" Simon spoke distractedly as he sought for an avenue to which he could flee before the imminent arrival of the other men and thus avoid their approaching proximity. "Unfortunately, I must be on my way-"

"Aw...! Don't be a party pooper! I was shy once, too. But once you meet new people you can find that you have a lot of the same things in common! There's my friend, Matt, over there. He's the fishing expert I told you about. Actually, he's a doctor by profession but fishing is like second nature to him. Anything you want to know about fishing: fishing rods...lures...tackle - he's your man. There's my cousin, Randy, over there and Pierre is the tall guy." Alex elucidated indicating them with a perfunctory nod of his head in their direction. "Pierre is French. He is great. He knows about treasure maps and pirates and everything. You'll get along fine. You'll get along fine with all of them. C'mon. Stay - please. Be my guest." he

SHARON ELIZABETH SARKISIAN

cajoled ingenuously.

"Alex!" Randmore called out loudly to his cousin who seemed to be having a conversation with the south-side of the barn. "What are you <u>doing</u> over there?" he inquired in exasperation flummoxed by Alex's seemingly odd behavior.

"Oui. What are you doing playing over there Alex while I am speaking? How RUDE. Si, you désires à trouver the gold I advise you to écoute à moi bien au lieu of talking to the chickens dedans cette structure-là." Pierre lectured austerely as he regarded the barn, miffed at Alex's lack of attention.

Pierre regarded Alex thoughtfully.... 'The pauvre garçon must have gone fou that he would find solace in conversing with a barn.' he thought sympathetically - yet still a bit grudgingly. Oui. He could commiserate avec the problèmes of the common man. Pierre relented. His anger against Alex diminished and he set his hard feelings aside. Pierre suddenly shuddered at an errant, ominous thought. If he did not know better, he might suspect that the spirit of Grand-mère Dûçot was the cause of Alex's aberrant behavior somehow. He quickly looked about him from side to side to assure himself that no spirits were lingering about - did they even come out in the daylight(?) - and then realized that he did not even know what a spirit looked like! Bien sûr, he had never seen one before! But according to Grand-mère's own description they were quite frightful. His attention returned to the present at the strident sound of Alex's whining attempt at protestation.

"I was not talking to a-" Alex started to explain to them all as Matt decided, at the same time, to add his own pearls of wisdom to the critique of Alex's odd behavior.

"Gadzooks, laddie!!! <u>Have</u> ye or ha' ye not set yer mind te seekin' out the gold? We ha' got te get busy, me boy! There be no time te waste! This be nary a time te be draggin' yer feet when ye know tha' we ha' got ground te cover! Time te step up te the challenge! This be the state o' do or die not a time te let the grass grow under our feet!" Matt lectured him encouragingly with boisterous gusto and much bluster while giving himself a mental pat on the back at delivering such an inspiring and stirring monologue.

At this point Alex threw his hands up in despair of ever being allowed to explain his position and then let them drop clapping at his sides resoundingly. Ah, well. 'SEEING,' he thought, 'would have to suffice as, BELIEVING.' However, when he turned to jostle Simon to the forefront for all to see and commence introductions he perceived that the man had…disappeared.

Edith Dûçot smiled brightly with satisfaction as she inspected the barn's exterior. The crew that Inspector Lahy had engaged to repair the damaged barn had completed their task splendidly. She peeked through a newly installed window pane and nodded her head with approval at the sight of a happy group of chickens strutting about within some bowing their heads down to the ground at periodic intervals and pecking at their feed. She had told Cari to go on ahead of her to the house while she conducted her nit-picking inspection but she had not found a nit to pick! She was thoroughly delighted with the end result. She chuckled to herself silently as she recalled how grudgingly Rafe Cordell had given in to Jim Lahy's hard-line "request" to send over a crew of city maintenance workers to clean up the damaged area, the exposed uprooted pipeline and the outbuildings on the property. She chuckled again - this time out loud as - WHAT! Edith stared aghast at the apparition, blinked her eyes in order to clear them, and on re-opening them the spectre from her past had disappeared. 'Could it be….' she contemplated staring wide-eyed with stunned amazement at what her mind told her was impossible but what her heart dared to hope for.

CHAPTER 19

Reining in Honoré in front of the "Laureltown Coffee Shop"
Pierre dismounted and tethered his mount to a hitching post.
How he longed for a cup of café. Laureltown, for all of his previous
reservations, was actually a quite charming place, he judged as he
noted the "French Pâtisserie" and various French restaurants dot-
ting the strip of the main street in the center of town. Peut-être,
after his café, he would pay a visit to the pastry shop on the corner
and give the pâtissier of the magasin the benefit of his expérience in
preparing croissants and pie pastry. It took skill to fold this dough
properly! He would generously share with him the secrets imparted
to him by Grand-mère Dûçot. Oui. He could be magnanimous when
he so chose…. But first, more to the point, he was tired and hungry
and needed sustenance after his hard day on the job. He entered the
coffee shop and was immediately struck by the noisy environment
- ATMOSPHERE this was not! The sound of the many conversa-
tions of those dining assailed him and - HOW Unbearable(!) - most
of them were speaking with their mouths full! How CRUDE! And
the random discordant clatter of the diners' utensils striking against
china as they ate left much to be said for gentility and gentle dining
on the whole. Pierre shuddered with distaste. Ces Américains! The
offensive social faux pas and infractions of etiquette of the patrons
gave Pierre pause and caused him to question the advisability of
dining at such a place. Nevertheless, the locals he had spoken with
recommended this place highly, a reservation was not required and,
most importantly, a variety of French entrées graced the menu.

He had already resolved to introduce himself to the chef. He must be French, mais, bien sûr! It would be quite pleasant to engage in a civilized conversation, for a change(!), with one of his country-men. Judging by the gravy dripping from one patron's chin to trail down the front of his shirt his reduction sauce appeared to be of the correct consistency. Pierre sniffed loudly and contemptuously with his nose up in the air in the direction of this blatant society of-fender at witnessing such sloppiness while the diner, on the other hand, merely regarded him momentarily and chomping down on his food noisily wondered at the stranger's odd behavior. 'In France,' thought Pierre, 'this definitely would <u>NOT</u> have happened!' he con-templated with patent disdain turning on his heel. Making his way to the back of the establishment where it was quieter Pierre se-cured an empty booth and opened the menu before him to note an adequate selection of food offerings from appetizers to entrées to desserts. After ordering from a stoic, monosyllabic waitress he sat back to relax until his food arrived. After working all day at the construction site his back hurt and he needed to rest. He sighed as he massaged his posterior briefly with his open palms. As an added precaution against viewing any more of the unsavory eating habits of his fellow diners he delved into a case of necessities which he had brought with him on this trip to produce a pair of black eye covers he often used when napping during the daylight hours to block out any bright glare or any stomach turning, nauseating sights such as the ones to which his poor eyes were being assaulted with at the moment. They were absolument nécessaire at times like this and he thanked his lucky stars that he had thought to bring them with him on this ill-fated journey. Pierre donned the sleeping mask fitting it over his eyes to cover them completely, securing it by pulling the stretchy elastic band over his head and then adjusting it there so that it rested comfortably in place. 'Pah!' he thought disdainfully. The band was not even cloth and most likely the cheaply manufactured elastic would ruin his coiffure! 'It read on the product label: "American Made". In France this never would have been allowed to take place. Cheaply made merchandise…uncouth behavior….' he grimaced at the thought that such inadequacies were allowed to exist. If it were not for his beloved Edi he would have left for France il y a depuis longtemps! Pierre yawned sleepily covering his opened mouth politely in order to stem his unseemly expelling of air from his lungs. As his thoughts drifted dreamily his head fell back against the booth's cushioned seating.…

"I saw a whole group of city employees crawling all over that land and I do not want any more indiscretions!" yelled the loud voice of Clyde's companion as he banged his fist in outraged fury on the table top before him.

Some of the diners had stopped eating and conversing to stare in the direction from where the bellicose rant was emanating and Pierre was jolted out of his slumbering state to jerk upright to a seated position from his slumped down posture on hearing such hollering. Pierre had come abruptly awake but he was slow to come out of his groggy state and was not yet fully alert. He was EXHAUSTED! He had not realized how tiring it would be to supervise all of those jokers at the construction site that Inspector Lahy had hired to perform tasks that to him were child's play. They were inept et très incompétent and they would have been aimless but for his direction. Perhaps he should teach some of the finer points of politesse to those loudmouthed people seated in the booth next to him. Pierre perked up at the thought. Why, his pauvre ears were ringing encore from the outburst of one of the occupants. How atrocious they were! 'Mais, bien sûr!' he emphatically concluded. It was quite obvious to him that they would benefit immensely from his instruction. He made his decision affirmatively. He sniffed loudly with contemptuous superiority, turned halfway around to face them and opened his mouth to address them only to close it again at the next words coming this time from the companion of the booth's table slamming occupant. Pierre's limbs froze as he listened in spellbound fascination.

"There won't be none!" Clyde assured his irate tablemate. "There won't be <u>NONE</u>! I already gave a piece of my mind ta that uppity French-foreigner and scared him good! He's so yella' an' shaken up he's not never gonna show up his face near that quarter ag'in!"

'It is that uncultured, Bohemian local!' realized Pierre recoiling in shock. THEY WERE PLOTTING AGAINST HIM! Pierre removed his hands from the protective sleep mask he had been about to take off - he must not unmask himself too soon! They had obviously not seen through his disguise yet! 'How unschooled they are! Not being able to recognize the esteemed visage, albeit masked, of the fameux Pierre Dûçot!' he contemplated in a mixture of smugness tinged with throes of disbelief. He recognized the voice of Clyde Barnett but not that of his obviously high-strung cohort. Pierre's attention returned to the present on hearing the barking response of the strange man's voice.

"Wrong!!! He was there early this morning and his friends were with him! Now, you better take care of them Clyde - or heads will roll!" threatened the bodiless voice in a warning tone as, horrified, Pierre's hands flew to his own neck to grasp it protectively and confirm that it was still attached to his shoulders.

'Imagine!' Pierre gasped at this new wrinkle of thought. 'THREATENING the life of Pierre Dûçot! These madmen must be stopped!' He craned his neck closer to hear them better but was careful to readjust his mask so that it covered his face more fully.

"Don't get yaself tied up in a bunch. I gots everything under <u>con</u>trol-" Clyde started to assert positively raising and lowering his palms toward and then away from his chest in a slow, soothing motion in an effort to calm and assure his companion of the certainty that all was well.

"You have NOTHING under control!" he nonetheless inter-rupted Clyde heedless of his conciliatory mien. "You can't even hold on to a rock sample." the anonymous boss man raged and ranted in critique while at the same time curbing his temper and lowering his voice as he noticed that his tirades were drawing the unwant-ed attention of some fellow diners who stared curiously in their direction.

"Look. The overgrown doofus thinks that those things are his blocks - HE ACTUALLY PLAYS WITH THOSE THINGS! He col-lects them an' stacks them up! -Less work for us - eh?" Clyde spoke derisively with a humorless laugh issuing forth from his throat on contemplating Elroy's gullibility and he nudged his lunch partner's shoulder in fellowship. "An' even if those other nitwits found the sample they wouldn't never know what it was!" he reasoned derid-ingly skeptical of the newcomers' mental faculties.

"Don't touch me you BLOCKHEAD! Of course they found SOMETHING! Otherwise they wouldn't be combing that field, wise guy! Maybe that big moron is no threat but those newcomers are a problem. Take care of them before I lose everything! Do it NOW!!!"

In order to vent his pent-up furor he threw down his napkin to strike the table sharply and then the infuriated diner slid in-delicately and unceremoniously on his seat along the length of the bench and out of the booth to rise clumsily to his feet. He stomped his way purposefully toward the exit of the establishment slam-ming the door behind him with a reverberating bang. Clyde, who had been following in his wake simpering and pandering obsequi-ously, reopened said door that had been slammed in his face and, quick as a jackrabbit, followed the boss man outside. After their departure from the restaurant and the coast was, que veut dire, clear, Pierre slowly removed his sleeping mask and laid it aside. He gulped convulsively in frigid fear, his Adam's apple bobbing north and south with the contraction and release of surrounding muscula-ture, as he swallowed hard down a throat that had suddenly become very dry. Clearly, the waitress had come bearing his order and gone while he had napped, leaving the plate of food on the table before him. He stared down at it listlessly. On finally lifting a forkful of the aliment distractedly to touch his lips he noted curiously that the entrée was cold.

CHAPTER 20

"Now, Elvie, dear. Tell me <u>exactly</u> what you have been seeing."

"I TOLD you, Edith. People appear and then they are not there no more!"

"You surely cannot mean that they just...VANISH into thin air? That is impossible."

"I don't know if it's possible or not. All I know is the cat appears after I've just cleaned an <u>empty</u> room. AND, when we first moved here, I seen a strange man comin' out of the floor! I can tell you I slept in the car for two whole weeks before Calvin, Dudley and Callie could convince me to step back inside this house! And I'm STILL spooked!" she concluded and looked around her for unknown eavesdroppers.

"Now, Elvie...! Think <u>very</u> <u>carefully</u>. What did this man look like?" coaxed Edith patiently seeking to jog the girl's memory.

"I can tell you I didn't hang around long enough to take a list down-" Elvira Green Maison started to reply definitively only to have her thought cut short by her companion.

"You mean "take an inventory", dear." Edith corrected her absentmindedly interrupting her as she found Elvie's answer unsatisfactory.

"You didn't let me <u>finish</u>." Elvie pouted at the unintentional slight.

"I am sorry, Elvie. Please, elaborate." she said closing her eyes momentarily in thought and sighing as she prepared to listen to Elvie's expectedly long-winded response. "Feel free to embellish at will!" Edith added coaxingly - if not a bit resignedly - to the invitation as an afterthought.

On not receiving an immediate response and on viewing the confused expression on Elvie's countenance Edith rephrased her response of acquiescence:

"Please, CONTINUE, Elvie." enunciated Edith simplistically.

"Oh…. Well. Why didn't you just say so?" queried the young lady uncertainly swallowing the lump forming in her throat. "He was terrible! Now, I didn't get a good picture, mind you, 'cause I was too busy hightailing it in the other direction. But. He dragged his leg behind him and he looked awful mean. An' his hair! It was all over the place! Red an' thick an' curly. When I went into the hall and saw him coming out of the floor I thought I was a gonner for sure! But, then Trudy showed up and I escaped while she distracted him!" Elvie said horrified with eyes which had grown large and had become as round as saucers as she looked inwardly inside seeing the bygone images in her mind's eye and she recalled the frightful events of that day.

"Elvie. You said <u>RED</u> hair - did you not?" Edith asked suddenly alert and dogged in her attempt to nail down the fact.

"I sure did! It was wild and red and-"

"And <u>CURLY</u>?" interjected Edith supplying the adjective ponderously and interrupting Elvie's otherwise copious reply to a simple dichotomous question.

Edith's response seemed to be of an interrogative nature but the connotation of her tone during delivery of the phrase was rhetorical and conveyed the implication that it was more of an established fact rather than one of a debatable bone of contention. All of a sudden, the vestibule door abruptly flew open wide swinging uncontrolled on its unoiled rusting hinges which screamed in protestation at this unwarranted abuse thereby startling the chatting pair who halted their conversation. They both turned simultaneously toward the shrill, discordant sound of interlocking metal joints grinding against themselves to see a perspiring, panting and discomposed Pierre Dûçot barreling through the entrance. Elvie stared aghast on viewing the Frenchman's harried disarray and noted his apparent condition of extreme turmoil. Edith, on the other hand, was not concerned on viewing his distress and had summarily discounted Pierre's agitated state out of hand. She knew of her husband's flair for the dramatic and had frequently borne witness to his melodramatic behavior in the past. His histrionic episodes always amounted to nothing and, if anything, were only of a minor consequence. Edith detachedly made a mental note that those door hinges needed to be lubricated and polished!

"Edi! Edi!" Pierre cried in patent alarm as he quickly entered the front door and shut it behind him sharply to lean his weight against it with terror showing in his eyes as he braced himself for an expected attack. "They are plotting against us! They seek to drive us off of this property! They are killers!"

"Oh, Pierre. Don't be ridiculous!" pooh-poohed Edith patently impatient with her husband's "flights of fancy".

She and Elvie had both rushed into the hallway intensely concerned at his impassioned calls and the slamming sound of the door but now Edith could only laugh on hearing Pierre's latest outlandish conspiracy theory. His wild, frantic looks, the eye shaped mask sitting askew half on, half off of his forehead and his rumpled clothing all contributed to his comical appearance and to the indubitable irrationality of his fearful statements diminishing his overall credibility. This dramatic display of Pierre's put everything in perspective for Edith. She was all at once ashamed of the way she had previously been acting - "grilling" Elvie for information, for Heaven's Sake! And the IDEAS she had been entertaining - how absurd they seemed now! Such unrealistic thoughts as hers were cause for embarrassment. Seeing ghosts…! Goodness she felt foolish! She was merely jumping at shadows, balking at bygone memories and mentally reliving a past which was just that - a PAST. Her brother had passed away a long time ago in that tragic accident with her eldest brother, Cari's father, Brandon Chesterfield and his wife. From Pierre's theatrical, emotional display arose: "SANITY" and the resulting epiphany which showed clearly to Edith the error of her ways. She had come dangerously close to becoming just as irrational and emotive as Elvie and Pierre sometimes were. Edith realized that she had almost let her imagination run away with her out of control!

"You cannot seriously believe that people are out to kill you?" scoffed his wife coming out of her reverie to readdress Pierre.

"US, Edi. US! We are all in terrific danger! Randy!" he wailed urgently to his nephew. "We must protect ourselves - we are under siege!"

Randmore McKinley who had just entered the house accompanied by his wife, Carina, had his arm about her waist laughing at a small joke she had made and whispering a response into her ear. He raised his head in bewilderment at Pierre's frantic comment at a loss for a reply not yet having had the time to fully digest its import.

"There is no one out there, Pierre - what ARE you talking about?" asked Cari who had heard her uncle's warning cry and on noticing the blank stare on Rand's face and the mute, nonresponsive women occupying the room spoke up to fill the silent void in the conversation.

"I HEARD them." insisted Pierre adamantly stubborn as he attempted to control the tenor of the discussion.

"Heard who?" Cari asked patiently as she prepared for one of Pierre's far-fetched, long-winded explanations.

"I was in the town diner taking my mid-morning siesta-" he began only to be interrupted.

"You were SLEEPING in a restaurant?" Cari queried sarcastically - yet with tolerant patience - as she shared a look of silent commiseration with Rand.

"Mais, bien sûr!" Pierre affirmed as if this type of behavior were par for the course. "Does not everybody? And then, as I was saying, I was awakened from my brief rest by the sound of these <u>COARSE</u> roughneck locals. Their interruption of my slumbers was <u>VERY</u> rude. They were loud and obviously inférieur - I could have suffered a heart attack! And they know about the GOLD!" Pierre stated with marked concern.

"Pierre. I think that you and Matt have gold on the brain!" Cari blurted out with unequivocal certainty.

"I totally agree with Cari." Rand concurred affirmatively nodding his head in agreement. "That brick Alex found only just happens to have a yellow tint to it. You have to remember, Pierre, that there was a lot of construction in the area Alex found the brick. It could have come from anywhere. There is no concrete reason to believe that it came from here or that there is gold on this property. And, you know, if you WANT to believe something hard enough, you start to believe it is a fact no matter how baseless any indicators really are!" Rand said reasonably.

CHAPTER 21

Matthew A. Flanderly, M.D. rubbed at the rapidly swelling bump on his head. It was extremely tender and sensitive to the touch and he howled in pain as he felt along the contusion's surface to assess the severity of the swelling protuberance. His fall had been quite unexpected and he had not even had the opportunity to brace himself for impact as he bulleted helplessly down the proverbial rabbit hole to be stopped by the hard surface below. He had, however, instinctively clung doggedly to his ever-present black medical bag from which he now withdrew much needed first aid supplies. He let forth many a strong oath as he gingerly swabbed at bumps and bruises with gauze sprinkled liberally with antiseptic and bound his more serious wounds tightly with clean, absorbent dressing secured in place by cloth tape. He tilted his head upwards to gaze wonderingly at the round opening high above him through which the bright light of day shone promisingly through. It was this aperture he had fallen through. It had been concealed from his view by long grasses and wet leaves and with one clumsy, bungling misstep he had plummeted downward from the heights to land… here. Wherever that was. 'OW!' Matthew inwardly exclaimed as a sharp stab of pain assailed him. He rubbed the back of his afflicted, aching neck and grimaced as dizziness overtook him and he had to avert his eyes from the sun's hypnotic glare. 'Where were Pierre, Randy and Alex in the thick of all this?' he wondered. He had merely been strolling about the grounds assessing the condition of the area here and there and if he just happened to stumble upon, by sheer accident, another gold brick he had every intention of telling them about it. He was not attempting to be duplicitous or sneaky a'tall. So when he needed rescuing from this terrible trouble which he now found himself in he believed that he had every right to expect that they should be there to rally to his defense. He limped on over to a rock favoring his right knee as he sat down on the boulder. How to extricate his person from this pickle.... 'There must be a way!' He pondered upon the problem while drumming his fingers upon his knee absentmindedly. Finally, he determinedly reached a conclusion. He decided that he must forge ahead. Grab onte the brass ring where he found it. And, most importantly, follow the Flanderly Code and never give up until he found a way out of his predicament! He would search for an exit immediately. With stalwart resolve he clapped his palms upon the tops of his thighs and pushed himself up off of them to stand up only to fall back down onto his seat with beads of perspiration popping out and accumulating on his forehead from the exertion required by the unsuccessful effort he had put forth. He would just rest for a moment - only for a moment, mind ye, and then he would go forth te find a way out of this underground prison. At least it was not totally dark down here with a modicum of illumination coming from somewhere. 'Begorra!' he thought. 'It was all over the place! And it became increasingly brighter farther along the corridor. It must be coming from somewhere!' he reasoned logically. 'Therefore, te my way o' thinkin',' conjectured Matthew thoughtfully, 'there ha' te be another way out!'

Simon stared at the scattered bricks littering the floor before him and loaded them, one by one, into his wheelbarrow. He sighed with resignation. How was he ever going to get through to that boy! He had told Elroy, time and time again, to confine playing with the blocks that his uncle had given him to the subterranean catacombs and <u>not</u> to bring them up into the house! But it seemed that the concept was too difficult for him to grasp. It had always been Elroy's habit to bring the bricks up into the house and so he had built a special ramp that wended downward first into the basement and then continued down to the tunnels so that he would not have to lug heavy bricks individually down the aforementioned two levels. He shook his head helplessly from side to side as he glumly considered the job ahead of him. 'Well.' he thought resignedly. 'I had better get started.' Once he had reached the lower level of catacombs he noted the coded aisle letter and row number on the side of each brick and advanced to each prospective cubbyhole where he replaced them, one by one. Each brick shone with luminosity because Elroy took care of his toys making sure to shine each of his blocks religiously and assiduously with a soft cloth. Simon reached for the final golden nugget which was more misshapen than the rest. 'Funny.' he considered briefly as he hefted it high. It had not been there before when he had left to replace what he had then perceived to be the final block in the wheelbarrow to its assigned resting place. 'Ah, well.' he acceded resignedly accepting what he could not change. 'I must not have seen it.' (Maybe he needed eyeglasses...?) He regarded the golden object's assignment code and realized that he would have to trek with it much farther down the tunnel to put it into its allotted cubbyhole than he had had occasion to do when replacing the others.

"Dang it!" exclaimed Simon nettled staring at the block's encryption and contemplating his unfortunate, untenable circumstance.

Simon rarely indulged in the exhortation of expletives rather than the articulation of credible speech. But it was <u>dusty</u> down here and the close quarters gave him the willies. As he plodded doggedly along pushing the wheelbarrow toward his final destination he saw the slumped over figure of a man sitting on a rock. He immediately dropped the handles of the wheelbarrow and rushed to the stranger's side. He took his wrist and felt for a pulse - it was imperceptible. Simon had been a doctor by profession. Was the man dead? He felt for the alternate pulse on the stranger's neck. Eureka! He felt something - a beat. It was throbbing, albeit, only weakly - but it was there! He noticed the little black medical bag beside the man. He lifted up his head to recognize a Matthew Flanderly who slowly raised fluttering eyelids at all the attentions he was receiving. Bleary-eyed and out of sorts Matthew rubbed at his teary eyes to clear them properly and then blinked twice in disbelief.

"Am I dreamin'…?" he asked in flabbergasted astonishment. "I MUST be dreamin', begorra." he concluded pinching his own cheek to elicit blood flow. "Is tha' <u>YOU</u>, Simon?"

CHAPTER 22

"From what I hear from Cari, Pierre has really lost it." Mary Jo enlightened Callie tellingly tapping the tip of her forefinger on her temple.

"I don't know...." her cousin replied. "He's been right about things before." she concluded contrarily coming to his defense while examining a hand painted ceramic casserole in the town's local cookery establishment.

"But this time is different." insisted Mary Jo. "He was having a bad dream. He <u>admits</u> he was SLEEPING when he heard those threats-"

"You mean COMING OUT of a sleep." Callie corrected her.

"Look. Pierre <u>always</u> thinks somebody's interested in cooking his goose or plotting against him. He's always crying WOLF!" asserted Mary Jo impatiently. "He just always has to be the center of attention - it's his ego!"

"Well, I for one <u>believe</u> him!" Alex asserted with conviction on entering the store and hearing Mary Jo's statements. "We've been looking for you two everywhere. You women and your shopping. Gee...! We don't need any of this stuff!" he whined in obvious frustration while peering down the chute of a food processor squint-eyed.

"Here's something we need." announced his wife approaching him and ceremoniously draping a cooking apron with a smiling pink pig face emblazoned on the front over his head to flow down past his shoulders and securing it with a bow behind his back. Stepping back from him to consider her handiwork she clucked approvingly and said, "I think it's you, Alex. Very attractive…and MASCULINE!" she reinforced her comment with a giggle momentarily edging closer to him to brush her fingers across each of his shoulders to smooth flat any wrinkled fabric.

"And this adds just the right finishing touch!" Callie added fitting a chef's hat atop Alex's bare head.

"Very funny, girls." Alex responded sarcastically removing said items and setting them aside. "Now we've got to find Randy and Cari and meet Pierre at the diner."

"The diner? What's he doing at the diner?" Callie asked as she knew he'd already had his lunch.

"He's going back over there to sit in the same booth he was in last time and see if those people he heard talking about us would show up again and reveal some clues about how they're going to run us off the property." he explained.

"But that doesn't make sense. He doesn't even know what they look like and they're not going to go back there again to sit in the same place anyway. Why would they?" Callie asked logically.

"Pierre says that all these 'seedy apples', as he calls them, always return to the scene of the crime! AND, that they all have their 'hangouts'!" Alex informed her forthrightly.

"AND even if they did go back there," interjected Mary Jo, pointedly ignoring her husband's steadfast, confident belief in Pierre's rhetoric, "they wouldn't talk about those things in front of him. If they are really serious about killing him, like he says, then they would HAVE to know what Pierre looks like and the red light would go off."

"He's thought of that." Alex readily assured her calmly. "That's why he's undercover." he stated smugly. Regarding the blank looks on both the girls' faces he elucidated, "He's in disguise!"

He smiled with satisfaction as he saw the understanding dawn on their countenances until he saw Callie's lips start to quiver and she burst out laughing.

"You mean he's got on those same raggedy clothes he was wearing on that "stakeout" for Jean Luc Paté?" Callie blurted out the question in disbelief.

"Frayed hat and all!" Cari answered as she and Rand located them in the store and adroitly wended their way around and between the displays of merchandise toward their friends.

Head bent over and torso hunkered down into his seat Pierre crouched and molded his body into the contours of the cushioned bench of the booth. His head jutted forward into the opened menu which he held out as a screen across the table with his lowered face hidden behind it. He was in the ultimate position for covert observation. His heart pounded loudly with anticipation in his chest. The blood coursed through his veins. He was primed for the thrill of the hunt. He was braced for any form of danger in any sort of situation which might arise. Attuned to all nuances around him and totally focused. His pricked up ears listened intently to detect any noises - no matter how slight - that might occur in the booth directly behind him. Therefore, he practically jumped out of his skin when the waitress in front of him stridently requested his order. She had appeared seemingly out of nowhere and stood before him at the ready with pencil poised over her pad and…waited. Pierre was speechless, irritated and angry at the same time. Did this serving maid wish him to, que veut dire, blow his cover? He looked up at her suspiciously with one eyebrow raised and eyes red-rimmed. He considered the possibilities. Given his distracted state of mind could he have possibly been unaware of her presence? Pierre finally decided that she did not mean to expose his presence and was not in cahoots with…des autres and relaxed. His one and only problème maintenant was that she was scaring away his, as these Américains would say, "pigeons".

"Des oeufs! C'est tous!" Pierre said curtly with a dismissive air wishing to send her quickly on her way and out of his ointment but then he suddenly realized that he was, in fact, quite hungry. Even though he had already eaten at LaurelsHeath his lunch had been less than satisfactory and he had hardly touched it. Joan Collins this Trudy was NOT and he missed Joan's wonderful food. Visions of her tasty sandwiches, opulent soufflés, casseroles and main dishes filled his head. He wondered if he might persuade Edi to bring her here…. He was immediately heartened by this new idea. After all, a man needed to keep up his strength, bien sûr! This process of waiting and watching that these Américains called, que veut dire, "surveillance" was a very EXHAUSTING activity! It made one hungry and il a très faim maintenant! 'The serveuse should have requested my order earlier!' thought Pierre conveniently forgetting that he had taken particular painstaking care to avoid her and to slip into the back booth unnoticed so as not to alert anyone to his presence. As he put his hand on her arm to halt her and amend his food order he noted the nameplate pinned to her bosom. It read "Annie". To compensate for his previously rude behavior and scowling, sour demeanor he sought to ingratiate himself. He smiled winningly and addressed her by name. Annie gave this ill-dressed, unkempt contrarian a strange look sideways. 'First, he was abrupt and dismissive and now he was being "folksy" and wanted her to stay.' Her radar told her that something was up. 'Was he looking for…a handout? Alms for the poor…?' she wondered. 'Or perhaps something else! Well!' she thought in a huff. 'I am NOT that kind of a girl!' On this note, Annie attempted to swiftly collect his menu without listening to him and stalk off. However, perhaps sensing her mood, Pierre had turned stubbornly mulish and would not relinquish it. A back and forth tug of war ensued with each of them refusing to give the other ground. The laminated menu was yanked roughly from Pierre's chest by Annie to her own then jerked firmly back from Annie's chest by Pierre to his own chest and vice versa.

"Pierre!" called Trudy as she spotted him before he could raise the disputed menu to cover his face once more to conceal his identity.

The waitress, taking advantage of this momentary distraction, snapped the menu from his grasp triumphantly again bestowing upon Pierre the same strange look with a backward glance as she beat a hasty retreat to the kitchen.

"I need your help-" cried the distraught lady who only succeeded in losing her balance for her trouble.

Trudy slipped on a slick spot resulting when the tussle between Pierre and the waitress caused the glass of water on the table to tip over and empty its contents onto the floor. She slid forward unbidden and unrestrained into the booth and landed directly onto Pierre's lap. Trudy turned contritely to apologize to him for her embarrassing accidental landing. As they faced each other nose to nose they saw the waitress turn to stare shocked at the spectacle they presented. ('So he WAS looking for a loose woman!' she thought, appalled.) The pair also heard a loud "click" accompanied by a bright light which flashed in their eyes startling them and shone on their faces. Their surprised and guilty expressions were now immortalized forever on film seen, as they were, through the lens of the camera's eye.

"Ah-Hah!" Clyde crowed at the top of his lungs as Trudy scrambled to her feet and out of Pierre's arms. "An illicit TRYST!" he exclaimed loudly with pleased satisfaction for all to hear. "An' all these WITNESSES, too! Shame on ya swami. For SHAME! Tsk, tsk, tsk!" scolded Clyde looking all the more like the cat who had just swallowed the canary. "Nows maybe ya'll quit tellin' ya nutty stories ta the police else I tell some stories te ya pretty wife! An' with these pixes ta back me up…who de ya think she'll believe? I got it all on film!" he said ominously tapping the camera meaningfully.

"So. It was you who threatened my person - who is your, comment dit-on, FLUNKY?" Pierre spat out the question contemptuously.

"More than yerself is gonna be threatened. How'd ya like ya pretty little woman ta know 'bout ya...involvement with the help!?" Clyde insinuated again warningly tapping his camera knowingly. "An' if ya don't stop spreadin' ya crystal ball theories ta Cordell ya wife won't be the only one ta see this picture. It'll be in the PAPERS!" he added smugly with overt satisfaction.

"My FANS!" cried Pierre in alarm his eyes bugging out of their respective sockets in pure horror at the thought. "The nom of Pierre Dûçot will be SCORNED!" he gasped audibly with the utterance.

"That's right, swami. Ya'll be famous." he confirmed sarcastically while involuntarily raising one eyebrow as he was a bit puzzled and taken aback by the overzealousness of Pierre's irrepressible spontaneous outburst.

Clyde was unaware that Pierre was not only speaking merely of the general public at large but more specifically of those who admired his dancing prowess and who attended classes at his dance studios. Nonetheless, he was still pleased with Pierre's frantic response even though it was a bit over the top of the reaction he had expected.

"An' I don't have no FLUNKY. If the boss man heard ya call him a flunky he'd make toast out a ya."

"TOAST?" Pierre timorously asked alarmed.

"TOAST!" repeated Clyde positively.

"There he is. He's speaking to Clyde Barnett." Cari said to her companions matter-of-factly as she and the others entered the eatery and she spied Pierre in the back booth. "And he's with Trudy, too."

"Wave ta ya friends, swami." Clyde advised Pierre in a nasty voice as he smiled his best crocodile smile in the direction of the newcomers approaching them.

CHAPTER 23

"Pierre, we've been looking all over for you! What are you do-ing dressed in that crazy garb?" Cari exclaimed petulantly while making the rhetorical inquiry.

"Trying to pick me up is what he was trying to do!" replied Annie in an insulted tone of voice as she deposited his plate of food before him on the table and fixed Pierre with a judgmental stare. "You should be ashamed of yourself, you geezer!" she flung the cen-suring comment scathingly at him in moral outrage before stalking away in a huff.

"I did <u>NOT</u> try to "pick" her up - she is not even my, comment dit-on - "type". And you KNOW that I am on a, que veut dire, stake-out!" Pierre said defensively as Cari pulled up at the brim of his hat enough to fully expose his eyes and he squinted against the sudden full glare of brighter light.

"Why do you persist on wasting our time with this stakeout nonsense? Honestly! These cloak-and-dagger games of yours never bring anything of importance to bear." Cari pooh-poohed impa-tiently as Mary Jo giggled at Pierre's chosen shabby attire and Callie leaned forward to pull down on his hat so that its brim covered his eyes once more.

"Very stylish, indeed!" Callie proclaimed in the best imitation of a polished highbrow accent that she could muster. "Quite the fash-ion statement!" she announced critically stepping back to survey her "work".

"Come on! Stop the joking around girls. Quit the tomfoolery!"

Randmore exclaimed impatiently. "We don't have time for this lunacy!" he concluded raising his voice to convey a withering tone.

"Yeah. We don't have time for these antics!" Alex concurred.

"Mais I did discover something - I did!" Pierre spoke up eager to defend both himself and his actions. "I discovered that cet homme, s'appelle Clyde-"

"Would ya care fer some TOAST with those there eggs, swami - I mean - PIERRE?" Clyde interjected sharply with a piercing look full of meaningful warning.

"Non, merci...I had better be going." said Pierre, almost too quickly it seemed to Cari, in a small voice while searching his breast pockets for the smelling salts that Matthew had given him - he was suddenly feeling faint.

"What's wrong with you, Pierre? You look sick all of a sudden. What are you looking for?" Alex asked solicitously concerned as Pierre abruptly ceased clapping against the breast pockets of his jacket and proceeded to frantically search through and empty his trouser pockets.

"Je cherche...." began Pierre distractedly. "I am searching for that...that witches' potion the médecin gave to me."

"You mean the smelling salts." Alex prompted knowledgeably.

Pierre abruptly halted his search in order to muster up as haughty a stare as he could on his gaunt, haunted visage and fix Alex with it as he spoke austerely: "Do not correct your elders, Alex."

"Pierre. There is absolutely NO hocus-pocus involved in the restorative properties of Matt's smelling salts!" Rand said reasonably. "It's all scientific. The elements work together and combine to form the appropriate degree of pungency in the fumes."

"That's right!" Callie contributed to the conversation. "Some things just go together." she finished simplistically.

"Like ya eggs and...TOAST!" Clyde proclaimed proudly in triumph while peeking obliquely at Pierre with a threateningly stringent glare.

Unable to locate his smelling salts to revive him and to calm his frayed nerves the Frenchman grasped at his throat and fell to the floor with Clyde's seemingly innocuous comment. Alex was the first to reach Pierre's side and knelt down beside him attempting to resuscitate the clearly overly stressed now unconscious man.

"Where is Matt in all of this when we need him?" Alex complained as he looked up at the faces of the others.

"But, Simon. They're yer kin!" argued Dr. Flanderly as his long-time friend bandaged a large bloody gash on his shin.

The second hand of the clock on the fireplace mantle tick-tocked in measured increments. Simon heaved a huge sigh of regret as he rose to his feet and leaving Matthew's side from where he lay on the cot walked to the small window of the cabin in which he resided. He scanned the verdant scenery outside as if searching for something which he knew he would never find. Simon had wheeled his virtually incapacitated friend in the wheelbarrow up the ramp from the damp recesses below to the charming little cottage above which he shared with his wife and Elroy. When he finally replied the ambivalent angst ringing in the tenor of his voice was clear to be heard.

"It is better this way. It is better that they do not know that I am alive. I weighed the pros and cons of it all a long time ago. The alternatives gave me no recourse. I would be an embarrassment to the family name - and you know how proud my sister is of the Chesterfield name. And little Cari...!" he cried mournfully.

His eyes teared over widening with his guilt and Simon was besieged by a flooding of raw pent-up, remorseful emotions.

"Though she is not so little anymore." he remarked absentmindedly while dashing the tears falling from his eyes with the back of his sleeve. "Cari would blame me for her parents' deaths."

"But tha' must ha' been nigh on twenty years ago, begorra! They wouldna hold any grudges agin ye!" Matt rallied to be positive and bolster his friend's sagging spirits.

"Always the perpetual optimist. You have not changed a bit, Matt. But, really. They are better off without me. Anyway, what am I now…? A broken man, that is what." Simon said answering his own question in a tortured voice as he hung his head in shame.

"Yer limpin' isna so bad." Matthew stated adamantly.

"I did not even want YOU to know I was still alive! No. Now my limp is not so bad. But back then I could hardly walk a straight line after the accident. But I could have at least tried to save them! I could have dragged them away from the edge of the cliff! But, in- stead, what did I do? I froze. I froze and then I saved myself!" he said overwhelmed with guilt as the former old feelings of helplessness and memories of the whole wretched affair came flooding back to haunt him once more.

"But, ye know tha' be nary the whole o' the truth! Ye were a- scared - an' who wouldna be with the ground fallin' away from ye an' the cliff crumblin' apart? Ye'd already thought tha' they ha' escaped. An' what about yer own condition? Ye said yerself ye could barely stand up straight!" Matt argued sympathetically taking up Simon's part and preaching to his cause. "It be clear te my way o' thinkin' tha' ye done everythin' ye possibly could. Ye pulled 'em both free o' the carriage - ye saw them get te their feet. Ye ha' no reason whatsoever te believe they wouldna follow ye." he continued to rally his spirits as he spoke judiciously.

"I TOLD you, Matt - I froze! I am a doctor. I was TRAINED to maintain a cool, level head and to keep a stiff upper lip in a crisis. It makes no difference that I, myself, was injured. I had a responsibil- ity to look after their well-being and instead I panicked - I ran!"

"Ye STAGGERED! Tha' is more te the like o' it. Ye had te look after yerself, man. One false, misbegotten step an'…POOF! Ye're useless te yerself let alone t'others!" Matt persisted doggedly in his defense.

"Do not try to make excuses for me, Matt. You are my friend and we both know that you would say anything to spare my feelings. They could take away my medical license if anyone found out that I shirked my sworn duty."

"Ye're makin' too much of it. A mountain out of a mole hill. All I can see is tha' ye were in shock. Ye were in the capacity o' a civilian. Ye're a <u>human</u> <u>being</u> first, man!" Matt concluded. "Ye say tha' when ye turned back they were gone?"

"Yes." Simon confirmed the fact. "If I had only had the presence of mind to pull them along with me.… Then Brandon and Jeanette would not have been standing on that platform when it collapsed!" Simon hung his head as he contemplated what might have been.

"A terrible business." Matthew sighed with regret mingled with sadness at the loss of his two friends and shook his head from side to side. "Where were they laid te rest?" he inquired.

"They weren't." Simon divulged uneasily casting his eyes down and shifting his weight nervously from one foot to the other.

"What de ye mean - "they weren't"?!" Matthew articulated stridently morphing his voice to ape Simon's two word revelation mockingly. "De ye mean te say te me their bodies werena interred proper?! Ye're my friend, Simon, but yer brother an' sister-in-law, they were me friends, as well! They deserve respect! Was there na' even a service te their memory - a requiem te mark their passin' o'er!?!" railed the Irishman passionately in outrage.

"Oh, there was a service, Matthew. But they were not buried because they could not find the bodies. In all that rubble it was impossible to recover anything. Their bodies, the bodies of the horses, the carriage, the luggage.… Everything and everyone was irretrievable: covered by tons of rock, dirt, trees, rubble. If my sister and

SHARON ELIZABETH SARKISIAN

niece learned how I had let Brandon and Jeanette just…slip away the way that they did without even <u>trying</u> to help them they would never forgive me. By golly, Matt!" Simon cried out grief-stricken wringing his hands in frustration at the futility of the situation. "I turned around and it was as if they had vanished, and everything else along with them, into thin air! It was as if Brandon and Jeanette Chesterfield had never existed!"

His tortured plea for understanding rang out as clear as a bell as the words of regretful remorse spilled forth from Simon Chesterfield's mouth. The scars of his mournful loss showed and now stood out markedly on a countenance that had suddenly become aged beyond its years.

"God rest their souls." affirmed Matthew piously.

CHAPTER 24

Cyrus Sykes rushed forward into the street to grab Cari around the waist and pull her into his arms and out of the path of the oncoming stagecoach rambling at a rapid pace in her direction.

"Why, dadgummit, can't these Neanderthals watch where they are going, jump into the present and install some stoplights!"

"I can hardly catch my breath!" Cari gasped the words out sputteringly stopping quickly to repeatedly gulp in scads of air.

"You should watch where you are going, little lady. You are not totally blameless either, you know!" observed the handsome stranger as he followed the departure of the retreating conveyance with his eyes as it barreled past them and disappeared into the distance.

Cari looked up at her "savior" wonderingly. He was so tall, she thought. Taller than Pierre. And although he was not stocky he was of a sturdy build which she found oddly attractive. Or, was it his arresting manner that she found so enigmatic? As she gazed into his hooded dark eyes she felt somehow at a loss for a response. She had almost been run down by a horse-drawn conveyance; while recklessly crossing the street in an unthinking rush; and he had come to her rescue just like that. Wow! She was floored! His arms were wrapped tightly about her and she felt so comforted and protected within their circling folds after almost meeting what could have been her untimely demise.

"I know I should have been more careful, but it's my friend.... You see, he is not feeling well and I am rushing to find a doctor."

"Well, Doc's office is around the corner." he informed her while marking her exceptional beauty and drinking it in shamelessly.

"Allow me to introduce myself. I am Cyrus Sykes."

As Cyrus smiled down on her engagingly Cari suddenly realized that she was still leaning heavily against him. She pulled away, embarrassed at such close contact with a total stranger.

"I am Cari Chesterfield McKinley." Cari pronounced flustered while quickly backing away eager to escape from Cyrus's presence and shrug off the unwarranted attraction she felt for a man that she had only just met. "Since I'm just visiting the area for a while I do not know my way around town and I won't be here long. I have to go now - bye."

Cyrus moved forward to stand in her path and said: "That's too bad. I was starting to enjoy the scenery." he commented flirtatiously favoring her with a sly wink as he eyeballed her shapely form from head to toe and back with his gaze finally resting on her bosom.

"If you'll excuse me Mr. Sykes-"

"Call me Cyrus, please!"

"Cyrus. I have to find the doctor-"

"Cari." Randmore called out to his wife who appeared to be vastly relieved at his unexpected interruption.

"Oh! It is my HUSBAND." Cari elucidated Randmore's marital status pointedly for Cyrus's benefit as she turned to see Randmore and Alexander approaching supporting a now less pallid Pierre Dûçot, whose cheeks were slightly more pink than at the coffee shop, on either side with their arms linked through his.

"Mary Jo and Callie decided to stay back at the diner to have a bite to eat with Trudy and Clyde - a regular foursome, huh? Meanwhile, Pierre is feeling much better but we figured to still take him to the doctor's office anyway." explained Randmore.

"He is going to get a complete checkup whether he wants one or not!" Alex asserted firmly. "We laid down the law!" he continued defiantly speaking directly into Pierre's gaunt visage as if daring him to open his mouth, put up a fuss and object.

Pierre picked up the gauntlet and rose shakily to the challenge: "I do not see the raison for this, comment dit-on, MANHANDLING. C'est ridicule. Tu sais - you <u>KNOW</u> I am tough as the hammer and nails." spoke Pierre with a sniff and as much grandeur as he could muster in his weakened condition.

Pierre's authoritative air crumbled, however, as his signature sniff lapsed into a masked groan. Cari also noted that he did not shake off the bolstering arms and gripping hands of Randy or Alex which were propping him up. An enormous wave of pity washed over her at the debilitated man's pathetic condition. In order to distract him and prevent him from sapping what little strength he still possessed and expending more energy with his boasting false bravado and airs she hastily interceded:

"I am so <u>glad</u> that you are feeling better, Pierre. I would like to introduce you, all of you, to Mr. Sykes. Mr. Sykes, this is Pierre, Alex and my husband, Randy. This is Mr. S-"

"Cyrus. PLEASE Cari. Call me CYRUS!" he said jovially. "It is nice to meet you fine gentlemen. And may I say, Randy, that you have a most charming wife!" said Cyrus buoyantly in the resounding voice of a statesman running for office and seeking to gain public goodwill by kissing babies.

"Mr. Sykes - I mean, CYRUS, was kind enough to point out to me that the doctor's office is right around that corner. Cyrus also saved my life. I was crossing to the other sidewalk and a coach almost ran me down. He pulled me out of the way." Cari admitted self-consciously remembering their erstwhile close contact and almost intimate proximity to each other.

"Oh, I was quite pleased to rescue a fair damsel in distress." Cyrus remarked modestly to the other men while he winked at Cari lasciviously and whetted his lips coyly in her direction.

"Do I KNOW you?" inquired Pierre perking up almost instantly.

"Your voice sounds very familiar to me. Perhaps you have a <u>French</u> relative?" he asked hopefully anxious to meet a fellow countryman and make the right connections.

Cyrus squinted sharply shooting Pierre a scrutinizing once-over glance of appraisal.

"You are French?" Cyrus finally asked in a colloquial, cordial fashion instead of addressing the Frenchman's question.

"Mais, bien sûr! Peut-être you have heard of me...? I am the fameux dancing instructeur Pierre Dûçot."

CHAPTER 25

"Hey, Barney! What ye doin' here? I never knew <u>you</u> was the reading type." Dwight Sanders said with a hearty laugh heartily glad to see his old friend. "Or are you just rememberin' our school days and our old hangout?!"

"Quiet, Sandy! Ya wants te get us in trouble with the management?" Clyde Barnett sallied jokingly as pretending mock concern he glanced at the librarians replacing used books to their allotted spaces on the bookshelves to make sure that their loudness had not caused offense. "They're likely ta throw us outta here!"

Dwight tittered as he considered their old antics.

"Our least favorite place to frequent but we did spice things up a mite during our little visits!" Dwight recalled grinning widely.

"Like the time we alpha-"bee"-tized everything in the card catalog backwards?" Clyde snickered with delight.

"Or…or the time that we <u>exchanged</u> the plaques on the doors of the "MEN" and "LADIES" rooms!" blubbered Dwight guffawing uncontrollably as the merry tears already filling his eyes sprang forth escaping the confines of their restraining orbs to slide down his flushed, reddened cheeks.

"Keep it down I said!" admonished Clyde noticing the librarians' irate stares now being directed their way. The mischievous twinkle suddenly re-entered his eyes: "Nows, Sandy - let's be fair 'bout all this…." Clyde gasped haltingly as his belly began to convulse with the throes of his mirth and his eyes seemed to dance and twinkle more brightly than before. "It was an EVEN EXCHANGE!"

"The way those prim and proper ladies was screaming on their way out of the bathroom when they realized that it was actually the men's inner sanctum was hilarious! We sure got an eyeful with that prank!"

"Yep." Clyde agreed. "But then, SO DID THEY!" he pointed out with a wicked grin pulling a wrinkled handkerchief from his pocket and mopping the accumulated beads of giddy perspiration from his brow. "They sure went in there like starched shirts: all prim and proper-like ladies. But whens they come out...! They wasn't actin' that way! Hee, hee, hee! They was fightin' ta get out the door!"

"We lucked out that day. That was the <u>whole</u> Ladies Historical Society visiting the library all staid and straitlaced for cultural research and then - BANG, ZOOM! Running like a bunch of clucking chickens out the door and into the street squawking with their feathers ruffled and all out of joint!"

Dwight stopped his reminiscing as he noticed all of the charts and property title deeds littering the desk before which Clyde was seated.

"What are these documents for, Barney?" inquired Dwight curiously picking one up to peruse it inquisitively. "Are you fixin' to join up with the Historical Society? You know, I hear they're visitin' in a few days, or thereabouts, to check out all the historical houses in the area. You know, you'd look kinda cute in one of those poufy, frilly hats!" he said chuckling at the mental image of his friend in a chapeau - the requisite headpiece that was a traditional part of the Society's official uniform.

"Ya always was a card, Sandy." replied Clyde in response to his mocking gibe while snatching the floor plan from him and slipping it into a folder.

"Was that some kinda maze, or something? With all those corridors and side exits it looked like one. What were those contraptions at the corners...trapdoors?" he queried pointing at the folder wherein lay the disputed document.

"Ya shouldn'ta seen that, Dwight." admonished Clyde sternly. "Now, don't ask no questions! I am workin' on a project fer my boss man - and don't ask who he is again 'cause I TOLD ya he's incognito!"

"Alright. You never call me by my first name, Dwight, unless it's serious, so's I'll mind my own business. But. If ever you need help with those plans you know I'm good with architectural stuff. I've been in construction work for years and that there layout looked complex!"

"Enough ta give ya a complex. But, did ya say that the Ladies Historical Society was comin' in ta town?"

"Yup. You know how they've been tryin' te get that old house yer boss is trying te get a permit te tear down declared a historical monument. I know I wasn't goin' te say nothin' - that I was supposed te mind my own business. But I presume that the reason you are researchin' all those papers ye put inte that folder is because you are lookin' for the title deed te that property which he needs te give the commission before they'll let him knock down the house and bulldoze the area."

"How did you know he was - what makes ye think he's my boss?" he asked innocently. "Never mind that!" Clyde said sharply losing his temper when his friend opened his mouth seeking to respond. "And a shopping mall would be the best thing ta come along ta this place in a long time!" Clyde asserted defiantly in order to stave off any prospective criticism coming his way. "It would bring jobs to this dead and drip of a town and bring in more tourists. Ya know that a mall will generate more revenue for the town and make us all more prosperous!"

"If you say so, Barney, but yer soundin' more like yer anonymous boss man te me when ye start spoutin' that rhetoric." replied Dwight in a patronizing, placating tone of voice that let Clyde know that he knew his justifications for building a mall were not his own ideas.

"Usin' all those fancy words, "RHETORIC", ya soundin' more and more like those squatters on the LaurelsHeath spread. Those newbies with all them high and mighty airs are too close fer comfort an' they's interfering with progress! Especially that Swami!"

"Swami?" asked Dwight in bewilderment.

"The French guy!" Clyde spat back angrily as he remembered Pierre's pompous mannerisms.

"Oh. Him. He's <u>bossy</u> but he's not so bad." responded Dwight noncommittally wishing to give Pierre's character and idiosyncratic behaviors the benefit of the doubt.

"No? Well, he is awful close ta that Trudy woman an' I'm sure he knows where her kid is."

"That Elroy should be put away."

"Don't I know it! He's always after the little kids and scarin' their parents ta death." Clyde said angrily.

"I saw some crippled guy with him one time and I think he was helping him - I wonder what that was all about."

Dwight Sanders cogitated on the question while scratching his head.

CHAPTER 26

"What, Alex, is...TOAST?" Pierre asked the young man casually.

"You've got to know what toast is, Pierre. You had it with your eggs this morning." Alex stated simply as he gave him a strange look.

"Je pense.... I think it translates to autre chose - something else. I heard...." Pierre phrased his words carefully, "Cet homme told this personne he would make toast out of him."

"Were they quarreling?"

"Oui." admitted the man timidly.

"Ah! Well. That's easy to explain. He was threatening to make dead meat out of him." interpreted Alex simply and succinctly.

"I thought so." said Pierre glumly as he drummed his fingertips upon the surface of the coffee table.

"Cheer up, Pierre. I know it won't be easy to tell Eleanor that Matt's missing but I'm sure she'll take it well when she learns everyone's out looking for him." Alex said slowly and thoughtfully misinterpreting Pierre's malaise as concern for Matt's well-being.

"Il apparait that many people are disappearing around ici." he replied grimly.

"You said a mouthful! First it was the kids and now, Matt."

Matt lay back as Trudy removed the lunch tray with the plate of half-eaten food upon it from his lap and left the room closing the door behind her. He watched her go with a sigh. His head was filled with so many conflicted thoughts and mixed emotions that he did not know how to feel. When he had learned, all those years ago, that his friends Simon and Brandon along with his wife, Jeanette, had died in a terrible accident on the road he had grieved and paid his respects to their memories. He had, with the passing of time, slowly but surely come to grips with and distanced himself from the heartache of the tragic event and sorrow which that day encompassed. Long after the fact, when he had met his wife, Ellie - then Eleanor Cartwright, he remembered how both Simon and his older brother, Brandon Chesterfield, had helped convince Edith to give her the position in the Chesterhollow kitchen where he had then first met her face to face. At that time he had remarked on this fateful coincidence. To his mind, it had seemed almost as if even though they were no longer living on the face of the Earth they had both reached out to him in spirit to guide him to Eleanor and love. An idealistic notion te be sure. But now, Simon had shattered his romantic illusion and revealed to him a more sordid and intricate tale. A tale of how he had failed to aid his brother and sister-in-law at the scene of the accident. How he suffered a form of shock and froze when he could have saved them. He had fallen into a black haze of darkness and when he had finally come to his senses it appeared that they had disappeared and a woman named Trudy was the one who had been nursing him back to health - out of his delirium and back to join the human race once more. In the background a small boy played with his blocks and he knew that his caregiver had a son. With every passing day Simon's admiration and love for his compassionate Trudy had grown ever stronger and flourished and since she did not have a husband to protect her and her son he henceforth married her in due course. After a great deal of deliberation Simon had decided that he would risk the humiliation which he knew awaited him at Chesterhollow and take Trudy and her son, Elroy, back to the ranch with him. However, she would not hear of it. Even as it became clear that Elroy was not developing mentally in stride with his other playmates and the court of public opinion had deemed it appropriate action to take him from her and commit him to a mental facility she still insisted she must remain at LaurelsHeath. She would not explain her decision but instead chose to hide Elroy from those who would take him from her and he had helped her secret Elroy from the general population in a small cottage he built on top of one of the rabbit hole entrances leading to the catacombs. Simon had acceded to Matthew that Elroy had always been a bright boy and he could not understand why Elroy became more introverted with each passing year and why he spent so much time in the lower catacombs beneath the house playing with his "blocks". The dust of the tunnels did not seem to bother him and he spent a majority of his time puttering about down there while it took Simon a conscious effort not to gag on the befouled air every time he went below to replace the yellow-colored stones which he referred to as "blocks" to each respective cubbyhole. Matthew also learned that Pierre knew of Elroy's plight as well. When Pierre had discovered the then cowering M.A. and Megan who had erstwhile been missing he was with Trudy in the kitchen. This fortuitous meeting between the children and the adults had taken place purely by accident. The young ones had been terrified of a "giant" they said had been holding them captive. The frightened pair had revealed how they had managed to escape the 'giant' by duping him into believing that they were playing a game of Cowboy and Indians. During the course of said game they convinced Elroy - the giant - that they must tie him up for the sake of adding realism to the game. After binding him securely they had then scampered off toward freedom when they heard someone enter the house, release Elroy from his trussing and then begin searching for them. They had wandered to the back of the house and spying the descending staircase before them planned to hide in the nearby basement until they could sneak out of the cottage undetected. But sadly this was not to be the case. Simon and Trudy related in turn what the children conveyed to them had happened next. Megan had fallen through the rabbit hole in the basement floor with M.A. following after to rescue her. At this point, they were found out and chased either by the unleashed giant or his nameless "goon" (Simon had smiled self-consciously at M.A.'s unflattering description of him and pointed at himself) through a maze. Charmer materialized out of nowhere and they had chased the feline to a cul-de-sac where the cat had mysteriously vanished. Feeling trapped and doomed they frantically searched for and located a release device in the wall which they manipulated and pushed through a panel and walked through a secret door on the other side of a kitchen broom closet. Once in the LaurelsHeath kitchen the wee ones had been apprehended by a startled Trudy who had been preparing a ham and Brie cheese hero under the strict supervision of Pierre Dûçot. Trudy explained how she had persuaded Pierre and the bairns to keep Elroy's hiding place a secret and played upon his chivalrous leanings to protect her son from those who would revile him. He had not refused her. She had appealed to his masculine male ego. Matthew chuckled as he recalled Pierre and Trudy exchanging secretive looks. He had presumed that perhaps they shared a romantic admiration for one another. What a ludicrous assumption to make on his part! 'What sensible sort of lady could be enamoured of that pompous, self-important screwball!' he pondered with amusement as he enjoyed a much needed moment of comic relief. Matthew had forgotten all about Edith.

CHAPTER 27

"How much longer are they gonna hug and kiss!?" said Alex impatiently at the train station while eyeing the overly long farewell taking place between Matthew and his wife and son.

"Give them a break, Alex. Eleanor has only just found her husband safe and sound and now she has to leave him to take M.A. to school." Randmore related patiently.

"Well, all this lovey-dovey stuff just is NOT my style. Look! Now she's reading him a list!" Alex uttered in disbelief as the trio next to the black locomotive puffing billows of fluffy, grey smoke from its vertical stack in preparation of its departure continued their exchange and the train's conductor collected tickets from last minute passengers.

"Alex, you know that if the roles were reversed and it were you and Mary Jo over there I bet that it would not be so easy to pry you two apart, either. And you have to give Eleanor some slack. She is only concerned about her husband and little girl. After all, Matthew has to take care of Megan all by himself and so she is just making sure that he knows her bedtime, Megan's daily schedule, what she should eat versus his low fat diet....That sort of thing...you know." Rand stated calmly. "Remember, she only just got them back after losing them. She is only looking out for their welfare. I am surprised that she did not object more strenuously to her husband's stance against accompanying her back home."

"Yeah! What is the deal with that? Look how tightly she is holding Matthew Alexander's hand — you would think that he was five

SHARON ELIZABETH SARKISIAN

years old! And why <u>aren't</u> Matt and Megan going with her? It just doesn't make sense!" Alex retorted defiantly. "Family should stick together! What are they staying here for?"

"It is true that M.A. <u>does</u> have to get back to school next week so he has to go back home but Megan does not attend school yet so Matt and Eleanor have no excuse to force the issue. You see, Matt claims that Megan just does not want to leave Charmer. He concedes that he will just indulge her for now since her education is not an issue at this point. Of course, I do not believe that is the sole reason he wants to stay. I suspect that it is more than likely Matt is staying because he thinks the yellow nugget that you found is gold. And with Pierre saying that the writing on the nugget is in Jan LaFitte's handwriting.... Draw your own conclusions, Alex. All he needed was Pierre's encouragement to "know" that there MUST be treasure or, as he puts it, "remuneration" in the offing." Randmore responded volubly.

"Pierre's been right before-"

"Laddie, whatever Pierre says ye canna take as gospel. We ALL can testify te the fact tha' the fellow be short a few marbles!" Matthew said jovially tapping his noggin with his knuckles to the young man as he joined the two men in time to hear Alex's last comment. "I woulda joined ye earlier," he explained to them urbanely, "but fer the fact tha' a group o' fair ladies comin' off o' the train who were in need o' me assistance descending the steps o' the exit. Quite charmin' they were, te be sure." he spouted boisterously to those surrounding him with a silly smile curving his lips as well as a rosy shade of lipstick staining his right cheek. "But they were definitely in need o' a gentleman's strong arm te lean against! I ha' te explain te them sternly tha' I only ha' two o' them available an' tha' they would just ha' te wait an' take their turns. After all, I be only one man!"

"Yeah, I saw them hanging on your arms. They wore these

130

pouf-y hats!" Alex noted looking sideways at the married man who quite obviously had enjoyed the close proximity of these fawning women a bit too much.

"There must be a convention in town." observed Rand blandly.

"Men. Men! Ha' ye no romance in yer hearts fer the fairer sex? Where be the fire in yer blood? Where be the passion in yer souls?! It is obvious te <u>me</u> that yer wives have ye <u>well</u> <u>trained</u>!" Matthew crowed smugly with a twinkle in his laughing green eyes.

"I see, Matt. You are right." Rand conceded thoughtfully musing upon the idea with his hands forming a pyramid below his upper lip as he ponderously tapped his fingers against each other in concert. "I will just have to bring this subject up in conversation when I next see Eleanor. It will be quite educational to hear from a fresh source a fresh, unbiased viewpoint on this subject."

"Now. Let us na be too hasty, lad!" Matt said a bit too quickly his erstwhile smile disappearing and his teasing, admonishing tone evaporating. "No sense te gettin' the little woman involved, ye know."

"That is right!" remarked Alex triumphantly as seeing Matt's discomfiture he chuckled. "I think Eleanor had already started to board the train with her back to yours <u>before</u> you turned away and rushed over to "help" the ladies."

"Now, laddie, dunna be smart with me!" Matthew retorted defensively.

"That is correct, Alex. Do not disrespect your elders! Were you raised par des loups?" asserted Pierre approaching from the nearby ticket office while simultaneously removing his hand from the inside of his jacket pocket and adjusting it to hang in line neatly with the rest of his complet.

"Ahhh! He can take it." Alex said to Pierre.

"Do not be coarse, Alex. Tu sais that Matthew has always been ton ami."

"Well...."

"He has always been your champion."

"But he-"

"Mais nothing! He has always supported you." insisted Pierre.

"Okay, okay! I apologize to you, Matt! I shouldn't have made assumptions." Alex said grudgingly.

"Good boy, Alex. Now, Randy," Pierre continued pivoting to face Randmore directly, "what has le médecin done cette fois-ci?" he queried expectantly craning his head toward him in anticipation of hearing the new gossip.

"He is CHEATING on Eleanor!" stated Alex playfully in strident tones recovering quickly from his momentary bout of apologetic sullenness and forestalling Randmore's response.

"Quoi?! Is that why she is leaving?" Pierre inquired scandalized stifling a gasp. "I am shocked, Matthew. JUST shocked! Alex was right to chastise you...you CAD!" Pierre finished pulling a white kid glove from the inner pocket of his jacket to slap it against each cheek on either side of his face.

"Ye blitherin' idiot!" Matthew yelled belligerently, smarting at the sharp, stinging pain initiated by the blows, pulling the glove from Pierre's grasp and throwing it to the ground. "I am not betrayin' me Ellie!" he asserted angrily shaking his fists.

Pierre backed away from his threatening presence in alarm and sought to redirect Matthew's ire.

"How could you say such a thing, Alex! It is clear to me that Matt is DEVOTED to Eleanor!" Pierre stammered nervously changing his spots as he hastily abandoned his former critique and stepped behind Alex pushing him forward, as if a sacrificial lamb, toward Matthew.

"Aww! I was just joking. And, anyway, he might have been betraying her in his thoughts! And you saw the way he was holding those ladies around the waist as he helped them off the train!" Alex said defensively yet guiltily to Randmore upset at the thought that his giddy, playful attempt at poking fun might have been misconstrued and taken seriously.

"Ye sanctimonious dolt!" Matt accused loudly while looking at Pierre defiantly his blazing eyes daring him to refute the statement as he smoothed back the ruffled, mussed hair on either side of his head which had been displaced by the impact of the offending kid glove.

"I told you, Alex, not to disrespect your elders." Pierre scolded nervously looking quickly at Matthew to make sure that he maintained his distance. "In any case, I too am about to leave with Edi – I just purchased the tickets. I have no desire to become toast!"

"'Twill be o' no loss te the rest o' us, te be sure!" Matthew stated loftily.

"What was that, Pierre?" asked Randmore quizzically shaking his index finger up and down in his ear canal to obliterate any blockage in order to hear him more clearly. "Did you say, TOAST?"

"Cyrus!" yelled Alex ecstatically in a high-pitched, gleeful greeting startling the other three and diverting their attention as he caught sight of Cyrus Sykes and approached him in welcome.

Cyrus had been walking along slowly contemplating his shoes while muttering under his breath when Alex cheerfully interrupted his dark, bitter thoughts. Looking up resentfully at the unwarranted intrusion and focusing his regard in Alex's direction he swore under his breath and spit on the ground before pasting on his finest crocodile grin to project an appearance of joviality which he did not actually feel. It was difficult to maintain his smiling mask when he remembered his meeting with the zoning commission this morning. They still refused to allow him to clear that ramshackle plot of land which he lived on temporarily so that he could build a shopping complex on the spot. As par usual the decision had been based on, what he thought of as, a mere technicality. Before he could bulldoze the property and the house they wanted to examine the deed of the house proving his ownership. They demanded it! They were sticklers on this point. The town's record office had burned down many years ago so the only way he could prove his right to the land was to produce his own copy of the deed. So he and the Commission were at a stalemate. However, they did allow him to occupy the house on the property as long as no one else provided any kind of documentation to the contrary to refute his claim to ownership. He paused as he smiled wryly and thought angrily of his hostages. After all these years they still would not relinquish the deed he needed to further his goals. He knew his father must have told them where he'd hidden it but they denied it. They also said that Roland would not want him to bulldoze Candlestick Manor. Clyde, on the other hand, asserted that this was not the case. He said they had tried to kill his father for the deed because they believed the property rights should go to them. However, their stubbornness and forthright, ethical dogma would all be for naught. In less than one year, and counting down, the land would finally revert to him by default. It was squatters rights, after all. And then he could do whatever he wanted. All he had to do was be patient. But now, those dang Historical Society Ladies had to come into town and reopen the old issue of the house being a historical landmark. They wanted to preserve the whole estate for posterity! He was so close to ownership he could taste it and now these women could ruin everything for him. Talk about putting a fly in your ointment! Plus, with those newcomers snooping around the place the chances were they might find something. Feeling the warmth of human flesh pressing into his palm jolted his consciousness back to the present reality.

Grasping Cyrus's hand in friendship Alex shook it with much enthusiasm: "It is great to see you again!" he said.

CHAPTER 28

"That Cyrus is a pretty cool guy." commented Alex in admiration looking through the dark lenses of the sunglasses Cyrus had given him and then putting them on and gazing and mugging for the full visual effect.

"You are not a fashion model, Alex, so stop that – you look ridiculous!" Rand said impatiently in exasperation on viewing his cousin's popinjay antics.

"Oui, Alex, you look ridicule. Now. Ce chapeau dont il me l'a donné est très stylish. Who knew that these natives had such excellent taste!" Pierre said admiring the shape of the brown hat with the sharp top center crease that Cyrus had gifted him.

The clean lines and narrow brim of the hat with its slim grey feather were very appealing to Pierre's sense of suave sophistication combined with benevolent manliness. Fitting it atop his head and adjusting it over the crown of his skull he stated with authority:

"I knew from the very start that his voice was familiar to me and conveyed an underlying je ne sais quoi. It is obvious to me that his bloodline is of a French strain!"

With the brim's edge between his index finger and thumb Pierre whipped these two fingers deftly downward running them swiftly along the track-like edge of the hat until they slipped off of the front rim slickly. He then raised his chin and showed to them his profile in relief.

"Bah! Ye overblown BUFFOON. Stop pickin' on the lad! He is appearin' te be sophisticated and grand in his new...eyeglasses whereas yer outlandish headgear just makes ye look te be <u>foolish</u>." Matthew said with much assurance while staring Pierre down and then harrumphed loudly with disapproving dismissal as he turned toward the local pub to whet his whistle. "Ye dunna all have te follow me." he said with irritation as Randmore, Alex and Pierre filed through the saloon's double swinging doors after him and sat down alongside of him at the bar.

"Mais, we cannot help this, vraiment, médecin." Pierre answered seriously with apparent ingenuous sincerity. "Alex doit have his milk and cookies. Il faut très nécessaire!"

"Would you STOP beating a dead horse, Pierre. That was a long time ago! Let bygones be bygones!" said Rand impatiently while endeavoring to hold Alex down on his barstool as he attempted to rise angrily to his feet to accost Pierre and contest his barb with his fists.

"Excusez-moi!" Pierre responded indignantly as if himself a miffed victim while he watched with trepidation Alex flailing his arms and struggling against his nephew's firm grip. "That is correct, Randy. You hold him back." He again regarded Alex cautiously to be sure that Randmore had him restrained securely before continuing, "It is just that I cannot forget how à cause de his milk and cookie break I almost perdu la capture of that pretender to French ancestry who tried to steal away my Edi!"

"He not be worth it, laddie. We <u>all</u> know that the man be a wee bit teched – and I say this conservatively." consoled Matthew successfully calming Alex down while motioning to a bartender to place an order for libation. "De ye per chance ha' some milk fer the lad, barkeep?"

With all of the best intentions in his heart Matthew, with this innocent query, had only just succeeded in inserting his foot into his mouth and inflaming Alex's angst once more.

"Now you have got <u>Matt</u> doing it!" cried Alex in exasperation addressing the Frenchman. "Look, Pierre. If you do not stop ribbing me about that day I'm gonna-"

"But, lad," Matthew interrupted him, "it isna a crime te be thirsty!"

"For the one hundredth time, Matt, I <u>was</u> <u>not</u> thirsty!"

"It is of no import in any case. Edi and I are leaving for Chesterhollow next week." Pierre elucidated stemming their exchange.

"Well, it couldn't be soon enough for <u>me</u>!" said Alex adamantly crossing his arms stubbornly and pursing his lips after shaking off his cousin's hold on his person.

"I assayed to acheter the tickets for the morning train demain mais ces uncouth Américains bought the last two tickets for the seats on the morning train bound for Charlottesville. They, how you say, "cut" the line. Incroyable. Ces gauche people stepped right in front of me when I was not looking."

"Oh, Pierre! They did not step in front of us!"

"Edi! J'ai cru that you had returned to LaurelsHeath. You should not be in a place like this! Vois. Such a SEEDY clientele!" he obsessed glancing about the bar until his eyes locked with those of a dangerous-looking semi-inebriated, hulk-y patron who took offense at his contemptuous, loudmouthed statement.

Horrified that this eye contact might lead to violent repercussions Pierre coughed nervously and discreetly looked carefully and quickly away from this person he thought of as a "hothead".

"Goodness, Pierre! Forget about that! You will never believe what a wonderful opportunity has arisen! I have come to notify you of the great honor which has presented itself. I have been invited to view history! And, by the by, you must remember that <u>you</u> <u>walked</u> <u>off</u> of the ticket line momentarily when that nice gentleman vendor in the white coat came by with his basket of freshly baked croissants and Danish pastry." Edith reminded her spouse.

"Edi-" Pierre interjected attempting to stem her explanation

SHARON ELIZABETH SARKISIAN

and silence her as he saw Matthew's lips contort into a sarcastic smile and he heard Randy stifle a chuckle.

"Oh! I do not <u>blame</u> you for wanting to sample the man's wares." she continued oblivious to her husband's agitated state of mind.

"Edi, it is not necessary to-"

"They were steaming hot right out of the oven of the eatery next door."

"Edi, you do not have to explain-" he said gazing into her eyes pleadingly, yet helplessly, as even Alex began to snicker.

"Who could resist such tempting treats?" she finally asked. "In any event, that is when those other people took your place on the line and purchased the last seats for tomorrow's passage."

"I <u>knew</u> it! I knew that there couldna be <u>no</u> way the clod could be in the right!" Matthew gloated with satisfaction wiping his palms one against the other to indicate that the case was solved and, there-fore, subsequently closed.

"You see what I mean?" Alex asserted the query vigorously. "He's <u>always</u> eating – but no one ever kids him about it!"

"Mais, <u>I</u> was not eating on duty! <u>My</u> obligations take precedence over all else! When that Tartuffe who tried to spirit away my Edi was escaping out the door-"

"The window." Rand corrected him with a small smile.

"Fenêtre ou la porte – quelle est la différence? This is second-ary. When that insolent pretender to French ancestry was leaping to freedom <u>this</u> one," Pierre indicated Alex derisively, "was drinking the laît and eating the cookies!" he concluded indignantly.

"For the last and final time – I was NOT EATING COOKIES!" said Alex adamantly in a frustrated fit of mounting rage.

"AND. That cochon would almost have gotten away had I not snatched him in time!" Pierre continued querulously in a rising high-pitched tone designed to drown out and forestall any further forthcoming objections on Alex's part.

Randmore had never seen the two of them so worked up and agitated before. Well, enough was enough, as far as he was concerned! He decided to take action and intercede – discreetly.

"Edith!!!" shouted Rand above their clamor in an attempt to change the topic and thus, hopefully, divert their attention – although, Matthew <u>did</u> appear to be enjoying their heated, bellicose altercation. "You were going to tell us your wonderful news!"

"Oh, yes! I have a rendezvous with culture! The ladies of the historical society invited me to see a quaint old estate not very far from LaurelsHeath. It is practically <u>STEEPED</u> in history and the unappreciative, self-centered <u>lout</u> who resides there wants to tear it down. Can you believe how uneducated and disrespectful some people can be?" she inquired in heated frustration.

Pierre, whose curiosity had been piqued by the thought of someone who might need education and instruction in the "finer things" of life – a subject near and most dear to his heart – abruptly turned away from Alex's opened mouth which was poised in retort and addressed his wife sympathetically:

"I know <u>EXACTLY</u> how you feel, Edi. Some people just cannot understand the concept of <u>HONOR</u>." Pierre commiserated authoritatively using his finest esoteric tone.

If ANYONE was qualified to rehabilitate the socially unfortunate it was Pierre Dûçot.

CHAPTER 29

"Auntie Jo? Can I tell you a secret?"

"Of course, you can, Megan." Mary Jo said dotingly to the little girl watching her frost a three layer chocolate cake.

Trudy was supposed to do all of the cooking but she hardly did any baking and a girl needed a snack once in a while. Her mouth started to water as she gazed at her culinary creation. She was almost finished enrobing the three story temptation in fluffy buttercream when she realized that Megan was whining in distress.

"You're not listening to me!" cried the neglected youngster as she watched Mary Jo pay more attention to slathering icing onto the baked confection than to her and her serious, heartfelt confession.

"I'm sorry, Honey. I must have drifted off. I didn't hear you. Now, what did you say?" asked Mary Jo self-reproachfully of the little girl with the pouty lower lip thrust petulantly forward.

"I shouldn't be telling you this – it's a secret." Megan began mysteriously slightly mollified now that she had captured the older woman's attention. "But-"

"Megan," interrupted Mary Jo with a knowing smile on a sudden realization after turning from her masterpiece to face Megan and actually taking critical full stock of her and, more importantly to the point, of her feline companion, "I think that Auntie Cari will notice that you've dressed up Charmer in her underwear and sweater!"

Tinkling laughter issued forth from the erstwhile solemn-faced little girl as she readjusted her hold on the complacent feline who snuggled obediently in her arms.

"Oh, we were just playing dress-up." she revealed ingenuously as Mary Jo patted Charmer's head and scratched behind her ears.

"She <u>likes</u> that." Megan commented with approval as wild and furious purring erupted from the house cat at Mary Jo's fond attentiveness.

"Well, Auntie Cari's <u>not</u> going to like you going through <u>her</u> drawers! Who gave you permission to go into her bedroom, any-way?" Mary Jo eyeballed her suspiciously.

"Well…. Kitty took me there." she explained nodding affir-matively. "We went through the wall." she further elaborated on receiving no reply from the nonresponsive face before her which regarded her dubiously on hearing her previous revelation.

Mary Jo had fallen completely silent. She was stupefied and stunned totally speechless. 'What a whopper! Megan must be lis-tening to Pierre's off the wall stories too much.' she surmised after her initial incredulity at Megan's absurd answer subsided.

"It's true! It's true!" cried Megan noting her "Aunt" Mary Jo's skepticism.

"Don't think that you can play me, Megan, just because I'm nice to you all the time. You know what your Mother would say if she were here and you told her a fib like that!"

"But, it's the truth – I'm not lying!" she insisted loudly.

"Okay." Mary Jo began rationally. "Let's imagine that Charmer did lead you to Cari's room. How did she turn the doorknob? You know that Auntie Cari and Uncle Randy always keep their bedroom door closed."

Megan giggled and adjusted the collar of the red crewneck but-ton-down-type sweater around "Kitty's" neck. She appeared to be thinking of what her answer should be.

"This is no laughing matter, Kiddo. Be honest, now." Mary Jo warned her little companion.

Mary Jo knew triumphantly that there was no possible way that Megan could have an answer for <u>that</u> question when she surprised her out of the clear blue sky with a somewhat cryptic reply.

"That's the secret!" she replied. "I wasn't gonna say a thing – they <u>told</u> me not to. But that was <u>before</u>. When it was just the broom closet. Now, it is Auntie Cari's and Uncle Randy's room and that's not right!" Megan said chattering away self-righteously non-stop in her childish voice attempting to imitate Pierre's supercilious pose which she had seen him assume many times before.

Mary Jo regarded the child in bewilderment. What was she to do? It was not up to her to mete out any kind of discipline to someone else's child but it was obvious that Megan was engaging either in a fantasy or in the well-honed art of prevarication. She'd probably learned that <u>tactic</u> from listening to Pierre. But of course, as Pierre would say, THAT was the explanation.... She got caught doing something wrong and was trying to avoid punishment by diverting her attention elsewhere. Megan was probably hoping that with her ill-woven tapestry of explanations she could convince her not to inform Matthew of her headstrong, disobedient behavior and improbable, far-fetched excuses for it. Well, <u>that</u> approach was not going to work. Matthew had to be told. He was the only authority figure available to her since Eleanor had left on the train with Matthew Alexander.

"You do know that I am going to have to tell your Father about this, don't you, Megan?" she informed the youngster sternly closing her mouth and setting her lips together rigidly to form one thin, straight line.

"But, I can explain! It's the wall <u>not</u> the door-"

Save all of the explanations for Matthew. Your Father will know what to do. And he's not as soft with discipline as you think, you know. There is absolutely no excuse for going through Cari's <u>drawers</u>!"

"Who has been going through my drawers?" Cari inquired with a laugh chuckling at what she thought of as her witty pun on words.

"THE GIANT!!!" Megan screamed in terror on an indrawn breath and then fell stonily silent.

Cari and Mary Jo exchanged stunned looks.

"Megan!" Cari finally found her voice to scold the child. "I am surprised at you! How could you be so rude! Just because Elroy is a little tall does not give you the license to ostracize him!"

Cari waited for Megan's reply. At the very least an apology should be forthcoming and, indeed, was owed to her newest friend, Elroy. Megan just stared at Elroy petrified while his eyes returned her gaze with an odd sort of recognition in their depths. Cari jumped at a slamming sound outside of the room in the adjoining hallway beyond the closed kitchen door. Observing the skittish pair curiously she pushed open the swinging door and poked her head through the aperture to crane her neck forward shifting her gaze first to the left and then to the right but saw nothing. Meanwhile, Megan wondered what the words "license" and "ostracize" meant. They had to be bad things. Elroy smiled at her and put his foot forward in her direction toward her as Megan's tremulous little jaw dropped in fear.

Trudy's skirt swished sharply at an angle in her haste to round the decorative, fluted pillar indicating the end of the hallway leading from the kitchen. Trudy approached the patio where Matthew and Pierre were raptly engaged in an earnest conversation. As she came abreast of them she spoke:

"We have got a problem."

CHAPTER 30

"**M**other?"
"Aye, son?"

"I'm worried about Meg…." M.A. confided seriously wearing a grim countenance that bespoke a world-weariness far beyond his young years and then he paused contemplatively. "Can I tell you a secret?" he finally inquired candidly suddenly deciding after much inner debate to come clean with his Mother and divest himself of the major burden of the information weighing heavily on his mind.

"Gracious, child! What's a mum fer if not te tell her yer secrets?" asked Eleanor of her son reasonably.

"I'm not supposed to say anything. Uncle Pierre told me not to." he confessed choosing his words deliberately.

"Oh, really?" said Eleanor starting to smile.

'So, the balmy French fellow ha' something te do with this mysterious secret!' she thought contemplating whether or not ignorance was actually contagious. The man was always imagining something nefarious be afoot! It probably ran in his bloodline. Te his mind the whole world was one big conspiracy – usually directed against him! She chuckled inwardly and visibly relaxed. She had not realized that she had been so wound up and tense in her morbid anticipation of hearing the worst case scenario.

"Ye know, Matthew Alexander, Pierre not be yer true "Uncle". "Uncle" 'tis more of a term o' <u>respect</u> fer yer elders. He be <u>NO</u> blood relation o' ours!" 'Thank goodness!' she thought privately relieved as she spoke the last sentence a bit too vehemently.

"Don't you <u>like</u> Uncle Pierre, Mother?" M.A. inquired savvy to the not so subtle change in the tone of his Mother's voice when she declared that Pierre was not his real uncle.

"Nooo…I like him fine, dear." she answered him carefully. "It is only tha' he isna me brother <u>or</u> yer father's brother and the distinction should be noted if only fer educational purposes." she bluffed convincingly successfully avoiding any besmirchment of the character of another human being with the secondary truth and thusly masking her genuine reason for disassociating Matthew and herself from Pierre's lineage.

The tall spires of the grand old house came into view beyond the hedges of thick, manicured foliage as Edith and her companions rode up the long and winding drive leading up to the old historic mansion. Its oval attic window panes framed by white moldings reflected the bright sunlight and seemed to peer in twinkling salutation at the newcomers as they approached. They became apparent next as the entire curtain of obscuring greenery opened up to fall away and fly past them revealing the entire grey structure. How striking it was in appearance. Its charming porch was edged by whitewashed spindles which swung around the front to the back of the edifice and a sign on a black metal post proclaimed it as Candlestick Manor. As they stepped out of their horse-drawn conveyance, Edith, Pierre, Randy, Alex and Matthew looked about them to see several other vehicles out front of the rustic dwelling in addition to theirs.

"Oh, dear! It appears that we are late. I <u>knew</u> that we should have started out earlier!" Edith said in obvious distress disconcerted that her tardiness might be construed as politically incorrect by the ladies of the historical association who she regarded as the cream of the crop of society. "If only we had not taken that wrong turn at that fork in the road." she fretted regretfully. "Let us enter Candlestick

Manor immediately."

"We're not that late." Alex said comforting her. "Look." he elaborated further pulling away from the others and stepping up onto the hardwood planking of the porch. "I can see through the window. They're still serving appetizers."

Alex pointed to the large picture window with the shades drawn exposing a cozy sitting room where occupants gathered in multiple clusters talking and laughing. A majority held champagne flutes while others nibbled on various hors d'oeuvres. Waiters carrying trays of savory fare and drink milled among the guests offering them food and drink. Several others sat by the fireside and chatted there while playing board games of checkers or chess.

"You see, we're not behind the eight ball by any means. We are merely fashionably late." Randmore observed calmly.

"Close yer mouth and stop yer salivating." Matthew chided Pierre who stared mesmerized at the treats being served inside. "Ye would think ye'd ne'er seen a bite o' food in the whole o' yer entire life. PLUS. If ye ha' na misdirected us <u>at</u> that fork in the road we woulda kept te the schedule an' been te the party on time!"

"I wonder who their caterer is." pondered Pierre aloud choosing to ignore Matthew's deprecating comments. "Without Joan ici to prise the command of the kitchen it is difficult to find a well-rounded meal around here!"

"Bah! Ye mean without Joan te take care o' <u>you</u> and fawn herself all o'er ye. An' Edith be right here te see it all. Ha' some respect fer yer wife, man – <u>have some dignity</u>!" Matthew admonished him.

"At least I do this, que veut dire, "fawning" in <u>front</u> of my wife – <u>not</u>, comment dit-on, <u>behind</u> her dos. I have absolutely <u>NOTHING</u> to hide from my Edi." stated Pierre alluding to Matthew's flirtatious behavior with the ladies at the train depot. "We keep nothing secret from one another." he spat back seething.

"Let us STOP all of this bickering!" Edith shouted in a loud whisper lest they be heard by those inside the house. "This is all so unseemly!" she said in frustration at Pierre's and Matthew's row and their lateness to the party at Candlestick Manor.

"I do not know about you people, but I am with Edith. Let us go inside." Randmore stated walking to the front porch to join Alex and ringing the doorbell.

"Yeah. I'm STARVING." said Alex with gusto as he moved closer to his cousin while Pierre noted his statement with a sarcastic look and opened his mouth to speak. "Let's go inside. I hope they still have some food left." continued Alex with hunger in his eyes.

On seeing Pierre's opened orifice poised in potential barb Matthew glared him into silence. Consequently, and with much regret, Pierre closed his mouth shut.

CHAPTER 31

Mary Jo knelt on the tiled stone floor in the middle of the main hall at LaurelsHeath examining the large decorative center tile emblazoned with the LaurelsHeath crest of a lion's head. She inserted her ten fingertips between the edges of the insignia tile and a much smaller adjacent background one. Digging her fingernails in as far as she could and pulling upward with all of her might only resulted in the flesh of her fingers glancing and scraping against the abrasive, hewn stone and then falling away from the meager narrow side surfaces as the center stone square would not budge or be lifted.

"Rats!" she cursed vexedly aloud at her failure as Cari approached to stand by her.

Although Cari stared down at her curiously wondering what she was doing on her hands and knees she was too preoccupied with her own troubling issues to remark on and make inquiry of her friend's strange activity.

"I just do not understand what has gotten into her. Megan is usually such a <u>polite</u> child. I just do not know how to handle this. I wish Eleanor were here – at least Matthew!"

"I know what you mean, Cari. I've never known her to tell such outlandish fibs the way she's been doing. Not to say that she tells fibs. And now, she's even got Elroy backing her up. What's the deal with that?" asked Mary Jo perplexed rising to her feet and massaging her hands.

"Elroy is only trying to protect her from getting punished." Cari said admiringly of Elroy's virtuous loyalty. "He is considerate that way. He does not want to see her get into trouble and so he is making excuses for her."

"Don't tell me that he's saying that HE can walk through walls, too, now." Mary Jo asked in disbelief.

"Of course not! He just says that it's part of a game that they sometimes play where they tell someone a riddle and then the other person has to guess the truth." Cari explained to her friend. "I would like to believe that Elroy is too old for games like that but he does appear to have difficulty grasping simple concepts…." she conceded a bit hesitantly.

"You mean that he is mentally challenged. Don't be afraid to say it, Cari. And don't try to put it delicately, either. He's a nice boy who has some problems, but we all have problems, and it does no good to go around sugarcoating things!" Mary Jo said pragmatically. "And, anyway, you should not go around encouraging him – you are a married woman. You know he has a crush on you." she admonished her in a scolding tone trying not to sound too much like Pierre.

"He does not, Mary Jo! We are just friends." Cari asserted adamantly firmly deflecting the suggestion of a crush impatiently.

"How can you say that? You see how goofy he gets around you. He stumbles all over his words. He gets all clumsy. He practically falls all over himself to please you when you ask him to do something."

"You, my dear friend, are imagining things."

"If you say so. But I am just letting you know what you can't see that's staring you right in the eye. You're LEADING HIM ON!"

"Mary Jo, stop it!"

"It's right in front of your face but you can't – no – you REFUSE to see it. It's as plain as the nose on your face the way he feels about you!"

"Enough!" yelled Cari in a high-pitched voice. "Okay. I will have a talk with him." she said guiltily in a lower, more balanced tone ashamed at losing her temper. "I will explain to him that although I appreciate his kindness and assistance with work around the house our relationship is merely a platonic friendship." she stated with tremulous emotion visibly shaken by Mary Jo's upbraiding tirade while cradling her throat, which had become raw from yelling, and pacing nervously back and forth.

Mary Jo felt abashed as she watched her upset friend pace back and forth as if she were a trapped animal in a cage. She had only meant to tease her a little bit when she had begun her taunts – not make her fall apart.

"Speaking of imagining things...." Mary Jo began tentatively. "With all of this talk of Megan's...." she halted speaking momentarily in order to consider her phraseology. "You know," she resumed speaking cautiously and sighed therapeutically to release her tensions while watching Cari pause and turn to look at her inquiringly, "about people walking through walls and stuff like that? Well, with all her talk of those things I think I've been seeing things. I mean, I HAVE been seeing things. I <u>know</u> it wasn't <u>real</u>."

"What did you see?" asked Cari with avid curiosity quickly forgetting her resolution to speak with Elroy regarding any romantic feelings that he might have for her and her own fretful feelings. "Come on, now – you can't throw out leading statements like that to someone and then leave a person hanging." she prompted cajoling Mary Jo to elaborate lest she fail to continue on with her revelation to its completion.

"It was only a trick of the eye I experienced because of all Megan and Elroy's talk about secret passages. I saw Trudy kissing a strange man and then I blinked to clear my eyes and...."

"And?"

"And then he was gone!"

"What did this man look like?"

"I'm not sure exactly. I only saw him from the side."

"Were you dreaming, Mary Jo? The power of suggestion could have put the seed of Megan's fantasies in your brain."

"No. I wasn't even in bed. And I already admitted that it had to be some sort of hallucination. You know, like when people see an oasis in a desert – a mirage, or something."

"So, is this "sighting" related in any way to what you were doing on the floor?" Cari hazarded the guess expectantly.

"Well…indirectly." she admitted shamefacedly. "You see, I was passing this room when I saw them and so I figured there might be a clue in here somewhere."

"You think this man disappeared into the floor?" Cari asked with a chuckle.

"Don't laugh at me, Cari. I feel ridiculous enough as it is." Mary Jo retorted quickly in chagrin. "And didn't Elvie say that she saw a man come out of this very floor?" she asked defensively in an attempt to lend credence to her position and to justify her unorthodox actions.

"Yes, she did." Cari answered stoically with a newly enlightened outlook that came with the realization that her friend's house of cards reasoning was built on the unstable foundation of Elvie's somewhat fanciful influence as well as a little girl's, who listened to a cat, and Elroy's. "She said that he had a limp. Did this man have a limp?" she inquired logically in an attempt to inject some concrete logic into Mary Jo's line of thinking.

"I don't know, but he did look kind of familiar even though I only saw him from far away at the other end of the hall and didn't get a real good look at him."

"Now that makes a little sense. All I can say is that if one imagines people I would think that they are usually going to imagine the faces of people they know. Because, I ask you, how can you imagine the face of someone you have never seen before? But. The surest way to put this issue of the "KISS" to rest, though, is to simply ASK Trudy if she was kissing a man in this room. Unless, of course, you want to get a crowbar and pry up that square tile with the crest on it and see what is underneath it." Carina suggested.

CHAPTER 32

"It's great to see a friendly face. I was so bummed out thinking that I would have to paste on a smile and make polite conversation with all those boring historical people. I got my fill of all that stodgy decorum in England. That's where I went to school. My Mother, Annabelle, thought that going to school over there would help me build character. Anyway, every weekend they would have these mixers where us students were all treated to lectures on science or linguistics and grammatical syntax. Sometimes, as a special treat, there would be these symposiums we were all required to attend where we would listen to classical music and then afterwards engage in thoughtful discussions with all these prim and proper experts on musical signatures, tempos, arrangements and composers. Then would come the speeches.... It was all so convivial but those gatherings were oh, so dry!" Alex said to Cyrus shuddering and shaking his head back and forth in distaste at the remembrance as he completed his monologue.

"I did not know that you were so opposed to CULTURE, Alex." noted Pierre inclining his head to one side and peering at Alex scrutinizing him loftily.

"Shhh...! Not so loud, boys. Don't want to cause an incident among these fine cultured ladies, you know." berated Cyrus jokingly with a serious air and then an outright chuckle as he burst into low, controlled laughter. "But I, mon ami," he said to Pierre, "happen to agree with Alex on this score. All these stodgy, highfalutin, opinionated women in one room trying to tell a man what to do with his own home can be daunting and is downright disgraceful, in my humble opinion! Someone should tell them their place. But, not today. It shant be today. So, you are English, are you, boy?"

"On my Dad's side. You see, he came over from-"

"Speaking of the, comment dit-on, BACKGROUND. Is there a possibility that you are from France?" queried Pierre quickly seeing his opening, and interrupting Alex, while putting one hand on Cyrus's shoulder and turning him in the opposite direction, steering him away from Alex's unfinished explanation.

"No." he said definitively. "I am not from France."

"You are très certain that you are not even a little bit French?" Pierre inquired inquisitively emphasizing the word "little" in a light, squeaky tone and squeezing together the index finger and thumb of his right hand in front of his right eye until the tips of them almost touched.

"No. I am not French."

"Just un peu French?"

"NO!" Cyrus said irritably.

"Not even un tout petit peu?" Pierre asked expectantly with a glimmer of hopefulness lighting up his eyes.

"Are you hard of hearing, mon ami? I said, "NO". Now let us go back to Alex over there. You were very, very rude to him. You do not just interrupt a person like that when they are speaking!" he roundly scolded berating an astounded Pierre Dûçot who had never – not ever – been spoken to in such a fashion before and, therefore, was reevaluating his previously favorable opinion of Cyrus.

Pierre decided that he was glad Cyrus was not French. The man was overbearing and boorish. He regarded him calculatedly. What was his, comment dit-on, angle? He must have one to speak so boldly and cavalierly to Pierre Dûçot!

"Now, Alex," Cyrus continued speaking while walking back to his side, "you were saying…. Ahhh! What are you doing you

BLOCKHEAD?!!!" Cyrus all at once bellowed at a waiter while shaking droplets of liquid from his hands and body like a wet cat would as the uniformed domestic who was carrying a serving tray on which rested multiple long-stemmed glasses filled with wine collided with him depositing the entire contents of the serving tray upon him and his newly cleaned and pressed three-piece suit which he had rented just for the occasion.

The bowl-shaped, handblown crystal stemware formerly decorating the tray's surface now decorated the floor's surface scattered across its expanse in semi-whole and broken fragmented pieces of glass.

"Heads will roll!" Cyrus again roared enraged as another server offering guests cream-filled pastries which rested in dainty, fluted paper cups on a large platter slipped on the fallen tray lying amidst the broken glass and slid into him from the back.

Unbidden, Pierre's hands rose involuntarily to encircle his neck protectively. Pierre became utterly immobile and could only watch horrified, as if from afar, in a stupefied trance as his mind cast back to his nap at the diner where he had been so rudely awakened and brought sharply to full consciousness by similar bellicose phraseology. 'THAT WAS THE VOICE! THAT is why it was so familiar! It was all so clear now…that…BEAST!' he railed inwardly.

"LE COCHON!" he spit out self-righteously at the man with wine staining his suit and whipped cream in his hair and on the back of his jacket.

"What do you mean, calling me a PIG?" asked the affronted Cyrus, who understood some French, angrily as he focused his full unblinking stare on Pierre his entire attention having been arrested by such a slur.

Cyrus waited for Pierre's response with bated breath along with the other guests who looked on with avid interest as the simple confusion of a household accident turned into a situation that seemed to portend something more. Even Alex appeared to look on expectantly in wonderment anticipating his forthcoming answer. Pierre's consciousness swirled in turmoil with a variety of emotions and possible rejoinders. He did not wish to become "toast". How could he avoid becoming "toast"? As he gazed into the narrowed, suspicious eyes fixed upon him noting his every facial expression and subtle nuance he could detect no quarter of mercy in the regard of Cyrus Sykes. His previous bravado when he tipped his hand of cards and yelled "COCHON!" almost revealing that he knew Cyrus for the scurrilous cad that he was from the diner was short-lived and had now dissipated. He cast about in his mind, now made more cunning by fear, for a suitable equivocation to disguise the fact that he was wise to the man's infamy. A lightbulb went off in his head as an idea occurred to him from out of the blue.

"Le Jambon!" Pierre clarified ingenuously with wide-eyed in-nocence. "J'ai laissé un jambon dans le four." he said enthusiastically grabbing on to this inspirational excuse and using it to prop himself up emotionally as he congratulated himself on the apropos, off-the-cuff prevarication and clung to it for dear life.

Alex appeared bewildered and Cyrus semi-skeptical.

"Vous voyez," Pierre obliviously continued in explanation, "I am having trouble with my English and plusieurs fois I speak à tort. Mais vous entendez bien. I said "pig" when the correct English is "ham" – I made a mistake." he concluded in simplistic resignation throwing up his hands and allowing them to fall clapping at his sides as if to indicate that no insult to his person or alter-meaning was intended.

"You don't have a ham in the oven, Pierre." said Alex unequivo-cally while looking at him strangely, puzzled by the untruth.

"I do dear, dear boy!" Pierre speedily affirmed as he saw Cyrus turn in interest to Alex attentively.

"But Trudy does all the cooking. And, besides, we don't even

<u>have</u> a ham in the larder." insisted Alex stubbornly vying with Pierre for Cyrus's attention as he saw him turn his glance Pierre's way.

"I bought one this morning, Alex." Pierre asserted in a tight voice which brooked no argument.

"When? You did not have time. You were at the train station picking up confirmation vouchers this morning and then-"

"I purchased the ham." Pierre said affirmatively.

"But you don't know how to cook ham properly." argued the young man.

"I used a recipe I learned from Chef Abrams, dear boy. It is foolproof. When I saw the ham at the boucherie I wanted to, comment dit-on, try it out." Pierre replied quickly in response in order to justify the existence of the fictitious ham to Cyrus.

"First of all, it's Adams <u>not</u> Abrams." Alex stated with a lawyerly bent seeking to set the record straight. "But anyway, you don't even <u>like</u> Chef Adams. In fact, you <u>NEVER</u> liked Chef Adams. Plus, he didn't care for you much either, especially after you sicced the dogs out on him. So why would he swap recipes with you? It doesn't make sense-"

"Alex, do not disrespect your elders! Do not contradict me!" Pierre snapped querulously losing his temper as he saw Cyrus fix him with an evil, piercing glare. "I must be going, maintenant." he said nervously. "Il faut take it from the oven before it becomes too crisp."

"You mean before it burns." Alex corrected him as he helped Cyrus clean the whipped cream off of his back with a red cloth napkin.

"I did NOT say that, Mr. Smarty Jeans. Now, come along!"

CHAPTER 33

'Où était cet Alex lorsque vous avez besoin de lui? Le traître! Staying behind to assist the enemy!' Pierre thought begrudgingly, yet miserably, as he inadvertently backed into a catering cart upsetting a group of lidded chafing dishes which fell clattering to the linoleum floor with a resounding crash before he could catch them all. And he <u>did</u> try to catch them all in a bizarre sort of dance which affirmed Jan LaFitte's characterization of him as l'oile – the goose. He ended up sitting on his posterior on the floor, however, after the rescue attempt failed with the newly cleaned metal containers – the lids crashing as cymbals – joining him to litter the stone floor of the storage area as they landed all about him in scattered disarray. Pierre stood up and dusted himself off while regarding the containers and lids now at his feet. Such an untidy mess! He recoiled slightly. However, this was <u>not</u> his responsibility. 'Let the catering staff clean up after themselves.' he thought. He turned and started to walk away. Then, experiencing a momentary pang of guilt at the "small" part that he had played in creating such chaos, he glanced back at the disarray of the kitchen behind him contemplatively wrinkling his nose and clucking in distaste. 'Non.' he thought conclusively as his fleeting moment of conscience evaporated. 'That désordre là-bas was most certainly NOT his problem!' he decided wiping his palms off one against the other as he divested himself of any previous qualms that he might have had with the action. That felon, Cyrus, had sent one of his henchmen to ostensibly "escort" him off of the premises so that he would not become lost in this

"maze of a house" but he had eluded the treacherous fiend. He stood up straighter proud of his accomplishment. Imagine! Believing that they could deceive the likes of Pierre Dûçot with that flimsy, transparent excuse! He was no fool! It must have been fate that while frantically searching for an exit to escape the manor and its evil patron he had somehow ended up in the kitchen. He tugged downward on the lapels of his jacket to straighten it. 'Yes! It must have been instinct.' he acknowledged with an affirmative nod of his head. 'Pierre Dûçot lost? PAH!' he thought disparagingly. He and Grand-mère Dûçot had spent many a treasured, happy hour in the kitchen when he was a young boy so it was just natural that he would unconsciously gravitate to this area of the house when he needed to experience feelings of comfort and solace. 'Those were les bons temps.' he thought reminiscently with a smile and a sigh as he longed for those bygone younger years. Of course, now, he had to be wary. Perhaps it was she who had drawn him back here....
His eyes bugged out of their respective sockets bulging forward as they glazed over and his palm rose to clap over a mouth which had simultaneously gone agape with his horror. When Randy, Alex and Matt had left him by himself on the other side of the cave that time, Grand-mère had come to him in spirit with the information that she was decaying and rotting but nevertheless longed to embrace him. The implication of the statement had been obvious. She wanted to take him with her to... THE OTHER SIDE! He gasped audibly in uncontrollable fear at the remembrance and shrank back against the wall only to become unintentionally entangled in the folds of the long drapes masking the horizontal window extending from the floor to the ceiling. 'What is this?' wondered the surprised man taken aback slightly as he pushed back on the restraining folds of curtain only to discover a flat panel. 'There was no fenêtre ici. How ridicule! Ces Américains sont fous.' he concluded haughtily as he lifted one eyebrow contemptuously and pursed his lips with

condemnation. And that Alex…he had no sense of loyalty. Instead of accompanying him out of Candlestick Manor comme un veritable ami he chose to stay avec un homme he had known for, perhaps, deux semaines seulement to help him instead! NOT that he could not find his way out of the house by himself, mind you. He sniffed contemptuously at the patently ridiculous idea as he summarily dismissed it out of hand. Et la pièce de résistance – or, que veut dire, the icing sûr le gâteau – was that he had recognized this Cyrus as the felon who had threatened his life! ALL of their lives! Pierre struggled against the enveloping folds of curtain like an insect trapped in a spider's web. And just like an insect pulling repetitiously on the silk strand which summoned the ravenous arachnid he yanked hard at the main cloth drapery panel engulfing his entire arm to free it from the hampering folds. Instead of securing his freedom, however, his action borne of frustration only succeeded in releasing a latch securing the ornate curtain rod from which the length of fabric hung flush against the wall. The curtain rod was pulled down at an angle by the pumping downward pressure on the drape causing the entire wall panel to twirl on a center spindle, like a top rotating on its axis, depositing the fearful man on the other side. Pierre experienced a state of vertigo he had never known before. He felt dizzy and nauseous. He was rendered inert and motionless by fear and the pitch blackness of this…place…he had fallen to. And then he realized that he was squeezing his eyes shut. He opened them tentatively, being prepared to close them again at a moment's notice depending on what he saw, to be greeted by a peculiar glow ahead of him. He had heard that one experienced this sort of illumination when one was invited to cross over to the "Other Side" and, therefore, he was loathe to move forward. He suspected that it was the wrath of Grand-mère Dûçot that had brought him here and reduced him to this uncertain state. Where was this place…? It was so cold and damp. Also, it was very dusty. Pierre sneezed three times consecutively before he could cover his nose with his handkerchief as was his usual wont. This type of atmosphere was definitely NOT conducive to the well-being of the delicate constitution of Pierre Dûçot.

"I have been a good boy, Grand-mère. Please, do not take me!" he called out in semi-hushed tones afraid of incurring more of her wrath after running away from her last time and fearing to, perhaps, wake the dead in case there happened to be any lingering about slumbering – he did not wish to alert them to his presence!

His voice only echoed back to him eerily, its sound magnified in volume multiple times as if spoken through a megaphone. He held his newly freed hands before his eyes and watched them tremble and shake unsteadily. He quickly lowered them and stood up cautiously. However uncertain was his situation he knew that he must needs overcome his apprehensions – he refused to characterize his timorous flights of fear as cowardice – and find a way out of this...spooky place! Pierre advanced slowly furtively glancing periodically about him with each step that he took. The particles of dust before him became denser, coagulating and coming together to form more of a fog-like, obscuring curtain in certain areas. Stacks as those which one would find in a library stood in horizontal rows resembling dominoes standing upright and he veered off to the side to examine one of these stacks more closely. What he saw ensconced therein made his heart leap with joy. He raised his hands to hover over the shiny, gold pieces reverently and then dared to give them license to dive downward and lift one out of its shelter to gaze at it in wonder. He all at once dropped it, as one would drop a hot potato, to fall back into its cubbyhole when he heard a faint moaning. The owner of the gold was obviously protesting against the would-be poaching of it – NOT that HE had any intention of poaching, mind you – and was asserting his proprietary ownership. He decided to investigate the source of the ghostly cries which seemed to grow louder and ring more eerily with his every faltering step nearer.

"Grand-mère?" Pierre called out timorously into the dimness as he advanced forward further down the aisle. "I.... I was not taking your gold." he said haltingly. "I was not <u>STEALING</u>. Non, non, non. Mais, bien sûr! I was only <u>looking</u>!" Pierre pledged solemnly as he crossed his heart and peered with trepidation around a crumbling corner wall composed of brick and mortar at which time the moaning escalated markedly to reach an almost fevered pitch. "Grand-mère!!!" shrieked Pierre his eyes flying open wide before collapsing in a dead faint.

The sharp, distinct sound of measured footfalls echoed hollowly as a pair of pointy-toed, black patent leather shoes struck the cobblestone floor of the corridor in methodical progression to halt at the crown of Pierre Dûçot's head.

CHAPTER 34

"I TOLD you." Alex said defensively. "I had to stay behind and help Cyrus. He told Pierre where the exit was and even asked his friend, Sandy, to escort him out so he wouldn't lose his way." he explained patiently in a harassed tone of voice as he detailed the events at the get-together which took place two days prior for the umpteenth time.

"The man even missed his train, Alex. We haven't heard from him for days. Don't you think his wife would be maybe a <u>little</u> bit concerned?" lectured Randmore. "He is always punctual. You can keep <u>time</u> by Pierre Dûçot for goodness sake! Breakfast at 7:30am, lunch at 12:15pm and dinner at 6:00pm. The man is a walking sundial! He has been gone for at least two days and everyone is worried about him except for you. Doesn't that tell you something?"

"Aw! You know how he is! He's probably just on one of his nature walks, again."

For the love of Mike, he wasn't the man's babysitter! But maybe he should've left the house with Pierre. Alex guiltily stole a glance at Edith her head bowed as she wept into a handkerchief. The other women surrounded her. Cari had a calming hand on her shoulder, Mary Jo looked on sympathetically and Callie said something which made her burst into a renewed fit of wailing.

"I was only trying to help. Gee-whiz!" Callie bellyached approaching Randmore and Matthew who were interrogating Alex mercilessly regarding the possible whereabouts of Pierre Dûçot. "Try to cheer a person up – you'd think I committed the crime of the century!"

Dudley laughed at her phraseology as he joined them in time to hear her use of language.

"She got that one from Calvin!" he boasted. "You've been spending too much time around him, Callie. I'm getting to think you'd be preferring his company to mine!"

"Oh, Dudley. Don't be a silly. You <u>know</u> that you're the only man for me!"

"This be nary a time fer jesting. Pierre be missing fer two whole days. Edith be grievin' her husband. So, I ask ye. What did ye say te her now, lass?" Matthew interrupted brusquely wishing to get to the crux of the matter. "The woman be out o' her mind with worry an' after just a few words ye've reduced her te an even graver state! Now, let us be gettin' te the brass tacks o' the situation."

"All I said was that she shouldn't be upset because we all had trouble finding our way around when me, Dudley, Elvie and Calvin got here. It's a big place out here, but it wasn't as if there were GRIZZLIES around every corner, maybe a coyote.... But, that was just when we moved here...."

As Callie spoke the men shared dumbfounded stares with Dudley looking increasingly embarrassed and uneasy. Cari saw the men bickering with Callie at the center of it all. Entrusting the care of her Aunt Edith to Mary Jo she walked over to confront them and to address the commotion.

"Never mind who is at fault. He will come back to us – if we do not find him first. Wherever he is I am sure that he is in fine fettle. But, of course, how could Pierre Dûçot be otherwise!" Cari asserted with a positive attitude.

"Calvin. Cal - vin!" whined Elvie pushing aside the fringe of dark brown hair from her forehead and then adjusting her hat gone askew with its bow drooping from the heat atop her head. "I'm fall-ing apart over here." she complained out loud as she leant on her pale green, ruffle-edged parasol with the sun's rays beating down brutally upon her and fanned herself with a folded map of the territory.

She was perspiring in the sweltering heat and now regretted at leisure her spur of the moment, impulsive attempt to appear glamorous by wearing a long-sleeved, three-piece ensemble. Elvie peered behind her but her errant husband was nowhere in sight. She hobbled awkwardly to one side on her high heels – the shoes which Calvin had warned her against wearing for the trip because they were not practical – and sat down on a large boulder. Sighing with relief she brought one of her ankles to rest upon her opposite knee and removed her shoe. After setting it aside she repeated the process with her other shoe and considered her situation. She had become separated from her husband; she could make neither head nor tail of the map she carried; and Calvin probably thought she was on her way to the house and was going to meet her there. Elvira Ana Green Maison waved her hand before her face to shoo away an airborne insect that she heard flying about. She glanced perfunctorily to the left and then to the right absentmindedly. She had absolutely no idea where she was.... 'There it was again!' she thought straightening her posture to attention. She could not pinpoint the location of the buzzing-type sound, exactly. She waved the folded map around her head to ward off a potential fly or mosquito. For all she knew they were poisonous and the size of oranges. She cringed at the idea and looked about briefly to assure herself that her wildest fears had not materialized and then slumped back in relief when she saw noth-ing of concern. She would never get used to life out here in this desolate place! She choked back a sob of futile frustration. She did not care if the house was Calvin's legacy! She undid the clasp of her purse and rifled through it for a tissue to dab at her eyes and blow her nose preparing to dwell on and immerse herself in the comforting blanket of her misery. How annoying. There was that disturbing noise again jolting her out of her complacent, dismal reverie which hung about her as a gloomy mantle of glumness. But, this time it sounded like the spray from the nozzle of a garden hose. Plus, it was louder – more urgent.

"Psssst! Pssssst! Pss.....t!"

The noise seemed to be coming from that group of bushes to her right. She rose reluctantly from her resting perch and stalked over to the shrubs to confront the greenery fearlessly and parted the intertwined twigs only to have her face met by a stream of hot air accompanied by additional hissing noises.

"Mr. Dûçot!" Elvie scolded while squinting and wiping away some steamy droplets of moisture from her face although she was relieved to see another human being. "What are you doing playing games out here and scaring me half to death? This is no time for hide and seek!"

"Elvie! Please, listen to me. You must help me to escape! I was... on the <u>Other</u> <u>Side</u>! Well...the portal, at least." articulated the man in frantic desperation.

"What? You were where...?"

"It was GRAND-MÈRE – she cast her spell over me. I woke up out here!"

"Are you alright, Mr. Dûçot?" Elvie asked doubtfully noting his glazed over eyes and frenetic facial movements and ticks as he peeked out over the leaves of a hedge.

"Mais, bien sûr! Of <u>course</u> I am fine!" he asserted unequivocally and curtly in reply to her question which he viewed as openly condescending, arrogant and overtly insulting – and did he not mention that he did not care for her overall attitude? "Cette fille est folle. Je le sais...." he began to speak to himself in French.

"Then, well...." Elvira said as she started to back away from the excited gentleman slowly. "Isn't your grandmother not living anymore?" she asked with an ingenuous lack of subtlety of the man she concluded had become mentally unhinged.

"Où sont – where are you going, Elvie." he asked her suspiciously. "DO NOT LEAVE ME!" he immediately cried in desperation on the heels of his query at the thought of being left alone in the wilderness.

"Nowhere. I am going nowhere." she replied in an even tone she studiedly sought to keep from quavering as she backed up against a tree trunk dropping her map and parasol to feel the trunk behind her searchingly with her palms turned backwards and slid herself off of it. 'No need to make any sudden moves.' she surmised nervously uncertain of Pierre's current mental sanity.

Elvie took in the man's tousled locks which stood up in odd places, the pronounced dark circles under his eyes and the grimy smudges of dirt on his cheeks. He looked like a wild man. She had thought once that he was a sea monster…but that was a long time ago. She reminisced. That had been under special circumstances. She had not known him then. Her mind wandered thoughtfully as unconsciously she quirked one eyebrow and regarded him dubiously.

"Je crois that you do not understand. I need your help to return to the maison to warn the others! They left me here –"

"You mean Grand-mère…?" Elvie interrupted Pierre with the leading question.

"Oui, Grand-mère. Mais, avec her minions, aussi! I know that this sounds crazy but I saw-"

"No need to tell me, Mr. Dûçot-"

"S'il te plaît, call me Pierre." he quickly interjected pleadingly in a fawning, obsequious tone of voice designed to ingratiate himself into her good graces.

"Okay, Pierre. I've seen things, too, you know so I can sort of relate to what you are saying." Elvie admitted stopping in mid-flight at his friendlier, more grounded tone of acquiescence and, perhaps, compliance?

Elvie regarded Pierre in all his agitation and her heart softened. Sympathy welled up from within her at the sight of his fragile, scruffy countenance his form being obscured by the foliage surrounding his entire body. She decided to accept his extended olive branch of friendship.

"There is no need to be afraid. Calvin always says there ain't nothing to fear 'cept the thought of being afraid. And <u>that</u> thought is just what makes your fear worse."

"Calvin is such a bright boy – did I ever mention that he is like the fils I never had?" Pierre said confidentially.

"My Calvin is big on being smart. You can learn a lot from him – I know I have! Well, what are you waiting for, Pierre?" she asked putting forth her hand toward him for the weak man to take hold of.

Pierre hesitated and then raised his arm to show her a large, green leaf in his hand.

"Let's GO!" she prompted him impatiently when she saw that he was not moving.

"I cannot. You see," he explained matter-of-factly as if nothing were out of the ordinary and adjusted the obscuring brush to expose more of his face and neck, "I am not wearing any clothes – Elvie, why are you screaming? COME BACK!!!"

CHAPTER 35

"I told you. It was <u>him</u>. That Cyrus is the même cochon who I heard threatening all of our lives at the diner. I knew that his voice sounded familiar to me. I was on my way to warn you when I was snatched by the spirits and taken to the Other Side. Once there Grand-mère cast her spell over me and I found myself out in the wilderness sans mes vêtements – without my clothes-"

"An' scarin the puir lass half te death, te be sure!" added Matthew acerbically closing the door to Elvie's room carefully behind him so as not to make any noise, save for a light click of the lock, and disturb his fitfully sleeping patient.

"Not to mention scaring all the wildlife in the vicinity!" Alex blurted out gleefully in an attempt at humor.

"Il n'est pas de nécessaire to feel so, comment dit-on…inadequate. Not everybody can enjoy the merveilleux physique of Pierre Dûçot!" he replied superciliously with as much hauteur as he could summon forth considering his weakened condition.

"Bah…! Yer just mighty fortunate Calvin and Elvie returned earlier than be expected and Elvie found ye afore ye caught yer death o' cold scamperin' about in the altogether like some degenerate! Ye can give us all o' yer far-flung theories an' yer highfalutin language but tha' makes NO excuse fer exposin' yerself te an' innocent young female!" he lectured scolding the Frenchman roundly.

"She is hardly innocent." Pierre responded in a huff to Matthew while eyeballing her husband, the laughing Calvin Mason – or Maison, whatever – meaningfully denoting what he considered to be the evidence. "Dans l'autre cas," he continued "I was not exposing myself to Elvie. Of course not! How absurd – such behavior is unthinkable." he asserted piously miffed that he was accused of committing such a vile act.

"Aye. Only Edith be subjected te <u>that</u> great honor." Matthew interjected sarcastically motioning to where Edith stood with a nod of his chin.

Various snickers and guffaws erupted in the room from those who appreciated Matthew's barb for the humorous sally that it was.

"As I was saying," Pierre continued over the mirthful noises staring down those in the room who, now embarrassed by the rebuke in his eyes, shuffled their feet, looked downward to regard their shoes or covered their mouths to cough innocently "Elvie only assumed that I was going to expose myself when I told her that Grand-mère had stripped me of mes vêtements."

"Someone ha' stripped ye o' more than yer clothes long before this! Grand-mère! Bah…! Yer Grandmother passed long ago. We already went through all o' this gibberish. There be <u>no</u> Grand-mère an' I be startin' te conjecture, though I be no psychiatrist by any means, tha' perhaps ye just be usin' her memory as a tool – a crutch – te blame fer all yer failin's. An', may I say,"

"You may absolument not!" Pierre interjected offended as he covered his ears with his palms refusing to listen to the objectionable analysis and Matthew spoke louder.

"THAT BLAMIN' yer mistakes an' inadequacies on a dead woman, an' by Jumpin' Jiminy, man, yer own GRANDMOTHER, te boot, just be cuttin' far below the belt!" Matthew stridently concluded as Pierre started to talk to himself loudly in French.

"Pierre Dûçot is NOT inadequate!" he finally blurted out yelling belligerently as Calvin, who had been exchanging guilty, meaningful looks with Dudley throughout the altercation, finally spoke up.

"Now, look guys." Calvin said entering conciliatorily between them into the fray and raising his hands before him in an appeasing gesture.

"This is none of ton affaire, Calvin. Stay out of it!" said Pierre hostilely in an overly brusque manner to his host.

Knowing that it was time to come clean and own up to the truth Calvin drew in a deep breath; looked quickly at Dudley; and then tried another tack.

"But I have a confession to make." admitted Calvin candidly eager to unburden himself of the secret.

Pierre, previously stone-faced in his rejection of Calvin's peacemaking efforts, became intrigued at the thought of hearing someone's real-life, honest to goodness, true confession.

"Continue." Pierre allowed patiently awaiting Calvin's thought provoking, mysterious secret.

"Remember when you were alone in the cave-" Calvin began slowly reluctant to feel the censure which would result after his revelation from the people he had come to like and respect.

"Do NOT be impertinent. What cave? Do not be ridicule, Calvin. There are no caves around here! You know this bien. Do not try to distract me."

"I am not trying to distract you. Look. I'm talking about when you and the other guys were following that treasure map. Before you found the gold you were alone in the cave and you heard some rock crumbling down and then you heard-"

"Grand-mère." Pierre, Randmore, Alex and Matthew recited in a simultaneous chorus sounding as if they were all sleuths who had just solved the world's most vexing riddle.

"So, what does this mean?" inquired Pierre impatiently. "It is clear that we all know this."

"The point is that I was Grand-mère. We were following you in secret!" Calvin articulated indicating Dudley and then himself with his index finger. "And when Dudley kept bumping into things and rocks were falling you thought it was your grandmother and so I played along."

Pierre was silent for the longest time.

"It's true." confirmed Dudley adding his corroboration to his brother's statements in the hope that he might jog the silent Pierre into speech.

Instead, Matthew was the first to speak.

"So tha' be it. Begorra. Ye done a good job o' it, te be sure. Pierre was a-scared te death. He be bayin' like a loon!"

"Like LeLoup." said Alex with a laugh. "Baying – wolf – LeLoup? Get it?" he asked the stoic faces before him which all regarded him silently – even Mary Jo! "IT WAS A JOKE, GUYS!!! C'mon – laugh a little with me!"

"Not so fast, Calvin. I know my own Grand-mère's voice. I appreciate your attempt to, comment dit-on, diffuse, the situation between Matthew and myself but-"

"Stop the nonsense, Pierre. Calvin just explained that there is no ghost of your grandmother." said Cari sternly attempting to inject some semblance of reality into the conversation. "Where's your common sense? Get a hold of yourself."

"Yes, Pierre, my love. Please get a hold of yourself. I just got you back and I do not want to lose you again, dearest!" exclaimed Edith earnestly.

"Why didn't you mention before that you pretended to be Pierre's grandmother?" Rand asked Calvin probing the veracity of his admission.

"Well.... It never came up. And we had all just become friends. We didn't want to mess that up. We were like buddies. I, we, me and Dudley, never really had that before. Sure. Everyone in our village looked up to us. But that wasn't because of US. You know? It was because of our looks and our family's reputation. We never had any real friends. And it felt good to have people around who really cared. I didn't want to take the chance of making you mad at us – me and Dudley. And, like I said, it never came up. So, why rock the boat? And it didn't start out as an intentional deception. Imitating Pierre's dead grandmother started out as a way to disguise that Dudley and I were in the cave. Then, it became a joke. Pierre sounded like he really believed my act and Dudley kept laughing. Their reactions kind of goaded me on. Not that it's any kind of excuse but once I got started their unknowing encouragement kept me going. Plus, I was afraid if I stopped I would get caught."

"This is all a very charming story, Calvin. Mais you cannot fool Pierre Dûçot. I KNOW my Grand-mère's own voice. I know, aussi, that this, Cyrus, is the cochon who threatened my life <u>and</u> obviously Grand-mère followed me here to take me back with her dans the case he succeeds in making me into "toast" – doing me in. But I will not go. Je refuse. Could it be that this Cyrus is working in, comment dit-on, <u>cahoots</u>, with Grand-mère? This is a legitimate question." Pierre posed his theory contemplatively.

"Pierre." Randmore broached the topic reasonably suppressing an exasperated sigh of frustration as he wondered if he would ever be able to convince Pierre of the fact that his deceased grandmother had not resurrected herself. "Alex tells me that there was wine at the party at Candlestick Manor. He also said that you had more than a few glasses. When someone over imbibes it's easy to become confused. You lost your way in a strange house and you conjured up your grandmother."

"I <u>heard</u> her!" Pierre stubbornly asserted to Randmore and the other members of the group adamantly adhering to his story.

"An' <u>this</u> be the same person. The very <u>same</u> person who be <u>seein'</u> dead people an' <u>hearin'</u> dead people sayin' te us – askin' us te believe – that <u>Cyrus</u> be a felonious character." Matthew asserted skeptically laying his arms across his chest with a disapproving harrumph.

CHAPTER 36

"Well, since all of us know about Elroy there is no reason he should not accompany us to the soirée. The boy is quite charming." Edith proclaimed using a tone of voice which would brook no argument.

"You do not understand, Auntie. Elroy has been in hiding for a reason. You see, we accept him as the thoughtful person that he is and know that he is helpful and endearing. However, there are others in the community who believe that his slower ways of thinking and difficulty in understanding make him a feared misfit." explained Cari. "And when Elroy interacts with children he does so on their level and it frightens them. So, they have complained to the sheriff and a warrant has been issued for his arrest. That is why he cannot make his presence here known! He could be sent to jail!"

"How preposterous! Who told you this?"

"Trudy did, Aunt."

"Trudy? That woman is an odd one. It is just a feeling that I perceive but sometimes I do catch her staring at me strangely and I just do not know what to make of it. Of course, she quickly averts her gaze before I can call her to task for her rude, curious behavior. In any event, I would hold little stock in what she tells you. Obviously she is mistaken. Who would want to put such a sweet boy as Elroy in jail?"

"Actually, they would send him to a mental asylum. I misspoke before." elucidated Cari correcting the misapprehension. "And Trudy is his mother – yes, I was surprised, too." she affirmed to an Edith whose mouth fell agape on hearing the bald revelation. "Yes. It turns out that Trudy is Elroy's mother and that is how she knows. She's been hiding him ever since he became an overly tall teenager and the parents of his younger playmates objected to his friendships with their children and ostracized him. It's funny that Matt and Pierre knew about his situation all along and they never said anything. In fact, it seems that Elroy is the one who originally abducted M.A. and Megan – although, it was all very innocent."

"Really?!" said Edith surprised that Pierre had not enlightened her of this previously.

"From what Megan tells me, she and her brother were intimidated by Elroy's size and felt compelled to follow him. Especially, when he hoisted Megan up and onto his shoulders and gave her a piggyback ride."

"I never! No wonder others are frightened of Elroy if he intimidates their children but he would not hurt anybody. And the intimidation is definitely not intentional. He must be taught that certain types of behavior are unacceptable and are frowned upon by others. All that kind boy needs is some simple instruction on proper social etiquette!" Edith diagnosed firmly.

"Did Pierre Dûçot hear that quelqu'un was in besoin de learning l'etiquette proper?" Pierre queried in obvious delight at the idea that someone might need instruction in the finer things of life – which was, of course, his specialty.

Carrying a tackle box in one hand and a string of fish in the other hand he entered the open back door of the kitchen and kicked it closed behind him. He wore a grey slicker overcoat and rubber boots. The gleam in his eye bespoke of his feeling of triumph at his successful fishing venture.

"I am heureux d'être à votre service dans ce regard. Maintenant, dis-moi, who is my nouvel étudiant? I will, comment dit-on, put him into shape, immédiatement!" he boasted gleefully with a bent indicating that he was unstoppable. "I will, comment dit-on, show him the ropes!" he further elucidated and then began humming.

"My, we certainly are in a good mood, my pet!" Edith chirped out happily as Cari looked downward feeling awkward whenever her Aunt and Pierre spoke endearingly to each other.

"Alors, ma petite chou I have come bringing you the fruits de mer." Pierre bragged depositing his "catch" into the sink.

Cari sighed inwardly as she considered the painstaking effort involved in gutting and cleaning those fish in the basin. How she wished that Eleanor were here! She could handle the task lickety-split with alacrity. Matthew was always out fishing whenever the seasonal weather and his schedule allowed for it and so she had, out of necessity, developed a knack for it and performed the task as if by rote. Maybe Trudy was adept at boning fish....

"Are you coming, dear? CARI?"

"Excuse me, Aunt Edith. What were you saying about a…party?" Cari hazarded a guess at the most relevant topic of conversation that she could think of hoping that she guessed correctly and could thereby disguise the fact that she had not been listening.

"The fish fry. Are you attending the fish fry, dear?" Edith asked persistently seeking to jog her short-term recollections.

"I would not miss the event!" Cari responded a bit too quickly relieved that her guess had been on point.

"I shall be preparing the fish personally and doing all of the cooking. Jusqu'à le moment you have goûté the cooking of Pierre Dûçot you have not, comment dit-on, LIVED. Your husband and Alex will be there with Mary Josephine. Matthew, Calvin, Elvie, Dudley and Callie will also be in attendance. Matthew has showed to me this wonderful fishing hole where we got lucky-"

"Wait a minute. One moment, please!" Cari interrupted him. "I thought that you and Matthew were not speaking to one another since your disagreement about Cyrus and Grand-mère Dûçot."

"Matthew and I have, comment dit-on, agreed to disagree. In any event, Edi and I will be leaving le jour après-demain so this soon will be a nonissue." said Pierre ebulliently in anticipation of leaving LaurelsHeath behind him and his wife.

Pierre cleaned the last fish in a carefree manner. He then packed it with the crushed ice in the cooler and lowered its lid carefully latching it securely closed.

"I have done all I can." he continued. "I warned you of the danger. This Cyrus is the cochon-"

"Who threatened your life in the diner, I know."

"Not just MY life. Your life, too. However, if you wish to tempt fate…choisis à ignore the sage wisdom of Pierre Dûçot, so be it!"

"Pierre! Cyrus SAVED my life. Explain that." Cari posed the question challengingly as if she were throwing down a gauntlet.

"I…cannot. But this is not ma responsabilité. Edi, however, is, as my épouse, dependent upon my protection."

CHAPTER 37

"It is of no différence à moi si you believe me ou not." said Pierre calmly squeezing the juice from half of a cut lemon over his fish. "Edi and I will soon be leaving this barbaric wilderness and you are free à rester ici and learn of the truth for yourself." Pierre said to Randmore as he adjusted the corner of the napkin stuffed into his shirt collar and hefted a forkful of food into his mouth.

"You are taking this the wrong way, Pierre. We are not trying to belittle you. Nothing could be further from the truth. But when we feel someone, especially someone we care about, is mistaken," pausing when Pierre stopped chewing and regarded him crosswise Rand amended his phrasing, "MAY BE mistaken about a set of circumstances it is our duty to lay out the facts of a situation so we can see things a bit clearer and objectively!" he said reasonably ending on a high note.

"You mean so that I will see things the way that you wish them to be seen. And who is this, WE?" argued Pierre as Alex approached them. "I hope that you are not speaking to Pierre Dûçot as if he were a child, nephew."

"He does that to me all the time." Alex complained offhandedly to Pierre. "I know what it feels like when no one believes you. Now, I do not know what went on after Pierre left me with Sandy at Candlestick Manor but I do know without a shadow of a doubt that Pierre doesn't even like to leave the <u>house</u> without a NECKTIE let alone without his clothes. I say that something fishy went on between the time he left me with Sandy and the time Elvie found him." Alex conjectured to Rand only to be interrupted by the approaching Matthew Flanderly.

"In the buff with a fig leaf in his hand. It must ha' been horrific. 'Tis nary a wonder the puir lass was rendered senseless!"

"And what, as you Américains say, stone did you crawl out from under, médecin?" Pierre addressed Matthew Flanderly coldly.

"Fer your information I just be informin' ye that yer playactin' te get sympathy dunna wash with me. Ye should be ashamed o' yerself, a grown man frolickin' about in the forest in his birthday suit. Well, nature boy, I'll na be buyin' yer snake oil excuses anytime soon!" scolded Matthew irrepressibly.

"I find it très intéressant that you seem obsessed with the unclothed form of Pierre Dûçot! This is very telling, bien sûr. This can only mean one thing...."

"Bah...! Get o'er yerself!"

"Quit it, you guys! I want to hear the whole story – just as it happened. Right from the horse's mouth. Let's sort this all out before you go so we can all part amicably." Alex pleaded earnestly determined to be a peacemaker.

"Alors. Si, you are interested...."

"Yes. I am." Alex affirmed with much conviction.

"No. I am NOT!" said Matthew contrarily despite the fact that Pierre's leading comment was not directed to him.

"YOUR opinion is of no conséquence, médecin." Pierre snapped curtly.

"Let us hear the man out, Matt. Then we can disabuse him of his fanciful notions one by one." Rand whispered to Matthew in a strategic aside to his friend.

"Aye. Let us do that, begorra." he replied.

Matthew stared across the lawn to where Cari emptied a fryer basket of freshly cooked crusty fish onto a large platter lined with paper toweling to absorb excess oil and Mary Jo was spooning freshly grilled vegetables onto Calvin's plate. Callie was ladling clam chowder into a bowl for Dudley. Matthew's stomach started to grumble hungrily and his mouth began to water.

"Matt? Matt?" Rand prodded the distracted man who had inexplicably fallen silent. "Do you agree?"

"Aye, aye. Let us get on with it, then." he retorted affirmatively licking his lips and turning his attention away from the festive, bountiful banquet of fare and toward Pierre and the matter at hand.

Confronted by and watching the up and down articulation of his jaws as he chewed the food in his mouth Matthew could not help but reflect upon Alex's descriptive dialogue where he referred to Pierre's mouth as a "horse's mouth" (he thought of Étonné and Eclatée). On further rumination Matthew decided that this was an apt characterization of his facial feature and that Pierre's mouth did, indeed, resemble that of an equine. Pierre was speaking.

"Tout à fait I realized why this Cyrus's voice was so familiar to me. It was he who had threatened us at the diner. He was speaking avec this Clyde bête and called him a "blockhead". Although, I do not fully comprend bien this correlation between a block and a head. Spacial relations suggest-" Pierre began to lecture on his point going off on a tangential consideration until Matthew interrupted him.

"Jumpin' Jehoshaphat! Get on with the crux o' the matter!" cried Matt in frustration as he watched Cari dispense a second helping of trout to Calvin while Mary Jo spooned more grilled vegetables onto his plate and he wondered if there would be any food left for him to eat by the time Pierre had finished recounting the events which had transpired that day at the party.

"An extremely inept description of human anatomy." Pierre resumed speaking his mind defiantly after favoring Matt with a scathing glance at being interrupted mid-speech. "However, ce mot was the telling word which struck the chord and caused me à souvenir that he was the cochon from the diner. I made the rare error of letting my emotions leap to the forefront and was ready to clap him in irons. But, one thing stayed my hand." quoth Pierre importantly pursing his lips thoughtfully and shaking his raised index finger in the air as he prepared to reveal his most pithy epiphany.

"Ye were too chickenhearted te confront him, te be sure!" Matthew interjected snidely.

"Then, I realized that he may peut-être have other minions hiding in secret!" Pierre continued speaking tapping his forehead knowledgeably with his forefinger to denote his savvy thinking prowess and totally ignoring Matthew's sarcasm.

"Wow! You think he has syndicate connections?"

"Alex, do not be ridiculous – and I thought you LIKED Cyrus!" Rand scolded his impressionable younger cousin.

"Well, I do, I mean I did like him until I learned he was a criminal." Alex replied ingenuously.

Randmore rolled his eyes upward toward the sky and then shared a glance of hopeless resignation with Matthew. Putting an arm about his cousin's shoulders he pulled him aside.

"We are trying to convince Pierre that Cyrus is not a criminal, Alex. We cannot do that if you keep encouraging him." Randmore explained patiently.

"Cet homme s'appelle Sandy is just one of his helpers." Pierre enlightened Alex confidentially. "He misdirected me, I could tell – Pierre Dûçot has le mieux sense of the direction. I eluded the mouffette and when I awoke I was in a strange world of darkness." he proclaimed eerily as he gazed between the spread apart fingers of his hands which he wafted periodically before his eyes in a hypnotic, undulating fashion for dramatic effect.

"Oh, BROTHER!" scoffed Matt in exasperated disbelief on hearing what he considered to be Pierre's contrived soliloquy of events and on viewing his hokey mannerisms.

Matthew wiped his hand across his mouth expressively after the unbidden exclamation issued forth from his lips.

"A beam of light beckoned me forward." continued the oblivious Frenchman who was clearly spellbound by his own adventures as he gazed afar heedless of Matthew Flanderly.

"Pierre. This kind of fanciful rhetoric proves what we discussed before. You had too much to drink and then collapsed. Sandy told us that you had wandered off with a lamp shade over your head-"

"That lamp shade was a disguise."

"A disguise!" Randmore said laughing in disbelief. "I do not believe you!"

"C'est vrai, c'est vrai! It is true. I was in a dark tunnel illuminated by a mysterious glowing light and as I moved toward it – Pierre Dûçot is fearful of nothing – I saw wooden bookcases of gold blocks. It was then that Grand-mère started to moan and I saw the forms of two denizens…."

"Stop the nonsense, Pierre!" Rand admonished reprovingly.

Matthew, who had previously opened his mouth with the intentions of spewing forth a sardonic barb regarding the idea of Pierre's "mysterious glowing light" instead closed it again at his subsequent mention of "gold blocks". Matthew's eyes gleamed with avarice and hope as he considered the possibility of prospective untold riches. Walking over to Pierre and clapping the Frenchman on the back in a gesture of close friendship he proclaimed:

"Now, now. Let us not be so hasty. Let us hear our bon ami, Pierre, out! <u>LET THE MAN SPEAK</u>!"

CHAPTER 38

"**M**y husband is very upset. Isn't there something that can be done?" Edith asked worriedly of the ticket agent as she watched in dismay from afar Pierre gesticulating and waving his arms at the train conductor as they engaged in heated argument.

"I apologize for the inconvenience, ma'am, but it just cannot be helped. An act of God is what it was. The entire Laureltown train trestle collapsed." Mr. Connors, the ticket agent, explained sympathetically. "It looks like your husband's blowing his stack!" he observed chuckling as Edith regarded him sourly. "Oh, come now. The joke was not <u>that</u> bad. Stack, smoke stack, blowing his stack - get it? And he will get over it!!!" he cajoled as she continued to tap her toe rapidly and regard him angrily.

"Pierre is very passionate and extremely sensitive. I seriously doubt acceptance will come to him very easily." she conceded resignedly as she watched Pierre throw down a white kid glove before the conductor and dared him to pick it up from the ground.

"What is going on?" asked Cari noting the commotion in front of the train as she and Cyrus joined her Aunt and John Connors.

"Our train trip has been canceled. The trestle has collapsed I fear and it will take at least one month to repair the damage."

"It does not appear that Pierre is taking it very well!" Cari noted concernedly looking on as the incensed Frenchman spat on the ground before him vexedly.

"At least he has got his clothes on." Cyrus quipped chuckling.

"How did you hear of that?" queried Edith sharply taking

umbrage that her husband's private business was being bandied about by a virtual stranger.

"Miss. Cari mentioned it in passing while we were chatting." he answered quickly wearing an awkward expression on his face.

"How COULD you!?" Edith chided her niece. "That personal type of information is Pierre's private business!"

"But, Aunt I didn't say anything. How DID you know about Pierre, Cyrus?" Cari turned and posed the question to him quizzically.

"You had to have mentioned it – or else how would I know?" he responded smoothly in an ingenuous tone of voice experiencing a brief moment of inward panic.

"I AM SURE that I did not tell you about what happened to my uncle."

"You told me this girl – Elvira, I believe you said her name was – was sick. You MUST have said it then." Cyrus's logic flowed reasonably as he spoke.

"Yes. I did mention Elvie…." Cari admitted looking from her Aunt's outraged countenance apologetically and then back again to face Cyrus doubtfully. "But I still do not remember-"

"YOU!" shouted Pierre interrupting and startling Cari out of her ponderous yet determined mood. "You destroyed the train trestle to keep me here! You will not get away with this sabotage. I will not allow it!" he declared enraged poking Cyrus with his forefinger as Edith laid a restraining hand which was meant to be calming on his arm.

"What is he talking about?" asked Cyrus taken aback by Pierre's sudden intrusion and frenetic state.

"You will have to excuse my husband. He is just a trifle disoriented. You see, he had his heart set on leaving on today's train. He has very important work to conduct at his Charlottesville dance studio." Edith quickly explained hedgingly in embarrassment not wishing to breach any social mores.

"I am <u>not</u> this disorientation." Pierre retorted to his wife shaking her hand from his forearm. "You are endeavoring to make me toast-" the irate man accused Cyrus swiveling around dramatically to confront him face to face once more.

"Why in the world would I make you breakfast? I hardly know you!" Cyrus interrupted Pierre in order to defend his innocence and to plead his case.

"Do not try to distract me. You, peut-être, can fool quelques personnes de temps en temps and toutes of the people all of the time mais you cannot tromper Pierre Dûçot any day of the week. I know of your devious intentions." he proclaimed wagging his finger accusingly at Cyrus. "AND, take your hands off of my niece!"

"Look, buddy." Cyrus said removing his hand from Cari's elbow. "I don't know what kind of pipe you are smoking but I'm just trying to help your wife out!" he said defensively self-righteously depositing an upright suitcase at Edith's feet and then retreating to a discreet distance from her.

"It's true, Pierre. Aunt Edith forgot one of her suitcases in the vestibule at LaurelsHeath. There was no one else available to help me and I knew that you two were coming here so I grabbed it to bring it to you. Cyrus happened to see me laboriously lugging this heavy piece of luggage. He saw that I was struggling with it and, gentleman that he is, offered to carry it for me. He took the time out of his busy schedule to help out a new neighbor, who he is hardly acquainted with by the way, to take it from my grasp and heft it all the way over here. I think you are being very ungrateful, Pierre!" stated Cari speaking plainly.

"Oh, la, la! I am being ungrateful. Alors, je pense que this Cyrus is in league with Grand-mère Dûçot and that is why he wishes to deny historical inspection of Candlestick Manor – he is hiding her there!"

CHAPTER 39

"**I** noticed that they haven't spoken to us since we confessed that we were the ones who were Grand-mère."

"Oh, Dudley, you're imagining things!" Callie scoffed negating the merit of Dudley's implausible suggestion as she arranged some furniture in the newly renovated sitting room.

The shape of the room was linearly unbalanced with the length of one wall being approximately four feet shorter than the one opposite to it. This lent the appearance of a trapezoidal shape to the space when someone first entered and noted that the adjoining walls capping them off at each end to form mitered corners were set at a diagonal. The cognac colored brocade curtains accented by a sheer tan overlay hung from the windows in the newly painted cream colored room gave one a warm feeling of understated elegance. The hardwood floors were of a honey-gold hue and a brown area rug denoted the central, main gathering area in front of the rustic brick fireplace with its brown and cream marble-topped mantle. Various accent pieces including a small gold clock complete with working pendulum and chimes decorated the projecting doily-covered marble surface.

"Now, if we put the mirror on that wall over there it will make the room look bigger!" she assessed judiciously. "I learned that little trick from a design magazine." Callie disclosed the tidbit of information to her husband proudly. "Then, we can put the maroon couch over there!"

"Maybe if we had told them about it sooner they wouldn't have held it against us...." Dudley conjectured thoughtfully to himself without hearing her as he was preoccupied with his own concerns.

"Don't be so sensitive!" Callie scolded her husband in an exasperated tone of voice. "They are just concentrating on convincing Pierre that his grandmother's ghost isn't out to get him. You know it is like pulling teeth to get Pierre to change his mind once he's got something into his head. The man just cannot admit when he is wrong. He can't stand it! It goes against his grain – his nature."

"Well, I hope you are right because Calvin is bothered by it, too. He doesn't show it but still waters run deep!"

"She is a CHESTERFIELD!" Clyde told Cyrus meaningfully and then he hooted with glee. "This could be the break we're looking for!"

"Her name is McKinley, doofus!" snapped Cyrus brusquely.

"That's her married name. Her maiden name is Chesterfield. Don't ya see? If we use her as leverage maybe we can get the hostages ta talk! Then, ya can have it all. The house is just the tip of the iceberg!"

Cyrus began to pace back and forth like a nervous cat. Lost in deliberation he gazed unseeingly before him contemplating the new revelation which had taken him completely by surprise. Finally, he stopped abruptly and broke the silence which hung as a thick, unseen veil in the air surrounding them both and spoke.

"Right under my nose and I did not see it. The hair, the coloring...."

"The birthmark, boss. The birthmark. She sure is a pretty little thing. I say we snatch her now!" Clyde blurted out zealously.

"Are you crazy, dummy? With all those relatives of hers around?" Cyrus noted as he spat contemptuously onto the floor and then shot Clyde a look of disdain. "The French guy is already suspicious!"

"Ahhh...." uttered Clyde brushing his exclamation aside with his hand. "Nobody's gonna take that guy seriously. He's seeing ghooo-stly visions of his dead grandmother!" he said expressively while waving his hands spookily in the air and metamorphosing his facial muscles into an expression of mock fear. "I say-"

"You have said enough!" roared Cyrus impatiently slamming down his fists on the oak table before him with a resounding crash as the displaced onyx chess set with its carved playing pieces jumped upward and then toppled to the tiled floor of the dayroom at Candlestick Manor. "That's another thing. How could you let him get close enough to see the hostages? Don't you have any brains?" Cyrus lashed out at him angrily.

"Now, that's not fair!" said Clyde defensively. "You <u>know</u> that weren't my fault. You can blame Sandy for that one. Though, he says the sneaky little busybody gave him the slip."

"All I know is he's too close for comfort. You take care of him, Clyde."

"Well, how's that? You know I didn't sign on for anything... physical."

"Are you getting soft on me, Clyde?"

"No. I'm not getting soft." he voiced the denial and sniffed to refute the allegation his manhood offended. "But first things first. We've got ta grab the girl."

"I do not believe it has to come to that." Cyrus articulated pensively as he wrinkled his brow thoughtfully.

"Don't tell me now that <u>you're</u> getting soft on <u>me</u>. I seen the way ya look at her when she looks the other way. Though, I don't blame ya. Like I said, she's a pretty little thing. Maybe ya can romance the information out of her." Clyde conjectured on a sudden inspiration.

"She does not know a thing." Cyrus retorted blushing a bright crimson at the suggestion as Clyde had guessed his secret inner feelings for Cari. "She was only a mere child when they came here."

"Ya mean, when your FATHER brought 'em here – an' you were just a kid, too, back then. I can tell ya are thinking about it – the romance angle, that is." Clyde teased him playfully. "An' ya are not much younger than Cari Chesterfield McKinley, either." he reminded Cyrus suggestively.

"You forgot one thing, bozo. Cari is in love with her husband." Cyrus replied brusquely in an unconcerned tone affected for Clyde's benefit which belied his true emotions and the gentler feelings which he felt for Cari.

Cyrus brooded on Cari longingly. 'Dare he hope...?' he wondered.

"An' don't worry about that foreign fella." Clyde assured him unaware of his boss's pensive mood. "He'd taken his clothes off – I heard it from my friend who works at the hospital – and he was caught running naked in the forest. Everyone thinks he's gone looney."

As he and Clyde vacated the house and he closed the door behind them both Cyrus for the most part ignored his friend's commentary and reflected on his chances with Cari. Dare he dream...? Elvie covered her mouth in horror as she inadvertently found herself eavesdropping on Cyrus and Clyde plotting and scheming. Pierre was right! Something was going on in that Candlestick Manor and Cyrus was at the center of it all! And Cari was in danger! She quickly moved from the open window through which Cyrus and Clyde's voices had emanated and frantically looked about her for a place to hide from them. Her eyes lit upon a gazebo. She hastened toward its concealing structure to crouch behind it. What should she do? She just did not know what to do.... She would tell Calvin. That's right. She would have to tell Calvin. He would know what to do. Oh, her head was spinning! Dr. Flanderly had suggested that she take this morning constitutional to clear her head. He had said that a walk outdoors would do her a world of good. It would help her clear her sinuses. The fresh air, the scenery, the flowers.... Well, she had gotten more than she had bargained for! She believed that this is what they called "irony". Elvie waited until Cyrus and Clyde left the immediate area and she was sure that they were far enough away so that she would not run into them before stepping out from behind the ivy-covered gazebo with its various overgrown foliage behind Candlestick Manor. Thank goodness that those villains had not seen her. Elvie breathed a huge sigh of relief while regarding her shaking hands and then paused to peer about her furtively to confirm that the coast was indeed clear. And that... <u>SNAKE</u> – she laughed thinking how much she sounded like Pierre – was after Cari! And who were these hostages...? How utterly...EVIL. Elvie stared down vapidly at the brightly-hued wildflowers she had been picking in the nearby vicinity which were clutched within her fist. She suddenly dashed the bouquet to the ground in loathing, glad to be rid of it, as if by virtue of the flowers' proximity of origin in relation to the manor the blooms were somehow tainted in nature and, hence, exuded a poisonous contagion. She set out to warn the others.

CHAPTER 40

"I will not go back there. I will not. And you cannot make me. I would expect something comme ci of you, Matthew and your nose for the gold pieces but not of you, Calvin. Did I mention that you are comme the fils I never had? I must contact my lawyers. I will have to revise my will...." Pierre said pensively as the two nudged and prodded him along against his will.

"We just want you to see that your dead grandmother isn't living at Candlestick Manor!" Calvin explained to him reasonably.

Pierre shook off the guiding hands of the two men pulling him along and straightened his jacket.

"You are right – did I ever mention that you were a bright boy?"

Pierre began pacing back and forth like a caged animal shaking his finger at various junctures for emphasis during his reasoning soliloquy while he spoke contemplatively.

"Maintenant that <u>Grand-mère</u> knows that <u>I</u> know of her presence at Candlestick Manor she will no longer wish to reside there. She will change her, comment dit-on, <u>strategy</u>. Now that Cyrus and Grand-mère have...que veut dire – joined forces together this sets a whole new complexion to the situation."

Pierre stopped his pacing. He paused motionless and tapped his chin thoughtfully. His eyes narrowed with his stubborn conviction before continuing.

"Therefore, nous devons be plus vigilant!" he proclaimed compressing his lips together to form one straight, steely and unbreakable line which refused to be neither daunted nor compromised.

Calvin and Matthew exchanged helpless glances. Would they ever be able to make Pierre understand and accept what they were telling him point blank?

"You're missing the point, brother. There is no "Grand-mère", period!"

"First of all, Calvin, I am NOT ton frère. Mais, bien sûr, who would not wish to be a blood relation of Pierre Dûçot? Second of all, you do not <u>know</u> my Grand-mère, Cal. Only <u>I</u> know how she thinks!" elucidated Pierre making the point triumphantly while tapping his temple with an index finger.

"Amen, te that." Matthew interjected mockingly.

"Do not make light of the spirits, médecin." Pierre said sharply raising an eyebrow and turning to fix Matt with a stern glare of condemnation.

"I was merely <u>agreein'</u> with ye, mon ami!"

"Do not patronize me, Matthew – you are tempting the fates!"

"Break it up you guys! Arguing is not going to solve anything." Calvin interjected interposing himself between the bickering pair. "I never meant to make anyone feel bad – honestly, I didn't. And I know you told me and Dudley that all was forgiven but it doesn't feel that way. You guys are making me feel worse by talking about this whole situation. Maybe you're not talking about what Dudley and I did directly but by constantly bringing up the subject of "Grand-mère", the whole experience with Hank Colden; the caves; the blowing up of the ridge – which almost killed you fellows who are now my best friends.... All the bad memories come flooding back and I feel guilty all over again! I feel guilty because we did terrible, crazy things to achieve our own selfish ends, Dudley and me and, yet, you guys forgave us. I'm humbled that you and everybody forgave me and Dudley. So, please Pierre. TRUST me when I tell you - when I PLEDGE to you that I pretended to be Grand-mère so you wouldn't backtrack to investigate when you heard the falling rocks in the cave." Calvin eloquently pleaded his case earnestly while simultaneously purging his conscience, as well.

Matthew and Pierre listened most respectfully to him and Calvin Maison took heart as he saw he had captured and retained their attention. However, when Pierre Dûçot spoke it became clear that he had only been humoring him out of politeness.

"Cal, you are comme le fils I never had. So, that having been said, I will not tell you the mensonge. Je sais that you are trying to, comment dit-on, keep the peace between Matthew and I. You are a good boy. Mais, this…cover-up, of the true facts will not be tolerated. I heard Grand-mère that day in the cave – it was her voice and I saw her here on the Other Side avec one of her minions sitting on a chair-"

"In the room with the gold?" Matthew inquired casually seemingly uninterested in or unaware of any potential monetary gain to be garnered as he kicked a fallen tree branch lying on the grass before him idly and Pierre smiled knowingly at his transparent attempt at nonchalance.

"Tu vois. I understand that you are concerned seulement sur the mental well-being of Pierre Dûçot and so you deny the existence of Grand-mère. However, I accept l'idée that there are des choses au monde that we just do not comprehend." said Pierre as he ignored Matthew and his query by putting a hand on Calvin's shoulder to turn him around and on doing so then steering him in the opposite direction that Matthew, himself, was walking.

"Aye! Ye canna be talkin' te mon ami, Pierre, in tha' fashion!" said Matthew slickly in order to curry Pierre's favor and agilely interposed himself between them as he needed to lead Pierre back toward Candlestick Manor and to the room where he had seen the gold.

Pierre halted and looked at Matthew suspiciously. Why was he being so tout à coup agreeable?

"Mais, you said à moi only a moment ago that you did not be-lieve Grand-mère existed."

"Tha', Pierre, mon dear ami is what we are goin' te find out! Now, come along." Matt said with feigned cheerfulness. "The GOLD – I mean – GRAND-MÈRE be waitin'!" he concluded tug-ging on Pierre's arm to lead him toward the house.

"Mais, I do NOT WANT to see Grand-mère. I just told you. I am trying to avoid her." stated the Frenchman firmly refusing to budge an inch.

"Now, now. Be tha' any way te speak o' yer own relation?"

"Could it be, médecin, that you are more interested in Grand-mère's gold than in our joyeux reunion?" demanded Pierre suspiciously.

Matthew opened his mouth several times with various replies on the tip of his tongue only to close it each time as he was at a loss for an appropriate response which was believable. As he considered for suitability and then rejected possible replies Calvin interceded.

"Of course good ole Matt has absolutely no interest in gold! How could you even suspect him of such a thing, Pierre, mon très bon ami?" asked Calvin in mock innocence gagging on his laughter as he rolled the last four word characterization off of his tongue facetiously.

"Dunna tell me yer na just as interested in the gold as I am!" Matthew bellowed in defense of his prevarication helplessly con-flicted as to what his reaction should be and woefully abashed that his true agenda had been revealed.

"Qu'est-ce que c'est...?"

"What the...?"

"Tha' be Elvie! The puir lass – she looks scared te death, she does."

Elvie was bedraggled and wet from head to toe. One side of her pinned-up hair had fallen down over one eye in one tangled, wet clump and she was missing a shoe.

"Pierre!" Elvira gasped out as she screeched to a halt in front of him swaying woozily and panted to draw air shakily into her lungs and to catch her breath. "You were right!" she clamored. "You were RIGHT!"

"Mais, bien sûr, I was right!" concurred Pierre buoyantly although more than a bit concerned when confronted by a lady in distress. "Maintenant. What am I right about?"

CHAPTER 41

"This is the perfect day for a picnic." Mary Jo observed as she regarded a flock of geese flying across the sky in a kite-like formation and sipped lemonade from an ice-frosted, tall glass.

"Yep. This is the life." replied her husband yawning loudly without politely covering his mouth and stretching out his arms open wide.

He wore a tan-colored straw hat with a wide brim which had stray shoots of the dry material poking out unevenly along its edge. Thick patches of white sunblock covered the freckles which spread liberally across his nose.

"Alex! You look like a goofball!" Mary Jo stated with a laugh.

"Awww.... Don't be such a stick in the mud!" he complained kneeling down to sit under a tree next to her.

"Did you find anything valuable with that thing?" she inquired motioning with her chin toward the metal detector which he had thrown down on the grass beside him.

"Only this...."

"Elroy's key!"

"You mean half-key." Alex corrected her pulling out his own partial key from underneath his shirt and dropping it to let it dangle once more from the chain around his neck.

"I know. He must've lost it again." replied Mary Jo.

"And Simon is probably looking all over for it. Once I find him I'll give it to him."

"How are you going to do that? Find him, I mean."

"Well," Alex said thoughtfully leaning forward to reach for a chicken sandwich deliberately avoiding the adjacent homemade biscuits, "I saw him near this cottage one time so I assume that's where he lives."

Taking a bite of his sandwich he chewed and swallowed.

"That's why I am going to head out there later and give the broken key to him. His son must have lost it again and he says his son considers it a good luck charm."

"You know I don't believe in luck." Mary Jo pooh-poohed. "And why don't you try one of my biscuits?" she inquired smiling slightly as she saw her husband's eyeballs glaze over with trepidation. "Oh, don't worry! I am trying out a new recipe – one I learned from Trudy, no less! When you look at her you would not figure her for the domestic type even though she is the house cook. Anyway, she walked me through the whole biscuit-making process. It was fun."

"FUN? With TRUDY?"

"I KNOW! Right? Yes, with Trudy! She's not as stoic and humorless as she appears to be. In fact, she went through the whole recipe with me several times showing me all the correct techniques to use. And to make the demonstrations real to me she would make little jokes up to help me remember stuff. For instance, when she found out I liked dancing she associated "cutting in" on a pair of dancers as cutting in a "pair" of shortening and flour with two knives. She called flour one partner and shortening the other one. She is really quite funny once you get to know her. And by the time we were through with our lessons we had flour all over our faces and the kitchen countertops, too. And she wasn't even mad that she had to clean up the mess we made. She said it was her job and besides that she enjoyed teaching me how to bake. The whole experience was fun. So at least try a biscuit, Honey. PLEASE…!" she cajoled him with sad, melting eyes and pleading expression as she poached one of them from the tray which rested on the red and white checkered tablecloth and held one of the biscuits to his firmly clamped together lips.

"SIMON!" Alex blurted out desperately half in salutation, half in relief as he jumped from his seated position near Mary Jo to shake his hand spastically in friendship.

"Hello, Alex. Hello, Mary Jo. It is such a fine day to be outdoors. You are on a picnic, I see...."

"Yes." said Mary Jo scrambling to her feet. "Would you care for a biscuit?"

"Mary Jo!"

"Don't mind if I do." said Simon. "I am a little hungry-"

"You don't have to eat that!"

"What's wrong, Alex?" he inquired his mouth full after taking a bite of the tasty creation. "Forgive me for speaking with my mouth full." Simon apologized for the faux pas in etiquette. "This is delicious, Mary Jo. So flaky. It almost tastes like...um, h-h-hum...." he cleared his throat and looked down.

"Like what, Simon?" queried Alex anxiously fearing the worst as Mary Jo nodded smiling triumphantly and favored him with an "I TOLD YOU SO!" expression.

"Buttery. My wife makes biscuits like these." he revealed tentatively uncertain as to how much of his personal life to disclose.

"You're married?" asked Alex with avid curiosity.

"I actually stopped by to ask you if I could borrow your metal detector."

"You're not changing the subject, are you? When do we get to meet her?" he pressed only to be interrupted by a loud, presumptuous voice:

"Mary Josephine you are an angel." Pierre Dûçot complimented Mary Jo as he swept in precipitately, picked up a napkin which he tucked into his collar and a plate and began to pile roast beef slices and fried chicken onto it. "How did you know I would be in the area? Ça fait rien. Never mind. It makes no différence to me. I always said that you were a very bright girl and too good for Alex!" he continued non-stop speaking conversationally as he dusted the dirt off of a boulder with his ever present mouchoir and sat down upon it. "You have ne quelque idée what I have just been through. Je…. Quoi?"

Looking into their astounded faces which were ripe with disbelief Pierre could not for the life of him tell what the matter was. He quickly glanced down at his attire to see that he was properly dressed. Quel mystère….

"Me and Mary Jo were just having an outdoor lunch and enjoying the weather. You're quite welcome to join us, Pierre."

"Excusez-moi." Pierre responded in an arrogant huff to hide his embarrassment at assuming that the picnic lunch was for his benefit. "I did not mean to intrude!" he added with standoffish hauteur not relishing the fact that Alex, of all people, was correcting him – without appearing to – and putting him in his place.

"'Twas not the first time ye've stuck yer big foot inte yer mouth an' 't willna likely be the last, te be sure!" Matthew interjected humorously as he caught sight of Simon with his back partially turned toward him and went pale.

"Well, you two must have gone through something." Mary Jo said as she jumped up and rushed to Matthew's side with concern coloring her voice. "Look how pale and drawn you both are!"

"I am more drawn than he is." asserted Pierre quickly vying for attention and deciding to settle for the sympathy vote. "That cochon has pulled on my last straw! He will think two times more before choisissant to tangle with Pierre Dûçot une autre fois!"

"Ye made more o' a colossal fool o' yerself, if tha' be possible." Matthew asserted matter-of-factly.

"It was a matter of honor! Sending his minions after the très fort personnage of Pierre Dûçot is one thing. Mais, to attack a gentle lady comme Elvie.... I had to draw the mark!" he professed with outraged dignity.

"Someone attacked a lady, sir? Where is the fiend? I'll help you dispose of him." Simon pledged assuredly.

CHAPTER 42

"That is my friend, Simon." Alex said to Matthew in triumph. "You remember him? My "imaginary" friend."

"I be contrite I didna believe ye, laddie. 'Tis only when ye spoke te him…he was ne'er in evidence." Matthew replied guiltily now that he knew Alex's friend not only existed but that, in addition, he could not reveal to Alex Simon's familial relationship to him as he had been sworn to secrecy.

"That's because he was either behind a barn or a tree when we were talking but Mary Jo had spoken to him, too. That's interesting. Him and Pierre seem to be hitting it off. I wonder what they're talking about."

Matthew's gaze shifted to where Simon and Pierre sat across from each other engrossed in serious conversation. Simon appeared to be bonding with the man who, unbeknownst to him, was his brother-in-law.

"It be hard te fathom what Simon could ha' in common with the loon. Let's go see." replied Matthew turning around and starting to walk toward the boulder where Pierre sat holding court talking to Simon.

"So, it's true about Elvie running hysterically in the woods?" queried Alex in a low, respectful voice which was mindful of Elvie's misfortune as he walked by Matthew's side.

"Unfortunately tha' be the case. The crux o' the matter be tha' she's uncovered some evil plot te kidnap Cari. While comin' te warn us all she was discovered red-handed by some unprincipled scalawag. She took te runnin' from the knave an' fell inte one o' the ponds surroundin' Candlestick Manor in her haste. She pulled herself out o' it an' barely eluded the scoundrel by the skin o' her teeth when she ran headlong inte Calvin, Pierre an' yours truly who happened te be movin' in tha' direction. I gave her a sedative te calm her down. Ye know I ne'er go anyplace without me trusty medical bag. Calvin took her back te the house with him and I was bound and determined te accompany them – ye know I ne'er leave a patient in distress! But tha' hardheaded buffoon o'er there insisted on confrontin' tha' blackguard, Cyrus, fer upsettin' a lady." Matthew imitated Pierre in a high-pitched tone of voice twirling himself around in a little affected dance while holding up his wrists and letting his fingers hang downward as if he were a puppy begging for a treat. "I was duty-bound te accompany him, o' course. Somebody ha' ta' protect him from himself! I must give credit te him, though. He let tha' Cyrus bloke ha' it with both barrels blazin', te be sure!" he recounted attempting to mask his grudging admiration for Pierre's gutsy behavior. "If ye ask me he was merely enjoyin' the whole situation. He told the man tha' Elvira was a fragile feminine flower and he did a dastardly deed by settin' one of his hooligans after her. He warned Cyrus te leave Cari alone an' te keep his lascivious thoughts o' perfidy te himself. An' he told him, as well, tha' he'd be watchin' him fer any slipups. The only thing be the fact tha' I canna be sure Elvie be rational at this stage. The way she was carryin' on when we found her I canna be sure how much o' what she told us be totally factual…. Now, I be no psychiatrist by any means but she was already recovering from one episode, fer lack o' better phraseology, and the current chain o' events may ha' been the catalyst required te <u>push</u> her o'er the edge, so te speak, an' traumatized the living daylights out o' the lass te the point where she could say or believe anything te be true. The lass be in quite a vulnerable state leaving her open te, let us say, <u>suggestion</u>." Matthew ended on an ominous note and then paused to catch his breath – he had said a mouthful!

"You mean, she's repeating what Pierre says about Cyrus being untrustworthy because grabbing onto his idea is a less stressful way for her to cope with what she's been through instead of actually facing head-on the unhappy truth of what really did happen."

Matthew paused tongue-tied preparing to be indignant at Alex's unexpectedly spot-on, succinct interpretation of Elvie's potential mental state. He tilted his head toward Alex gauging his analytical assessment and searching his visage for signs of offending pomposity but could find none.

"Aye." Matthew finally said slowly. "That be what I be referrin' te. But next time," he advised critically, "leave the diagnosin' te the professionals!"

"But, I just figured-"

"Dunna be smart, laddie! Ye gave an oversimplification o' a complex mental phenomenon. There be a reason ye matriculate through the laborious rigors o' medical trainin'!" Matthew further admonished Alex as they approached the others.

"I told him that was no façon in which to treat a lady. Mais, bien sûr! I let him, as you Américains say, have it with both barrels. I told him that I would be watching him closely and one more indiscretion with the fairer sex, even the tiniest infraction, faux pas or misstep on his part, and I would have to, comment dit-on, bring the hammer down on him!" Pierre lectured feelingly point on point and then leaned back as far as he could on the boulder and crossed his arms over his chest. "There was terror in his eyes." he concluded with finality satisfied that his points had been taken loud and clear.

"BRAVO!" cheered Simon in praise clapping his hands in applause. "That was quite stirring. I applaud your convictions. My hat's off to you. I never approved of the way Roland Sykes, Cyrus's father, treated women and it appears that he has imparted the same disgraceful ethic to his son."

"Mais, bien sûr! The apple does not fall far from the arbre! This Cyrus and his minions must be taught the leçon."

Pierre halted abruptly and cogitated.

"Vous savez, you remind me of quelqu'un." said the Frenchman suddenly.

"Bah! Every person ye see reminds ye o' somebody!" pooh-poohed Matthew quickly interrupting their conversation. "An' tha' 'terror' in his eyes ye be so keen on describin' most likely be the indication o' the man suppressin' a belch!" he added irreverently.

Pierre had been positively glowing under the influence of Simon's praise and Matthew was a little worried about him deducing the similarity between Simon and Edith. Their temperaments and expressions were very similar as well as their interests and views on topics such as history, etcetera. Edith and Simon were also twins and so besides their similar mannerisms they did resemble each other and, although Matthew did not want to give him too much credit, he believed that Pierre was already starting to subliminally recognize this. Matthew knew that he had to distract the Frenchman's attention somehow!

"Je suis très sûr that you are someone I have seen before." he asserted doggedly adhering to his chosen topic, ignoring Matt and drumming his fingertips in measured metronomic succession on his knee as Mary Jo yawned slightly in the intoxicating warmth of the sun and began sipping more lemonade from a tall glass. "Are you...peut-être French?" he suddenly inquired expectantly regarding Simon hopefully with large, inquisitive puppy dog eyes.

Simultaneous bursts of laughter erupted from Mary Jo – who expelled lemonade from her mouth in a most unladylike fashion, Alex and Matthew. Matthew's laughter was of the nervous kind. There was no humor in its depths.

"Pierre always thinks that people who agree with him and

compliment him are French." Mary Jo explained away their laughter to Simon as she wiped the tears of mirth from her eyes and the droplets of the fruity drink from her dress with a paper napkin.

"This is not vrai." Pierre asserted the protestation seriously. "I was merely curious regarding your ancestry. You are such a gentilhomme en comparaison avec some people!" he stated firmly while fixing Matthew with an accusatory stare of condemnation. "It was wise of you to make friends with Simon, Alex. C'est très important to, comment dit-on, "hang out" with the <u>right</u> crowd. Not, par exemple, with des personnes comme le faux médecin, ici!" he commented superciliously on concluding his remarks.

At this juncture Simon and Matt exchanged humorous smiles. Matthew had already explained Pierre's attitude toward him to Simon. Matthew shook his head in private musing. It was difficult for him to come to grips with the fact that Simon was actually Pierre's brother-in-law.

"You are welcome at Chesterhollow any temps." Pierre extended the invitation graciously to Simon while pointedly turning his coldest shoulder to Matthew.

Simon appeared bewildered and somewhat flustered by his statement.

"Chesterhollow...?" queried Simon in an unsure, slightly shaken tone of voice as he posed the open-ended question.

"Pierre is married te Edith, the mistress o' Chesterhollow ranch in Charlottesville. Ye see, after her former husband, Mr. Norden, passed she remarried...." Matthew explained 'And THIS is the result!' he seemed to say to Simon as he indicated Pierre with one fluid, upward introductory gesture of his upraised palm immediately followed by a swift, sharp, downward hand motion a few inches lower of the same appendage, the palm automatically rebounding to its original upward position to hover momentarily before he let it drop uncontrolled to strike his side.

"Simon is not interested in our family history, Matthew." Pierre said inflamed as he was offended by Matthew's deprecating gestures and his insulting implication.

"REALLY, NOW?" he responded caustically. "It seems te me tha' ye're interested in everyone else's family history!"

CHAPTER 43

"Il pleut!"

"What're ye talkin' about – I be gettin' soaked!" yelled Matthew irascibly as lightning bolts rippled across the cloudy morning sky and raindrops began to pelt down in an unrelenting deluge. "If anyone were te ha' the gift o' understatement ye'd sure 'n' away take the prize!"

"Quick!" yelled Alex with sudden inspiration. "Let's head for Elvie's gazebo!"

In a mad scramble for cover both Pierre and Matthew darted after Alex toward the structure to jog up its trio of steps and take refuge under the gazebo's roof.

"Boy, that was close!" cried Alex in relief as he shook out the wet blazer he had been holding over his head as a shield against the rain and laid it carefully and neatly across the projecting built-in seating which ran along the back railing of the high and dry shelter. "Mary Jo would have a fit if I ruined this jacket!"

"Brilliant, Pierre! Ye're just brilliant! Now, we're trapped here an' ye're the only one te blame. Dunna try te deny it! First off, ye ha' us searchin' all o'er the grounds fer only <u>yer</u> lame brain knows what and now we're hold up in this small space – toe te toe, we be – an' I'll likely be missin' me supper!"

"You are free to leave here whenever you wish." Pierre offered the invitation curtly extending his arm and waving to the pouring deluge outside of the gazebo's cover. "I told you I will not rest until I find the evidence that will put that Cyrus behind bars where he belongs! The Cochon's behavior cannot be overlooked! He threatened the life of Pierre Dûçot which is bad enough. But now he threatens the feminine ladies of our families. He has designs on my niece; has driven Elvie to the cliff of insanity and seeks to poison the suggestible mind of this naïve young boy!" he lectured piously indicating Alex.

"Hey!" cried Alex in objection to Pierre's characterization of him as an impressionable, naïve boy – he was a man! "And the space here is not small, it's kinda comfortable!" he spoke judiciously with an authoritative air about him.

"Ye can blabber all yer self-righteous falderal all ye wish but I say tha' Cyrus isna no way bound te hurt Cari – if ye noticed the infatuated glances he be givin' her ye'd see tha' – an' if ye'd only mind yer own business we'd all be better off! We'd be home in dry clothes with food in our bellies an' relaxin' afore a cracklin' fire!" Matt remonstrated Pierre while ignoring Alex completely.

"Vous savez la seule raison that you followed me out here was to look for the briques d'or. And Simon agrees with me!"

"He agrees with yer defense of the ladies ONLY. But he dunna know tha' this conspiracy o' yers isna bona fide."

"LOOK. Will you two stop arguing? You're hurting my eardrums. We're stuck here so let's just make the best of it!" Alex advised sensibly. "And you guys aren't the only ones with problems. My metal detector is lying out there getting rusted right now. It probably won't even work anymore. And what about Mary Jo? I hope she got back home alright. I <u>knew</u> I shouldn't have left her to carry all those things back all alone!" he lamented concernedly second-guessing himself with aforethought removing his straw hat and throwing it to the segmented wooden floor beneath their feet in frustration. "I don't know why I have to follow you guys anyway. You always get me into trouble!" he stated grimly with a helpless feeling on the inside and a worried frown wrinkling his brow as he thought of his wife's safety.

"Dunna worry, laddie. Yer lady be a hale an' hearty lass! She'll be fine, te be sure!" Matt asserted assuredly with hollow bluster in a sympathetic attempt to sound convincing to the younger man and allay his fears as he, himself, sat down on the bench behind him knowing full well that if the shoe were on the other foot and it were Eleanor out there fending for herself against the elements he would be frantic with worry.

"Well...I hope so." Alex said slowly somewhat mollified by Matt's encouraging words and demeanor. "I know Simon will be alright, he can take care of himself! Boy!" he exclaimed while re-garding the pouring rain. "We're lucky this gazebo is steps off of the ground on this wooden base otherwise we'd be standing on the ground that would eventually become muddy. And, as I said before, the place is pretty big, too. Nice and wide and we've got these nice places to sit on. Pierre...what are you doing?" Alex inquired of the man who was stomping the floor of the gazebo at various junctures with his booted foot and harrumphing in disapproving satisfaction whenever the wooden floor section beneath his feet gave slightly under its pressure or creaked hollowly in protest at the uncalled-for battering.

"Pah!" he responded pointing downward to the abused surface as he looked up at him triumphantly. "American made! In France such poor construction would not be tolerated. Écoute! Hear how the foundation groans and makes the rude, unseemly noises? In France there are genuine craftsmen who actually take pride in their work and enjoy the perfection of their finished products!" Pierre lectured to the mesmerized younger man who was clearly overawed by his fervent address with a final stamp of his foot almost tripping over both of his feet in the process. "Quoi?" he asked dramatically raising a hand to cup his ear in an exaggerated fashion to denote a feigned interest. "Médecin? Médecin, did you say something?" he inquired with a blatant challenge in his voice which dared the Irishman to speak as he heard a potentially insulting gasp issue forth from Matthew Flanderly's throat. "Matthew? Matthew…?" he cajoled but after still receiving no response his face suddenly became drained of all color. "MATT!!!" he yelled anxiously on receiving no reply from his friend while swinging around to confront Matt and almost losing his balance on the uneven flooring before catching himself to stand totally erect. "Gone…. He is GONE! Just as I suspected…. Grandmère…. She has spirited him away!" he said ominously. "What shall we do? Alex?" he called out in query as he swung around again to confront his unresponsive companion. "Matt is missing. He…was… Alex?" Pierre asked hesitantly shifting his gaze from left to right in search of the vanished Alexander Caine who was now suddenly in absentia. "I am losing my <u>MIND</u>!" he bellowed in fearful desperation as he was concerned about himself and the fate of his friends – but mostly about himself.

Pierre raced down the steps out into the pouring rain and then ran back up the steps of the gazebo, under its arch and under its sheltering ceiling. He wiped the water off of his face and slicked back his wet hair with his hands. The pelting slap of the cold raindrops had brought him back to his senses. He then glanced about to confirm that no one was lingering in the near vicinity and heard his last statement.

"No!" he shouted even louder lest one of his many admirers had trailed behind him in the hopes of meeting the fameux Pierre Dûçot, heard the shocking revelation and was scandalized. "I am not losing my mind!" he yelled to the surrounding foliage as a further precautionary disclaimer just to be on the safe side – one could never be certain whether or not one of his zealous, die hard fans were hovering about for an autograph.

Mais, bien sûr, Pierre Dûçot could not exhibit any weakness and risk his, comment dit-on, IMAGE in the community. He would be ruined otherwise and he had a reputation to uphold!

"Pierre Dûçot does not lose his mind!" he continued to rant staggering around the perimeter of the gazebo as if he were a man possessed and almost tripping over his feet several more times.

'Thanks to the goodness that none of my ardent fans are about to witness my…clumsiness.' he ashamedly observed inwardly. 'What is this?' he asked himself in curiosity. That loud creak. Where had it come from? He turned about in a circle regarding the confines of the gazebo while meticulously cataloguing every point of interest and aspect of the empty structure surrounding him. Open latticework fencing bordered the structure's perimeter and was practically covered with green foliage which had grown onto and woven itself into and around its framework of whitewashed wooden slats. Four columns evenly spaced apart around the gazebo's circumference rose regally upward from its foundation to support its roof which curved into an overhanging arch in four places. Ivy and various clinging vines spread across the four columns intertwining as they climbed reaching for the sky. The ceiling of the structure depicted the image of a multitude of laurel leaves caressing the head of an adult male lion residing in the center against the backdrop of a clear, blue sky. The image of the lion gave Pierre courage. Pierre stood up straighter. He pulled the mouchoir out of his jacket pocket and blew his nose. The handkerchief was wet with rainwater but this did not faze him. As he mindlessly stuffed it back into his pocket he came to a stunning realization: He was a DANCING INSTRUCTOR. Pierre Dûçot does not trip over his feet!

CHAPTER 44

Randy McKinley was not a happy man. Tethering his stallion inside of an old, abandoned shed in order to spare the steed from traveling across potentially muddy fields he pulled the hood of his rain slicker over his head and took a deep breath before striding out of the shelter and into the rain. What had started out as a pleasant, temperate morning had quickly turned into inclement weather. When Cal had come to LaurelsHeath earlier supporting a fainting and teary-eyed Elvie on his arm they had all been concerned about her health. When they listened to her erratic, sometimes incoherent, frantically pieced together story they all were concerned regarding her lucidity. Then, when Mary Jo returned sans Alex from their late morning picnic brunch and apprised them that Pierre was on his way on a reckless rampage, with Alex and Matt in tow, to search for clues of criminal intent and to confront Cyrus a second time to defend Elvie's honor they had all agreed that he should head Pierre off at the pass and inject some reason into the situation. It was concluded that although Cal wanted to meet with Cyrus to give him a piece of his mind it would be best if he stayed with his wife to comfort her and give her moral support rather than adding fuel to an already lit fire. Also, Cal had acceded that Rand had a better knack of getting through to Pierre and making him listen to reason. The fact that both Alex and Matt were accompanying Pierre had not inspired adequate confidence in their abilities to keep the confrontation civil. Between Matt and his lust for gold and Alex with his impressionable nature and propensity to become

overawed by fancy rhetoric it was clear that someone with a de-
tached point of view was needed to help lend a balanced spin to the
issues in contention. Luckily, Randmore had neglected to remove
his slicker from the last big rainstorm from his saddlebag. He had
forgotten how storms like this one could kick up in even the sun-
niest of weather. Rand ducked under some bowed tree branches
absentmindedly. Hopefully, the ground would stay hard enough so
that he could find the guys quickly, convince them of their folly and
they could all make it back safely through the glen by nightfall. As
he assessed the soaked condition of the area it was clear to him that
whatever condemning physical evidence against Cyrus which Pierre
intended to uncover he would not find tonight! Mary Jo had informed them that a friend of hers and Alex's by the name of Simon
was behind all of this lunacy. (Where did those two meet up with
these people from?!) Maybe it was not Simon's direct intent to encourage another confrontation with Cyrus but Mary Jo said that he
was so encouraging and supportive of Pierre's first confrontation
with Cyrus that his praise egged Pierre on. She said that the two
had bonded like brothers and Simon's approval of him for defending Elvie's honor coupled with the admiration he had expressed for
such "chivalrous" behavior on his part had worked Pierre up into
a self-righteous fervor. He had noticed that during this particular
revelation of Mary Jo's recounting of events Edith had shifted uncomfortably and a stricken, abashed expression took possession of
the facial features of her otherwise placid countenance so embarrassed was she of her husband's susceptibility to flattery – and she
was usually as cool as a cucumber! By the time Simon and Pierre
had finished speaking Pierre felt it was his duty as a gentleman to
return to Candlestick Manor once more and favor Cyrus with another "dose of his own médicament". Rand pushed aside a bunch
of wet branches which had been displaced by the gusts of howling
wind. At last. The manor house was in sight. The torrents of rain

were abating a bit and it now was easier to see more clearly. 'They just might make it back in time for dinner.' Rand thought heaving a weary sigh. He didn't look down at his brand new pair of boots. He had just picked them up and brought them home yesterday from a specialty shop in town which specialized in handmade leather footwear. The hand-tooled items had been rubbed to a rich sheen. They had been custom-made to order and he had waited about a month for them to be made by the town cobbler who, as a special favor to him, had rushed the order. This was his first time wearing them and they probably looked about two years old now. Of course, he hadn't expected them to look new forever and he had purchased them mainly for their purported comfortable fit and function – but still...! Rand swallowed his disappointment and put forth a stiff upper lip. He would assess the damage to his footwear later, he decided. For right now, he would spare himself the heartbreaking sight. This weather was definitely fickle in nature. Although it was true that when he had left the house a mile, or so, behind him it had started to drizzle a bit he had not expected anything long-term, let alone anything like this storm! How was he to know that what he had thought to be a temporary light rain would turn into a downpour like the one he was now experiencing. He should have turned back at the first sign of the rainfall worsening and donned some heavy rain gear and particularly...rubberized boots! Rand raised his right foot out of a muddy patch and, against his previous resolution, regarded his footwear with dismay. On seeing their woebegone condition his regret overwhelmed him and he could have wept. He had tried to behave in a noble fashion. However, in his fervor to prevent Pierre from potentially embarrassing himself and them all with his off-the-wall rhetoric he had paid the price: he had sacrificed his new riding boots. He considered the adage "Discretion is the better part of valor.". He saw the truth to it and accepted the wisdom of the proverb. It just proved the point further, he had acted in haste and now he had time to repent at leisure. Hey! Wasn't that a proverb, too...? Randmore broke through the cloistering group of trees and foliage before him and observed a sheltering oasis in the form of a roofed structure which rose from the ground approximately one half mile from where he stood. He ran toward it thankfully. Although the stormy weather was abating to showers and the sky was lightening with the promise of clearing he had to rest! That shelter could not have made its appearance at a more opportune time in his journey – he had to take a breather and catch his equilibrium! Unless, of course, the newfound haven was merely a mirage...? A figment of his mind which he had conjured up out of extreme dog-tired desperation? He needed to know immediately! Randmore plodded faster toward its welcoming arches and that is when he saw him. It was a tall fellow storming about the perimeter of the structure waving his arms and talking loudly to himself. As Rand hurriedly drew closer he saw that it was...PIERRE! A wide grin spread across his face combining with an expression of relief that he had found him in time – before he caused a bad blood incident with the local landowner and neighbor. He closed his eyes and drew the back of one weary arm across his wet face – he had been cutting and pushing aside plenty of thick overgrown foliage to come to where he was now standing! Of course, Alex and Matt were not with him.... Randy opened his eyes to greet Pierre but he had...disappeared! What had happened to him? He had been there a second ago. Maybe this truly was a mirage. He had taken his gaze off of him for only a moment.... He had closed his eyes for only a moment but in the blink of an eye HE WAS GONE!

CHAPTER 45

"It looks te me te be some sort o' root cellar." Matthew deduced critically holding up what appeared to be an old, desiccated, dried-up turnip to the meager light.

"I don't want to sound mean because I would not ever wish you trapped down here but I'm glad you are with me. It's spooky down here – I wouldn't want to be all alone!" Alex said with a fearful shiver. "And where is that weird glow coming from?" he asked looking about him curiously for its origin but also at the same time with trepidation dreading that someone unsavory might be behind him.

"I dunna know, laddie. But, one thing be fer sure. Next time I'll be takin' the steps!" Matthew responded indicating the wooden staircase leading upwards with a nod of his chin in its direction while simultaneously rubbing his sore backside. "Fell right on me keister, I did, when that clueless buffoon released the trigger fer openin' the trapdoor."

"Well.... That's funny because I landed in that pile of hay over yonder. It broke my fall." Alex said shyly with a crooked, apologetic smile as he contrasted his good fortune at not being hurt with Matthew's hard fall to the ground.

"You were in a different place then I was when the floor swallowed me up."

Matt stopped moving forward as a loud click sound caused him to look above him and raise his lantern up high as he regarded the ceiling above him:

"Methinks Pierre will be joinin' us soon. Now, as I be figurin'.

This place was also some sort o' storm shelter...."

"Wait. What do you mean, Pierre will be joining us?"

"It be only a matter o' time, lad. Only a matter — AH!" he hooted with satisfaction raising an index finger upwards as a loud thump resounded behind them. "Our visitor has arrived!"

Smiling, Matt turned unconcernedly in the opposite direction of the sound and continued his thoughtful pacing as he resumed surveying the contents of the chamber before him.

"Ye see, this old water bottle an' the lantern ye found," Matt raised the lantern to show it to Alex, "bear out me theorizin'. This lantern ye found be exhibit "C" an' the turnip an' the water bottle be exhibits "B" an' "A" most respectively. 'Twas a stroke o' sheer genius yer bringin' those matches otherwise we couldna have lighted the candle in the lantern." he noted with admiration.

"Well, I can't take full credit. Pierre always taught me to be prepared.... SEE?" Alex bragged as he pointed to the waterproof wallet attached to the belt at his hip. "And if that thump was Pierre back there we should go back there to help him!" he asserted stalwartly.

"Bah! If the roles were reversed; if the situation were t'other way around; de ye think the bloke'd help US?"

"Yes. He WOULD!" Alex said without hesitating a moment.

"I believe yer right." Matthew consonantly agreed and turned to stroll leisurely in the other direction where the sound came from.

"And he could be injured. Why are you walking so slowly for?!"

"Injured? Bah! Dunna ye know tha' the good Lord protects numbskulls like that? The fool be so hardheaded he canna be in any true peril." responded Matthew stepping up his pace nonetheless despite his cavalier words.

"And you are a doctor. You are supposed to help people. You took an oath-"

"Alright! Blast it! Dunna push yer luck. I be agoin', laddie – aren't I? Ye see me walking, dunna ye?" Matthew responded

SHARON ELIZABETH SARKISIAN

attempting to mask the concern in his voice and heart for Pierre's well-being that Alex's admonishing provoked. "I KNEW that it be ONLY a matter o' time afore tha' goofball be joinin' the party!" he added in conclusion pursing his lips.

"Why do you always talk about him like that?"

"Like what?"

"You're always talking about how he disrespects you, but you're always disrespecting him. Why do you do that?"

"Ye see, laddie, Pierre always be telling everybody how smart he be. He always be actin' so infuriatin'ly superior an' then – BOOM! He be sayin' somethin' all-out foolish. For instance. He be seein' his dead grandmother. Or, imaginin' people be followin' behind te take his photograph. Or, he be spinnin' his conspiracy theories an' tellin' his tall tales. Or,"

"But usually he's right!" Alex pleaded in Pierre's defense.

"OR. He be poisonin' the minds o' me young impressionable bairns!" Matt said loudly to accent his point and finish his thought.

"There he is!" Alex interrupted him pointing to the fallen figure of Pierre Dûçot lying on the ground a few yards ahead.

Next to Pierre was a fluffy white cat licking his cheek and me-owing. The two hurried to reach his side with Matthew opening and delving a hand into his ever-present medical bag to pull out his bottle of smelling salts.

"Hey! I'd know that fluffy little furball anywhere!" exclaimed Alex bending over to scoop up Charmer into his arms and stare into the cat's alluring blue eyes. "How did you get in here?" he asked the feline rhetorically as she shook her head causing the charms on her collar to knock against one another in a flurry of tinkling music. "Well? What're you waiting for?" Alex inquired impatiently as Matt just stood there with the vial of the potent mixture in his upraised mitt.

"I be just cogitatin' tha' 'twould be a shame te wake him – he looks te be so peaceful!"

"Matt…!"

"An' it be so nice and quiet in here without his caterwaulin'. Why spoil everything?"

"Matt!"

"Well once he be awake 'twill be on your head – dunna say I didna warn ye." he foretold grimly kneeling down beside the head of the unconscious man, uncapping the bottle of the reviving potion and waving it beneath his nose so that its fumes escaped and wafted upward into his nostrils. "Charmer most likely fell te this place the same way tha' we ha' come te it. The feline likely tripped the release lever – wherever it was – and fell through the trap door. It be quite interestin' te note that both Pierre an' the cat found the trapdoor's release mechanism." Matthew tapped his forehead. "They say it takes one-"

"Look away…!" Pierre warned choking and coughing.

"Hmmm…." Matthew grunted regarding the vial in his hand curiously. "He should ha' come to consciousness earlier. I just may ha' te replenish this bottle with a new mix." he observed sniffing its rim cautiously and wrinkling his nose at the acrid odor which was not pungent enough.

"LOOK…AWAY!!!" gasped the semi-conscious man who, with a sudden spurt of strength, pushed Matt aside and attempted desperately to sit up.

"It looks like he be talkin' te YOU, Alex. I wonder what he wants." Matt puzzled to himself as he recovered from Pierre's shove.

"Do not look into its eyes, Alex!" cried Pierre as he rose painfully to his feet and limped toward him. "It is trying to mesmerize you!" he elucidated encircling his hands around the cat's body and roughly pulling the feline away from the arms of the young man who was still admiring her sweet face and azure blue eyes.

Dropping the cat to the ground Pierre wiped his palms one

against the other to symbolically clean them and shuddered.

"Thank HEAVENS I saved you in time! I have suspected this for a long temps mais now I am certain that...that CAT is one of Grand-mère's minions! It is spying on us and has likely spirited us to this place – wherever we are!" Pierre garrulously imparted to his companions as he looked about in fear while dusting off his clothing and straightening his tie which remained askew despite his several well-meaning attempts.

"Balderdash! De ye understand what I told ye, Alex? It was nice and quiet down here only a moment ago!" Matt said thunderously as Charmer scampered away to sit in a corner and gaze at them watchfully without blinking. "Then we could hear ourselves think! Then we could think about how te get outta here!"

"And…. And…where is "here"?" Pierre asked fearfully as he jumped in fright startled by seeing his own shadow on a wall and wiped at a cobweb clinging to his hair.

Matthew bestowed Alex with an "I told you so" smile and then addressed Pierre's question, "Well we're not in Grand-mère's secret lair, tha's te be sure. When ye went about bangin' yer feet all o'er the floor o' the gazebo ye must ha' triggered some sort o' device because the bench I was restin' on collapsed inward and I fell on me keister te this place we are now. There must ha' been a different type o' knob ye triggered subsequently because as I be lookin' upward, bewildered and puzzlin' upon what happened, a section o' this ceiling on t'other side o' the room slid down at an angle depositin' Alex te the ground o'er there." Matt summarized as he pointed to the space behind Pierre. "Silence ensued, fer the most part, while we tried to get our bearings when suddenly we heard a bunch o' caterwaulin' and loud stampin' goin' on above us which ended in one big "KABOOM" and we knew ye must ha' landed-"

"Succumbed to the same fate." Alex corrected Matthew.

"Aye." affirmed Matt with an irritated glance at Alex for

interrupting him. "I was all fer proceedin' te find a way out o' this dungeon but Alex convinced me tha' we had te retrace our steps te look fer ye."

"Merci mille fois, dear boy. You are my true friend." Pierre said gratefully to Alex while looking at Matthew reproachfully.

"Matt was afraid you might be hurt." Alex translated while Matt favored him with another irritated look.

"An' here ye be. Not a scratch on ye an' sleepin' like a newborn babe in the woods!" Matthew spit out the words as he folded his arms with finality.

"Mais…." Pierre eked out and then lowered his chin gulping down hard with his Adam's apple bobbing up and down during the process. "But," he continued meekly, "where are we now, médecin?"

Matthew threw Alex a silencing look and then considered his answer carefully. Looking at Pierre he decided that the man looked tortured and penitent enough at having caused this predicament and so he answered frankly.

"I neglected te mention that little detail, now, didn't I? I apologize te ye, Pierre." he acknowledged to the man with the large fearful eyes. "It appears te me tha' this be some sort o' a combination root cellar and storm shelter. An', as I said, we fell inte it by accident."

"If this is true, then what is…IT, doing here?" Pierre asked outstretching his arm and pointing with his shaking index finger to the corner where Charmer crouched regarding him warily while he flicked it up and down several times in loathing.

Matthew chuckled outright.

"The laddie an' I were just conjecturin' on tha' very same circumstance and we ha' come te the conclusion tha' the puir animal merely fell te this spot by chance. Just like us, the feline be seeking cover from the rain, triggered the release lever and fell through the trap door te where we be now."

CHAPTER 46

"I <u>do</u> hope that Elvie is all right!" said Edith wringing her hands anxiously.

"Well, she's been through a lot lately." Cari rejoined with a compassionate smile handing her aunt a cup of coffee.

"If you are referring to that fiasco with Pierre in the woods I hardly see any humor in it." Edith said misinterpreting Cari's smile. "And if you are implying that Elvie's experience there played any part in putting her in a hospital bed I am ashamed of you. Just ashamed! How dare you speak so disrespectfully of your uncle. I knew that Jeanette should have taken a firmer line of discipline with you when you were growing up." she scolded Cari before collapsing into a fit of weeping.

Cari watched helplessly as she handed her aunt a tissue from the box on the side table in the hospital waiting room. She had already suspected that her aunt's nervous concern for Elvie, though genuine, masked a different, underlying seed of sorrowful agitation. She was not sure how she should broach such a painful topic, but after some forethought and deliberation on the matter Cari decided to ease into it indirectly.

"The doctors say that Elvie's case of pneumonia is not very serious and they have already got the high fever under control. All she needs is some rest. Calvin is in with her right now but we will be allowed to visit with her after he comes out of her room. You know, I saw the look on your face when Mary Jo mentioned her friend, Simon.... I know that it must have hurt. I know that you two were very close."

"Not just <u>close</u>, Cari." exclaimed Edith sniffing and dabbing at her tearstained eyes with the tissue Cari had given to her. "We were twins. Twins run in our family, you know." she shared with her. "Although he was only two minutes older than I, he was my older brother and I looked up to him!" she continued shakily again patting gently at a renewed bout of tears falling from her eyes and letting forth one final sob. "And to hear Mary Jo speaking of this Simon bonding with Pierre like a brother.... <u>Our</u> Simon should have been the person bonding with Pierre as a brother. Oh, they would have found so much in common, Cari. Simon believed in honor and moral behavior – Pierre believes in that, too." she said sniffing loudly and blowing her nose. "Simon loved sailing and fishing – so does Pierre. Oh, and CHILDREN. Pierre and Simon both love, in Simon's case – loved, children. Remember how Simon loved children? He said he was going to have four or five when he found the right woman to marry and settle down with. Remember how he was with you, Cari – do you remember…?"

Cari sat down at a table in the cafeteria of the LT General Hospital and mindlessly followed a lonesome, floating tea leaf in her cup of brew with her eyes. A warm, masculine voice jogged her out of her apathy.

"Cari? Cari, are you alright?" Cyrus inquired as he sat down uninvited.

"Oh. Yes, I'm fine. Hello, Cyrus." she said cautiously without lifting her head or establishing eye contact as she did not know how much of Elvie's story to believe or disbelieve.

"I heard of the illness in your family. Elvira has taken ill?"

"Yes." she said shortly as she started to rise from her chair to stand upright.

"I brought these for her. I thought they would brighten up the room a bit." he said hurriedly raising a large bouquet of flowers to forestall her departure. "But, when I went to her room they wouldn't let me in. In fact, her husband – Calvin, is it(?) – was downright rude." he complained as he tried to capture her gaze with a tilt of his head toward her face.

"I believe the doctors will only allow one person at a time to be at her bedside. And she is still slightly contagious." Cari stated aloofly with the added warning as she pushed back her chair and walked away from the lunchroom-style table with Cyrus following on her heels.

"Could you at least take them to her for me and extend to her my best wishes for her speedy recovery?"

Cari regarded Cyrus thoughtfully. He sounded sincere but could she trust him? She had always been taught to judge not lest she her- self be judged but did this mean that she could not at least be wary? She knew that Elvie would never accept flowers from Cyrus, that is if Calvin ever let them get to her bedside, and she would throw a fit of hysteria at the mere thought of the man she considered her dire enemy being in the hospital. But, then, she felt for Cyrus. He seemed to be such a nice man. He was only reaching out in friendship. And he looked so sad and bewildered at why they were ostracizing him. She let out a deep sigh and took the flowers from him.

"Thank you for the flowers, Cyrus." she said as she separated from him abruptly and rushed down the hall only to collide with a bearded gentleman who also carried a large bouquet of flowers. "Oh! I'm terribly sorry, sir." Cari apologized sincerely.

"Quite alright. Excuse me!" he responded brusquely pulling his wide brimmed hat down lower over his head to cover his face.

"Do I know you…?" she called out in inquiry to the stranger as he walked quickly down the corridor.

"Who was that?" queried Cyrus as he caught up to her.

"I do not know. But his voice sounded very familiar.… Well." she concluded shaking her head to clear it. "I must bring this sandwich to my aunt in the waiting room. She is so distraught over Elvira's condition and…other problems that she will not eat. And she has to put something in her stomach! It's not healthy to go without food for so long and she needs her nutrition! They will not let you eat in the waiting room, but maybe she can sneak a bite!" she replied in a suddenly garrulous response.

"Cari!" exclaimed Edith shocked at her niece's choice of company. "What are you doing consorting with this man?"

"Excuse me, Mrs. Dûçot, I meant no offense. It seems everybody is taking offense at me today and I don't know why. But I was just about to extend an invitation to you and your whole family to come over to Candlestick Manor for a tour of the house. I heard from the society ladies how interested you are in historical sites and I thought you would enjoy it. I thought that, maybe, afterwards, you could offer to me your opinions on historical matters."

Edith regarded him dubiously. Was he truly sincere or the monster that Elvie had made him out to be? She could not tell. Looking at him now, seemingly so humble and unsure of himself – so eager to please, he did not seem so dangerous an individual. And she would love to see the rest of the house. When she had been there previously she had spent most of her time in polite conversation with the ladies of the historical society. Perhaps she could sway him from his intention to tear down the manor. If she could change his attitude and make Cyrus see the light she would actually be performing a public service for the community. She did believe in giving people the benefit of the doubt and it would not be the first time that Elvie had become a victim of her own flights of fancy…. She had made up her mind.

"What a cordial invitation." Edith exclaimed. "Of course, we would love to attend!"

CHAPTER 47

"I told you. They have to be missing longer than overnight in order for us to begin an investigation into their disappearance." Inspector Lahy explained to Rand calmly.

"I KNOW that. Procedure. Bureaucracy. But we are dealing with people's lives here and my wife's aunt is going out of her mind with worry. Plus, my cousin is missing, too, as well as my best friend." Rand uttered urgently. "I am already searching the area for them. You and your men know this land better than I do. If you could just start looking a few hours earlier-"

"Protocol is protocol. Hope you understand. Come and see me later, though, and I'll be happy to help you." Jim Lahy assured him despite his objections as he ushered Rand to the door guiding him with a friendly palm on his back. "Don't forget to come back." he reminded his involuntarily retreating back.

'Same as in Charlottesville.' he thought to himself. Where did these kooks come from!? He waited a few seconds monitoring the second hand of his watch and when he was sure that he would not be seen he pulled back the curtain covering the police precinct window. He watched Randmore depart down the street. That guy had some kind of nerve throwing his weight around and asking him to make an exception just for him. He was doing it all around town – asking favors, that is. Anson Davis, the cobbler, told him that McKinley had prevailed upon his good nature to do a rush job on a custom pair of boots. Boy! Anson had just been bragging to him about what a beautiful job he had done making big shot Randmore

McKinley's boots. He had used prime leather, cut to specification. He had sewn the seams stitch by stitch; tooled by hand strategic sections of the leather and on completion of the footwear had buffed and polished each boot to a high sheen. Well, look at them now! 'What a lack of respect!' he noted clicking his tongue disapprovingly. He had asked Anson to do a rush job on the dress boots as if it was absolutely, positively imperative he have them right away – as if he needed them for a special occasion. Yet practically the next day after he picks them up they were crusted with mud, the leather was discolored and weatherworn and they looked about five years old. He was about to let the curtain loose to fall back into place when he saw Cari. You just could not miss that flowing auburn hair. She was walking with Cyrus Sykes. He owned half the town. That McKinley had better be careful or he'll sweep her off her feet. He could potentially lose her to Cyrus as he lost Callie to Dudley. Now Dudley was in and he was out. He closed his eyes in pain as a pang of grief assaulted his heart. He still thought of her with her silken blond hair and musical laughter sometimes. How he missed her companionship! Yes, McKinley better be careful or next time it might be him who's out and Cyrus who's in....

Joan Collins looked at Cari and Cyrus with cagey contemplation as she caught sight of them crossing the square together with his hand on her arm. That two-timing harlot. She had heard her swear to poor, dear, sweet Randmore that after her flirtation with LeLoup that there would be no one else! Yet, now here she was doing it again! How he put up with her indiscretions was beyond her! 'He was so forbearing.' she contemplated in admiration. If only Randmore had married her beautiful and faithful daughter, Jocelyn, he would have had a wife he could depend on! A wife who would not embarrass him or two-time him when he wasn't constantly holding her hand! Cyrus Sykes…. She sure knew how to pick 'em. When she was arranging for a cab at the train station someone had pointed him out to his traveling companion and she overheard him say that he owned half the town. He seemed a little young for her but she supposed that for a woman like Cari who was just looking for a fling it didn't matter much. She probably liked 'em young. Robbing the cradle wouldn't prove to be any obstacle to her. At least that Aunt Edith of hers had learned her lesson with that Paté philanderer – it was in all the papers. Even Cari had been involved with him. He had a wife he was cheating on and kids, to boot! Joan thought a bit then cocked her head. Paté. The name sounded like an hors d'oeuvre…. But the article in the **Daily Trumpet** said that wasn't really his name. It was Falzigger. Anyway, Edith never strayed from Pierre again – and who would want to? It seemed that Cari, however, had not yet learned her lesson. Well, she was here for Mr. Dûçot and not to engage in intrigues or gossip. Edith knew that she would do anything for Mr. Dûçot after he helped bring Jocelyn's rapist to justice and saved her, Joan, from his crazy brother. They were like two criminal peas in a pod, those two. Although, she heard tell that Chris Colden had turned to God. As a God-fearing Christian she hoped that he truly was born again. Now, Mr. Dûçot needed her help. It seems that the cook at the house here was unable to cook well enough to satisfy the taste of Mr. Dûçot's sophisticated palate satisfactorily. He had expressed his dissatisfaction with the food preparation to Edith and, good wife that she was now trying to be, she called her to come to the rescue. Well, she would not fail him. 'Hang on, Pierre,' she thought, 'I am coming!'

CHAPTER 48

"I'm STARVING!" announced Alex while kneeling over some rubble in a corner to sift through it as Matthew groaned aloud in hunger and Pierre laid a hand on his empty belly.

Alex had put a voice to something that they were both trying not to think about. They had been in the root cellar an indeterminable amount of time with every minute and hour passing at a snail's pace.

"Look! I found a can of tuna fish!"

"Lookin' te feed the cat, are ye now, laddie?" Matthew said in jest irritably as his stomach grumbled at the mere mention of food.

"Peut-être he can find some milk and cookies in there, aussi." Pierre quipped idly pointing a finger at the pile of debris while Alex picked up a rock and started to strike its jagged, pointed end against the top of the metal can making small dents in a circular pattern.

"You're both just jealous because I found some food and you did not!" Alex said scraping at the metal harder with the rock in an attempt to open the can more quickly.

"Are you...peut-être planning on sharing the contents of that can of poisson?" Pierre asked Alex while yawning with prefabricated boredom.

"Why?" Alex asked suspiciously suddenly halting his assault and battery upon the now pitted and pockmarked container to squint his eyes distrustfully at Pierre as he wondered at his angle.

Pierre casually pulled a pocketknife from his pocket and allowed the small can opener tool to dangle from its case. He smiled slightly as he saw Alex's eyes widen covetously as he watched the opener swing back and forth and licked his lips.

"Odds Bodkins! All right! Mon ami, Pierre!" congratulated Matthew as he patted him on the shoulder and with a sharp, graduated meow Charmer trotted over to sit on his lap and purr adoringly to the man who had once thrown her to the corner of the room.

"Aww.... Now, that's not fair! I won't have any left for myself." Alex whined. "Three against one? Aww, man!" he concluded in defeat knowing that he needed to use Pierre's can opener but not wishing to relinquish shares of tuna fish for the favor.

"A bite o' food is better than none at all, laddie." Matt reminded him.

"And I have always shared my food avec you, Mr. Small Fry. And, anyway, it is your own fault. I have told you toutes les fois to be prepared!" Pierre refreshed his memory illustrating his point by shaking the pocket knife at him teasingly.

"Well...what has she done?!" Alex said glumly pointing at Charmer resentfully as she rubbed against him purring violently and eyeing the unopened can in anticipation.

"Canna ye ha' compassion fer the puir beast, laddie? It be obvious it be as hungry as us." Matthew pleaded lobbying on Charmer's behalf.

The cat continued to purr wildly at this statement and moved to Matt's side as if voicing consummate agreement with his plea and her appreciation, too.

"Dunna ye try te get on me good side ye furry little charlatan. Yer bamboozlin' ways willna work on me. I only be lookin' out fer ye fer Megan's sake. She'd break down in tears if ye came te an ill pass." he said gruffly as Charmer climbed onto his lap and snuggled against his chest.

"That cat is a fair-weather friend. All right, all right! You can ALL have a share." he relented staring down the self-serving feline.

"But I," Alex said to Pierre defiantly as he snatched the pocket knife from him by the can opener, "get the first piece!"

"Mais, bien sûr, you will get the first goûte." Pierre assured him as he watched Alex pierce the edge of the can and force the blade along the rim until it separated the top from the body of the container to reveal a small piece of tuna steak.

The tuna was slightly grayish and Alex regarded it dubiously. He sniffed it to ascertain its freshness and then raised the container to eye level to study it curiously.

"What ye be lookin' at, laddie?" Matthew asked impatiently – but holding his temper – while his stomach grumbled noisily at the wait in a protest saying: "feed me".

"The expiration date." he elucidated causing Matthew to wail in frustration and tear at his hair. "But it smells funny and the color doesn't look too...wholesome. I was only making sure that it was safe to ingest." Alex explained.

"The boy has gone fou." stated Pierre with a slight smile as Matthew got to his feet wiping his mouth with an unspeakable incredulity he could not express and the displaced Charmer jumped from his rapidly disappearing perch on Matt's lap to push the now opened can of tuna from Alex's hands and upend it along with its contents onto the dirt floor.

"She did that on purpose!" Alex exclaimed to the others accusatorily as they all watched the cat insinuate the tip of her nose under the edge of the container and finally nose it over and away exposing the fillet.

"Why that greedy little animal. She wanted tout the poisson for herself!" stated Pierre in angry surprise.

The tuna fillet was peppered with dirt and the three men looked at it – Matthew in particular – regretfully.

"She seems more interested in the can than in the tuna fish." Alex pointed out heartsick at the loss of his dinner and trying to keep his mind focused on something other than his lost meal.

"The laddie be correct. The dratted varmint be playin' with it!" said Matthew in disbelief.

"Now that Charmer's turned it over, though, she seems to have lost interest in playing with the can." noted Alex. "She's just standing next to it."

"Peut-être…she wanted to turn it over." Pierre said quirking an eyebrow as he watched Charmer stand at attention triumphantly as if she had just completed an important mission.

"Ye know what ye are, Pierre?" Matt asked him rhetorically. "Yer akin te the boy who cried wolf!"

"Qui est ce garçon who cries: WOLF?"

"Ye mean te tell me ye've ne'er heard the tale o' the boy who cried wolf?" asked Matthew in incredulity.

"Alors. He must have been a very bright boy because if he cried for LeLoup he would have come."

"Canna ye believe this…? I canna believe me own ears! Such colossal-"

"He is right, Matt." said Alex interrupting him while bending down and picking up the upended can only to have Matthew gawk at him stupefied.

"Dunna encourage the feebleminded, lad." Matthew admonished him indicating Pierre with a nod of his head.

"Or he may be close to right." Alex corrected himself. "There's a note in here signed by LeLoup." he revealed lifting out a cellophane wrapped paper from the bottom of the can. "It COULD be just a coincidence-"

"Let me take a gander at that piece o' paper." Matt said curtly taking the paper from him; liberating it from its cellophane protected confines; unfolding it and reading the note aloud. "Take twelve steps te the north wall and then take the third staircase te yer right. What be the meaning o' this? Some sort o' riddle?"

"Look! Charmer went to the wall over there! Didn't Megan say that Charmer knew the way through underground tunnels – maybe that's the north wall!"

"Alex, ONE, you are, TWO, imagining, THREE, things." Pierre remonstrated him as he navigated several long strides to the wall in front of him while counting them aloud between the words of his admonishment. "And I will prove this to you. Observe!" he said shaking a leg up high and continuing to punctuate his words with enumeration for each of his ongoing strides. "It, FOUR, is, FIVE, obvious, SIX, to me, SEVEN, that, EIGHT, there is no, NINE, truth whatsoever, TEN, in that, ELEVEN, message, TWELVE...." said Pierre slowly in flabbergasted astonishment as he knocked the tip of his nose against the wall in front of him and then looked behind him to lock eyes with Matt questioningly. "How could this be?" he queried.

"Bah! Purely coincidence. Purely coincidental. And what is it with tha' animal!?" he asked angrily choosing to take out his wrath on the one animal smaller than he was who could not talk back. "She be constantly shaking her head to and fro and tha' jingle-jangle noise be wearin' on me nerves! Who's te say what creepy-crawlers be down in this unclean hole an' she likely ha' got all o' them!" proclaimed Matthew with finality.

CHAPTER 49

"I got a postcard from Eleanor the other day." Cari revealed as she sat down at the breakfast table in the pantry with a tray of sandwiches, mugs of coffee for each of them and a full creamer and sugar bowl.

"Boy! If she ever found out that Matt was missing she'd go nuts! Are you gonna write back to her?" Callie asked with big, round eyes filled with a mixture of concern and curiosity as they all reached for their sandwiches and coffee.

"I'll have to. She will get suspicious if I do not."

"Well, it's your own fault, Cari. If you hadn't been so polite throughout the years we wouldn't have this problem. But no.... Miss. Manners, Cari Chesterfield McKinley, always answers her correspondence.... She always returns telephone calls and reciprocates visits. And, heaven forbid, she forgets to send someone a thank you card! So, of COURSE, she's going to expect you to write her back. You have established a pattern of politeness, here. You're practically OBLIGATED to send her some kind of response." Mary Jo enumerated hammering home her point.

"Okay. Okay, Mary Jo. I get your point. However, in my letter to her I just will not bring up that Matthew is missing and may be lying out there somewhere helpless, or worse. But the jig is going to be up eventually when Matthew does not respond to the missive that she sent to him." Cari replied whipping Matthew's letter from Eleanor out of her pocket which she had just picked up from the Laureltown Post Office and waving it in the air for her to see.

"Could you pass the creamer, please?" Callie interjected.

Cari watched as Mary Jo passed Callie the cream and she poured all of it into her cup. Callie glanced up to notice not only Cari's but Mary Jo's gaze upon her.

"I hope no one wanted any." she said guiltily. "I apologize for indulging but I never could get used to the taste of just plain coffee – it's so bitter." she said squinching up her facial features.

"Well, then why do you drink it?" Mary Jo inquired taking the empty creamer from her and turning it upside down over her mug in the hopes that at least one droplet of the liquid might be left to fall out and dilute her coffee.

"Do not worry about it, Mary Jo. I will get you some more fresh cream out of the refrigerator." Cari said standing up to walk across the room to the icebox.

"Could you also get me a Danish pastry from that platter on the counter?" Mary Jo requested somewhat meekly.

"And one of those chocolate chip muffins for me?" Callie added her order to Mary Jo's sheepishly.

"What am I, a waitress?" Cari asked over her shoulder as she bumped into a familiar adversary.

"Joan! Where did you come from?" Cari queried with surprise wondering if their shaky, temporary truce was still being reciprocated.

"Your Aunt Edith called me over. She told me you needed help in the kitchen over here."

"We sure do need help!" Callie piped up dolefully. "Trudy's not much of a baker. Those pastries over there are all store-bought."

"AND. They are also very GREASY." Mary Jo added to spite her cousin, Callie, who was responsible for their purchase.

"We'll have no more of that! It seems I got here just in time!" Joan said with a repressed smile.

"Not soon enough, Joan. Thank you for coming. My husband

claims that he has not had a decent meal since he left Chesterhollow and your cooking." Edith asserted matter-of-factly as she swept regally into the room.

"How is Mr. Dûçot? Where is he?" Joan inquired avidly of the suddenly silent and solemn quartet looking at them expectantly.

Finally Cari spoke up, "Pierre, Alex and Matthew Flanderly are missing."

"NO!" she gasped. "I hope those Coldens aren't at the root of all this trouble. They hate Pierre for being so cultured and honorable!"

"Yes...." Cari said with a suppressed smile and chuckle at the complimentary statement as she suspected that Joan had a small crush on Pierre that she was not willing to admit, even to herself. "Well. What I do know," she finally admitted when she was able to contain her mirth and speak simultaneously, "is that Pierre went to berate this gentleman, Cyrus, for inappropriate behaviour toward a lady and Alex and Matt accompanied him. The lady in question is Elvira Maison. She was Elvira Green when you first met her. She married Calvin Maison since then."

"Calvin is the brother of that Dudley who rescued me and Pierre – I mean Mr. Dûçot." Joan said shyly and blushed a bright crimson as she knew Edith did not care for her familiar use of her husband's first name.

"Yes. Exactly." she concurred pretending not to notice Joan's heightened coloring. "So, he went to confront him on that score with Alex and Matt and they never returned. They-"

"Oh! I hope dear Randmore – Mr. McKinley – isn't missing, too!" exclaimed Joan in distress worrying her lower lip.

"No, actually, he is out right now looking for them. The police have yet to list the case as a missing persons situation, so they are not actively searching for them but Calvin and Dudley-"

"The hero?"

"Yes, the hero who rescued you and Pierre. Calvin and Dudley have both joined Rand in the search and we are <u>very</u> certain that Pierre, Alex and Matt will turn up soon safe and sound!" Cari said assuredly.

"YES. I am certain as well." proclaimed Edith. "And that is why I need to enlist your help, Joan, to arrange a beautiful welcome home dinner party for the three of them."

"I will make all of Mr. Dûçot's favorite foods!" said Joan eagerly.

"I am counting on it, Joan. And, I need you, Cari, to rent a suitable hall for the party to take place in. I need you, Mary Jo, to arrange for appropriate music and dancing for the evening – as I know that is your forte. And I need you, Callie, to arrange for appropriate floral arrangements."

"Where would I go for that, Edith?" asked Callie who felt like a shy little girl once more whenever she spoke to her.

"Well, dear…perhaps Cari can help you. You know, by the by, I bumped into a man at the hospital when I was visiting Elvie and he was carrying a very large, impressive bouquet. He did not even apologize for his faux pas but merely raised the arrangement higher to shield his face from my justifiably irate scrutiny and hurried along without saying a word. It was almost as if he were running away from me! He was very rude. Most definitely a motley and uncouth sort. REALLY!"

"You know, I believe I encountered the same man, Aunt Edith. He almost knocked me down – but he <u>did</u> excuse himself. And it was not even his fault. I tried to apologize to him because if I had been more careful I would not have collided with him. His voice sounded very familiar…."

"And what will you be doing, Edith?" asked Callie.

"Pardon me, child?"

"What will you be doing for the party!?"

"Oh, I will not be doing anything for the party per se, dear. I shall be out searching for Pierre because as all of us know there can be no party without Pierre!"

CHAPTER 50

"Charmer may be shaking her head, but she's not scratching herself." Alex was quick to point out to Matthew as he approached Charmer at the north wall, picked her up and inspected her neck for fleas or other vermin amidst a sudden purring noise which erupted from the cat at the human contact.

"Then tell us, I dare ye, why the feline be shakin' her head." Matthew challenged him folding his arms one over the other across his chest.

"Well. Maybe it's sign language."

"Laddie. Yer in danger o' bein' as unbelievable as Pierre. Ye dunna want tha', do ye?" he pleaded. "Then, not only would I be trapped here with no food, no water, no warm fire te relax by, an' no means o' escape, but I would be alone in me sanity, as well. Say ye wouldna do this te me – say it." entreated the distraught Irishman.

"Why would Charmer be shaking her head? Why?" Alex asked himself aloud ignoring Matthew's obvious attempt at humor with the insincere plea which was mainly espoused for Pierre's benefit.

"Mais, bien sûr. You can figure this one out – you both wear a collar." observed Pierre with a crooked grin as he noticed Alex's neckchain which had come out from under his shirt and lay exposed against his chest for all to see. "As you Américains say, it takes quelqu'un to know one!"

Alex looked at Pierre. He then looked at the collar around Charmer's neck. Pausing in thought for a moment Alex looked down at the chain around his own neck from which dangled the key

MAISON LEGACY

from the tackle box which he had salvaged from their last vacation together. There was silence in the cold, dank room.

"The seule différence is that you, Alex, wear <u>one</u> key and the cat has many, comment dit-on, ornaments. Peut-être she is proud of them and wishes to show them off." Pierre speculated sarcastically sharing an amused look with Matthew as they both of them considered the thought processes of the inexperienced man many years their junior and lacking in savoir faire attempting to be a super sleuth.

"Pierre...you're a GENIUS! You've just given us the answer!" Alex said to the man patronizing him. "Just as <u>I</u> am wearing a key around <u>my</u> neck," Alex explained while sorting through the charms on Charmer's neck, "maybe the cat is wearing a key around <u>her</u> neck!"

A burst of laughter from the other men followed his out-of-bounds theory as Matthew and Pierre both looked fondly at the ingenuous "whiz kid".

"Laddie. Ye're sounding like me daughter. Tha' puir beast ha' not a clue te what we're searchin' fer. I hate te say it, but it looks te me like we're trapped down here an' we'll not be goin' nowhere until someone up above comes te rescue us!" Matt said solemnly, suddenly serious.

"That is correct, Alex. Quelqu'un must find us or we will be trapped here...hopeless...and eventually starve to death. Where is that key?!!!" cried Pierre in self-induced panic rushing to Alex's side and practically choking Charmer as he grabbed at the feline's collar.

"And here it is! Let go, Pierre, you're going to make me lose it!" Alex fussed as he wrestled with Pierre for control of Charmer's collar. "Now," he said clearing his throat with a grunt after winning control of the cat and inching slightly away from him as he attempted to remove the pet collar, "it makes sense that the keyhole should be around here somewhere because it would correlate with the clue! That's funny...." Alex said bewildered as he fumbled with the collar on the cat's neck.

"What are you playing with, Alex? Don't you réaliser that Pierre Dûçot is becoming, que veut dire, claustrophobic! I feel faint.... I have a very delicate constitution. But then you would not be expected to know that. Would you stop playing with that cat!" he clamored impatiently at what he believed to be was Alex's inaction.

"I am not playing with the cat!" Alex explained while continuing to rotate the collar in a circular motion around the exceptionally thick fur of her neck as Charmer let forth several throaty moans of protest at his manhandling. "I can't find the buckle of the collar so that I can undo it and then take it off. But, the good news is that I have located the keyhole. It's a small keyhole, so I almost didn't see it, but it's here. And if Charmer would only hold still so I could get the key into the lock-"

"Arrête! Stop your struggling you horrible animal!" yelled Pierre as Alex finally maneuvered the cat into the appropriate position and was able to insert and turn the key in the lock.

A twelve inch by twelve inch square door pulled down to form a ledge. Inside, in a horizontal row, were three round, yellow knobs. The numbers on each knob were almost rubbed off. A faded number "2", though practically indistinguishable, could be recognized on the center knob, however, the numbers on the first and third knobs were indeterminable. Matthew moved to the fore to study the knobs.

"'Tis no wonder I couldna find the release at the top o' tha' staircase! The buttons te push-"

"Or pull." interposed Pierre meekly.

"are o'er here!" Matt finished his sentence in the face of Pierre's interruption.

"When we were coming this way I saw two other staircases on either side of this storm shelter." Alex added helpfully.

"Tha' makes THREE stairways altogether. Aye.... Now, this be makin' perfect sense! So. All WE have te do is press the button-"

"Or pull." Pierre reminded Matthew a second time.

"marked "3" and then exit via the third stairway – if tha' message be correct." Matthew concluded casting Pierre a slightly disgruntled look for his consistent interruptions.

"And we can get out of here! Finally. Mary Jo must be worried sick about me – about ALL of us." Alex noted cheerfully for the first time since this ill-fated misadventure began.

"Me thanks te ye, Miss. Charmer. I be in yer debt." Matthew acknowledged appreciatively to the feline who seemed to understand and trotted over to rub her body against and walk between Matthew's legs purring wildly.

"It will be merveilleux to leave this place. Without the proper sanitary facilities available.... To put it delicately.... Let us just say I need the fresh air." Pierre said looking meaningfully in Matthew's direction as Alex smothered a laugh.

"Why ye four-flushin'-"

"Interesting choice of words, médecin. In any case, we must focus on the problème before us-"

"Yer quite right, mon ami." agreed Matthew stepping up to Pierre and peering at him closely with the implication that he was the problem.

"Do not be childish, Matthew. I merely wish to point out that the numbers are rubbed off two of the knobs. How do we know which of the two is number one and which knob is number two?" Pierre asked.

"That's right! Suppose we choose the wrong knob?" Alex said.

"Dunna worry, laddie. 'Tis simple. We already know the center knob be number two. It is obvious, therefore, that the knob te the left side be number one and the knob te the right o' it be three. Ye see? Left te right. Perfect," Matt paused to let the echoing vibrations of that one word reverberate and hang in the air and linger a bit before completing his phrase, "sense!" he ended walking back and forth with a methodical gait and a scholarly bent to his logical approach.

"Mais. I say that the knob to the right of the center knob is number one et the knob sur the gauche of the center knob is number three!" proclaimed Pierre adamantly throwing his own contention into the ring for consideration and thereby adding a fly into Matt's ointment.

"But tha' makes no sense, dunna ye see? The whole country reads and writes from left to right!" argued Matt.

"C'est vrai. This is true...." he admitted reluctantly.

"I have to say, Pierre, Matt does have a point. I'm behind him one hundred percent." said Alex stalwartly as he put his hands to the knobs one after the other. "But, we can release each button and try them all out!"

"Do not touch ces choses, Alex! The wrong knob could be, comment dit-on, booby trapped!" warned Pierre in alarm.

"I was only trying to be helpful."

"Please, Alex. Keep your helpfulness to yourself."

"I hate te admit it, laddie, but Pierre may be right. Not about secret traps an' such, mind ye. But look around ye.... This whole chamber be in disrepair an' disarray. The cellar be an old refuge an' any false move could have a dire consequence!"

"Hey! What's this?" Alex asked with curiosity unearthing a worn leather pouch from the brown pile of dirt beneath the three knobs.

"Would you put that down, Alex! You are always playing with something!" complained Pierre peevishly as he pulled the faded brown rectangular briefcase from him and threw it back to its original resting place.

"You are a big bully – do you know that, Pierre?"

"Excusez-moi for wishing to concentrate on the matter at hand!"

"Well, I say we press the third button!" said Alex with a challenge in his tone of voice as he reached for the knob.

"Arrête, Alex!" Pierre exclaimed pushing his hand aside. "I say we must pull the first knob!" Pierre said authoritatively as he started to pull the first knob.

"An' I say, we investigate the situation further. Those two other stairways Alex saw be the bones o' contention te address primarily!" Matthew admonished Pierre as he sought to hold back the knob that Pierre was attempting to pull.

"Alex!" Pierre shouted. "What are you doing?!" he demanded heatedly letting go of the first knob in order to grab hold of Alex's wrist to prevent him from pushing the third knob.

Pierre's abrupt release of the first knob to the left of the center knob labeled "2" caught Matthew off guard and, therefore, with the resistance from Pierre's pulling action suddenly taken away Matthew fell forward thus pushing the knob inward with his unrestrained force. A rumbling erupted from somewhere above them.

"Now ye've done it! I dunna know what ye've done but it canna be amountin' te any good!" Matthew scolded Pierre as he gazed upward at the ceiling; heard the sound of rocks pushing against each other and felt the firmament beneath his feet move. "Now, dunna touch anything further – laddie?! What're ye doing?" he roared as Alex started to push knob "2" and, also, the button-shaped knob to its right.

"I am trying to compensate for the first button-topped knob on the left side having been pressed." he replied.

"Ye're gonna make it worse – so stop it or else we will ha' nary a chance o' ever gettin' out o' here!"

"C'est correct, Alex. Matt is right. Mais, you must pull the knobs, in any case. Comme ça." Pierre said seeking to demonstrate with his hand gripping knob "2".

"I said dunna touch that!" Matt cried in frustration stamping his foot repetitively to accentuate each of his spoken words.

Matthew saw Charmer slide under his upraised descending foot and swerved to avoid stepping on the feline. However, this spur of the moment maneuver caused him to unwittingly lose his balance and fall backwards. He grasped onto Pierre's upper arm for support as he tumbled yanking it backwards as he sought to steady himself consequently causing Pierre to inadvertently pull out the knob marked "2" which he held within the grasp of the hand of that very same arm. Pebbles, rocks and dirt began to fall from the now collapsing ceiling above them. All three men sought to shield their heads from the falling debris.

"To the staircase!" Matthew yelled above the din of oncoming debris as he turned and ran back toward the original chamber he had fallen to.

Charmer and Pierre followed hard on his heels with Alex hesitating, looking toward the crumbling box-like depression in the wall which was rapidly disappearing wherein lay the three knobs and then at the fleeing threesome who were fading into the distance. He knew he was in danger of being left behind. Finally, he made a decision. Alex made his way over fallen debris amidst the onslaught of descending rocks to the panel of knobs, which hardly resembled a panel any longer, and lifted out the brown leather pouch. Turning, he paused to avert more falling rubbish while he coughed violently, surrounded as he was by clouds of thick dust. Stuffing the pouch under his shirt he hurried to catch up with the others. Through the various chambers he flew ducking and dodging until he saw the other three. Charmer let forth a high-pitched meow of unbridled urgency with her paw on the first step of the staircase.

"We were waitin' on ye, laddie. What took ye?"

"It is obvious. Alex stopped for his milk and cookies."

"Dunna mind him, laddie. Pierre was just as concerned about ye as I. Scaredy-cat tha' he be he was goin' te go back fer ye."

"I would have gone back for you, too, Pierre." Alex expressed the sentiment through parched lips as he gave the Frenchman a hug.

"Do not listen to the médecin, Alex. He is tout fou!" Pierre said hugging Alex quickly with an affection which belied his words.

"It's okay, Pierre. I'm afraid, too." Alex responded with earnest emotion.

"I confess I was a bit confused as te which staircase be the correct one te take." Matthew admitted sensing Pierre's embarrassment at the sentimental moment and thus seeking to change the subject. "But me daughter says tha' the cat always knows the way out o' tunnels an' showed her and Matthew Alexander the way when they were lost in the catacombs."

"So, that story of theirs is true?" inquired Alex in amazement. "Are there really-"

"We dunna ha' time te explain now, laddie." he said pointing from Pierre to himself and then back again. "We must follow the feline an' hope she knows what she be doin'. Our young lady be likin' the steps o'er here." he continued indicating the staircase Charmer had chosen to climb to the very top of to gaze back at them pleadingly with a come hither aspect from her perch there. "Go ahead, me boy.... Follow her lead. Go ahead!" Matthew prompted Alex.

"Why do I always have to go first?" whined Alex petulantly.

"We be doin' ye a favor, laddie, te save yerself first. However, I willna force ye. I will go first-"

"Non, non, non!" Pierre objected suddenly shunting Matthew aside with one arm in a panic all at once realizing the full import of the very tenuous position they found themselves in and various perilous scenarios flashed clearly before his eyes. "I wish to save myself. I will go first!" he cried climbing to the top of the ascending planks which formed the staircase where Charmer stood waiting and disappeared along with her through the opened aperture.

"Well. It be obvious te me tha' this be nary a time fer arguin'.

It be yer turn, Alex. Time te get out o' this place!" Matthew encouraged him as he helped move him along up to the first step of the ladder-style staircase and Alex climbed to the top. "Ye'd best hurry!" he warned as the horrendous rumbling noises started anew and grew louder and the staircase began to move from side to side. "Who's te know what tha' balmy Frenchman be doin' out there on his own an' bein' unsupervised!" he said in jest as Alex clung to the rickety structure until the shaking stopped.

"It's your turn, Matt. C'mon!" Alex called out above the noise in the chamber.

"I be comin'. Ye see me climbin', dunna ya?" he said with feigned brusque bravado planting his foot on the next higher rung and pulling himself upward as the steps behind him began to come apart falling to hit the ground below. "Go on," Matt yelled bravely as Alex looked on transfixed in openmouthed horror, "who knows what trouble Pierre may be gettin' inte on his own!"

"Matt!" Alex cried out as the plank Matthew was standing on collapsed underneath his weight and he held on for dear life to the step above him.

"Go back, lad – save yerself!" he shouted as Alex began to climb back down to clasp his wrist and pull him up.

"If only I had a rope!" moaned Alex in despair.

CHAPTER 51

Rand was absolutely furious at the way Jim Lahy had patron-
ized him. They had known each other for quite a few years
now and friends did not speak to friends like that. He sighed. Well,
complaining about the situation wouldn't do him any good. This
gazebo was the place he'd seen Pierre. He reined in his stallion and
dismounted tethering his horse to one of the columns supporting
the roof of the graceful structure and jogged up its steps to walk
upon its boards. He looked about him with trepidation as he experienced an eerie feeling. He was sure he had seen Pierre here last
night but in the blink of an eye he had no longer been treading the
boards of this very platform. Rand did not believe in ghosts, but all
Pierre's talk about his dead grandmother must have gotten to him
to the point where he had been hallucinating yesterday and now was
letting his imagination run wild. The storm of yesterday had cleared
up and he had revisited this spot this morning before seeing the
inspector. He had hoped to find some clues or evidence Pierre had
been there.... Maybe a dried footprint – something. It was when
he had left Jim's office that he realized he did not have his lasso
with him. He'd had it with him this morning when he was helping
Calvin and Dudley bring in some stray cows. He was already in the
area after he'd finished so he figured he would take a gander in this
direction. He could have SWORN that he'd left his lariat here. And
now that he was here he was breaking out in goose bumps thinking
that maybe something had happened to Pierre and he had actually
seen his restless spirit on this very gazebo last night. He shuddered

as chills of foreboding erupted within his body. He just could <u>not</u> look any further.

"There I was, comment dit-on, nose to nose with death. I was staring it right in the face. Bien sûr! I was dodging the boulders to the left and then to the right; choking with my last breath. Yet I carried them both, tous les deux, on my back to safety. I barely escaped alive." Pierre related with world-weariness in a strained, affected tone of voice to Simon as he listened raptly enthralled and spellbound.

"You are just fantastic, Pierre. Unbelievable." Simon applauded him.

"This is true." he replied humbly as under his breath Matt simultaneously interjected "Ye got that right." and cleared his throat. "But in the difficult situations what is one to do?" Pierre concluded modestly with upturned palms while bestowing on Matt a disparaging glare for making his off-the-cuff sarcastic comment.

"Fortitude, Pierre. FORTITUDE! No wonder my sis- I mean, my boy, Elroy, looks up to you!"

"Malarkey! Dunna be believin' him, Simon. He was the first te run fer the exit when the chambers began te collapse! An' 'twere it not fer his childishness we wouldna have had any trouble a'tall!" Matt articulated baldly.

"Souviens-toi! It was you, Matthew, who pushed the wrong knob-"

"That was a mistake and you know it, Pierre! You were trying to activate that same knob. Matt was trying to stop you. Because you were mad at me you stopped trying to pull it out and so Matt who was performing a balancing act by trying to prevent you from pulling by pushing ended up pushing the knob all the way in when you let go of it. In summary, you were <u>both</u> jostling for control of the first knob and you were <u>both</u> being childish!" Alex said in Matt's defense. "But in the end you did save us both with that lasso – talk about being prepared!" he marveled in complacent idolatry.

"I always keep a spare one, as you Américains say, <u>tucked</u> <u>away</u> for emergencies." he fibbed convincingly while all the while truthfully not fully knowing where the lasso had come from – it had just been lying there – but not wishing to detract from his reputation as a hero with an admission to this effect. "This is not the first time that I have preserved the bacon for you and Matt!" Pierre reminded him as Alex smiled slightly at his incorrect wording of a fairly well-known idiom.

"Matt said you were going back to save me when I was caught back in the collapsed chamber. I'm glad you're my friend." Alex noted gratefully.

"Mais, bien sûr I was going back to aid you. But the médecin held me back."

"'Tis true, laddie. I be sorry te say't. I was figurin' it'd be too perilous fer him amidst the avalanche and there'd be nary a hope te find ye. But Pierre was very fierce."

"This is très true. I would have helped you no matter the cost!" proclaimed Pierre staunchly.

"An' no matter tha' ye were tremblin' in yer boots with fear." Matthew elucidated beneath his breath.

"What did you say, Matthew?" Pierre asked him sharply.

"I be merely extrapolatin' tha' if me Eleanor heard even a mere whisper o' this conversation we're havin' she'd be a-tremblin' with fear." Matthew replied smoothly as Pierre regarded him somewhat skeptically.

"So would Mary Jo. As soon as Matt's feeling better after his near death experience we ought to go." Alex piped up anxiously.

"You are a bright boy, Alex. Edi must be in the church right now sick with worry and devoutly praying for my safe return."

"Yes, she was always one for prayer." noted Simon.

"What do you know of Edi's habitude?" asked Pierre in surprise.

"Oh, I mean from what you have <u>TOLD</u> me about her I am sure that she is very religious and deeply devout." responded Simon quickly to allay his suspicious curiosity.

"Edi is a wonderful woman – you would like her. However, she a besoin de a firm hand or she will, comment dit-on, run wild. C'est la même chose avec toutes les femmes. They will, how do you Américains say, walk all over you(?) if they have the chance. You must show them their place!" Pierre elucidated earnestly to Simon as Matthew, Alex, Calvin and Dudley listened attentively. "Merci, for letting us rest ici after our ordeal."

Matt and Alex who had been for the most part solemn and quite humbled by the lesson of their own mortality and Calvin and Dudley who knew of the other three men's near death experience in the root cellar had listened respectfully to Pierre's slightly skewed tales of his own bravery and heroism. But on hearing his statements regarding Edith and women as a whole they exploded into fits of full-blown laughter.

"Do not let Edith Marie hear you say that!" Simon exclaimed while wiping the tears of mirth which were falling from his eyes. "She will blow a gasket!!!"

"Oh! HO! HO! Me heart canna stand it! Edith would throw a fit!" cried Matthew once his laughter had subsided.

"As well as all the breakables in sight!" Alex added remembering when his cousin had questioned Cari's pregnancy.

"Ye'd better hide the family heirlooms!" Matthew quipped to Alex's jest.

"She <u>does</u> reach for the crockery when she wishes to "express" herself!" Simon conceded in agreement.

"And don't forget what happened to LeLoup!" noted Calvin recollecting the incident. "Elvie had him in that headlock and Edith-"

"Edith had that rifle trained on him!" Alex finished the sentence for him lightheartedly. "I remember – you told me. I <u>wish</u> I had seen it!"

All the while during the time that the others were conversing amongst themselves Pierre remained uncharacteristically and markedly silent. One could tell from the look on his face that he was thinking. One could practically see the wheels spinning behind his forehead and in that brain of his cogs were turning. Even Matt stopped his revelry of rocking back and forth to cock his head and regard the Frenchman suddenly gone mute strangely as one by one the other men, taking their cue from him, followed suit and fell silent as well. This moment of quiet attentiveness appeared to be what Pierre was waiting for because at this lull in the conversation he spoke abruptly:

"How did you know that my Edi's full name was Edith Marie?" he asked with the savoir faire of a supersleuth discerning a tell-all clue – all he needed was a pipe to put in his mouth; clamp down upon and hold between his teeth for realism. "And how did you know that she throws – er...things "slip" from her hands when she becomes excited? I have also noticed that whenever Edi is entering the same room, you leave.... If she is anywhere in the area you go "POOF!". And when we invite you to dine with us, you decline! Maintenant, I am not stupide." he illuminated tapping his temple with his forefinger and staring down Matthew's 'That is debatable...' visage. "So, why are you avoiding Edi?" Pierre asked Simon pointedly.

"Bah...! Maybe Simon be avoidin' <u>you</u>. <u>An'</u> ye be hearin' things again! Ye was mistaken!" asserted Matthew with finality.

"I was <u>NOT</u> mistaken. Marie was aussi the nom of ma grand-mère." Pierre maintained his ground stubbornly.

"Ye've just proved me point. Ye've got 'Grand-mère' on the brain!" he countered.

"But…. Matt? I heard Simon say 'Edith Marie', too." Alex said in corroboration inserting the proverbial fly into Matthew's ointment.

"So did we." concurred Dudley speaking on behalf of himself and Calvin as they both looked at each other in nonverbal agreement.

"OW…!" Matt yelled suddenly. "I am in terrible pain. Pierre, could we set this parleying aside fer just one moment, only, so ye can fetch me medical bag…? It contains me mixture tha' I use te dull pain." he fibbed convincingly. "PLEASE?" he quickly entreated him imploringly as he saw Pierre open his mouth angrily and sensed that he was about to deny the request. "I savvy that <u>YOU</u> know how it feels te be in PERFECT agony, Pierre, mon ami. Would ye please retrieve it fer me – me bag be just around back?"

CHAPTER 52

"I will not do it. I will not lie to Pierre!" said Calvin obstinately.

"But it not be lying, Calvin, me boy. Dunna ye see? I just be askin' ye not te…mention certain things. There be no sense in gettin' Pierre all worked up o'er nothin'. He'll be overreactin' – as usual! Ye know how the man carries on!" Matt replied vociferously.

"Cal's right!" Dudley concurred with his brother. "Pierre's been good to us. He's forgiven us for the unforgivable. He trusts us and we've become friends. I won't betray him. Friends don't betray friends." he said adamantly.

"Oh. And thank you for the flowers you left with Alex. Elvie really liked the blooms." Calvin interposed to say grudgingly to Simon.

"You are welcome, Cal. And admittedly, it would be very unfair of me to ask you to keep my secret. Also, your loyalty to Pierre is not only justified, it is admirable. But at least let me tell my sister that I am alive in my own way. She should hear it from me. Please. Do not let on to Pierre that you heard me call her by her full name. I only ask for your silence and then only for a few days at most." Simon begged Calvin urgently.

"But, then Pierre would think he was really hearing things!" objected Alex.

"He be already hearing thin's!" Matthew asserted to help justify the prevarication.

"Now, you know that is not true, Matt! I am not certain why you do not get along with Pierre – it is unfortunate. But Alex, Cal and Dudley know Pierre better than I do and if they collectively feel that revealing to Pierre that I am Edith's sibling is the best course of action to take in this circumstance then I must concur with them and defer to their decision." Simon interceded addressing Matthew reprovingly.

"Let me ask you. Would you even have <u>told</u> Edith if you had not made that slip of the tongue in front of Pierre?" Cal asked Simon accusingly as he had learned the hard way to his own detriment how his and Dudley's previous deceitful behavior had set in motion a chain of events which had caused mental anguish and physical injury and he did not relish the idea that, with this current deceit of Simon's, history might potentially again repeat itself to some degree.

"Would you even have told <u>US</u>?" Dudley added his query to Calvin's.

"Auntie? I doubt that Pierre would be in this field." said Cari as she saw her aunt push aside some brush and gaze behind it searchingly.

"Ah-hah!" she exclaimed triumphantly as she knelt to examine a footprint in the dried mud while unzipping her shoulder bag to rummage through it. "Pierre must have made this footprint!" Edith elaborated in an excited voice as she located the item she had been seeking and unfolded the tape measure, stretching it out to span the length of the hardened imprint from its heel to its toe. "I am coming my beloved! I knew it. It is his exact shoe size!" she trilled happily.

"You cannot be sure about that, Auntie! That mud was very soft last night and the force of the rains could have affected its size." Cari said reasonably.

"My dear niece. You have not seen Pierre's naked feet! <u>I</u> have and this impression in the mud is definitely his footprint! No one's feet are as large as Pierre Dûçot's!" Edith mimicked him playfully.

"You sound just like Pierre!" Cari laughed. "But, even if it is his footprint," she pursued, "what about the others? Where are Alex and Matt's footprints? And, how do we know which direction they took?"

"Cari. You are putting a damper on my investigation...! Ah, here." Edith said picking up a broken twig to hold it before her eyes and gaze at it critically in the light. "Do you see this twig?" she asked rhetorically. "This is proof positive that Pierre, Alex and Matthew toddled off in that direction." Edith determined as if this statement were an established fact pointing ahead at some other fallen tree branches and snapped twigs while Cari regarded her doubtfully.

"Those broken twigs on the ground that you are pointing to could have been made by anyone – even by some animal. So, how do you figure that?" Cari asked moving closer to her aunt.

"Elvie taught me how to track people down." she explained.

"Elvie taught you?"

"Yes, dear. It appears that Calvin learned tracking skills during the war and imparted his expertise in this regard to her. She was also taught the art by a genuine Indian."

"Really?" Cari queried with piqued interest.

"Oh, yes!" Edith guiltily assured her omitting the fact that the Indian in question was part of a side show in a local carnival which Elvie had attended.

"Well, I cannot pooh-pooh all that know-how. Okay," Cari allowed extending her hand to grasp her aunt's elbow and help her to her feet, "let us proceed." she conceded walking forward with Edith.

"I told you that you did not have to come but you insisted on following me." said Edith as she and Cari sloshed through a muddy tract of land that had not dried yet and she slipped landing unceremoniously on her rump.

"Someone had to keep an eye on you." Cari responded pushing against the ground beneath her to come to her knees and rise to stand upright on her feet. "We've lost and found people enough times on this supposed leisurely visit to LaurelsHeath that it is unbelievable and I do not wish to lose you, too! It only makes sense that we should all go places in groups of twos so we can keep an eye on each other."

"Pierre, Alex and Matthew – three people – went off with each other and it did not help them from disappearing off the face of the earth." Edith observed worriedly a frown creasing her brow. "Pierre had not wanted to come here in the first place. It was I who had convinced him to visit this place and now he is missing. It is all my fault! This place is just a tourist trap! Randmore!" she cried as she caught sight of her nephew-in-law approaching and left her niece wiping the mud off of her clothes with a handkerchief behind her to greet him.

CHAPTER 53

"I'm glad I caught you two." Randmore said. "I assume that you are searching for Pierre, Alex and Matt as well. I just spied a cottage to the side of that stream over there and I was about to go over to investigate. You two can join me. Perhaps those people can tell us something. Maybe they saw the guys and can tell us where they've gone to or the residents of the cottage may have seen nothing. But it's worth a try, anyway." he conjectured as he, Cari and Edith trudged toward the house in the distance.

"I am just glad to see you, Rand. It is so desolate and quiet out here. It is like me and Aunt Edith are the only people alive. It is good to see another soul!"

"So, you would be glad to see anyone. Is that what you are saying? Well, that's not much of a compliment, is it?" he queried.

"Oh, you know that's not how I meant it!" Cari objected laughing. "Stop playing with me!" she added in cheerful admonishment her spirits buoyed up by her husband's light teasing.

"Let us stop playing period and hurry on to that cottage." Edith prodded urgently. "We must find the boys. We are certainly at a disadvantage out here on foot but we felt it wise to tether our horses at the lean-to back there as the ground is not yet fully dry in places and there are still some watery puddles and slick muddy spots." Edith loquaciously articulated anxiously.

"I see that Cari knows about those particular spots!" Rand commented humorously observing his wife's suddenly miffed openmouthed countenance and muddy disarray.

"Well, she is certainly no fashion plate to be honest with you." Edith said sternly with a smile and a playful wink in Randmore's direction belying her harshly spoken words.

"Pierre!" Randmore cried jubilantly as they reached the cottage from the rear aspect of the house and found the Frenchman bent over assorted farm machinery and feeding troughs.

"And why don't you address him as 'Uncle Pierre', Cari?" Edith scolded her niece in a low voice continuing without waiting for a response. "I can partially understand Randmore calling him 'Pierre'. After all, he is an in-law and so he and Pierre may feel a bit awkward with such formality. But, you, Cari, have no such excuse!"

"Je cherche Matt's medical bag." Pierre revealed with irritation to Randmore. "Mais, je ne le trouve pas! This crazy médecin est tout fou. Dans le premier instance he argues avec Pierre Dûçot – as if Pierre Dûçot is ever wrong – and then in the second time he is pleading with me à trouver le médicament pour sa maladie. Il est complètement fou!" Pierre told Randmore in irritation, intent on his purpose, as he approached him to squat by his side.

"Pierre! We're so glad to see you!" Rand clapped him on the shoulder.

"Yes! We were all so worried about you!" cried Edith throwing her arms around the back of his bent over shoulders until he gave up his search and stood up to face her and give her a hug.

"You need not have been concerned about my well-being, ma petite. Pierre Dûçot knows how to take care of himself." he boasted with savoir faire sniffing importantly and adjusting his posture to stretch to his full height.

"But, nevertheless, we were worried – Uncle." Cari added along with the familial title when she felt her aunt's piercing gaze upon her.

"Where are Alex and Matt?" Rand asked Pierre with concern.

"Those helpless children are in the house with Calvin, Dudley and Simon." he replied deciding it was fruitless to resume his search for Matt's medical bag and, instead, led them around to the front door of the cottage while explaining how he, along with Alex and Matt, had fallen into a ghastly root cellar and due to his heroism above and beyond the call of duty he had led them all to safety.

Cari and Rand listened patiently to Pierre's fantastic recount of events and his bravery with its grandiose embellishments with a large grain of salt. They shared a commiserating glance with one another which seemed to express: 'Same old Pierre!'. Edith, however, hung on his every word as if gospel. As they drew closer they were met with the sight of Cal and Dudley rapidly exiting the cottage throwing up their hands and gesticulating in disagreement. Alex followed closely behind them with Matthew and Simon running to catch up to the other three men. Something about Matt's companion struck a chord with Edith and stirred her recollection. The shoes; the trousers; the jacket; the hat.... All of these garments captured Edith's attention.

"How deplorable. It is that rude fellow from the hospital. Goodness! Where do these uncouth...."

Edith's remark petered out and came to a stop as his aspect from under the wide brim of his hat came clearer into focus with his approach. Was she seeing an apparition? A ghost? She stared at Simon's face hypnotized as her hands involuntarily rose to cover her cheeks and then her fingers lowered to cover her gaping mouth.

"Simon?" Edith whispered before falling backwards into Pierre's arms in a dead faint.

Cari looked at her aunt and then at the man before her who had abruptly come to a halt on discerning her aunt's practically inaudible, pitifully disconcerted one word query; vacillated momentarily and then seemed to come to life rushing to Edith's side to hold her hand within his own.

"UNCLE SIMON!?" gasped Cari.

"Matt! Get over here – NOW!" Simon yelled distraught.

Matt was already two steps ahead of him as he swerved and ran back inside the house to retrieve his medical bag from where he had secreted it on the lower shelf of the side table to the left of the couch where also resided the forgotten unstructured leather briefcase, overlooked in the shuffle, which Alex had risked his life to salvage.

CHAPTER 54

"Dunna be jealous, Pierre. We all o' us knew tha' sooner or later Edith would come te her senses an' leave ye fer another man!" Matthew teased smiling as Pierre watched Edith and Simon convivially conversing tête-à-tête with smoldering eyes over a coffee cup raised halfway to his lips.

"Very amusing, médecin. Forgive me for neglecting to laugh. WHAT ARE THEY TALKING ABOUT?!!!" Pierre spontaneously blurted out angrily as Matthew burst out laughing heartily at his friend's unfounded concerns at being neglected by his wife.

"Edith dunna mean te leave ye outta the loop! She hasna seen her brother fer years. They're just catchin' up with one another!"

"It is not just that. Let us speak plainly, Matt. We are being, how you say, SNOWED. Mais, you are not the idiot and I am not the simpleton, either. Cet homme Simon lied to Edi. He pretended to be dead. When she was grieving he turned his back on her. Edi, if you remember, lost deux frères et une soeur that jour. Instead of being a gentilhomme of honor and coming forward to comfort her he chose, instead, to cower in the dark. He hid amongst the shadows and let her suffer alone with a small niece to care for. He did not lighten her burden and, how you say, come out from the gloom. He allowed her to mourn him in silence."

"What yer sayin' dunna make sense. Simon suffered a trauma te his mind. Ye can understand that — can ye? He was afraid o' what people might think o' him. If ye dunna mind me sayin' I seen ye many times in abject fear and runnin' fer yer life. So, I know yer nary a much different than Simon. Maybe that be why I put up with yer antics!" responded Matthew interpreting the situation in a way he hoped that Pierre would understand.

"Mais, I am different. I may – under extraordinary circonstances – display certain…vulnerabilities…."

"Ye mean cowardice." Matthew asserted while Pierre looked down upon him haughtily.

"Pierre Dûçot is not a coward-"

"Yellow streak! Ye got a yellow streak! Now, dunna deny it." Matt defied him.

"Pierre Dûçot does not deny the <u>caution</u> he exhibits. Bien sûr! This caution is symbolic of wisdom. It is a virtue. Finalement, I always recover from my momentary caution and come through with the bacon. And I toujours, comment dit-on, <u>own</u> my responsibilities."

"Hey, Pierre! Why aren't you mixing with your new brother and sister?" Alex asked curiously as he sauntered up to them with his head bent over a napkin to catch the crumbs falling from the brownie dusted with powdered sugar he was eating.

"Pah! My new brother et soeur…. Where were they when that pretender to French ancestry tried to steal my Edi? Where were they when you, Alex, were dangling in the cave? Where WERE they when that Colden cochon was cooking my goose? WHERE WERE THEY WHEN WE WERE TRAPPED IN THE ROOT CELLAR??? Hmmm? You, Matt, Randy, Dudley, Calvin… YOU people are my family. NOT those two who lured Pierre Dûçot into their confidence only to laugh at him behind his back!"

"Pierre has himself a point, Alex. At least I laugh at him te his face!" grinned Matt mischievously after making the admission.

"Do not attempt to make small of me to mask the bad behavior of others. US three." Pierre pointed to Matt, to Alex and then, lastly, to himself. "We disagree tout le temps. But, we always talk about these differences out in the open and agree to, how to say, disagree.

This is the characteristic of civilized behavior." Pierre concluded with an air of finality to his voice.

"Bah! Get off yer high horse and smell the coffee. Ye know they be only protecting Elroy from bein' taken away from the bosom o' his family. And Simon was feelin' the shame o' na' tryin' te rescue Cari's parents, as well."

"That…is no excuse!"

"Bah…!"

"Did quelqu'un ever tell you, Matthew, that you sounded comme the mouton?"

"Yer full o' malarkey, de ye know tha', Pierre?"

"Merci mille fois!"

"Ah…. C'mon, you guys. Stop quarreling! Simon's a great guy, Pierre. You two were getting along famously until you learned he was your brother-in-law. You know…. We're not deaf over there." Alex informed Pierre. "That's why I thought I'd mosey casually on over here and see what was up with you guys and now I think that I know." he said sitting down on one of the chairs at LaurelsHeath.

"And just what do you think that you know, Mr. Small Fry?" Pierre inquired somewhat snidely.

"I think you are jealous of all the attention that Edith is paying Simon."

"The laddie be spot on! Tha' is what I been sayin'."

"And, you're using Simon's mistake of not telling Edith he was alive – not that I think it was the right thing to do – to hate him on second sight and not give him a second chance to show he was a good person. That way you can justify being mad at a great guy like Simon without admitting that it's really for the immature and silly reason that you want Edith's affection all to yourself. And how do you think Tru feels about not having Simon all to herself? She has to share him with Edith. And, what mother wouldn't want to protect her child? Tru, that's what Simon calls her, really sacrificed her own

SHARON ELIZABETH SARKISIAN

desire to be honest about her sister relationship with you to be true
- no pun intended – to her husband and not tell on him when he
asked her to protect his secret!" Alex expounded wisely.

Pierre regarded Alex coldly. How dare the young man speak
to him in such a condescending manner after all that he had done
for him. The insolence! Pierre could hardly believe his impudence.
Yet.... What if les choses he said had some grain – just a very, very
small tiny grain – of truth to them? Wouldn't it be le meilleure
chose to examine his feelings just as a precaution – just so that he
would not embarrass Alex by calling him out to account for his
impudent speech? 'Oui. I am very fond of the boy.' he concluded.
Therefore, he would give Alex's highly outlandish criticisms the
benefit of every doubt!

CHAPTER 55

This party was supposed to be for <u>him</u>! Pierre watched with anger boiling over as his dinner companions all pushed back their chairs to get up and rush forward to crowd about Simon as he entered the room with Trudy on his arm. Well, he refused to join them. He had been very forgiving up until now and "go with the flow", as these Américains say, but enough was enough! This was <u>his</u> party – mais, bien sûr, it had been arranged by Edi expressly for his homecoming; this was <u>his</u> family; these were <u>his</u> friends and, he watched as Simon and Trudy took canapés from the platters the caterers' assistants milling among the guests offered them, this was <u>his</u> food! Joan had prepared it for HIM! He slammed his clenched fist into the tabletop before him with a resounding blow causing the guests at the circular tables nearby to stop conversing with one another momentarily to stare at him, the guest of honor, curiously before resuming their revelry. Well, at least Joan had planned the menu and supervised its preparation. Mais, bien sûr! She could not be expected to make all of this food by herself. However, at least she had taken over the position of chef at LaurelsHeath from Trudy for the length of his stay there. That was one bright spot. Trudy's cooking skills were rudimentary at best and left much to be desired, as far as he was concerned, while Joan's cuisine was très magnifique by contrast. He sighed contentedly slightly mollified at the thought of ingesting her marvelous food at his next meal at LaurelsHeath. Pierre shifted his weight in his chair and gazed at the well-heeled ladies from the historical society to his right and Jim Lahy, Rafe

Cordell and other new acquaintances that they had interacted with in Laureltown with their companions to his left. The ladies wore long evening dresses. The gentlemen wore tuxedos or other formal evening attire. A small orchestra played in one corner while dancers glided across the parquet floor. Bunches of flowers decorated the walls at strategic junctures and paper streamers festooned the upper corners of the ceiling in the elite rented hall. Sparkling silver and gold streamers hung from the ceiling. Crystal chandeliers lighted the large room and the guests laughed as champagne flowed freely among their crystal flutes. Cari had had difficulty in securing a large enough party space for them on such short notice. But Edith was able to rent this hall last minute due to the ladies of the historical society who gave her an "in" with the management via their recommendation of her. Pierre looked ahead miserably at the group gathered around Simon and Trudy. They were his family – not theirs! He narrowed his eyes with resentment. Out of the blue Joan Collins sat down beside him.

"I hope that you approve of the menu, Mr. Dûçot."

"Toutes des choses you perform is perfect, Joan." Pierre said listlessly without taking his eyes off of Simon and Trudy who were laughing as Edith wiped some cream cheese which had oozed out of a canapé from his cheek. "And, I told you to call me, Pierre!"

"Okey-dokey, Pierre." she assented to the unhappily distracted man. "He can't hold a candle to you." Joan said indicating Simon. "And, after all, she's just doing the HONORABLE thing by attending to her brother after finding him after all these years." she said reasonably attempting to lift his spirits out of the doldrums. "She's just doing what's expected of her – how would it look to others if she ignored him? Of course, it took ME a while to understand that when I saw Edith fawning all over him – I disapprove of one who doesn't cleave to their spouse. Of course, a famous man of the world such as you are knows how people do talk about what's absolutely NO business of theirs so you probably figured out her fear of being gossiped about before I did."

Joan's voice was very soothing and as he glared in Simon's direction her words slowly penetrated his consciousness and voilà! They made sense to him. Especially when she referred to him as a "man of the world" – which was what he was! Pierre was reminded of his responsibility to the community. This was a responsibility encompassing tolerance and leniency. He was, mais, bien sûr, a role model to those directionless souls who looked up to him for guidance. And, also, he was a role model to his fans who admired his professional dancing skills and work as an instructeur of the arts. Oui. Edi obviously recognized this, too, and, clearly, she was only taking pity on Simon who – even Matt had agreed – was suffering from a trauma to the mind. Edi was merely seeking to protect him and stave off any unwanted criticism from others which might possibly deflect upon his distinguished person. He, Pierre Dûçot, should have realized this sooner and it had taken the common sense words of Joan – elementary as they were – to open his eyes to the real reason that his family pandered to Simon and Trudy. Pierre suddenly felt very small. A pang of fear suddenly struck a chord in his heart as an unbidden thought came calling. How would it be construed by his fans if he did not show a similar compassion and embrace his new in-laws publicly? He quickly began to rise to his feet with the intention of rushing over to greet them only to be stopped by Joan's next words:

"Now, if you don't mind me saying. I'd be more worried about those two if I were in your shoes. NOT, that anyone can fill YOUR shoes...Pierre!" she said indicating with a flick of one delicate finger a pair of dancers as they swept across the edge of the dance floor and blushing as she articulated his proper name. "I mean, I do not approve of gossip, but what are people going to say?" Joan asked innocently watching as Cyrus held Cari tightly within the circle of his arms and whispered intimately into her ear.

Pierre's eyes glazed over in wide-eyed shock turning to anger as he watched his niece with her body pressed closely against the form of someone other than her husband. His jaw dropped leaving his mouth agape as he watched Cyrus provocatively dip her backwards in his arms before whisking her inwards in a half arc to disappear amidst the throng of dancers.

CHAPTER 56

"It is a trick! I tell you, it is a TRICK!"

"Oh, Pierre! How can you say that? Cyrus just invited us to a dinner party at his house – there is nothing mysterious about it! It is merely a friendly gesture-"

"Was compromising my niece a "friendly" gesture?" Pierre countered interrupting his wife, incensed.

"Not that again! So, they danced and then had a cocktail. It was a social event, for heaven's sake!" Edith exclaimed.

"It depends on how you define a social event! You saw the façon he held her – the way that he TOUCHED her. It was almost as if he were, comment dit-on, SAMPLING her. It was indecent and quite unseemly. You are putting your desire to see Candlestick Manor above Cari's reputation as a happily married lady!" Pierre stormed relentlessly

"I am surprised at that kind of innuendo. You are reading more into this than there is!" replied Edith defensively her voice cracking slightly.

"Il n'est pas important what is MY innuendo. What matters is Randy's innuendo. HE is the one who found them alone together in the anteroom seated closely together on a couch and drinking alcohol!" Pierre elaborated unhappily tapping his temple meaningfully.

"It was wine not hard liquor! And Randy understands that they were just socializing and-"

"And that is why they are sleeping in separate bedrooms." Pierre interjected finishing her sentence for her, although, not in the way which she had intended.

"And just how do you know that?" Edith inquired of him challengingly irritated that he had interrupted her.

"Simple deduction, ma petite chérie. Trudy asked Cari how she liked the bouquet of carnations she had placed in the vase on her bedside table!" he explained in triumph as Edith looked at him expectantly waiting for him to elaborate.

"And…." prompted Edith impatiently seeking to draw forth some sort of a response as she waited for him to continue.

"C'est incroyable…." Pierre mumbled to himself before resuming coherent speech. "Mais, bien sûr it is clear. Don't you see?" he queried as she shook her head negatively from side to side. "Non? I will explain myself. Cari said that the carnations were a nice touch. She told Trudy that their floral scent was very soothing during the nuit! However, Cari is allergic to the carnations! You should know this!" he admonished her.

"Dearest. I do not wish to put a monkey wrench, as the younger generation would say, into your theory. But it is most likely that Cari was merely being polite. Cari did not wish to hurt Trudy's feelings by telling her that she did not care for the flowers." Edith imparted to him logically and patiently.

"Mais, Cari also said that pink carnations were her favorite flower. Joan told me that she had removed the carnations soon after she saw Trudy put them at the bedside before Cari saw them there because she knew of Cari's allergy and that they were a "tacky" red color. So. Why would Cari say that they were pink quand she never saw them in the first place? Joan informed me that the carnations in the single guest bedroom down the hall were pink!" Pierre elucidated triumphantly tightening the knot of his cravat with a final flourish as if putting the "check" to his "mate".

"Randy, I've told you over and over again that there is absolutely nothing between Cyrus and I! He was just trying to be friendly and mend fences between our families." argued Cari leaning against the fireplace's left stone border in the living room at LaurelsHeath.

"Oh? Is that all that he was doing?" Randmore asked sarcastically. "Then, tell me. Out of all of us why did he have to do it with my wife!? I'm beginning to believe that Elvie is right. Cyrus has designs on you!"

"But, Matthew says-"

"I don't care what Matt says. He's not an expert on psychological disorders! Elvie's very clear on what she heard. She hasn't changed her story once."

"She also thought Matt, Pierre and Alex were sea monsters. She did not waver from her story at that time, either. And then the truth finally came out on its own!" Cari stated argumentatively shifting her weight uncomfortably as one of the many offset stones in the simulated rockface ornamentation of the stuccoed panels on either side of the fireplace dug painfully into her side – it seemed to move of its own volition!

"That was a long time ago, Cari, and you know it. She's proven herself to be loyal and trustworthy. Not to mention, a good friend! So why are you defending Cyrus over one of our own?!!!"

"I am not defending Cyrus! It is just that he extended a very cordial invitation to see his historical residence and Aunt Edith really wants to take him up on the invite!" Cari said defensively.

"Cari. Think about it. The man is half your age!"

"He is not! Cyrus cannot be more than five years my junior – the most ten!"

"So you <u>have</u> been thinking about it!" Randmore pounced jealously with his response on hearing the new evocative content of her indignant reply.

"Why do you have to keep coming back to me and Cyrus?" Cari

stridently queried distressfully through quivering lips.

"Because you keep talking about you and Cyrus. And what were you doing with him at the dance which was held in Pierre's honor? Don't you think that people were talking? I even saw Joan Collins point you out to Pierre while she talked to him a mile a minute. She looked shocked and I do not blame her – I was thrown for a loop, too! When I saw the way that he was holding you so closely I headed straight for you two to tear you apart but he must have seen me coming because he ducked with you into the crowd of dancers before I could get my hands on him! And then, on top of that, later I catch you with him in a secluded side room!" Randmore ranted while punching the left palm of his hand with his right fist. "You said that after that incident with LeLoup you wouldn't do this again." he argued further.

"Do what? I have done nothing." she choked out tearfully at the accusatory jab.

"Cari. You are consorting with another man! And, he is a much younger man. Plus, anyone can tell he is smitten with you. Alright. So your Aunt Edith is a history buff and she wants to see the whole of Candlestick Manor. But what's the sense of it? Jim Lahy says that it's only a matter of time before Cyrus can tear it down. If a deed doesn't turn up showing that someone else owns the house he will have every right to do what he wants with it once his squatter's rights vest. Or, something of that nature…." Randmore reasoned impatiently as Cari turned her back to him and folded her arms across her chest obstinately. "Look, Cari." he sighed in capitulation. "Your aunt is an avid fan of history. But you are NOT. Candlestick Manor has nothing whatsoever to do with you or US!"

CHAPTER 57

"You see? These bricks are not REAL gold! They just <u>resemble</u> gold. If you rub them lightly, after a while you will see the yellow color rub off onto your skin." Simon revealed to his attentive audience.

"So, ye be sayin' tha' the brick the laddie found be worthless?" Matthew enunciated to Simon in hopeless disappointment – a woebegone broken man he did appear to be – as he stood next to Pierre, Randmore and Alex, his dreams of wealth and glory dashed away in a cold, cruel world!

"Not to my boy, Elroy. He loves stacking them up in different designs, building forts and whatnot....You know what I am talking about. Sometimes he even plays dominoes with them." chuckled Simon fondly at the thought of his son's exploits.

"The block looked gold to me. It felt solid like gold, too." Alex piped up crestfallen.

"I told you that colored block could not be gold, Alex." Randmore admonished his younger cousin. "You have a tendency to romanticize things. Valuable objects just don't fall from the sky, you know. And no one just leaves them lying around for someone to find. Things like that just don't happen and there is no such thing as getting rich quick!" he lectured realistically while he looked about him at the orderly horizontal stacks holding a multitude of bright yellow compressed metal blocks lying side by side consecutively as orderly as soldiers on each of their multiple shelves.

"But, that's not fair! You mean that these bricks have absolutely no value to them at all?"

"I believe tha' we have already established tha' fact te be true, laddie." said Matthew sadly yet grudgingly unwilling to let go of his dream so easily but resigned to knowing that he must.

"Alex, Alex, Alex! Do not take it so hard. You cannot control Mother Nature. She is a fickle mistress at best!" Simon chimed in laughing heartily on viewing Alex's comically outraged expression.

"Attends un moment, Simon!" Pierre finally interrupted as he was tired of waiting patiently for someone to ask him <u>his</u> opinion and also miffed that no one had sought his esteemed point of view thus far. "There is extreme value to these pieces of, comment dit-on, hardware. You have all, especially you, Simon, have overlooked one crucial factor that is so obvious that it cannot be ignored. Mais, bien sûr, you could not be expected to know this!"

"I <u>knew</u> it! What is it, Pierre?" Alex asked eagerly in admiration with an expectant aspect to his countenance. "Tell us!" he prompted demandingly as the Frenchman paused and pursed his lips pensively before speaking for dramatic effect.

"C'est the signature, of course."

Pierre looked about him relishing the aura of suspense which he had created with his theatrics. Four inquisitive faces looked up to him in anticipation of his next words. The men stood in the section of the catacombs which extended downward from the stairway in Simon's basement. A strange glow illuminated the area and the semi-acrid air irritated the delicate interior linings of Pierre's nostrils and pharynx. He cleared his throat.

"As I have said avant. This is the handwriting of Jan LaFitte! And wherever Jan LaFitte is an element we know that there is a…je ne sais quoi to the "mix". Something different. A twist, one could say, that leads one to know that the choses are not always as they appear!" Pierre said mysteriously.

Matt licked his dry lips all the while during Pierre's drawn-out response to Alex's question. He found Pierre's explanation, however, to be totally unsatisfactory and not to his liking – he had, after all, heard such similar rhetoric before! But, at the same time, he felt his previously dashed and desiccated dreams slowly coming back to life to bloom with their sudden resurrection aided by this infusion of hope.

"Get te the point o' what ye be talkin' about, Pierre, mon ami!" Matthew ground out in frustration from between gritted teeth as he sought to prevent his temper from spiraling out of control with the impatience which he felt. "Ye always be speaking in riddles!"

"For your brain, Matt, I will make it clear. Wherever there is the evidence of Jan LaFitte there is always <u>profit</u> involved in the transaction!" he replied.

"Now, was tha' so hard te express?" queried the rejuvenated Irishman with a huge smile spreading across his face and greed exploding inside his chest via his rapidly beating heart now that he received the answer he wanted to hear.

"WOW! So my golden nugget can actually be worth something!"

"Not you, too, Alex! Do not get bogged down in these farfetched fantasies of Matt's and Pierre's again! You almost got killed <u>TWICE</u> last time because you were helping them with their prior treasure hunt! Now. <u>They</u> are so hardheaded and stubborn that <u>I</u> <u>know</u> I cannot sway <u>them</u> from pursuing their pie in the sky shenanigans. But, I am appealing to you to exercise some common sense and save yourself from all of the aggravation involved in this fruitless chase for riches and glory." Randmore appealed to his young cousin.

"You know that Pierre is always right about these things. Remember last time…? He has a sixth sense about these things! It's in his blood-"

"This is vrai." Pierre interrupted Alex smiling all the while and drinking in his flattering words of confidence regarding his savvy.

"I have the blood nose!" he bragged assuredly tapping his proboscis with an index finger.

"You mean, the nose of a bloodhound, don't you, Pierre?" asked Alex correcting him.

"Do not be impertinent with your elders, Alex." reprimanded Pierre.

"Well. I give up! It looks like you're all going to pursue this wild goose chase no matter what I say – no pun intended, Pierre." Randmore added apologetically as Pierre looked at him affronted at the possible reference to his "alter ego" of L'Oie.

"Alors, Mr. Simon says…" Pierre swiveling sharply to face him inquired abruptly of his notably silent, nonresponsive host who gazed pensively ahead of him, lost in thought, "what is your point of view concerning this topic – or do you have none?" he challengingly goaded Simon, whom he still viewed as a competitor for Edi's affections, in a nasty voice.

"LaFitte was Tru's maiden name." Simon mused aloud reflectively.

CHAPTER 58

"Let me help you with that, Trudy. Une gentille lady, such as yourself, should not have to lift the heavy objects!" gushed Pierre taking the dinner platter of roasted chicken, baby potatoes and carrots from her hands to walk it over to the dining room table and set it down in the center. "It is a pity that Simon and your dear son, Elroy, could not join us ce soir. And what a merveilleux dinner you have prepared for us all – it looks quite tempting!"

"Oh, brother!" said Cari in exasperation behind her hand in an aside to Mary Jo and Callie. "As soon as Pierre found out that Trudy's maiden name was LaFitte and figured that she might be related to Jan he has been fawning all over her! It's so transparent it is embarrassing!"

"I will admit it. The way he's ingratiating himself into her good graces is pretty tacky." Mary Jo agreed.

"Joan did the cooking. I only brought in the platter, Mr. Dûçot."

"Mais, you did it so GRACEFULLY." he promptly responded as he pulled out a chair for her to sit down upon. "You must have been on your feet all the day. Please. Sit and enjoy your dinner." he said ingratiatingly as she sat down and he pushed in her chair, took it upon himself to unfold her cloth table napkin and placed it in her lap.

"I think I am going to be sick." said Callie incredulously as Pierre solicitously offered to cut Trudy's meat for her.

"Callie, my child. You are not feeling well? Peut-être the méde-cin can offer you some médicament." Pierre suggested helpfully on overhearing her comment while Cari and Mary Jo hid their smiles behind their hands.

"No, thank you, Mr. Dûçot – I mean Pierre. I'm feeling much better now!" Callie objected stumbling over her words in confusion as she saw Pierre waving Matthew over from across the table.

"Dunna be shy, Callie, lass. We'll ha' ye fixed up in two shakes o' a lamb's tail!" said Matthew making his way around the table to stand before her, but with his back to the rest of the diners, as he regarded her with twinkling eyes and winked knowingly at her – yes, he was familiar with the frustration Pierre's blarney could cause a person to feel – while producing a water pill placebo from the miniature medical kit attached to the belt around his waist. "This little tablet," he informed her holding it up to the light, "be me cure-all te everything tha' ails ye from soup te NUTS!" proclaimed Matt cheerfully nodding his head slightly in Pierre's direction letting Callie know that he knew she was not really so much <u>physically</u> sick as she was repelled by Pierre's toadying behavior as he presented her with the useless pill and poured her a glass of water from the nearby carafe.

"So. Matthew," began Pierre, oblivious that he was being mocked by Dr. Flanderly, "où est our poor, sick Elvie?" he queried noting her empty chair at the table along with Calvin's absence while he sat down next to Trudy, totally ignoring his wife's welcoming pat of the seat of the chair next to hers and also not noticing her slump back against the back of her chair in vexed disappointment at his unintentional snub.

"She was afraid to stay here. She was too scared of the threats she heard Cyrus make to stay!" Callie elucidated. "And, truthfully, I wanted to go with her. The people around here are creepy! Except for you and your family, Trudy." she amended. "But Dudley wanted to stay and hold down the fort. You know.... Keep an eye on things. Protect and defend our territorial rights!"

"It be only temporarily tha' Elvie be gone off on holiday." Matthew interrupted Callie. "More te the point, I suggested it te help the puir lass clear her head. New surroundings can oft times help a person gain a new perspective on life. A new outlook on the common sense of the entire situation. An' when she returns she will be as good as new – refreshed! Aye…. There be the word: REFRESHED!" Matthew rolled the word off of his tongue lingeringly.

"Elle est une fille qui est très intelligente. Her only mistake will be to return to this lieu. In the Laureltown diner I aussi heard this Cyrus avec son cohort, Clyde, threaten our lives. Mais, comme les gens inférieurs that all of you are – except for you, Trudy, my long, lost sister – you refuse to listen to me. We should ALL follow Calvin and Elvie's good example and leave for the hills!" Pierre strongly recommended with all the educated hauteur and impetus of a witness to the looming threat.

"I dunna see ye runnin' fer the exit yerself, Pierre, mon ami. Could it be tha' perhaps yer stayin' fer some sort o' other reason?" Matthew inquired slyly with his leading question.

"I dunna, I mean, I do not know what you are speaking of…." Pierre stated innocently nonchalantly observing the tips of his fingers intently – he believed he had a hangnail!

"I take yer answer te mean then tha' yer theory o' the handwriting on the gold bricks ha' absolutely nothin' te do with yer all fired up determination te stay previously! ADMIT IT, begorra! Ye see remuneration on the near horizon an' yer afraid someone else will get te it first!" Matthew hammered out in an impromptu rage.

"Alex, you are just the personne I wanted to see-" Pierre broached eagerly as Alexander Caine entered the dining room ready to eat after washing away the daily grime from his hands at the bathroom sink.

"Would both of you just sit <u>down</u>?" Cari scolded Pierre, who was rising from his chair to approach Alex, and Matt, who stalked over to dip his hand in Alex's jacket pocket and withdraw the golden brick he had taken to carrying there as a keepsake and as a good luck charm – hey, if Elroy believed in luck why shouldn't he, especially after his, Matt's and Pierre's narrow escape from the root cellar? "Let us enjoy our dinner!"

"Yes! It is getting cold and Joan went to so much trouble! I know that we did not really get along at first when she came to Chesterhollow but she came all the way out here because I asked her to for you, Pierre. So she could prepare your favorite foods. And I must admit that Joan has really outdone herself!" Edith, silent up until this point, asserted eloquently only to be ignored by the three men standing.

"Hey! I didn't mean to be so popular." Alex admitted in jest as he watched Pierre grasp the other half of the brick Matthew was holding onto and pull at it.

"What de ye think yer doin'? I mean te examine this piece o' evidence that the laddie found te get at the crux o' the matter!" Matthew argued to Pierre.

"You do not know what you are looking for." Pierre responded quickly.

"An' I suppose yer just the bloke te make tha' evaluation?" he inquired peevishly pulling the contested item back in his direction.

"Mais, bien sûr, Matthew. I underestimated your intelligence! I am pleased that you recognize this FACT!" he retorted pulling the brick toward himself once more.

"I were set te take a gander at it first!" he replied gruffly yanking the brick in his direction.

"You do not know the première chose about the, comment dit-on, puzzles!" Pierre argued knowledgeably pulling the block of gold to his chest.

"Oh, an' you do, te be sure. I, on t'other hand, understand

YOU, dunna I!" Matthew contested sarcastically.

"Matt, it's my brick! I found it so stop arguing!" Alex pleaded.

"Ah, HAH!" cried Pierre who took advantage of Alex's distracting plea of conciliation to snatch the golden item from Matthew's momentarily loosened grip. "Maintenant," explained Pierre as he shielded the metal block with his body, "I can tell you that this, comment dit-on, inscription is hand engraved-"

"Hey! Where did Charmer come from!" said Alex in surprise scooping her up in his arms as she purred wildly at the human contact — or was it at his gentle touch?

"Unfortunately, laddie, yer beginnin' te act as beguiled as me daughter when it comes te tha' animal. Thank goodness she be upstairs te bed sleepin' else we wouldna hear t'end o' it with all the cooing an' other assorted gobbledygook!"

"That animal saved our lives, Matt!" Alex responded with vitriolic fervor.

"Forget about that cat, Alex. Has tout le monde gone fou? Écoute à moi! Maintenant. Cette inscription-"

"I didn't notice this before. This charm matches the inscription...."

"Will you arrêtes interrupting your elders, Alex?! I am explaining-" Pierre attempted to continue speaking only to be ignored.

"The lad be right!" said Matt gazing at the charm on the cat's collar which Alex fingered between his thumb and forefinger.

"Maybe it's a clue!" Alex said in excitement as he locked eyes with Charmer and they stared at each other unblinkingly.

"Ye might be right, laddie. Ye might well near be right!" Matthew articulated pensively with a couple of slow and thoughtful affirmative nods of his head.

"See if it fits into the engraving, Alex! You know.... Like that key from the tackle box fit into Elroy's good luck charm key!" prompted an excited Mary Jo who had risen from her chair between Cari and

Callie to rush over to stand beside Alex and gawk at the charm on the feline's collar which read LEROI in raised gold letters soldered in succession onto a miniature flat, rectangular, gold plate.

Even Pierre could not contain his curiosity and crept over, however casually, with curiosity to view the charm.

"Let's see the block, Pierre." urged Alex as Pierre slowly held it out. "Turn it over to where the engraving is." he asked in excitement as Pierre complied and Alex fit the embossed letters of the charm on Charmer's neck collar into the debossed letters of the golden block. "Nothing happened." Alex noted in disappointment. "Aw, SHUCKS!" he lamented woefully.

"Alors, of course nothing happened. When will you STOP playing, Alex, and listen to me? Maintenant. As I was saying…what was I saying? Ah, oui-"

"But, wait, silly. Don't you see?" Mary Jo interposed addressing her husband.

"Are you people in the habitude of interrompant others?" Pierre articulated in frustration. "I do not blame YOU, Mary Josephine. It is obvious to ME that Alex's penchant to interrompre his elders has set for you a mauvais exemple. Or, as you Américains say, has rubbed off on you the wrong way."

"No, Pierre." Mary Jo said facing him. "That's not it! TURN IT! The key is that it's a KEY. The charm is a key, so turn it clockwise!" she enunciated triumphantly.

"But, there's no possible way the charm can turn in the engraving. The brick is solid metal." Alex argued to his wife. "The metal will never budge!"

"At least try. TURN it!" Mary Jo demanded eagerly.

As Charmer meowed in protest at her neck being held in position awkwardly at an angle Alex decided that he would appease his wife and accede to her demand. He, therefore, turned the charm on the feline's collar which had already been fitted into the debossed letters of the misshapen block of golden metal. To his surprise, a piece of the metal which he had just deemed "solid" twisted clockwise and the circular marking of a cylinder, previously undetectable, appeared with the rotating motion. The sound of a click resounded in the suddenly silent room as all watched with bated breath. Alex's eyes became dark, as huge as saucers and suddenly awestricken as a seam encircling the object sprung into evidence with the "click" of the turning key when it finally reached its destination. He slowly separated the upper half of the block from the lower half. Clear pieces of icy, faceted stones brimmed forth to fall to the carpet while the others remained nested in their confining metal prison.

"DIAMONDS!" breathed Pierre.

"DIAMONDS!" Alex breathed.

"I be rich!" Matthew uttered.

Crossing over to them purposefully after rising from his seat beside Edith, Randmore picked up one of the sparkling stones and went over to the expensive new portrait mirror on the side wall and dragged it across its pristine, unmarred glass surface leaving one long, scarring scratch trailing in its wake.

"DIAMONDS!" Randmore concurred.

CHAPTER 59

"Such uncalled for behavior – REALLY!" Edith proclaimed vehemently and gawked with animosity as she watched Pierre lay his jacket across a puddle of muddy water so that Trudy could step onto it to cross the street without soiling her shoes.

"It is a very gentlemanlike act, you must admit, Mrs. Dûçot." said Joan respectfully knowing that Mrs. Dûçot disliked it when she addressed her by her given name. "Of course, since he has not known the woman for that long it is quite unseemly." she added as Edith handed her the two heavy grocery bags Pierre had deposited in her arms when he had spotted Trudy at the curb of the sidewalk attempting to skirt the deep puddles of rainwater which had accumulated from last night's rain and ran to her aid.

"I just do not know what has gotten into that man. TOTALLY ignoring me for another woman! He never ruined a jacket for ME!" Edith complained watching the pair cross the street without taking her eyes off the two long enough to notice Joan struggling with the weight of the household groceries which included, for the most part, "essential" delicacies required by Pierre Dûçot. "Not that I would ask him to or ever allow him to ruin a perfectly good jacket on my behalf. Money does not grow on trees, you know!"

"I am sure that once the newness of having a new sister-in-law wears off everything will get back to normal and Pierre will pay his full attention to you once more." Joan surmised backing through the door of the CONNOISSEURS gourmet shop to follow Edith outside with difficulty as her arms were wrapped around the aforementioned grocery bags and Edith had exited the store without holding the door open for her to pass through unobstructed so engrossed was she with the activities of her husband and Trudy.

"I do not believe that it is appropriate for Trudy to allow Pierre to hold her about her waist!" gasped Edith oblivious of the situational irony of her talking to and treating Joan Collins as a trusted confidante when she had never felt friendship for her or cared for her as a person before this incident.

"Hi, girls." Alex greeted them cheerfully as he rushed forward toward them with Rand following in his wake. "Fancy meeting you two here. Isn't it a beautiful morning? It's a great day to be alive. It's a great day to be rich! Right, Randy, buddy boy?!" he asked jubilantly of Rand who had just caught up with him and who immediately jabbed him in the ribs with his elbow to silence him and remind him of their pact of secrecy.

All of the diners at LaurelsHeath the day that they had discovered the diamonds secreted inside Alex's brick had been sworn to absolute secrecy about the discovery. It had been agreed that they were just protecting their interests by doing so. Matt especially wanted to keep everything hush-hush. He felt that if others heard, or even suspected, that there were diamonds at LaurelsHeath – and possibly even more in the bricks in Simon's basement – before they could gather them all the area would be overrun with prospectors. And he was likely correct in this belief! Of course, Rand had every intention of consulting with Inspector Jim Lahy to establish the legitimacy of their claim on the diamonds. The diamonds really belonged to Simon, when you thought about it, as the misshapen, large nugget-like golden blocks were below his basement. But, Matt had his mind set on the idea that he would be willing to share his newfound wealth with them – hopefully with him being the major recipient of Simon's largesse. After all, without Alex – with Mary Jo's help – deducing the relationship between the charm-sized key

on Charmer's collar and the impression on the block which ultimately led to him discovering the diamonds they would never know
that they existed in the first place. To Matt's way of thinking, Alex
was entitled to at least a finder's fee, and Alex was ALWAYS willing
to share.

"Rich?" queried Joan bewildered as she looked to Alex to clarify
the meaning of his evocative, upbeat exclamation.

"He means, "rich", because we have just discovered Simon,
Trudy and Elroy are part of our family." Edith improvised the on
the spot prevarication off-the-cuff. "He and Simon hit it off quite
famously from the very start. When he and Mary Jo first became
acquainted they had no idea that they were family."

"I know what you mean Mr. Caine." Joan said turning to Alex
and addressing him in a forthright manner. "Being away from Jed
isn't so bad in that he's just a hop, skip and a jump away by carriage. But I do feel rich-er when he's around close. And with my
girls all moved out.... Well, I <u>do</u> miss them something terrible." she
admitted to Alex haltingly and then paused pensively. "It's so good
to have your family around you!" Joan suddenly resumed speaking
with impassioned fervor and emotion. "Yes, you are very fortunate,
indeed, Mr. Caine."

"You know that you can call me Alex, Joan. After all the travails
of life we've been through we <u>definitely</u> do not have to stand on
formality here!" Alex responded looking comically beneath each of
his shoes as he heaved an inward sigh of relief that he had not inadvertently given up the ghost that they were guarding an important
secret. "Nope. No formality here!" he affirmed aloud with jocularity after his cursory inspection. "See? I checked. Get it? Stand
on...feet...formality...? Well, <u>I</u> thought that I was being clever."
Alex griped grumpily out of sorts and disappointed that no one had
found his jest humorous or even smiled in recognition of his sally.

"Excusez-moi, Alex. Have you...stepped in...something?"

Pierre asked discreetly on his approach as he turned to regard an overweight horse chowing down on some hay at a nearby feeding station and then turned slowly to openly consider some others at a watering trough.

"No, Pierre. I have NOT "stepped" in something." Alex replied in a huff at being so obviously off the mark misunderstood.

"Oh. I see." he said shortly and discreetly to Alex who was clearly out of sorts today – imagine, being flippant with Pierre Dûçot (how rude)! "Trudy wishes to consult with you about some household matters, Joan, dans le magasin là-bas." Pierre announced turning to address her and pointing to the shop on the next corner.

"I am on it, Pierre. I'd better hurry, too. The last time I left Trudy alone she bought the wrong type of tart tins and who knows what she'll do this time!" Joan fretted as she hurried off quickly to catch up with Trudy and hence stave off pending disaster.

"Be careful with her, Joan. Her feelings are extremely delicate! Do not offend her!" he nervously called out after her retreating back as she ran hurriedly down the avenue to disappear into the place of business Pierre had previously exited.

"Pierre?" Edith addressed him in query and moved to stand in front of him to garner his distracted attention.

"Oui, ma chérie?" he queried distractedly while continuing to peer in the direction of the shop where he had left Trudy. "Perhaps she needs my aid. In a big city such as this one she may feel over-whelmed…." he conjectured ponderously.

"Pierre, this is just what I wish to discuss with you! You are overly concerned with Trudy! You are NOT her Sir Walter Raleigh! She has lived here for years. Why would she feel overwhelmed?" Edith pronounced in exasperation.

"It is a gentilhomme's responsabilité to faire certain that ne personne takes advantage of the feminine ladies."

"But, Pierre. You are taking this to an extreme – you have

SHARON ELIZABETH SARKISIAN

become her toady!" Edith admonished her husband who felt less than masculine at being upbraided by his wife – and in public, too!

"Pierre Dûçot is no one's, comment dit-on, sidekick!" he informed her in a huff to repudiate her allegation and, seeking to change the subject and deflect attention from himself, he turned to Alex abruptly. "Maintenant, Alex, what are you playing avec encore!?" Pierre asked in irritation. "You are always…fiddling with something or other!" he said as he snatched a smooth knob with a number "2" depicted thereon from his hand.

CHAPTER 60

"We MUST convince her te take just a wee bit o' a vacation. After all, she be workin' hard at beautifyin' this old house. The puir lass be toiling herself into a frazzle! I dunna want te have another patient on me hands!"

"I'll ask her again, Matt. But you already asked her once and she said "no". Once she has made up her mind it's not likely that she's going to change it. She's stubborn that way. I appreciate your concern for her health, though." Dudley said earnestly to Matt as he reflected upon Callie's well-being. "She has been looking pretty tired lately." he conceded.

"Mais, bien sûr! Our dear Callie has been travaillant dur pour quelques semaines-"

"He means te say tha' the lassie be working hard fer weeks-" Matthew translated Pierre's comment irritably – couldna the man ever speak proper English?

"The dear child is, how you say, dead on her chaussures!" Pierre interjected assertively, displeased at being interrupted so rudely and seeking to regain control of the conversation.

"Feet, Pierre. FEET!" Matt expounded teary eyed and out of patience.

"Those, too." he agreed seriously with a profound look on his face.

"Baaah!!!" Matthew cried in dumbfounded frustration as Dudley laughed at the innocent misunderstanding.

"The feet are inside the chaussures, Pierre. And so, the phrase you meant to use is: Dead on her feet." Dudley corrected gently as Pierre opened his mouth with an indignant response only to wordlessly clamp it shut again as Dudley cluelessly continued speaking unaware of the Frenchman's angst. "But, I will try to convince her to take some time off."

"Tha' be all we can ask, Dudley, me boy. That be all we can ask." Matt said approvingly as he slapped Dudley on the back of the shoulder affectionately before Dudley exited through the screened side door of the sunroom. "We ha' te make sure tha' Callie be far out o' the picture o' things before she can leak the information of our diamond find te the populace at large!" he said urgently rushing to Pierre's side from his lookout vantage point at the window after peering outside at Dudley quickly to confirm his departure, releasing the folds of curtain he held aside to fall back into place concealing the image of Dudley's retreating form, and hearing the closing door click shut as it fell back into alignment with the doorjamb. "We all o' us know she canna fer the life o' her keep a confidential secret!" Matt continued fretfully subsequently rushing back to the door again to lift up the frilly red curtain covering the adjacent window a few inches to peep through it anxiously reassuring himself of the fact that Dudley truly was out of earshot before agilely flitting back to where Pierre stood and resuming his complaint. "She ha' no head fer business. We canna take any chances! Callie is what ye would call a blabbermouth! Not te be less o' a gentleman, but I had te state it! She just canna help it. I dunna even think she know what she be sayin' when she be tellin' all o' our confidential secrets. Hopefully, Dudley can convince her te leave the area fer other purposes – but, we needs handle this cagily fer if she were te find out the real reason we want her gone the lass will ne'er leave. What de ye think, Pierre, mon ami?" he asked the silent man with the compressed lips forming a straight line who regarded him belligerently and looked as if he were about to blow his stack.

"The utter impudence." stated Pierre indignantly while controlling his anger.

"That's exactly what I be sayin', mon ami. I be totally concurring with ye."

"The undisciplined…pip-squeak!"

"I be agreein' with ye one hundred percent. I asked politely. But, we canna be too harsh on the lassie-"

"How DARE Dudley correct Pierre Dûçot? After all I have done for him…. Showing to him the, comment dit-on, ropes…. To act so disrespectfully! C'est incroyable!"

"What's all this about someone being disrespectful?" inquired Rand as he entered the sunroom letting the screen door slam shut behind him.

"C'est this Dudley. He actually has the temerity to correct Pierre Dûçot! How shameless!"

"Would ye quit yer complainin' fer the life of us all! Dunna ye see tha' yer hot temper is only goin' te bite off our own noses te spite our faces? We need te keep ourselves te Dudley's good side so that he'll be amenable te our cause. So tha' we can enlist his aid te convince the lass te leave the area!" Matthew retorted to Pierre before Rand could respond to the irate Frenchman.

"Wait a minute." Rand interjected. "What do you mean? Who's the "lass" – do you mean, Callie?" Rand proposed the guess as she was Dudley's wife.

"Randy, me boy, of course, I mean, Callie."

"But that's absolutely ridiculous. Why would you want to get rid of Callie?"

"Because, my dear fellow," Matt explained to the ingenuous Randmore, "Callie be a newspaper!"

"What ARE you talking about?"

"Matt is saying that Callie is an open book!" Pierre began to explain only to be interrupted by the doctor.

"Ye see. Even though all o' us in the room the day Alex uncovered the gems were sworn te a pact o' secrecy, Callie just canna be trusted not te blurt out the information unintentionally. The lassie canna keep nothing close te her vest! Tha' be why we all are better off if she go somewhere else fer a little while – just until we've had the time te gather all o' the precious baubles from Simon's basement." asserted Matthew with only an assuredness borne of greed could muster up.

"The mind does not connect to her loose lips." Pierre added to convince him of this truth as Rand started to laugh at Matt's single-minded, baseless worry and Pierre's inept use of colloquialism.

"I should have known. Is <u>this</u> what this is all about? The diamonds? You, Matt, are something else!" Rand choked out between his chuckles.

"C'est vrai! It is true. Souviens, avant? Callie told Dudley toutes les choses about our treasure map from the tackle boîte." Pierre reminded Rand in an ominous tone of panic as Dudley, who had jogged back to the sunroom in order to retrieve his forgotton set of keys which he had left lying on the table, halted at the door on hearing mention of his name to listen to what was being said.

"An' then, when Pierre was in a debilitated state, she stole into me private papers an' filched the map out o' me briefcase te show it te him outright!" Matt added.

"And c'est certain that if she remains she will, comment dit-on, spill her beans to the first outsider engaging her in conversation."

"Okay." said Dudley red-faced with pent-up anger and all riled up pushing open the outer door to charge through it. "All bets are off! I get the picture. I thought you had forgiven me and Calvin for our part in the past fiasco. I stupidly thought that we had left the past in the past – that it was all behind us. Well, now I know better!"

"But, Dudley, you know these two-"

"No, no, no. You don't have to make excuses to ME, Randy.

But, Callie deserves better than this negative opinion you have of her. She's honest and true – which is more than I can say of you, Pierre, or of you, Matt, considering what I heard you just say about her. She's your Hostess, for goodness' sake – and here she is going to stay!"

CHAPTER 61

"**D**id she say anything about me?" Cyrus asked Clyde as they gathered the dinner dishes from the hostages' evening meal.

"Ya didn't have ta follow me all the way down here ta find <u>that</u> out. She's all hot dang ta join her aunt at your party."

"But what about ME?!" he prodded as overeagerly as a young schoolboy involved in his first romance and oblivious of any listeners other than Clyde at that moment.

"She said ya were a generous person ta open your house ta them!" Clyde responded while cocking his head at an angle and scratching his scruffy, bearded chin thoughtfully.

"You leave her alone, you evil, evil man!" cried out a feminine voice.

"Now, now, dear. Do not call him that. He is evil, but, he is merely the mouse. Roland is the rat. <u>He</u> is only doing what he is told." her masculine counterpart informed her soothingly with an open taunt directed solely at his captor.

"Don't you speak of my father like that!" exploded Cyrus in anger at his restrained guests. "You are the ones who put him in that coma! Didn't know that – did you?" he yelled in defense of Roland Sykes at the openmouthed man who was obviously at a loss for the appropriate verbiage with which to express his shocked surprise and subsequent sympathies. "Well, you'd just better be <u>glad</u> he is in that coma because he wouldn't be as nice to you as <u>I</u> am being. Why do you think you've had it so easy these past couple of years? Because he's not at the helm – that's why! You are dealing with his softhearted weakling son. Dad collapsed after you nearly killed him during your burglary attempt!"

"That is not how it was! If you had chosen to listen to <u>us</u> at that point, instead of your lying, poor excuse for a parent, we could have explained-"

"Gag them, Clyde. I'm sick of listening to these insulting lies." Cyrus said scornfully cutting short the protestations of his restrained inmate.

"Gotcha, BOSS." Clyde responded as he stuffed cloth kerchiefs into the mouths of both hostages, knotted the ends of each respective square cloth behind their heads and resecured their wrists to the arms of their chairs with ropes.

"All you two had to do was to decide to come clean with those documents that my father wanted from you two and hand them over. But, no. You had to be stubborn and incapacitate an innocent man. And <u>all</u> of your attempts to disparage his good name will not change the facts! Well, the doctors say Dad's vital signs are improving and he's getting better. You had better hope that they are right because if he dies because of you, you will see how fast this soft, lenient, bumbling <u>mouse</u> becomes a raging bull thirsty for vengeance!" threatened Cyrus in a hard, cold voice as he gazed at his prisoners through bloodshot orbs filled with fire.

"But, I think a vacation is a great idea!" Callie said brightly as Dudley regarded her with wide-eyed astonishment while she calmly dropped two sugar cubes into her cup of hot coffee as they sat in front of the counter of the beverage kiosk where Danish, muffins and newspapers were also vended.

"But, they want to get <u>rid</u> of you, Callie." Dudley stated, fuming at the very idea, as he swiped the banana-nut muffin from her hand before it reached the lips of her opened mouth.

"Dudley! Come on, that's my lunch!" exclaimed the bemused young lady as she regarded her husband who was seething with rage. "Honestly, Honey. Why should I mind if they want me gone or not? I could use a break. I'm tired. All this getting up early to meet with contractors – dealing with their flubs, supervising deliveries.... Listening to Pierre's problems, Elvie's problems, worrying about the guys – they almost got killed! I am pooped! All I'm saying is that a little time away is not such a bad idea about now."

"Where is your pride, Callie?! Matt and Pierre called you a blabbermouth! I think you should stick to your principles and stay – show them they can't intimidate you!"

"I don't <u>have</u> any principles, Dudley – well, not like <u>you</u> mean. It's worth it if my going helps ease the tension, for now. And with me gone, if something "leaks out" information-wise they won't be able to blame me for it! Don't you see? It's the perfect scenario. They'll have to blame someone else for a change."

"The worst part of it all is that I thought they'd forgiven us for past events. I thought that they understood that we, Calvin and I, were penitent and had no intention of ever crossing the line again. I thought that we were friends!"

"Ahhh.... So, that's what it's all about. It's all about you. <u>You</u> are feeling guilty. This attitude of yours has absolutely nothing to do with me. You are feeling slighted because you feel Matt and Pierre's stance concerning me somehow reflects on you. Well, I have got news for you, my handsome husband – it doesn't! <u>You</u> are the one projecting it on yourself!" she elucidated rooting through her bag for some money to pay the vendor with. "Here you are – keep the change!" Callie told the cashier as she handed him the approximate amount of paper currency to cover her lunch check.

"That is so much hogwash! And, you know it, too. I don't know about you, but I have no intention of being forced out of <u>my</u> own house just to please the whims and fantasies of two greedy men who prize wealth over the cultivation of honest relationships!" Dudley said piously as he watched Callie throw the other end of her scarf around her neck and followed her quickly moving form across the street. 'It was almost as if she were deliberately attempting to elude him!' he thought.

"My, oh, my, how sanctimonious art thou, Dudley. Well, if the diamonds are all that Pierre and Matt can think of that's their problem. I have nothing to do with it. All that aside, my place is with my husband and if you're staying, my love, then I'm staying." Callie proclaimed affirmatively as she saw a lull in the oncoming traffic from the island of pavement she had reached and hurriedly made her way across another side street to her buggy with Dudley trailing in her wake.

Discreetly following the pair in order to eavesdrop on their conversation Dwight Sanders' eyebrows shot up from behind the shield of his newspaper at Callie's mention of diamonds. His surreptitious attempt at gleaning information had paid off big time! So, that was what Barney was always alluding to when he talked about his boss' lucrative plans! He would just have to confront Clyde and let him know he knew all about the score. Maybe Clyde and his boss would cut him in for a share. This was big...BIG!

CHAPTER 62

"I don't understand why ya keep those two around – they tried ta murder your father!"

"They claim otherwise. They say it was self-defense. I did not see the altercation and I need to be sure. I need proof!"

"So, now ya are disbelieving ya own father – ya own flesh and blood?" Clyde asked Cyrus indignantly. "Now, I can see as how ya don't blame the girl – she was clear in the next state! But, ya has got ta know that your pa would never lie ta you." he asserted in outrage.

Hunkered down on the floorboards of the gazebo, Cyrus shook his head from side to side and scratched his chin while he looked up at Clyde contemplatively. For an employee he was getting a little too pushy. However, his father had trusted him and Clyde was the only link to him that he had. Until Roland woke up to direct him otherwise he supposed that he would just have to keep Clyde around.

"Dad used to spend a lot of time in this gazebo just thinking and pacing the floor. I often wondered when these old floorboards would wear out!" Cyrus reminisced chuckling with the memory. "Now, these floorboards are torn up all right. Only, the culprit was last week's storm and not my Dad doing the damage. How's that for irony? Now, here's the impasse, Clyde. Those historical ladies are breathing down my neck and my Dad is in a coma; the gold bricks are a mystery to me and I do not know what he would want me to do."

"Well, when Roland was writhing on the ground after that

murdering skunk shot him — the smoking gun sitting right there on the barn floor by his side — did he tell ya anything unusual? Did he happen ta mention anything like where the deed ta the house is?" asked Clyde offhandedly with a penetrating stare.

"We have been through this all before." Cyrus spoke wearily rising and dragging his arm across his lips. "He said to "take care" of Elroy — which I did…. I got him on the wanted list with the police. And he mentioned that the bricks were the key."

"De ya 'memba anything else?" Clyde prompted him anxiously, jogging his memory.

"He pointed at the man and said: "He shot me.". Then, he started rambling about the cat. Soon after that, he fell into a coma and I called Doc. I still can't figure why he was holding those two hostage to begin with. I don't know what to do with them and I had no choice at the time then to put the man back into his restraints and hide the man and his wife — with your help — until Dad comes out of the coma and tells me why he was holding them as hostages in the first place. They could be one of those husband and wife criminal duos for all I know and until I <u>do</u> know I can't rightly release them into an unsuspecting public. I can't even inform the police of their existence because they might say something damaging about my father that is untrue and he is not able to defend himself against false allegations in his condition. Arguably, the male hostage should be arrested for attempted murder! You do not happen to know anything about what they had been arguing with my father about — do you Barnett?" inquired Cyrus irascibly as he had worked himself up into a worried frenzy with the weight of the world resting upon his shoulders and his hands figuratively tied.

"Me? I don't know nothin'. Elroy is the one who let those two louses loose, though. Otherwise, they could never have gotten ta ya father in the first place. So, indirectly," Clyde said, stressing the second "i" in indirectly, "Elroy is partly ta blame for your father's woebegone condition! That's probably why ya pa said ta take care of him!" Clyde finished innocently as he gazed through the yawning opening in the floor and whistled disbelievingly at the enormity of the breach. "That's a drop." he noted as he let a pebble fall from his fingers and marked the time until he heard it hit the bottom with a sharp "ping". "Man, it's dark down there, too! We just might be able ta lower a rope ladder down there – of course, we would need a strong post ta hitch the other end ta. Then, we could climb down-"

"Whatever for, bozo?!" Cyrus snapped at him curtly, annoyed that his concerns about his father were being taken so lightly and were being so casually dismissed out of hand.

"Ta investigate down there, of course! It looks ta be a room below." Clyde observed directing the beam of a flashlight through the opened hole. "There just might be something to this floor – there just might!"

"Dad did spend a lot of time here. Maybe you are right, Barnett." Cyrus relented thoughtfully as he lowered his body to rest on his stomach, stretched it across the floor of the gazebo and poked his head into the opening while Clyde held the light strategically to illuminate the dark interior. "Wait a second. There's something here...." he said with surprise at the unexpected find reaching down into the hole to retrieve a man's shoe from a small upper ledge. "It's a shoe.... Someone's been looking around down there – maybe my father...?" speculated Cyrus as he looked to Clyde for a guiding opinion and handed him the leather article of footwear for inspection.

"Naw." Clyde scoffed in negation. "This shoe isn't his size, anyway. This shoe's too modern. Not his style...not his style. You know those old-fashioned, gentlemanly-type two-tone shoes your pa always wore.... Hey!" he suddenly exclaimed snapping his fingers with his excitement as he tried to jog his own memory and finally succeeded in doing so. "I saw that dang outlander wearing hip-hop shoes like these ones. Ya know, the young one with the blond wife who's so buddy-buddy with that fella who's got the single name: Simon. I shoulda known he'd be poking all around here. He thinks he's some kind of detective. He was already poking about the construction site. Alex. That's his name. He is trouble with a capital "T", that one is. I never for a minute trusted that little-boy face of his from the moment that I saw him. And now I'm proven right — vindicated. Well, we'll take care of him fer snooping around where he don't belong.... I know! We'll get him fer trespassing! This shoe is the proof he was here — Cordell can't dispute that and neither can he." Clyde said cheerfully holding up the shoe and shaking it in the air triumphantly while expressing his approval of the situation with a gleeful hoot and holler. "Ya already, like a good son, took care of Elroy like ya daddy, Roland, told ya to.... Ya got him nice and blackballed out of the community. Next, we'll teach that Alex Caine a thing or two about minding his own business! Sandy! What are ya doing out this way abouts?" he inquired good-naturedly of his friend who had momentarily startled him out of his long-winded tirade with his abrupt appearance.

"I was looking all over for you, Barney. I know all about what you and Mr. Cyrus are up to," Dwight Sanders asserted, halting to tip his foreman's cap to Cyrus, "and I want in!"

CHAPTER 63

"Come this way. I have something to show you." Simon said gravely as he shepherded the four other men to the basement stairs and they all descended them together rank and file, one man after the other.

"Begorra!!! What went on here?" Matthew expostulated flabbergasted at the thick layer of dust which had not existed previously covering the floor and surrounding askew, upended objects as well as the unnaturally brown particles which hung as if a curtain suspended from above, polluting the air.

"It looks like a bomb exploded in your cottage, Simon!"

"Randy, you're not far off." Simon concluded grimly.

"I cannot breathe!" Pierre suddenly shrieked shrilly taking them all by surprise so that they stopped and stared. "How could you bring me here? You know that Pierre Dûçot is claustrophobic!" he complained bitterly in a frenetic panic as he held the upper flap of his jacket across his nose as a shield against the choking particulate dust matter.

"This is even worse than the root cellar!" Alex proclaimed in the midst of Matthew's unbridled laughter at what he considered was Pierre's unwarranted discomfort.

"I can feel the walls, comment dit-on, closing in!" the Frenchman proclaimed in abject horror as his eyes bulged from their sockets.

"Quit yer complainin'!" Matt admonished him lightly chortling heartily at Pierre's unfounded theatrics as he dabbed at the tears of mirth trembling in his eyes and rolling down his cheeks with a handkerchief. "Ye sound just like an old lady."

"May I show you the rest of the damage?" queried Simon some-what gravely in order to capture their attention as they looked to him expectantly and he pushed aside the screen masking the stairway leading downward to the catacombs revealing that it was blocked by imploded debris from below.

Matthew was crestfallen on viewing the blockage. There seemed to be no way around the wreckage. Not even a crack or small chink in the obstructing debris was evident. Excavation of the matter appeared to be impossible. He had already been calculating how to spend his share of the proceeds of the remuneration. Drat it all...! His dreams were shattered. Matt felt drawn up as taught as a bow string – he was that tense. The children's educations were at stake, BLAST IT! Matthew suddenly chuckled to himself at the double entendre and relaxed his tight muscles a bit. He decided to concentrate on solving the problem at hand. There had to be a solution to this somehow! He snapped to attention as he heard Simon speaking to them all.

"I do not know what caused the explosion. Trudy and I were fast asleep last night when suddenly we were awakened by what sound-ed like a huge explosion the quaking of which shook us right out of our bed. We did not know whether the house was on fire or if the center of the upheaval emanated from a point outside of the house. We immediately went to collect Elroy from his room and then exit the house to a safe area. However, to our surprise, his bedroom was empty and we descended to the first floor to see him escaping from the basement just as another explosion erupted from beneath the basement and shook the entire foundation of the house with its force propelling him along with it and hurling him clear across the room." Simon expounded.

"Was Elroy badly injured?" Rand queried with marked con-cern coloring his voice and a solemn expression transforming his habitually calm countenance.

"Thank God, he was fine. In fact, when we had rushed over to his side to help him to his feet he had this huge mischievous grin on his face. He had thought of it as a huge adventure! I must confess to you that at that point I briefly considered the possibility as to whether he might have had something to do with the upheaval and, however inadvertently, have caused the explosion somehow." he admitted guiltily.

"You don't say...." commented Rand rhetorically.

"Oui." said Pierre abruptly regaining his composure and suddenly coming back to life and rejoining the conversation. "Do we know any autres personnes comme ça, Alex?" he asked of Alex affectedly with a nonchalant, wide-eyed innocence while he stared at him unblinkingly.

"Hey! Just because I have an inquiring mind doesn't mean that I'm foolhardy." snapped Alex indignantly, miffed at Pierre's supercilious implication. "NOT that I am saying that ELROY is foolhardy." he decried apologetically to Simon, rejecting the very idea vehemently. "It is just that Pierre likes to pick on me from time to time because I am the youngest AND, dare I say, the handsomest!" he concluded defiantly turning his back to Pierre in order to accentuate the fact that he was slighting HIM this time.

"Pah!" Pierre responded with resounding derision. "I present to you the evidence. Alex is tous les fois playing with something for, how you said, adventure. He plays with the cannons; with the stocks in the field; with the-"

"With the cat who showed te us the direction out o' tha' root cellar!" Matthew quickly inserted into the commentary as a reminder.

"And, who carried the key on her collar that opened the golden brick containing the diamonds. And remember, Alex found that brick on one of his, what you call, adventures!" Rand spoke forth pointedly and proudly in defense of his cousin.

"Et, voilà. Maintenant he is playing with quelque chose d'autre in his pocket!" persevered Pierre in defense of his point, continuing to speak disregarding Matt and Rand's observations in support of Alex, catching at Alex's wrist to pull it from his pocket and expose a yellow object clasped within his clutching hand.

"We all o' us, except Simon, are quibblin' now te no end. Simon and his family just survived a near tragedy in the makin' and fer this reason we must all be thankful. Yer a shining example o' what a husband and father should be, Simon!"

"Thank you, Matt. But you know what this all means – don't you?"

"Aye, Simon. I am sure'n afraid that I do!" he responded grimly. "This kind o' explosion canna only mean one thing: SABOTAGE. Someone else or some persons unknown te us know of our treasure an' mean te keep us from it with this obstacle! The crux o' the matter be how can we dig through all o' the rubble blockin' our access te the blocks below which contain the diamonds."

"But, wait a second. Aren't you jumping the gun, Matthew? We do not know for sure that the explosion was anything but an accident. If others knew of the diamonds, then why have they left them down there for so long? Obviously, if they had access enough to plant explosives down there and set them off they could have taken the gems whenever they wanted. Why the explosion now?" Rand asked.

"Dunna be lookin' fer logic in this case, me fine-hearted fellow. The nefarious mind works in strange ways.... It not be functionin' like yours an' mine. Tryin' te fathom it is near te impossible!" stated the Irishman with absolute certainty and a scholarly bent to his manner as he folded his arms with assured finality.

"Maybe, they didn't know how the nuggets and blocks were valuable. After all, it took us a long time to figure it out and that's only because I saw the charm on Charmer's collar and Mary Jo and I figured out that it was a key." Alex conjectured.

"You could very well be correct, Alex. But, isn't it baffling how they figured it out now? After all this time...." Simon pondered aloud.

"I think that maybe <u>they</u> knew about the diamonds but didn't think that <u>anyone</u> <u>else</u> knew of their existence. So, now it's only a matter of who gets to the bricks first. And that means that we have just got to figure out some way to get down into those catacombs before they do!" Alex surmised triumphantly.

"Only we know about the diamonds." Rand asserted. "There is no conspiracy or hocus-pocus going on! If any others did know about the diamonds they would have had to have been tipped off and there is no one among us who would betray our secret!"

"Attends. One moment, s'il te plaît. You all are forgetting one crucial element. This is the one key straw which is breaking the camel's hump!" interjected Pierre solemnly raising his index finger for emphasis of his forthcoming point to be made as the other men watched him expectantly.

Funny.... All in the basement waited on Pierre's word and yet he remained silent. He seemed to be waiting in anticipation for someone to finish his thought for him and, therefore, stared back at <u>them</u> eagerly awaiting a response which he considered to be elementary. This unorthodox, out of the ordinary face-off continued until finally a dense, impenetrable cloud hanging over Matthew's head dissipated, vanishing into thin air; his wrinkled forehead with the knitted eyebrows cleared and he blurted:

"Callie!" Matthew said bitterly.

"Callie." affirmed the other men simultaneously as if this were a foregone conclusion.

CHAPTER 64

"We be needin' te ascertain whether the explosion in Simon's basement was set off deliberately or was purely by chance. Edith happened te mention ye had dealt with demolition devices durin' the war and so.... Ye see, me dear boy," Matthew shifted his weight uncomfortably from one foot to the other as he prepared to ask his favor, "ye bein' an' explosives specialist an' all o' that, yer expertise would be invaluable te knowin' if this be a natural disaster or one thought out an' prefabricated." Matthew explained, broaching the topic to Calvin in a gingerly fashion.

"Dudley told me that you wanted to shunt him and Callie to the side and send them off on some trumped-up vacation to get them out of the way while you harvested the diamonds solo." said Calvin accusingly as he regarded Matthew with a semi-hurt expression.

"That be soundin' pretty ugly the way ye just put it." Matthew conceded guiltily and lowered his gaze to regard the ground shamefacedly. "But I didna mean no disrespect." he said quickly. "The diamonds be fer all o' us – Simon an' Trudy be willing te share. I was only tryin' te protect our interests so we <u>all</u> can be rich an' prosper."

"Then – if so – you should have brought it up straightforward to them, like you just did with me, instead of playing sneaky mind games with Dudley. You were USING him to manipulate his own wife. And all of this chicanery after you got him to trust you, too, and make him think you were his friend; had let bygones be bygones and had Callie's best interests at heart!"

"Calvin, dear boy. I be deeply penitent an' truly remorseful…. Canna ye forgive me? I apologize te ye. Canna we just forgive me lapse in judgment in this circumstance and forget?" pleaded Matthew with ingratiating sincerity.

Calvin regarded Matthew circumspectly. He <u>sounded</u> very sincere and humble…. He relented and relaxed his stiff stance and demeanor, disrobing himself of his combative manner.

"Okay, Matt. Dudley can be a little sensitive at times, I will admit. I admit it. I know you well enough to realize that you meant no harm. So, let us go to Simon's and we'll see what we can find. If there's something fishy in the mix I'll find it — there's nowhere to hide!"

"Ahhh! Thank you, me boy. Thank ye fer yer understandin'. Ye see," said Matthew sighing with satisfaction on digesting Cal's response as he clapped a hand behind Cal's right shoulder and continued speaking while they walked to Simon's house, "when I called Callie a blabbermouth I didna mean te be harsh."

"You called Callie a <u>blabbermouth</u>?!" Calvin said in rhetorical disbelief. "No wonder Dud was steamed!"

"An' when Pierre an' I were speakin' te each other the fact that Callie be akin te a daily newspaper may ha' come up in the conversation — but 'twas only because she canna control her chatter." he added quickly to soften the criticism. "She be a very givin' person — dunna misunderstand me by no means. But sometimes she be givin' too much!" Matthew asserted in frustration. "Sharin' our personal, confidential information in such top secret circumstances just will <u>not</u> do."

"And you said <u>that</u> to Dudley?" Calvin queried appalled in an offended tone of voice.

"Of course not! He overheard us, Pierre an' I, talkin'."

"I see. Of course, that makes it alright, then!" Calvin shortly ground out vexedly incredulous, wondering at the unabashed insensitivity surrounding Matthew's justification.

Matt spoke as if because his potentially slanderous comments were spoken behind Dudley's and Callie's backs this made the act condonable and, therefore, acceptable when it was not!

"I hardly believe the lassie knows that she be blurting out our private secrets. It just comes naturally te her." Matthew continued unaware of Calvin's tempered disapproval.

"So. You are saying Callie is a loose cannon who can't be trusted to keep her mouth shut." Calvin said from between taut lips attempting to control his anger and maintain his resolution of forgiveness.

"Ye understand, then?" Matthew inquired hopefully in a worried tone oblivious to his companion's angst and barely cloaked sarcasm. "Although, ye are puttin' it a bit bluntly, te be sure."

"And what do you think of Dudley, then?" asked Cal without addressing Matt's question.

"Well. He just canna see the forest fer the trees. He canna see her faults. He needs te be more objective."

"Matt," Calvin said controlling his outrage at Matt's criticisms of his brother and sister-in-law admirably, "I think that we could ALL use a good, healthy dose of objectivity." he concluded pointedly as he knocked on Simon's front door.

"So, are we going to that shindig at Candlestick Manor next week?" Mary Jo asked Cari as Alex trailed alongside them repeatedly pitching an object up into the sky and catching it with one hand as he kept pace with the two women.

"Yes, we are. That is why we are on the way to town to buy us both new dresses on Alex's and Rand's credit account at the department store. Alex is cosigner and so we need him to okay our transactions there. Rand said he was otherwise occupied or else he would have been glad to come with us instead. But, in my opinion, though, I believe that he was glad he was busy and did not have to follow a couple of girls around on their shopping excursion and carry their packages. But at least we have Alex."

"Such as he is...." jested Mary Jo as she observed him catch his flying projectile backhanded and turned to Cari shrugging her shoulders in feigned disappointment.

"You know, Randy did not want me to go to the dinner – he was that jealous. I think Pierre had been filling his head with ideas of Cyrus trying to whisk me off of my feet and spirit me away somewhere! It took a lot of my feminine wiles and quite a bit of persuasion on my part to convince Randy that this was not the case and to allow me to attend the dinner party. But, then, who could resist these pleading eyes?" Cari rejoined as she opened her eyes wide and thrust out her pouty lower lip.

"You're bad – do you know that, Cari?" Mary Jo teased her as they both enjoyed an unrestrained, uninhibited bout of laughter.

"Yeah! You know, you women give us males of the species a hard time? You just have to act all injured and get all teary-eyed and us men have to go groveling for your forgiveness. Aw, man! It's so unfair!" opined Alex breaking his silence.

"Oh, poor Alex. Did little Mary Jo hurt your feelings?" she asked in jest as she walked her index and third fingers up against his chest until they reached his collar and then touched the tip of his nose playfully with one of them.

"Would you stop playing around, Mary Jo?!!!" Alex said pushing her away. "I am serious. You should be serious, too, for a change. Pierre and Matt are sure that someone is on to us and purposely blew up the entrance in Simon's basement to the diamonds. In fact, Matt is going to ask Calvin to investigate the site in question at Simon's house to see if there's evidence that the explosion was deliberate!"

"Don't get so agitated, my darling. How could anyone possibly know about the diamonds?" she asked in exasperation.

"Pierre and Matt think that Callie let it slip somehow!"

"She did not!" Mary Jo cried out in defense of her cousin. "Do not be ridiculous. How do you let something like that slip somehow? Please, enlighten me." she asked challengingly as she dared him with her piercing eyes to gainsay her and Alex subsequently fidgeted.

"It <u>is</u> possible, Mary Jo." Cari said taking pity on Alex's plight of being caught between defending "the guys" and caving in on his convictions to please his wife. "Callie <u>has</u> told.... I mean, she <u>has</u> said.... Well, you have to admit that she <u>has</u> given out – what THEY consider to be – our privileged information before." Cari said haltingly as Mary Jo turned her judgmental gaze in her direction.

CHAPTER 65

"Hey, Chrissy! How's things going on in your neck of the woods?" Clyde asked with genuine jocularity on seeing his old friend as he pounded the last nail into one of the new floorboards of the gazebo.

"Better than ever since Roland helped me see the light of the Lord. I am doing all right. Now that I am born again I see beauty and light in all around me. I am thankful and grateful for living this glorious existence."

"Well, ain't that a hoot. I'm rightly glad ta see ya. But, I reckoned ya was working with the underprivileged children down at that orphanage.... They didn't <u>fire</u> ya, did they?!" jested Clyde with an overeager laugh as he rose from his knees to admire the neatly finished repair work he had just completed of the gazebo floor and stamped his right foot over its new surface in several places for good measure to test its strength and ability to support weight.

"Nawww – tee, hee, hee." he chuckled lightheartedly. "You are a card, Clyde. You sure are! I am here to visit Roland, of course." Chris Colden elucidated his voice lowering and suddenly becoming solemn. "I heard he was hurt badly in an accident and I wanted to see him and offer him some solace – if I can."

"Well, that's awful nice of ya. Awful nice. You're such a good fella. How <u>could</u> they have ever come ta think of ya as a convicted criminal?!"

"I was not always this grounded and serene, Clyde. I have made many mistakes in my life and, I am ashamed to say, that during those dark times in my life I enjoyed unspeakable...activities. But that type of life is all behind me now. From the day Roland took me under his wing and turned my life around I started to live clean and I am resolute that I will not slip-slide back into my old ways. Roland was my rock THEN and he is my rock NOW."

"I admire that attitude. I surely do." stated Clyde methodically putting away his hammer and nails into his toolbox; closing its lid; securing its latch and lifting it off of the bench with its handle paying careful attention to each step of the procedure.

Clyde's mother had always taught him that neatness was a virtue from the time that he was a small boy wearing knee pants.

"But, Roland is in more serious condition than I reckon ya done heard. He is in a coma." Clyde elaborated. "And it was no accident, either. Shot. He was shot – and by people he trusted, too. They'd turned bad somehow – like rabid curs biting the hand that feeds 'em. They was tied up in the house. I saw them there and I feel guilty because I was the one that let 'em loose. They told me that Elroy was the one who tied them up during one of his games of Cops and Robbers – or was it Cowboys and Indians.... I forget. But that's not important! I let 'em loose and went to berate Elroy for his bad behavior – for something that he didn't even do! The irony of it all!" he cried in mental anguish shaking his fist with emotion and then he continued speaking. "I scolded Elroy for – ya know – for tying people up like that and leaving them that way when the game was over. He denied it though, like most kids would. Said cops and robbers had nothing to do with it. And then I saw that things was missing. Roland's expensive statuettes were off the shelves.... I heard a tussle going on out back so I grabbed my rifle and ran ta the barn where it came from. Roland was lying bleeding on the ground with a handgun and a club beside him. And the two people that he trusted most, looking guilty as all get out, were there next to his poor broken body. The woman stood over him just watching as the man knelt next to him with his hands on his throat looking ta finish him off. It was a terrible sight." concluded Clyde with much gravity shaking his head from side to side with pity at the memory. "They would have gotten me, too, if I didn't have Bessie, that's what I call my rifle, with me. And ta clinch it all, for one brief, shining moment Roland woke up. He pointed his finger up and said the condemning words: He did it. Roland was my best friend. I felt terrible."

"That is the most heartwrenching story that I have ever heard. My mentor.... Oh, my mentor. There can never be another Roland Sykes!" Chris wailed piously in a grief-stricken fervor of desolation.

"Yes siree. And ta my way of thinking if Elroy was telling the truth, as I 'spect he was, Roland may have tied those two people up himself! He probably found out that they were traitors to him and were really after something material. Maybe he had tied them up for interrogation purposes and I, without knowing any better, let them go by mistake and they did Roland in before he could find out the vital information. That's what I am thinking. But here's the kicker: they claim that it was self-defense. They say that there was a third person there and that he was the one responsible for trying to murder Roland only this third party ran away afore I came in and they was only attempting to revive Roland with resuscitation instead of chasing after the perpetrator of the dastardly deed!" Clyde recalled the couple's reasonable excuse for their actions sarcastically mocking its sincerity with his scoffing tone of voice.

"Why don't they just admit their guilt and ask forgiveness for their actions? Doing penance for your crime, I have found, is more liberating than covering it up."

"There's ya answer, Chrissy, plain as day: LIBERATING. There'll be no liberating when they are locked up for good!"

"Is there a slim chance that they could be telling the truth?" prodded Chris. "A person is innocent until proven guilty, you know."

"None. Chris, yer being too kind. I know Roland taught ya that.

But look at the evidence. I was right there! The man was throttling Roland – his hands were around his throat-"

"Perhaps, he was just loosening Roland's shirt collar to give him air – to allow him to breathe."

"He was holding his nose so he couldn't draw breath!"

"Perhaps, he was performing cardiopulmonary resuscitation?"

"Tsk, tsk, tsk! You're being too kind, ya know? I think Roland did too good of a job reforming ya!" Clyde conceded chuckling with delight at his own observation. "Yer always being inclined ta give one the benefit of the doubt! Here's the down and dirty: Those two no-good murderers claim that there was a third lawbreaker. One who had it in for my boss, Roland, and was lying in wait for him in the barn ta hijack him. They were walking outside after I'd re-leased them from their bonds and saw Roland and the other man arguing something fierce inside of the barn through the open barn door as they were passing by. Assuming skullduggery 'twere afoot they backtracked and entered inside and by that time the man and Roland were wrestling amongst themselves. The unknown assail-ant picked up this piece of kindling on the spur of the moment of seeing them and started to club Roland with it. The two of them then jumped in ta help and started ta grabbing and hitting at the anonymous perpetrator, who fought them back, until he got over-whelmed and ran away. Meanwhile, they stayed behind ta help poor Roland. Soon after, they heard a gunshot ringing through the air from an undisclosed location and Roland's life blood started ta spurt out of his body."

"That is a reasonable story." responded Chris judiciously.

"That is all it is – a STORY! I told ya. I saw the gun right there at Roland's side! It was smoking – freshly fired. My boss pointed at the guy directly."

"How could he have pointed at him if he was on his back?" Chris inquired perplexed.

"Of course, he could not point DIRECTLY at him." Clyde spoke in exasperation. "He was as near ta losing consciousness as it was! But he definitely raised up his pointer finger ta the ceiling of the hayloft, clearly meaning ta finger him, and announced most unequivocally: 'HE DID IT.'!"

CHAPTER 66

"I have just received this missive from me Ellie. She has informed me tha' that bloody scoundrel, Chris Colden, is out on reprieve from prison." Matthew announced in concerned alarm.

"When did this happen?" asked Mary Jo with concern for everyone's welfare as she finished darning one of Megan's socks, snapped the end of the thread between her teeth and raised her fearful countenance with its fear filled eyes inquiringly.

"Accordin' te her sources he has been on the loose fer about a year, now." Matthew informed her as he adjusted his reading spectacles and continued to peruse Eleanor's letter in depth and at length.

"He had better not attempt coming to cette région avec his criminal activities because I shall then be forced to discipline the cochon moi-même!" Pierre stated with supercilious certainty as he intertwined his fingers, inverted his hands and cracked his knuckles outwardly causing the Irishman to lower the sheet of paper before his face and address his daughter playfully.

"Ye hear that, Megan? Yer Uncle Pierre be goin' te protect us! What a relief!" Matthew told his little girl as she giggled and took her newly mended socks from Mary Jo's lap and ran to the doorway only to be halted by the words of her father. "Say, thank you, te yer Aunt Mary Jo." he admonished her before she could make her escape through the exit.

"You sound just like Mother!" Megan cried stamping her little foot petulantly at the gentle reminder.

"I am glad te hear it. Yer Mother isna here now, young Miss.,

and she be countin' on me te make ye mind yer manners and not te
allow ye te behave like a young hellion. So, say, "Thank you, Aunt
Mary Jo." te yer Aunt Mary Jo!" he snapped at her so sharply that
Megan's mouth fell open wide in surprise.

She was used to being the apple of her father's eye. He had
never raised his voice to her in anger before. He had always shielded
her from her Mother's sharp-tongued discipline.

"Then, ye can go outside an' play." Matthew told her in a softer,
gentler tone on viewing the hurt in his daughter's eyes as she stood
still as a frozen relic suspended in amber.

"Thank you, Aunt Mary Jo." Megan parroted before turning and
running from the room.

"There was no reason to become angry with the child, Matthew.
Cette parodie de justice is not sa faute. Mais tu peux reste calme.
I have no intention of letting that rotten apple fall farther than the
tree. I have a strategic plan which will-"

"Hold yer horses, mon ami general. I be readin' here in this
letter that the Colden fellow has changed his ways. It says here"
Matthew informed Pierre as he continued reading "he be working
at the monastery with the children, o' all things, and is trainin' an'
studyin' te be a…minister!" he gasped in disbelief as he whipped off
his black-rimmed reading eyeglasses and looked over the top edge
of Eleanor's letter at those about him to note their reactions to this
startling news.

"It absolutely boggles the mind. After what he did to Jocelyn?
And they are letting him go? And they're letting him work with
CHILDREN, no less!" Mary Jo said shuddering in a mixture of fear
mingled with distaste as she expressed her potent disbelief of society's loose moral boundaries which she did not deem as stringent
enough.

"It would appear tha' he was released on a parole te a mentor
who convinced him of the error of his previous ways and convinced

him te change his path fer the good." Matthew further expounded. "Through the high caliber connections of his parents and the influence his mentor had on the higher-ups he is now workin' at a monastery nearby! Begorra.... Could it be true? I fancy that none of us can be certain of our safety fer sure!"

"I <u>told</u> you." Pierre preempted Matthew's dramatic summation. "I will handle this, Matthew. I will ferret the cochon out. I will leave no stone on the ground upside down until I-"

"Would ye stop yer senseless chatter? Dunna ye see tha' the misbegotten rogue has the backing o' the government o' the town? There be nothing we can do.... Randmore!?" Matt cried as he and Cari entered the room arm in arm after returning from their walk. "Have ye heard the dire tidings te date? CHRIS COLDEN is near te the area an' on the prowl once more!"

"Are you certain of this, Matt?" Rand asked him with concern as he protectively pulled Cari closer to him.

"But, if he has truly changed his ways...." piped up a feminine voice grudgingly but decidedly determined to give the reformed criminal the benefit of the doubt.

"For shame on ye, Mary Jo." Matt admonished her as he rushed to a window with a watchful eye to those attempting to breach the perimeter of LaurelsHeath.

"C'est seulement Alex dehors." Pierre divulged the intelligence to Matthew as he observed the younger man outside throwing a yellow knob up into the air to catch it behind his back as it fell, impelled by the force of gravity, toward the earth. "<u>Et</u>, he is playing avec quelque chose, encore!"

"If he has truly changed his ways," stressed an exasperated Mary Jo forthrightly in her crusade for fairness, "then he should be given the benefit of the doubt so that he can start a new and productive life free and clear without constantly having to look over his shoulder and wonder if people are whispering about him and his past behind his back!!!"

"After the crime he has perpetrated against the puir Collins' lass?! How can ye be defendin' tha'...scourge o' humanity? I am all fer fergivin' an' fergettin' but I am shocked tha' ye can be so fergivin' so soon. The proof o' the pudding would be in his conduct from this day forward." Matthew opined in a scholarly fashion. "We shall just have te <u>wait</u> and <u>see</u>!"

"Edi!" Pierre shrieked suddenly in alarm as all eyes in the living room turned to focus their attention on him on hearing his fearful, piercing cry. "I see Calvin, Elvie, Dudley and Callie out there with Alex!" he explained in a panic.

Pierre's explanation, although intending to educidate and make clear his reason for angst, ended up puzzling the listeners about him. Stunned and with no clear guidelines or cues from the Frenchman on how to respond they remained silent. Finally, as she was his closest relation in the room, Cari blindly hazarded an attempt to soothe and ease his troubled mind. She felt it was her duty!

"Calm down, Pierre. Calvin and Elvie returned last week – we all know that. And there is no reason why Alex, Callie and Dudley should not be out there. They are staying here, too, you know." Cari said reasonably seeking to calm the perturbed man.

"Mais, do you not see? You foolish, foolish child! If you are here. Matt, Randy, Mary Josephine, Alex.... If everyone is <u>here</u>. Edi is out <u>there</u> all alone with that...ANIMAL!!!"

CHAPTER 67

"I never knew that you were so good with plants, Elroy. You have a green thumb." Edith praised the young man appreciatively as he showed to her his prize flowers growing and flourishing under his loving care in his greenhouse. "He must get his love of plants from me!" she concluded happily to Simon as she turned to Elroy and gave him a hug. "Even though we are not related by blood there must be a spiritual connection between us somehow!" she said in an aside to Simon as she turned to her brother briefly. "I have the smartest nephew in the whole world! You know, Elroy, horticulture is a <u>very</u> highly esteemed science. It requires a lot of dedication but the end result," Edith said enthusiastically and paused as she held some potted flowers to her nose and deeply breathed in of the intoxicating perfume emitted and savored the scent before exhaling, "is <u>SO</u> worthwhile!" she concluded beaming with familial pride as she reached up to catch at a few of the curls atop Elroy's head to arrange them more attractively. "There!" she proclaimed with satisfaction as she stood back to admire her work – the stunning effect even bedazzled her! "Now, doesn't he look handsome?" she inquired of her brother as Simon burst into laughter on viewing the effeminate way Elroy's curls cascaded over his forehead. "Oh, pooh! Men!" she exclaimed derisively. "What do you know about style, anyway? The male of the species is so cut and dry. No flair for the dramatic. Tasteless.... No soul. You just have no imagination to speak of – Trudy, dear girl. What do <u>you</u> think of Elroy's new hairdo? I am in need of a <u>woman's</u> opinion." said Edith pointedly as she glanced briefly at Simon. "I arranged his hair myself." she announced somewhat boastfully as Trudy coughed to mask her chuckle on first seeing the bird's nest atop her son's head and held her hand in a fist over her mouth in order to disguise her mirthful smile.

"It is very...unusual." commented Trudy judiciously dutifully analyzing Elroy's new coiffure respectfully. "I have never seen anything quite like it!"

"Isn't it wonderful, though?" Edith gushed.

"It certainly has a...style."

"My thought exactly." she asserted definitively, taking what she considered to be a compliment in stride, as she glared triumphantly at Simon. "Nothing but the best for my favorite nephew!" Edith continued on speaking choosing to overlook the fact that Elroy was her ONLY nephew – at least one who was not an in-law. "And I have chosen just the cutest outfit for him to wear at the dinner next week."

"Dinner...? What dinner?" asked Trudy taken unawares by this new piece of information.

"Well, the one at Candlestick Manor! Of course, you have been invited...? If not, I shall have to speak with that nice Cyrus Sykes to get you on the invitation list. I am sure it will be no trouble for him at all to set a few additional place settings at the table for you, Simon and Elroy to attend. Oh, dear! Elroy, your jacket has come undone – and we are starting to experience a slight nippy chill to the air!" clucked Edith as dotingly as a mother hen would approaching him and pulling up his collar; bringing the plackets of his outerwear together and buttoning up his overcoat.

"ENOUGH!" Elroy objected suddenly as his smiling grin disappeared and the hovering cloud of fog composing his ever-present vapid gaze dissipated as if he were emerging from a trance. "Let us put an end to this foolishness." he heralded assertively shunting Edith's helping hands aside. "I am no one's plaything!" he proclaimed majestically gathering himself up and thrusting out his chin.

"What has come over you Elroy?" scolded Trudy. "Your Aunt Edith is only looking out for your welfare!" she said as Edith stood as still as a wide-eyed statue, taken aback, startled at Elroy's vehement stance and at a loss for words. "You would not want to catch a cold, would you? Or, be embarrassed at the dinner party because you were wearing attire that was inappropriate for the occasion. Now, apologize to your Aunt Edith immediately!" she ordered the obstinate young man before her.

"Oh, that is quite alright, Trudy. The boy is quite right." Edith said snapping out of her temporary frozen state of surprise to interject graciously. "Pierre is always chiding me for coddling him too much, as well. I suppose I never <u>have</u> found it too easy to cut the apron strings!"

"There is no excuse for bad behavior." she replied sternly. "And Elroy is old enough to know that he is acting rudely and behaving like a truculent little boy. In fact, he has not caused such a fuss or acted out this way in years! He almost sounded just like his uncle – my brother, just then. Elroy has been giving me such similar back talk for the last few days. And I never know when to expect his… sass. He just…blurts it out! It is almost as if he circumvented puberty and is only now just growing up!"

"Do not speak of me as if I am not present. Uncle J.L. is a man of strong character and you would do well not to disparage him or make light of his unashamedly-voiced convictions!" Elroy warned.

"Let me remind you, my impudent young man, that no one loves and admires your Uncle J.L. as much as I. And, I have known him quite a bit longer than you have." replied his mother.

"I have remained docile for far too long. I am at a loss as to why I have never taken exception to your suffocating methods of parentage before this. But, I am putting you on notice now, Mother, that I am a force to be reckoned with!"

CHAPTER 68

"The reason I be convenin' this meeting is te discuss the perplexity of our dire straits! All o' us here be knowin' – an' I have apprised Simon and Trudy o' it – of the compartment containing the diamonds in Alex's chunk of metal. Now that the access through Simon's basement to the other golden blocks be stoppered-up we have te put our heads together te think o' a way te get te those gold bricks some other way!" Matthew announced urgently as he made eye contact with them one by one with his gaze falling lastly on Pierre who hugged Edith closely to him for fear that Chris Colden might suddenly materialize and abscond with her.

"But, wait." objected Mary Jo. "Even if there are other bricks as you say, how do we know for sure that any of them contain more diamonds? Maybe Alex's brick was the only one?"

"Mary Jo. Canna ye ever be anyway but pessimistic? Does there always have te be a "Why" an' a "Wherefore" te everything on all accounts? Lassie! Ye've got te learn te think big! Te imagine the glowing picture in the distance an' reach fer the prize! That be what it be all about!" Matthew cried unequivocally as he rose from his chair at the oval mahogany table in the family room and pounded his fist down upon its surface focusing his gaze solely on the woman who dared to put a damper on his quest and hopes for untold wealth and riches until he had stared her down.

"O...kay." said Mary Jo a bit meekly after having been the victim of Matt's reprimanding remonstrance. "But where are Calvin and Elvie in all of this scenario – I know that they came back from their sojourn a few days ago? And, what about Callie and Dudley? Those four actually own the house. Any roundtable conversation, as this one is, should include them, too. You <u>DID</u> call them – didn't you? I guess…. Maybe…they couldn't make it…." Mary Jo concluded tentatively with her lonely voice trailing off into the ensuing quiet of the room as Matt's eyes shifted guiltily away from hers and refused to meet them directly.

"Matt does not want Callie here because he thinks that she will leak any plans that we make here to an outsider." Cari finally informed her breaking the tensely mounting silence.

"Are you for REAL, Matt? Callie would never do anything like that!" spat out Mary Jo angrily her normally dulcet brown eyes now shooting sparks of fire as she spoke in defense of her relative.

"Now, calm <u>down</u>, lassie! I be one of yer cousin's biggest fans-"

"Dunna ye be puttin' any o' yer Irish charm to the test on me, Mister!" she railed furiously imitating his pattern of speech. "I will not be sweet-talked. You cannot call my cousin a traitor and then expect to smooth it over-"

"Alex, can ye not control yer wife?" Matthew asked turning to the younger man with a pleading expression washing over his countenance.

"Sweetheart-" began Alex suavely rising to his feet calmly before being pushed down by his wife as she rose up adroitly.

"Control his wife? You call Callie some kind of Benedictine Arnold or Mata Harietta and expect me to sit back and take it? This is CALLIE'S HOUSE and she's your HOSTESS! And how <u>dare</u> you tell Alex to control his wife. He is not your puppet – sit down, Honey, I'm talking-" Mary Jo chided Alex again pushing him back down into his chair as he sought to stand up a second time with open mouth to voice a peacemaking suggestion, "and he needs no instruction from you!" she concluded in a hurricane of loquacious fury.

As they witnessed the spectacle in the family room all sitting at the table remained silent fearing that they would be excoriated by Mary Jo next.

"Dunna get so excited, lass!"

"Excited? Excited. If you think that I am excited now, you had better think again! Just you wait!"

"Mary Jo, didn't you tell me once that you were frightened because you saw a man disappear into the center emblem of the floor of the main hall? You were scared to death! Do we even know who that person was? And, perhaps there is some way that the center emblem can be used as an entryway into the catacombs." Cari loudly interjected seeking to change the subject and curtail Mary Jo's escalating rant directed at Matt.

"Oh, goodness. I apologize for causing you any distress, Mary Jo. You see, that man was me. The center square in the entry area is really the trap door entrance to a tunnel which leads to the first floor fireplace of my house. You exit and/or enter through the façade of the fireplace which swings open and closes shut via a latch mechanism at the side!" Simon explained resolving the mystery.

"Wow!" breathed an overawed Alex Caine. "This house sure does have a lot of secret passages."

"That is quite right, Alex. In any event, I frequently use that tunnel as a shortcut when I wish to visit Tru. It also seems to make our tête-à-têtes feel more romantic somehow." he explained as he glanced surreptitiously at Trudy and they shared a secretive smile. "I also use it in inclement weather, as does Trudy, when I need to travel between houses and do not wish to have to battle the elements. I never meant to upset anybody. I am deeply sorry for any unease that I caused you, Mary Jo."

"That's okay, Simon. I wasn't really afraid…." Mary Jo acceded to him politely.

"Are you kidding me?" crowed Cari. "Mary Jo was spooked

out of her mind! I have never seen anyone so out of her skull. She thought she was going CRAZY! She was actually on her hands and knees trying to pry that square center tile out of the floor with her fingers! I have never seen anybody so gullible." she ended laughing at the abashed expression on Mary Jo's face.

"What about the broom closet in the kitchen? Me daughter, Megan, be talkin' a mile a minute o' the adventure she and Matthew Alexander experienced when Elroy be chasin' them through the tunnels where the gold bricks be nestling. Perchance, we can access the gold blocks through there?" hazarded Matt choosing to steer the conversation more directly back on point.

"I had considered that." Simon conceded. "But I don't recommend the broom closet. The panel ofttimes sticks and if you are able to open the panel and access the main tunnels where the bricks are it is almost impossible to find your way back out. Tru and I tried it once, on a lark, when we'd first discovered the entryway and we were lost down there for three whole days – just wandering about hopelessly before we found the way back to the kitchen entrance purely by chance and fell through it. The fear that we felt during those three days down there we could never wish on our worst enemy."

"Kitty knows the way!" piped a high-pitched and guileless girlish voice as Megan entered the room hugging Charmer to her chest.

"Megan. Dunna ye know tha' this be the time when wee ones are supposed te be snug an' cozy in their beds?" Matthew admonished his daughter gently in surprise at seeing the young one he had only just put to bed an hour ago now downstairs in her pajamas.

"I forgot to give this back to Uncle Alex. He let me play with it today and I came to return it." she explained as she produced a yellow knob with a number "2" etched upon it. "Kitty knows the way. Kitty knows the way. Kitty knows the way!" Megan parroted as Matthew looked up from his small child and stared at Pierre.

CHAPTER 69

"Hey, Rafe, thought we'd get a couple of beers! What was he doing here?" Jim Lahy inquired curiously on entering the office with a backward nod of his head to indicate the departing Cyrus Sykes, who appeared to be in an inordinate hurry, as he barreled out of the same door shoving past him without a word of greeting. "What's eating him?" Jim groused rubbing his manhandled, sideswiped arm.

"You tell me. It's anybody's guess. He's been breathing down my neck to let him tear down Candlestick Manor and bulldoze the entire area and its environs. Now, at the drop of a hat, he comes in today and withdraws all of his paperwork that he has filed to date to that end. He tells me to forget the whole thing. That he has changed his mind. That he has seen the light and that the historical ladies have been correct all along. I will never understand these landowners as long as I live. Capricious, that's what they are.... ECCENTRIC. That's the word I'm looking to use. Eccentric and quirky!"

"Not so fast, sherlock. Not so fast.... You are ignoring an age-old dance of nature that has played out through the annals of history and will continue to perpetuate itself into the future until the end of time...."

"Don't wax poetical on me, Jim. Not only do you <u>sound</u> ridiculous but your conduct is not that of one befitting a law enforcement officer." Rafe rejoined in a joking form of banter. "Now that we've gotten <u>that</u> settled you can speak plainly and tell me what you mean to say. Or rather, what I know that you are chomping at the bit to tell me."

"Cari Chesterfield!" Jim elucidated gleefully with his eyebrows raised anticipating Rafe Cordell's response, as if the import of his meaning was now made transparent and could be derived solely by the expression of Cari's name, only to be met by Rafe's very blank, obtuse stare. "Haven't you noticed the way Sykes looks at her when she's in the room? -Like at the diner…or, when she was here with her family that day at the station? His voice gets all shy…. He stumbles over his words…. And when he does talk at length – you know how curt he usually is – he gets all gushy. He is crazy about her!" Jim clarified to him pointedly on noting his befuddled stare.

"But she is married to that McKinley fellow!" Rafe reminded him.

"I know that and you know that but do you think that is going to stop him? I may be new to this burgh but even I have seen that the man usually gets what he wants. All the store owners cater to him when he comes into their establishments. He is the most eligible bachelor in Laureltown! All the single girls stare at him when he walks into a room – sometimes, even the MARRIED ones! Anyway, Cari is one hundred percent loyal to McKinley and won't give him the time of day. So, Sykes probably thinks that if he backs off on the idea of bulldozing the historical mansion he might make some inroads into her good graces and score some points with her. Gratitude is better than nothing, after all. And we all know she is going to be so grateful he has changed his mind about leveling that precious historical mansion. Her Aunt Edith Chesterfield Norden Dûçot has been like a mother to her since her own mother passed away. Her aunt is going to be extra grateful the manor will stay intact and we all know that the way to a girl's heart is to please her relatives."

"You can't be serious, Jim." Rafe scoffed in skeptical disbelief.

"Well, it's only a theory but stranger things have been known to have happened. And look at how the almighty Cyrus Sykes withdrew his complaint against that Elroy fellow McKinley's wife is so fond of…. One minute, Elroy is a menace to the community, the next, he's an innocent, self-effacing young man who means no harm to anyone. That alone is sure to soften Cari Chesterfield's heart towards him and score him some major points with her."

"Why does she keep her maiden name, Chesterfield, when she's married to Randmore McKinley?"

"I used to wonder about that myself, at first. But then I heard there were two reasons. Reason one, is that the ranch her father started in Charlottesville called Chesterhollow was established with the idea that a Chesterfield would always be at the helm, so to speak, running it. Since he passed without leaving a son to take over the reins she feels that she has to keep the name and the tradition alive. How can you have a Chesterfield ranch without a Chesterfield running it…? She's got to keep the bloodline alive. Number two, it's a sentimentality issue. She keeps her unmarried name in memory of her parents who died so young. It's her way of keeping their memory alive in her heart and honoring them."

"That's some kind of devotion. That's someone who stays true to her roots – what a woman!" Rafe said in low voiced admiration.

"Indeed…. You do know that I was kidding about the beers, don't you? I know that we're not allowed to drink while we are on duty. I just like to shock people once in a while…you know, shake things up…. It relieves the boredom." Jim said as he opened the door of the mini-refrigerator in the office and grabbed a bottle of apple juice. "Would you care for some?" he asked Rafe as he poured himself a glass of the thirst quenching libation and then took a drink. "It's nutritious…!" he coaxed Rafe exaggeratedly smacking his lips together to accentuate his satisfaction as he savored the juice's taste in his mouth.

"No. That's alright. Actually there is something you can assist me with, though. You might know this guy." Rafe said as he walked over to him and he showed Jim a man's picture. "He was convicted in Charlottesville of rape. He served his time and now he's turned preacher. Roland Sykes turned him around. He mentored him – showed him it was better to give than to receive, and all that.... Now, he lives at a monastery in the area and is working part-time at an orphanage. You worked and lived in Charlottesville.... Do you know of him? And, if you do, I was wondering if you think his turning over a new leaf routine is on the up and up. I have to lookout for the safety of the community."

Jim Lahy regarded Chris Colden's photo pensively. Had he turned over a new leaf? And was he, as Rafe put it, "on the up and up"? That was a good question. He regarded Colden's mugshot warily as he remembered the trial, Colden's damning testimony and his off-the-wall, oddball family. A big chunk of the evidence in the Colden rape trial had been hearsay and a large deciding factor of the ultimate verdict was based on the testimony of one Pierre Dûçot.... Chris' brother, Hank, never forgot about that and retaliated not only against Pierre but his family, too. Hank Colden even had him fooled into thinking that he was an upstanding citizen who was ashamed of his brother's crimes and apologetic toward the victim's family – that is until he showed his true colors.... It appeared that he was not as good a judge of character as he had thought he was. And now Rafe asked <u>him</u> if he believed that Chris was truly penitent for his crime.... Was Chris as duplicitous as his brother?

"I do not know, Rafe. I honestly cannot say." admitted Jim Lahy as he took another slow sip of his apple juice.

CHAPTER 70

"Sleeping on the job. Is that your new work ethic, Barnett?" asked Cyrus as Clyde's eyes flew open wide at the sound of his booming voice above him and the pressure of the prodding toe of his shoe and he pushed himself off of his bed of misshapen blocks of golden metal he had been hacking at with a pick in an unsuccessful attempt to break them apart.

"I was just taking a rest." Clyde grumbled yawning and mumbling to himself as he rubbed with the knuckles of his clenched, chisel-holding fist at the side of his cheek which had a dented impression in it from one of the blocks he had used as a makeshift pillow to support his head as he indulged in his unscripted and unscheduled mid-morning catnap among them which had taken him by surprise. "I was gonna try ta chisel 'em this time – after my nap."

"You were taking a rest in the morning…? Do you normally take a nap after just getting to work?"

"This hacking is hard work. I don't know what these things are made of," Clyde said disgruntled stifling another yawn and then irritably throwing down the hammer and chisel he was gripping in his fists, they seemed glued to his hands, when he forgot that he was holding the items and almost hammered his open mouth inadvertently in his attempt to politely cover it during the deed, "but they are indestructible. Boy! I feel like Rip Van Winkler!"

"You are getting old, Barnett – and it's Winkle."

Cyrus chuckled as he watched Clyde rubbing the sleep from his eyes and then the soreness from his bent over back with his bony hands and fingers.

"Don't laugh, youngblood. You're getting older, too!" he said irritably as he came fully out of his groggy trance and raised his lowered eyelids to look his boss fully in the face. "Well, doggies!" he exclaimed whistling as he perked up. "Look at you all manicured up! Yer nails are all buffed and shiny – ya got a haircut, too. My, my, my!" he observed walking around Cyrus in a circle and studying him from head to toe unwaveringly without even bothering to disguise his piqued interest. "We must be trying ta impress someone.... Someone in particular...? Ya shoes are all spit and polish and where'd ya get this flashy suit?" Clyde asked reaching out to finger the lapel of Cyrus's handsome, new dark jacket admiring the weight of the fabric and the opulent thread count.

"Do not touch the material, you blockhead! You will mess it up. Instead of me and what I am wearing, concentrate on opening those metal chunks! Use your head! Try melting them down!" Cyrus yelled at Clyde as he pulled away from the man who was obviously taken aback by such a strong negative reaction.

"Do I look stupid?" he responded in retaliatory angst. "Wait. Don't answer that. YES. I have tried melting them. I told you. The things are, like, indestructible! All that happened when I applied heat to 'em was fumigation. I almost choked to death from the fumes! Big clouds of smoke erupted everywhere – big!" Clyde shouted in his own defense as he paced back and forth on the dirt floor of the root cellar beneath the gazebo with arms stretched out before him and his hands spread apart wide to indicate the breadth of the clouds. "I pretty near passed out from lack of oxygen!" he complained.

"So, you naturally took a nap." Cyrus said sarcastically.

"I needed ta relax!" said the peeved man in defense of his action. "I was only putting my head down for a second but I lost track of time and before I knew it I was out like a light! I couldn't help myself.... It was like I was drugged. Yeah...that's it. It was just like I'd been drugged. There was this gold-colored DUST falling from those blocks in the first place. It was all over them. Maybe, that Elroy put some kinda sleeping powder on 'em. I couldn't help sneezing and coughing. Anyway, I am thinking that maybe next time I will apply more heat ta the metal ta ooze it down good. Of course, I don't want ta do it too much 'cause I don't want ta melt the diamonds."

"Could you be that dim-witted? Diamonds are the hardest substance known to man! They are not going to melt – it is an impossibility! Are you sure that Sandy knows what he is talking about?" inquired Cyrus.

"Course he does! He heard 'em sure as shooting. The girl, Callie, said that the bricks were loaded with the gems and that they was supposed ta keep the info secret! Ya know he wouldn't lie ta us. He's our friend – yours and mine. And he has a stake in this same as you and me. He has no reason ta give us a bum steer! Ya know, there's writing on each of these bricks? An' it's the same on each one." boasted Clyde proudly sharing the information.

"You noticed that, genius?"

"Don't get sassy with me so much, boss man. I am not the one who's practically handing this land over ta them historical people so I can cozy up ta a woman. Once they get a foothold in the door of the house they'll be poking their ladylike noses into everything and who knows what they'll find."

"They will find nothing." Cyrus assured him adamantly. "They are an inquisitive bunch but they are a prissy, stuck-up group of women. They will not deign to get their dainty hands dirty by exploring every nook and cranny of this house. But we, on the other hand, shall be free to examine these bricks and determine how to get the diamonds out of them unhindered with none of the historical ladies wise to what we are up to. Plus, we will not have to worry about any competition from them for the diamonds. In fact, the historical declaration and classification will provide us with the perfect excuse for keeping Candlestick Manor standing instead of destroying it. Everybody knows that I always pushed to have it torn down. People would not understand if, all of a sudden, I decided to keep it standing without a reasonable explanation. They would be suspicious of my motives. Now, we have the explanation to please all of the idle curiosity people would naturally have because of human nature. It is the perfect cover. All we have to say is that we tried to get the permit to tear down the house but the influence of the historical society is too strong. We lost the fight to get appropriate rights to the land and Candlestick Manor and must accede defeat gracefully. I will be admired for being a good sport. Perhaps, people will even feel sort of sorry for me because I did not get my way in this instance because, if you think about it, I was fighting for my home. I really wanted rights to my abode and fought for the property rights for so long – poor me. Then, we wouldn't even have to worry about competition from anyone in the community, either!"

"Except for that nosy, Alex fellow. He just might come back looking for his other shoe!" Clyde warned narrowing his eyes.

CHAPTER 71

"Ye mean te tell me. Tha' ye had this in yer possession all o' this time?! An' ye never thought fer one – no, no, no, let me finish." Matthew said in negation to forestall Alex from speaking and held up his palm between their faces to reaffirm his request that no excuses would be accepted at this time. "Ye ne'er even considered fer one wee, small, tiny bit o' a moment, te inform us of yer find. It took me little daughter – without even knowin' what she be doin' – te show me the solution te all our prayers. The solution, may I add, tha' ye purposely chose te keep secret from yer brethren. Ye kept yer friends in the dark, laddie. We," Matt said as he pointed first to Rand, then to Pierre and then to himself, "are very disappointed in ye. Now, what de ye have te say fer yerself?" he concluded halting in his tracks, with Alex and the other two men following suit, folding his arms across one another to cover his chest and fixing Alex with a judgmental frowning stare.

"You guys are always picking on me for collecting things, so I just neglected to mention it." Alex said simply shrugging his shoulders.

"Now, have either of ye ever heard o' anything so purely selfish?!" Matthew said to the others in a voice which would brook no argument as he looked from Pierre to Rand and back again.

"Hey! I just didn't think about it – okay? Pierre is always razzing me about the things I find, and how I'm always picking things up, and how I should respect my elders. I was practically conditioned to keep quiet about things – conditioned to repress my emotions and hold my true feeling inside and suffer in silence!" Alex bemoaned his fate flinging out his tragic sob story, as well as his arms, to emphasize his pathetic state of mind.

All at once speechless, Matthew paused momentarily in astonishment before expelling his breath.

"Oh, brother!" Matthew articulated in disbelief as he resumed, along with the others who now followed his lead, walking.

"Aren't you pouring it on a little thick, Alex?" Rand inquired with a smile after just having borne witness to Alex's first theatrical debut.

"Oui. Alex, you are buttering the bread a little too thick. This can only mean one thing: you are intentionally misconstruing the facts so that you can blame Pierre Dûçot for your failure!"

"Pierre, mon ami, I do believe tha' yer English is gettin' better – yer argument is impeccable!"

"Merci, Matthew."

"However, ye do tend te connect every situation te yerself."

Pierre regarded Matthew sourly as he mentally reviewed the intended meaning of the tail end of his backhanded compliment.

"Alex is right, you know. You two <u>have</u> been coming down pretty hard on him for investigating situations and picking up meaningless doodads." Rand said to Pierre and Matthew, who readjusted the pickax he toted in a canvas bag strapped across his shoulder and the hat with the clip-on light attached to it which was falling down over his brow.

"Pierre Dûçot has merely drawn attention to the facts. If anything my, comment dit-on, criticisms, highlighted the existence of the yellow knob Alex was playing with. This was all the, how you Américains say, kick in the pants that Alex needed to cause him to see the number deux sur the knob and à réaliser that cette knob was the <u>same</u> knob from the root cellar and that when the root cellar collapsed a porte was opened between the root cellar and the maze in Simon's basement. This is an elementary conclusion to arrive at because Alex found the knob in Simon's basement. Even the simple mind of the médecin, here, understood immédiatement the important meaning of such evidence. The significance was indisputable. And because the root cellar and the catacombs are connected we can access the golden pieces in Simon's basement through the hole in the gazebo – if we can climb down the opening after Matthew <u>damaged</u> the stairway through the entrance leading downward." Pierre concluded quickly glancing peripherally at Matt surreptitiously to see if he felt the sting of the retaliatory barb to his backhanded "compliment".

"I was in peril of losin' me life! I was hangin' on by a mere thread!" Matt replied in potent outrage. "How can ye say I would do somethin' akin te tha' destruction by me own choice!" he queried indignantly.

"I lost a shoe…." volunteered Alex causing both men to turn and stare at him briefly in annoyance before resuming their heated exchange.

"In any event, this is why I brought the lariat which," Pierre articulated grandly without attempting to tone down his boastful triumphant demeanor or make any effort at all to appear humble, "SAVED YOUR life!" he pointed out piously shucking any perceived besmirchment off of his shoulders as he deftly removed a coiled-up length of rope with a loop on one end of it from his backpack.

"My lasso! I was <u>sure</u> that I had left it at the gazebo – and I was right." exclaimed Rand as he took the lasso out of Pierre's hand. "I am so glad that it was there when you needed it or you might not be here with us, Matt! That was close! Forgive me for waxing so philosophical. I do not normally indulge in such speculation – I usually leave that to others – but maybe that was the reason I laid the lasso down and forgot it in this particular place…. I forgot it here so that it would be available for Pierre to find and use to save your life! Fate is so fickle, you know? Thank God it worked this time to keep you safe and here with us, your wife and your children. Amen!"

"Amen!" Alex, Matt and Pierre echoed him and his sentiment.

Pierre stood there looking uncomfortably embarrassed that his previously uncontested fib had been exposed and, therefore, remained notably silent after this heartfelt affirmation.

"See? This is my signature loop." Rand continued speaking as they approached the gazebo steps.

"So, that's why it held so well! You know, with other loops you step into them and they immediately tighten all around when you pull them no matter how slight the tug and squeeze you to death. But with this loop you have more control over how much you want to tighten it. It's the best!" Alex explained to the others proudly praising his cousin's innovation.

"Well, Alex." Rand said modestly. "It depends on what you use it for. It is all in the tension of the slip knot. Sometimes you need a lasso where the loop pulls closed the second you pull on the other end of the rope. It all depends. In my case, I only needed this type of lasso for my chore."

"And in our case, we were able to use it as a kind of step ladder to go around our bodies to hoist us up." said Alex.

"Aye." Matthew agreed. "As a fisherman I know all about the importance of using the proper knot. It always be good, sound judgment an' practice te be PREPARED!!!" Matt said blandly but with silent implication as he stared at Pierre before bursting into laughter with Alex following suit and Rand wondering at the humor of his statement.

"What is so funny?" Rand inquired as he regarded first them and then the uncharacteristically cowed Frenchman who remained silent.

"Ye see, Pierre be representin' te us tha' that be his length o' rope!" Matthew explained to Rand after his laughter had subsided. "He always be contendin' that he be the one cornering the market on preparation fer staving off the straits o' adversity!"

Matthew's buoyant mood quickly evaporated, along with Alex's, as they ascended the steps of the gazebo to find the entrance to the root cellar was neatly and almost seamlessly repaired. Matthew walked on the surface of the new floorboards and stamped upon them at strategic junctures. The birds chirped happily unaware of the seething anger simmering, percolating and about to erupt.

"It be clear te me that this be war! Drastic times call fer drastic measures! It now be such a time!!!" blustered the inflamed Matthew Flanderly clamping his lips tightly together in one unbreakable, hard seamless line.

CHAPTER 72

"This be the perfect time te investigate the catacombs: under the cloak o' darkness!" said Matthew lifting the low over-hanging branch of a tree to walk under it and then letting it drop behind him after he had passed. "We can locate the bricks tonight and then, with the party in full swing tomorrow providing appro-priate distraction, we can swoop in tomorrow an' collect them with no one bein' the wiser. It just be fortunate tha' I recalled the fact that because I fell te the root cellar through a trap door mecha-nism when I was seated on the bench it dunna matter tha' the hole we exited from be boarded up because we can enter through the bench!" he triumphantly whispered to Randmore, Alex and Pierre, pleased with his deductive reasoning powers as he attempted to al-lay their qualms about the advisability of their foray and summarily he turned his flashlight in their direction. "An' why did ye have te wear that ridiculous cat burglar suit?!" he queried in exasperation as the light cast its illumination on Pierre who was wearing the same close-fitting, black one-piece leotard complete with matching face mask that he had worn when he had "guarded" Eleanor's virtue from the unwanted attentions of Jean Luc Paté.

"It is obvious to <u>me</u> that you know nothing presque the stake-outs. C'est simple. Je me suis habillé dans ce costume for stealth purposes. Je suis portant ces vêtements pour camouflage.... Alors, I will blend into the background – I will not be seen!" he elucidated demonstrating by jumping swiftly from side to side with cat-like swiftness.

"Aye.…That be a bonne idea, mon ami, Pierre. I hope I <u>dunna</u> see ye. Because if I ever <u>were</u> te see ye in that getup I'd lose me lunch!"

"If we were not on cette importante covert expedition-"

"Hey. Hey. Hey! Pierre, what's that?" Alex asked loudly in his attempt to curtail an argument between him and Matt.

"Matthew asked me to carry it." he responded only to be rudely interrupted by the ill-humored Irishman.

"I'll take that!" said Matthew sharply wresting the carrier from a resistant Pierre who refused to release its handle voluntarily. "THIS be me secret weapon!" Matt interjected quickly before Pierre could expound upon his answer.

"Mee-ow!" cried its angry occupant in a protracted wail as she skid from one side to the other and back again like a table tennis ball in motion during Pierre and Matt's small scuffle.

"Charmer! What's she doing here?" cried Alex in bewildered query as he regarded Matthew quizzically.

"I brought the animal along for insurance purposes. Me daughter told us that she be knowin' the way through the catacombs an' so I be bringing her along as a guide. In the event tha' we find ourselves in need of direction we can rely on her te save us — similar te how she did prior. Also, I could not remove her collar and who knows whether or not we shall need one of her charms." he explained to Alex.

"But, Matt. That is patently ridiculous! That cat does not even know where we are going. And, need one of her charms — do you hear yourself? REALLY! And everyone knows that dogs are much smarter than cats are." Rand asserted.

"Balderdash! Because o' her charm we opened the gateway te the diamonds!"

"But that was a special case! A onetime occurrence. You cannot hope to attach any significance to that singular happenstance!"

"Randy, me boy. Yer problem is that ye ha' no imagination…no fire in yer blood tha' will spur yer mind onte higher things! An' if me daughter an' son vouch for this feline's directional capabilities I'm inclined te believe in them, too! Especially after what she did fer me, Alex and Pierre." Matthew admonished him stubbornly.

"I tend to agree with Randmore, médecin." interrupted Pierre deciding to let bygones be bygones and speak to him despite his previous insulting comments. "The cat is nice to look at but she does not appear to be très intelligent. She let you put her in that little box, didn't she? That is the telling point!" he concluded, tapping his temple knowledgeably amidst Charmer's low, prolonged rumbling growls and hisses of protest.

"Now look what ye done, ye bungler! Ye offended the feline lass. And such commentary o' yers be coming from a man – an' when I say "man" I speak loosely – who believes horses be purposeful and his dead grandmother be comin' back te life!" Matthew reminded Pierre as he put down the pet carrier carefully and opened it to pull the fuzzy creature into his arms to stroke her head lightly.

With a frenzied cry, Charmer's ears flew backwards and flattened to the sides of her head. She hissed at Matthew loudly and long, spitting out saliva. Without warning the bedraggled feline jumped from his arms to run to Alex and rub against and weave in between and around his legs.

"What have you done to her, Matt?" Alex asked in accusation as he picked Charmer up and cuddled her in his arms.

"I had te get her in the box somehow, laddie." Matt replied defensively as Charmer hissed at him when he reached out his hands to take her from the fold of Alex's arms.

"WHAT did you do to her?!"

"It was an accident, laddie. A sheer accident! I just put down me glass o' water fer a moment te pick her up an' put her in her carrier. 'Twas not me fault tha' she tipped it onte herself." he elaborated innocently.

"Water? No wonder she looks so scruffy! So, you are honestly telling me that she tipped a glass of cold water on herself? C'mon, Matt! I wasn't born yesterday, you know. You doused her with water to get her into the cat box more easily! Now, she'll never help us." said Alex glumly as Charmer began to purr and look up at him trustingly.

"But, she'll do it fer you, me boy. Why, she's taken te ye like she's taken te me Megan."

"So you want me to use her, to take advantage of her, for our benefit?"

"Dunna put it so harshly, me lad. Ye know well enough that we all love the precocious little feline." Matt said ingratiatingly as he bestowed multiple fawning stares on the feline and attempted to pat her head.

Charmer, perceiving no imminent threat from Matthew while she was in Alex's arms, snuggled more closely against his chest and ignored Matthew.

"It might help to win her over a little bit if you try to make amends with her by drying her off – she's soaked!" exclaimed Alex, indignant on the afflicted cat's behalf, on noting the growing wet spot on his shirt as it absorbed the seepage being let forth from her fur.

"Now, be sensible, laddie. How am I supposed te do that!" Matt asked as Charmer growled menacingly when he approached her with both of his hands extended.

"How about with that handkerchief in your pocket?"

"Me handkerchief! De ye mean te tell me tha' ye think I am goin' te use me clean – freshly washed an' pressed, mind ye – handkerchief te rub against tha' filthy animal?!" Matt asked him angrily, outraged at the very idea of doing so.

"If you want to mend fences with her and show your sincerity to that end I think you should do it!"

On hearing herself referred to as a "filthy animal" Charmer's ears perked up and flattened against either side of her head. She stared at Matthew warily and let forth a low hiss.

"You see?" Alex asked rhetorically. "You got her all riled up again by calling her a filthy animal. But, she is ready to make up and be friends, if you are."

"An' just HOW de ye figure that?" queried Matthew.

CHAPTER 73

"**E**lroy is getting awfully aggressive." Cari commented as Mary Jo helped her zip up the uncooperative zipper of her dress. "I am not exaggerating." she said to her nonresponsive friend who was fixated on unsticking the teeth of the dress' stubborn fastener. "The other day, for example, we were just talking when out of the clear blue sky he put his arm around me!"

"I should have your problems." stated Mary Jo distractedly. "I think the zipper is stuck. Where's Randy in all of this? We could use his help. Or, better yet, maybe Elroy would like to help."

"I should know better by now than to tell you anything, Mary Jo. Anyway, it's funny how we need a man's muscle to unstick, of all things, a stuck zipper!" Cari observed laughing. "Well," she said in answer to Mary Jo's question as she attached the final earring to her earlobe and Mary Jo continued to struggle with the stubborn zipper of the dress, "Randy went over to Simon's house – something about getting to know his new uncle-in-law better. It would be a boys' night out for them, so to speak. But I suspect the real reason Rand is visiting with Uncle Simon is because that the prospect of a boring evening touring the rooms of an old house does not thrill him. It certainly had something to do with the timing of his visit with my uncle. Rand kept me up so late last night that I was too exhausted to argue with him about it in the morning when he said he was skipping the dinner party. Otherwise, I would have insisted that he accompany us to the manor. I suspect now that is the real reason he kept me up 'till all hours last night dancing at that club – so that I would be too tired to argue with him. What did you think that we were doing, Mary Jo?" Cari asked as she noticed Mary Jo's mischievous smile and noted her reluctance to respond in a timely fashion.

"I am not thinking anything – I plead the Fifth!" Mary Jo affirmed solemnly.

"You are bad, Mary Jo!" Cari said to her friend who had finally correctly realigned the tracks of her zipper and, raising her head to regard Cari innocently, deftly pulled it all the way up.

"You didn't have to stay up past your bedtime last night if you didn't want to." Mary Jo responded simply. "Anyway, Alex had the same excuse. It seems that he really wanted to get to know Simon better, too. So, when he heard Randmore was going, of course, he had to tag along as well. Honestly, those two go everywhere together!" she exclaimed as she and Cari exited her bedroom to stand in the carpeted hallway and closed the door behind them.

"That means we are all without dates. Pierre informed me that he could not attend either." said Edith glumly as she met the other two at Cari's bedroom door. "I came to find out what is taking you two girls so long! Come along, now. The driver is waiting!"

"My zipper was stuck, Auntie, and Mary Jo-" Cari began to explain only to be waved aside into silence by Mary Jo.

"What excuse did Pierre give you for not going, Edith?" Mary Jo asked Edith.

"He said that he had to polish his gun collection." replied Edith.

"His...gun collection? Since when does Pierre Dûçot own a GUN COLLECTION?!" Mary Jo asked rhetorically. "I have heard a lot of whoppers in my time but this one takes the cake!"

"Since when does Pierre own a gun collection?" Cari prodded her aunt with genuine curiosity following up on Mary Jo's previous question as they walked along and exited LaurelsHeath manor.

"Would it hurt you so much, Cari, to address him as Uncle Pierre once in a while, dear? In any case, I asked him the same question and he said that since he has been living in the "wild west" and come up against "des criminal elements" he started a gun collection."

"Elvie! Callie, Dudley, Calvin.... What are you all doing here?" Cari inquired happily glad to see them and delighted that they could all be together.

"Edith invited all of us to a dinner party at Candlestick Manor." Calvin explained.

"And that is the ONLY reason I came – for Edith's sake." Elvie stated emphatically. "After what I heard that Cyrus Sykes say, or what I thought I heard him say, I don't know how all you people could want to sit at his table and break bread! Despite what Dr. Matthew says I don't fully trust him."

"If me Eleanor had been here, I wouldna been able te come to-night. She be not as easy te hoodwink as your ladies. Eleanor can see right through me. She woulda insisted I attend the party."

"Well, what excuse did you give Edith for having to be absent from the party tonight?" Alex asked Matthew.

"None at all, laddie. No one asked if I were attending the festivities!"

"That's not fair, Matt! Pierre, Randy and I had to give excuses to our wives! Of course, Randy and I shared our excuse. We said we were going to stay with Simon. We are not going to be there, of course, but Simon is staying at his house tonight to cover for us just in case someone shows up asking for us. Pierre had to make up his own excuse, though." Alex clarified.

"Aye. I heard his lamebrain excuse." Matt informed him. "We couldna all o' us had the same alibi – the women would ne'er have believed us. But, cleanin' his gun collection? Bah!" he scoffed at what he deemed to be an unlikely, if not transparent, excuse. "Next, you'll be claimin' that ye have te wash yer hair!"

"It is a plus better raison than yours!" Pierre replied defensively. "You had no excuse at all!"

"True…true. I can confess te me flaws. I must admit that ye do have a valid point." Matthew conceded graciously. "But, now to the matter at hand. It would appear tha' we would have te come down here a multiple amount o' times te get out all o' these bricks!"

"I agree, médecin. You, Randy and I can carry maybe deux ou trois bags of blocks in one swoop. However, Alex here, can barely carry one full bag at a time." Pierre complained.

"If you were as smart as you think you are Pierre, you would know that we don't have to carry all the bricks to the surface. So, figure <u>that</u> one out!" Alex responded in a huff at Pierre's deprecating skepticism regarding his ability to help out in a meaningful manner.

"Alex, you are one smart cookie!" Rand affirmed.

"Please, do <u>not</u> mention, cookies, in front of <u>this</u> one!" Alex said, slightly mollified at the compliment from his cousin, while simultaneously pointing his finger at Pierre.

"It is not polite to point at others." said Pierre reaching out and grabbing hold of his accusing finger to thrust it aside of his face. "And may I point out that if these bricks were indeed cookies c'est certain that you would be able to carry quite a few bags of them." he commented to Alex casually attempting to mask his eagerness at hearing Alex's solution to their problem of transport.

"Stop verbally sparring with others, Pierre, and, Alex, tell us your solution to our transport problem! Do not hide your light beneath a bushel, Alex." Rand prompted Alex enthusiastically.

"Aye, laddie. Enlighten us!"

"Well…okay. Only because you and Randy want to know." Alex said to Matt. "We can use the key on Charmer's neck collar to open each brick and empty the diamonds in them out into the sacks."

Matt's eyebrows rose abruptly in astonishment at the elementary aspect of the solution. He was stupefied. He was absolutely speechless as he regarded Rand and Pierre taking note of their similarly flabbergasted expressions. Such a simple solution to their "complex" problem and it had taken Alexander Caine to put it forth and make them wise to it. Where were their brains in all of this...?

"The lad be a genius!!!" cried Matt feeling it was incumbent upon himself to finally say something to break the palpable silence existing in the musty cellar beneath the gazebo as he clapped Alex on the back of his shoulder in a congratulatory manner. "He has done it again! It be fortunate I brought Charmer along. I told ye she be me secret weapon!" he crowed victoriously.

CHAPTER 74

"I don't see Matt." Cari noted to the girls as Cyrus's butler hung up their coats and they moved forward to greet their host and then join Calvin, Dudley and Elroy up ahead.

"How much do you want to wager he's with Rand and Alex?" Mary Jo whispered to the others as they advanced forward.

"And Pierre is probably with them, too. I swear, those four men stick together like glue! Of course, there is safety in numbers." Elvie stated matter-of-factly as she regarded Cyrus warily and with trepidation.

"You are probably right. Dudley told me that when we were almost at the manor he saw four men, one of them as tall as Pierre, headed for that gazebo in back of the house." Callie added as Edith worried her lower lip wondering what mischief her husband might have become embroiled in.

"Auntie! Don't bite your lip like that! It will start to bleed!" Cari warned her aunt.

"Plus, you'll ruin your lipstick!" Mary Jo cautioned Edith.

"Oh, Mary Jo! Could anyone be more superficial?! Can't you see that she is worried about her husband?" scolded Cari.

"Leave her alone, Cari. She is perfectly correct. It would not do to look undone." said Edith as she quickly creased her lips together rubbing them one against the other to evenly smooth out her lipstick across them and patted at her hair rescuing a few loose tendrils falling out of place on her head. "I do hope that Pierre does not cause any trouble tonight of all nights! Whenever those boys get together there is sure to be some mischief afoot. And what an excuse he gave me for not being here – cleaning his gun collection! I should have seen right through it! That is what love does to you.... It blinds you to the truth. He probably knew that I would absolutely forbid whatever tomfoolery he is up to and that is why he was not forthcoming with his true plans!"

"Don't worry, Edith. I am certain they cannot get into too much trouble outside of the house." Trudy contributed to the conversation in a soothing tone of voice to calm her agitated newly realized sister-in-law who had removed a white lace handkerchief from her purse and began twisting it between her hands.

"You do not know my husband that well as of yet!" Edith informed her.

"Well, speaking of shallow people and lipstick I am going to the ladies' room to check on mine!" Elvie affirmed positively as she went off in search of the lavatory.

"Cari, dear, you should go after her." admonished her aunt as Elvie disappeared around a corner. "We were only here once before and she might not remember the way and become lost! She is still very fragile!"

As Elvira Maison reapplied her lipstick in front of the bathroom mirror she chided herself for coming to the dinner party at Candlestick Manor. She did not trust that Cyrus Sykes one iota and even though he was acting so nice and proper to them all she was sure he had one of those ulterior motives. She glanced about her quickly to make sure that the place was not booby-trapped and then, mentally shaking herself, took a firm hold on her emotions. She was becoming, what that nice Dr. Flanderly called it, paranoid. He had insisted she call him, Matthew. He had explained to her that from listening to Pierre's fears and conjectures she has developed a sort of sympathetic suggestibility to his way of thinking and most likely misconstrued the meaning of everything she heard Cyrus Sykes say when she was listening to him and his friend from behind the gazebo because of Pierre's slanted outlook and influence concerning Cyrus. Well...maybe so, but she would keep her eye on him. She twisted closed the bottom dial of the circular tube of lipstick watching the bright crayon of color as it swiveled in a downward spiral to the very bottom of its case and snapped the top cover onto it decisively, covering the cosmetic completely. Placing the cosmetic in her purse she closed her handbag with a click of its clasp and turned to leave the room. 'What's that?' wondered Elvie, feeling compelled to stand rooted to the spot, as a sound inside of the room became evident. She looked about her. Perhaps it was the sound of the guests conversing in the room down the hall.... The lavatory walls were probably so thin that you could ascertain sounds emanating from the nearby rooms. 'Yes.' Elvie concluded resuming her walk forward. 'That was a plausible explanation.' she comforted herself on reaching the door.

"Help! Please.... Help us!"

Elvie froze with her hand on the doorknob poised to turn it. Someone in the room needed help.... But there was no one in the room. 'Am I going crazy, again?' she wondered fearfully as she looked down at her hands and saw that they were trembling. She just couldn't let anyone know about this relapse. She had just better keep this between herself and the four walls. Calvin would think he had married a crazy woman. He would feel like a pitiable laughingstock. She couldn't do that to him. She resolutely turned the doorknob and exited the lavatory closing the door carefully behind her as if it would break if greater force were applied only to turn and walk directly into Cari. Goodness. She had hoped that she would not run into anyone until she had a chance to compose herself.

"I see that you found the bathroom all right." Cari said pulling away from her. "Aunt Edith was concerned that you might get lost and so she sent me after you. My aunt can be overprotective sometimes — but that just means that she cares.... What is the matter? You look white as a sheet." Cari exclaimed as Elvie threw herself against her and clasped her arms around her neck as if it were a lifeline.

"Cari, I think I am going bonkers, again." Elvie revealed candidly finding that she could not maintain her resolution to contain her feelings. "That nice Matthew Flanderly tried to help me but it didn't work. I was not gonna tell anybody but.... But I just have to confide in someone. What should I do, Cari? What should I do?"

CHAPTER 75

"I be thinkin' tha' this be the last batch o' the pieces te open. An' that be all thanks te ye, Charmer, me little darlin'." Matthew said fawningly as he patted the feline's head.

"Stop that, Matt! I am trying to fit the key on her collar into the depressed letters on the brick!"

"Take yer time, laddie – take all the time ye need. We'll soon be rich men, laddie. Respected. Respected an' revered.... Aye. All the populace will be agog an' lookin' up te us."

"Wealth isn't everything." said Alex.

"Aye. But it sure an' begorra helps when the tax man comes te callin'. Wouldna ye like te buy yer Mary Jo nice things te make her life easier?"

"I give her nice things."

"Well, wouldn't ye want te give her <u>more</u> nice things?!" Matt asserted irritably, annoyed that Alex was gainsaying him and downplaying the virtues of his dreams of prosperity.

"<u>And</u> we are lost." Alex reminded him. "So if we can't find our way out and are stuck here, what good are riches going to do for you?" he posed the question in a challenging tone of voice, daring Matt to answer it.

"Tish Tosh!" he scoffed unconcernedly. "Dunna be so negative, me boy. Once Randmore an' tha' clod, Pierre, return from deciphering the tunnels we shall be off an' on our way!" Matt replied in a jolly timbre.

"But what if they cannot find a way out?" asked Alex worriedly.

"Since the debris closed off the exit to Simon's basement we can't go through there and we can't go back the way we came in – it's too risky! The whole place is falling apart literally!"

"Tha' kind o' thinkin' will ne'er get ye anywhere, laddie. Ye must always look te the rainbow an' ne'er lose sight o' it or yer bound fer failure. An' there be nothin' risky about climbin' up the way we came. In my opinion, all o' you three people are alarmists. It be a mere hop, skip an' a jump to climb that wall."

"But we have these sacks to carry. And what about Charmer? How are we going to carry her up with us? Someone has to hold the handle of her carrier. We can't just <u>leave</u> her down here!"

"Charmer, as I elucidated prior, be me secret weapon. She be knowin' these tunnels like the back o' her hand – dunna ye, me darlin'?" Matthew asked rhetorically as he faced the feline and gave Charmer his friendliest smile. "An' she'll find the way out fer Megan's sake! So the child not be fatherless an' can see her daddy once more!" he concluded tearfully.

"Well, we did not find a way out but Pierre and I did find this." said Rand dryly pushing a belligerent Elroy forward to stare at them all indignantly.

"I wanted to be on your mission, too - whatever it is. Why should I have to be left behind with the girls?" Elroy complained.

"Je comprend bien how the boy feels. There were plusieurs des temps when I, believe it or not, was left behind while the big boys went off in groups.... I was tout seul and all alone. Overlooked and my prowess disregarded.... Cast aside and my worthiness denied...! It was horrible!"

"Is he for real?" Elroy queried of Rand, Alex and Matthew who stood there silently in various degrees of bewilderment until Matt finally addressed his query.

"I be askin' meself that very same question every day. He be the real article, all right." replied Matthew. "May I speak te ye in private,

Randy?" asked Matt pulling him aside to ask: "What have ye told the boy regardin' our…project?"

"I just told him that we wanted to explore down here because we were curious. Nothing more."

"Calm down, Elvie. Now, tell me <u>where</u> you heard the voices." Cari requested of the distraught young woman as they entered the bathroom together.

"I don't know – I can't tell! It was booming all over the place. I thought I was going out of my mind. After Matt told me that I was mishearing things-"

"Misinterpreting things." Cari corrected her.

"Misinterpreting things and talked me down from it all I thought I was okay. Now, I'm hearing voices…. What am I gonna do, Cari? What am I good for? What will the others say when they find out? What will Calvin say? Will his feelings stay the same for me? Will he HATE me?"

"Do not panic, Elvie! That is the absolutely WORST thing you can do. We will get to the bottom of this – believe me!" said Cari assuredly to the sobbing young lady. "Now, let us take it step by step. Where were <u>you</u> when you heard the voices."

"I was standing right here, in front of this mirror. I washed my hands, refreshed my lipstick and then I heard this sound so I stopped and listened. Nothing happened. So I went to the door to leave and then I heard someone cry for help."

"The voice had to have come from somewhere. Let's look around the room and see if we can find something – anything that might be a clue-"

"Clue? Did I hear someone say, clue? A clue to what? Edith sent me to find out what was taking you two so long. I think that every-one was going a little stir-crazy waiting for you two. Trudy is acting odd. She is giving Cyrus goo-goo eyes when she thinks nobody is looking and sticking to him like white on rice. Maybe she thinks he's going to disappear next. Though why she should care is a mystery to me.... Anyway, they decided to start without you. Edith, Trudy, Calvin, Dudley, Callie and Cyrus are touring the house and they sent me down here to collect you both and if all else failed to physically <u>carry</u> you two back to the living room to follow their bread crumbs, so to speak. Or, in other words, follow in their tracks. Elroy went off on his own. BORING! But, now we finally have something interesting going on! So, tell me about this clue!" Mary Jo demanded.

"Can I tell her, Elvie?"

"Might as well, the cat is out of the bag anyway." she replied.

"Mary Jo..." Cari stole a corroborating glance at Elvie before continuing, "Elvie has heard someone in this room cry out for help and I was just saying to her that we have to find some sort of clue that would explain where the cry came from because no one else is in this lavatory but us."

"Uh-huh.... Are you sure this was a real, human voice?"

"Mary Jo!!!"

"No, that's okay, Cari. That is a fair question. It was a booming voice, Mary Jo. Kind of like a megaphone."

"Megaphone.... Megaphone, megaphone, megaphone. What could sound like a megaphone? Let's see...." Mary Jo walked around the room looking like a detective tapping the tips of the fingers on her opposite hands together and scanning the area at each quarter turn. "Who, what, where, when, how. <u>Who</u> uses a megaphone...? Someone who wants to be heard. <u>What</u> is a megaphone? Usually metal...a speaker projecting your voice.... You speak or blow into it so the sound may be projected. <u>Where</u> is a megaphone? In an area where the listeners are farther away from the speakers.... <u>When</u> is a megaphone used-"

"Mary Jo, stop being silly. This talking out loud doesn't serve any purpose." Cari stated impatiently. "So stop stringing Elvie along with what is probably false hope!"

"You're right, Cari. I have the answer, anyway."

"Mary Jo, really? Please. What is the answer?" Elvie pleaded hopefully.

"The air vent. All we have to do is to find the air vent in the room and we have found our megaphone." she said as she looked behind the sink cabinet and then the toilet bowl. "And, here it is!" Mary Jo said triumphantly. "But, I wonder what this button next to it does." she said ponderously looking up at the other two ladies from where she stood bent over to examine it and touch it tentatively.

Cari appeared more than slightly surprised and dumbfounded at Mary Jo's find and the accuracy of her educated guess. She reflected upon the positive, and sometimes unexpected, results that conjecturing aloud upon a problem could bring. Elvie appeared grateful and started shaking as she burst into thankful tears and in her newfound relief ran to hug Mary Jo where she now knelt on the floor to edge closer to the toilet to further consider the vent. Unfortunately, she slipped on a sheet of toilet paper on the floor and careened into Mary Jo in a half-hug, half-attempt to halt her uncontrolled forward impetus as she barreled into her body. In turn, Mary Jo braced herself against the wall inadvertently pushing the button she had been examining curiously. A panel in the wall opened revealing a dark, uninviting passageway.

"Oh, thank you, Mary Jo. Thank you, thank you, thank you! I did hear a real voice, after all! I wasn't imagining it!" cried Elvie joyfully as Cari gasped in astonishment on viewing the passageway and pointed to the opening in the wall which remained unnoticed by the other two girls. "I thought I was losing my mind!" Elvie continued speaking to Mary Jo heedless of Cari's wordless gesturing.

"GIRLS! Come to attention – LOOK!" Cari commanded in the

tone of a drill sergeant as, shocked at Cari's stringent interruption, both ladies followed her pointing finger with their eyes. "It's a passageway." Cari stated needlessly.

"Think of the poor person trapped down there who needs our help!" exclaimed Elvie staring fixated in awe at the opening in the wall.

"Or, imprisoned down there…."

"How can you even think that, Mary Jo? Do you honestly believe that Cyrus is capable of something cruel like that?"

"If you saw him clearly instead of seeing him as an attractive flirtatious flatterer with an obvious crush on you…." she replied suggestively, questioning Cari's objectivity with her open-ended statement of implication.

"I knew it! I knew there was something dangerous about that Cyrus Sykes. Pierre was right all along!" Elvie espoused firmly with a stiff upper lip. "Well, I don't know about you two but I am going to help that person!" Elvie resolved firmly as she rose and passed through the entrance in the wall.

"Elvie, wait! You do not know what's down there – wait for me!" Cari called after her. "I'd better go after her, Mary Jo…. Where do you think you're going?" she asked as Mary Jo followed so closely on her heels that Cari had to halt in her own footsteps to stop Mary Jo's progress forward. "You have to go back to find the others and tell them where me and Elvie have gone."

"Are you kidding me, Cari? Stand aside. I'm going with you and Elvie. I wouldn't miss this adventure for anything! This is the most excitement I've had in YEARS!" replied Mary Jo marching forward and past her into the murky gloom ahead.

Cari paused to watch her friend as she pulled a miniature flashlight from her purse while continuing to walk into the distance. She wondered if she should take it upon herself to inform the others of their whereabouts. Finally, recklessly deciding to throw caution to the winds she turned acutely on her heel to hurriedly follow in Mary Jo's dust, literally.

"Wait for me!" Cari called out into the dim emptiness.

"Elvie just came back relaxed and refreshed and you let her go roaming around all alone in a strange house!" Calvin berated Callie as he strode to the lavatory with Callie, Dudley, Edith, Trudy and Cyrus following in his wake. "Use some common sense. She probably got lost in this maze of a house!"

Calvin was clearly incensed and one could practically see the steam shooting out of his ears.

"It'll be okay, Cal. Mary Jo just went after her and-"

"That's easy for you to say, Dudley, when it's not your wife who is missing. And Elvie is in a fragile state of mind!"

"Cari is also with them." Edith reminded him. "And I am not worried. My niece has a good head on her shoulders. She is extremely responsible." she continued speaking as they finally reached the lavatory and Calvin flung open the closed door and she fell silent as she stared, along with the others, at the opening in the wall.

CHAPTER 76

"**I** don't know how you find your way around down here, boss man." commented a clearly distracted Dwight Sanders who had lost his sense of direction.

"I used to play down here as a child. I vaguely remember it.... But somehow, subconsciously, I seem to remember the way." Cyrus explained slowly and ponderously as he paused to reflect upon a forgotten memory. "I seem to recall a playmate at that time.... It was a pleasant moment in my childhood – but, oh, so brief."

"That is all very nice, Mr. Sykes-"

"Please, Edith, I asked you to call me, Cyrus!"

"Thank you. That is all well and good, Cyrus. But, I wish to ask Mr. Sanders a question, if I may."

"What would you like to know, Mrs. Dûçot?" Dwight asked.

"Wouldn't it perhaps be better judgment if we split up into groups to search for the girls? We could increase our efficiency that way. The tunnel seems to branch off into three different directions at this point. Perhaps, each group could explore one of the tunnels and then we could meet back here, at this starting point, if we locate the girls or find something which might lead us to Elvie, Cari and Mary Jo and share the information about it. Then, we could all of us go forth in force and find them together. Of course, we would need a way to signal-"

"Take cover! Take cover all of ya civilized people!"

Edith and the others turned to see a harried, half-sleepy-eyed Clyde Barnett rubbing the somnolence from his eyes and running toward them in a panic. A large gold nugget was in his hand and gold dust in his mussed-up hair. He presented them with quite a sight.

"Those murderers are loose and they are armed an' dangerous an' they are coming this way! I was examining those blocks – just like ya told me to – and I got the tired feeling again. So, I figured I'd take a little rest. I laid down my rifle – " Clyde turned from Cyrus to engage them all in the conversation, "I only use it to shoot at cougars and wolves – " he qualified piously, "and before I knew it I was snoozing. I heard a click and opened my eyes ta see those criminals who tried to kill your father standing over me with my own rifle trained on me. I swear the man was looking at me with blood in his eyes and one of those evil glints!" Clyde told Cyrus turning back again to face him directly.

"MURDERERS!!!? You mean that Elvie is out there with murderers on the loose?" Calvin hollered in incredulous outrage with the sound of his voice echoing and reverberating throughout the corridors of the underground enclosure.

"Shoo----shush!!! Be quiet! They might hear ya – ya dolt! I was lucky ta escape with my life!" Clyde addressed Calvin with fear in his voice, rushing over to face him, jumping up and down and gesturing in an attempt to replace yelling in fright with his body language and also to relieve his stress. "Ya will give up our LOCATION!"

"You are correct. I shouldn't be directing my anger at you. I should be directing it solely at SYKES! Tell me, Mr. Sykes-cho. Do you normally keep murderers confined in your house? Or, is this just a hobby of yours?"

Cyrus could not meet Calvin's eyes. Instead, he looked down guiltily. There had been a better way to handle this. An option which he had ignored.... To go to the police and let them figure out if it was truly attempted murder they were dealing with or a matter of self-defense. It could even have been an accident.... They could have shot his father unintentionally when they really meant to shoot at or ward off his real attacker. Actually, it had been his first inclination to turn the two perpetrators over to the police but he had let Clyde convince him otherwise. Yes, Clyde's opposing rhetoric had swayed his judgment but the ultimate decision had been his and now the lives of three innocent young ladies, one of whom he cared for deeply, and, perhaps, all of their own lives, too, were at risk, lay forfeit or hung in the balance because of his poor decision. He shuffled his feet as Trudy watched him sympathetically. It was at least clear to her that he was torn apart about it inside.

"Well, Sykes-cho? We're waiting…." Calvin articulated tapping his foot impatiently to keep time and hurry it along until he could contain his ire no longer. "What do you have to say about it!!!" he snapped sharply and belligerently as he shook off Dudley's restraining hands and moved toward his tongue-tied target.

"You leave him ALONE!!!"

Trudy's outburst came unexpectedly as she rushed hurriedly, moving forward swiftly, to interpose herself between Cyrus and Calvin's rapidly advancing form. No one had ever seen Calvin that angry before – or Trudy so protective, for that matter.

"Cyrus is doing the best that he can guiding us through this maze and I am certain it is not his fault-"

"Randmore! What are you boys doing here?" Edith exclaimed in astonishment interrupting Trudy and running to Pierre's side simultaneously to clutch at his arm possessively. "Thank goodness you boys are here. Have you seen Cari, Mary Jo and Elvie? We are just frantic looking for them and now Mr. Barnett, here, has informed us that there are two murderers on the prowl down here!"

"Cari's missing?! And there are murderers on the loose?!" Rand asked her shouting the question in an appalled fashion.

"Mary Jo's down here, too?!" Alex fumed loudly in a worried fervor.

"And Elvie. And it's all this hotshot's <u>fault</u>!!!" Calvin asserted angrily.

"They had no business roaming around unescorted in a strange house. It is truly unfortunate that they became lost but they only have themselves to blame!" declared Trudy pragmatically while she unconsciously moved closer to Cyrus and placed a protective hand on his forearm.

"Are you honestly making excuses for Cyrus's behavior, Trudy? Why, he has potentially placed all of us in a perilous situation!" Edith said as she stared at her unbelievably and her eyes took note of how tightly and familiarly she clutched Cyrus's arm. "And, may I remind you that you are married to my BROTHER?"

"I noticed this touching, too, Edi. <u>Quite</u> unseemly for a married woman – even if her maiden name is LaFitte!" Pierre said dramatically before his hand flew to cover his mouth on realizing the possible repercussions which could arise from what he was saying meted out by Jan or one of his emissaries if Jan chose to take offense to his brash declaration.

Pierre glanced about him furtively to quickly ascertain if there were any niches from where someone could perhaps be listening while Elroy stood back and listened to all of them in amusement.

"There is no need to worry about those others! I set them free. They are not murderers!" Elroy said calmly, unflappably unperturbed by their needless concerns and assorted folderol.

"You set those ferocious twosome free?!!!" Clyde shouted loudly forgetting about his previous caution to Calvin that he remain silent. "Get a hold of him, Sandy, and take him away!" he commanded Dwight. "I told ya, boss man. I told ya when Roland said ta take care of him it could only mean one thing and one thing only! The kid is a danger! He is a bad seed! Ya done good originally when ya took the step of putting an order against him with the police. And then, at the drop of a hat, disrespecting your own father's wishes ta get rid of this wrongdoer," he pointed an accusatory finger of con-demnation at Elroy, "ya went and had it removed. And, why? Ya did it ta impress some girl!" he spit out disparagingly. "Well, we got him all physical-like and in the flesh, now.... I say we take him back ta the sheriff and get him locked up for good!"

A sudden plaintive wail of protest issued forth from the pet car-rier in Matthew's hand.

"Roland did not mean to have Elroy restrained when he asked Cyrus to take care of him, Mr. Barnett."

"Oh, now look who we got here talking. Miss. Trudy over here calling Roland by his first name like they was on familiarity terms and cozying up to his son. Putting and rubbing your hands on him – ya should be ashamed of yourself. An old married lady, if that descriptive can apply, looking ta rob the cradle. What do you know about it – what do you know about anything?" scoffed Clyde derisively.

"Mr. Barnett. If Roland asked Cyrus to take care of Elroy he meant it at face value. You see, Elroy is Cyrus's younger brother." Trudy revealed to the surprise of all present, especially to the sur-prise of Elroy and Cyrus, both. "Before you and Roland became acquainted, Mr. Barnett, and before I met Simon, Roland and I were married. However, neither Roland nor my brother approved of one another. There were constant arguments between Roland and I about my brother's influence on Cyrus given my brother's activities which Roland deemed questionable, at best. The conflict put a terrible strain on our marriage which ultimately led to our divorce. When I discovered I was pregnant we agreed that Elroy would stay with me and Cyrus would remain with him. My brother named Elroy." she expounded.

"I knew I recalled a playmate. When I was a little boy we would play down here all the time – it is slowly coming back to me now!" Cyrus reflected on his younger days aloud.

"I, too, recall a childhood friend with whom I used to cavort with among the blocks down here. But then he...disappeared and I remained in the catacombs to play with the gold blocks alone." Elroy concurred with Cyrus's tentative recollections. "I remember that I felt bereft at what I then considered was your unequivocal desertion and rejection when you no longer came to play with me anymore. I was very lonely." he dejectedly told Cyrus, as he remembered his hurt feelings.

"It was not of Cyrus's choosing that he left, Elroy. Do not blame him. Roland and I separated the both of you. At that time, Roland did not believe that it was wise that you two should play together. You and Cyrus would become too attached to one another and wish to be together all the time. Then, it would be harder on each of you when each of us took one of you to live away from the other. Therefore, to avoid this possible scenario and to spare you two the anguish of pining for one another, Roland thought it best that you two should be separated early in life with neither one knowing that the other existed." Trudy expounded with open frankness.

"Brothers! Well, I'll be dogged!" breathed Clyde in amazement as the cogs of his brain began slowly to turn; his blood started pumping vigorously – as evidenced by the rapidly pulsing vein on the temple of his forehead – and a lightbulb exploded, figuratively, above his head. "That explains ya foggy memories – don't ya see? But, then Cyrus left early so it didn't affect him...." he said in excitement to Cyrus and Elroy. "Elroy, I noticed you are using big words now...and acting your proper age. So," he stated revealing his sudden epiphany, "those bricks must've affected your thinking just like they are making me go ta sleep! And now that ya can't be near them anymore 'cause your cellar's blocked up so ya can't reach them and be near to 'em ta breathe their dust, ya are coming back ta normal smarts! Ooops!!!" Clyde let forth the expletive and then covered his mouth with his hands on the realization that he had just let the proverbial cat out of the bag and admitted that he had been in the portion of the tunnels which stretched out beneath Simon's residential property.

"Don't worry." Randmore assured him. "We know all about the bricks and had already suspected your underhanded involvement in vying for exclusive possession of them."

"They be on <u>Simon's</u> division o' the property an' they belong te him." Matt inserted the fact quickly into the conversation to make sure that Simon's claim to the misshapen blocks was not overlooked.

"Trudy? I am curious. You said that your brother named, Elroy? Claude Fauste told me of someone who had named him." began Edith.

"Edi!" Pierre said warningly and gasped lest she divulge anything further regarding Jan LaFitte's agents or his business affairs.

"Do you mean, LeLoup, Edith? Yes, Pierre, my brother is Jan LaFitte. Do not worry. We are all family now!" Trudy said soothingly to the jumpy Frenchman who appeared to be on the very verge of experiencing an attack of the vapors.

"I've been thinking…" said Callie, broaching the topic thoughtfully, "about the name, Elroy, and the letters on the backs of the bricks…."

"So have I, dear. So have I." Edith agreed. "Elroy and LEROI sound quite similar."

"That is because, LeRoi, is my true name. This, Elroy, is a nickname…there is no need to kneel before me, Pierre Dûçot." Elroy demurred to the Frenchman who had dropped to his knees before him.

"La personne qui est appelé, KING, deserves le plus grand respect and I bow to your superiority, my nephew." Pierre replied with flowery exuberance – despite the fact that he was Elroy's elder!

Pierre mentally sniffed haughtily beneath his submissive façade and regarded this young upstart superciliously. He cataloged Elroy's strengths and weaknesses as he knew them. Coming to his feet, he decided that Elroy didn't present much of a threat to his status with Jan.

"You know, Elroy?" Dwight spoke up suddenly. "I think Barney is right. You are like a different person, now. I have been watching you the last few days since you have not been playing with those dusty bricks and I, too, have noticed that you are more confident and self-assured. So, it makes sense" he surmised, "that now that you are not in proximity to the bricks en masse your mind has cleared up and it's like you have come out of a kind of trance. And the fact that Barney is in a dumb trance every time he is with those dusty bricks en masse bears out the theory! And, you know, when you are down there, in the stacks, those weird nuggets actually glow? It is a creepy feeling to have all that eerie illumination around you – ooooh!" Dwight gasped with fright involuntarily and shuddered as chills moved up and down his spine.

"Is this your ring, Monsieur Sanders?" inquired Pierre abruptly removing a gold pinky ring with the initials D. S. from his finger and showing it to him.

"Why, yes! It is!" Dwight replied, startled, as Pierre's unbidden question caught him off guard. "I have been looking for this. Where did you find it?" he inquired taking the ornate ring with sapphire chips around its border and filigree work on its sides from him and fitting it onto his own pinky finger.

"Calvin gave this ring to me when I had admired it on his hand. He had found it among some wreckage he and Matthew had been foraging through in Simon Chesterfield's basement. Vous savez, Monsieur Sanders – alias Sandy – je crois que vous êtes correct in what you say. Mais, I find it interesting that Calvin found your ring in Simon's basement. So, I ask myself, how did Dwight Sanders' ring come to be in Simon Chesterfield's basement? It was not found inside the tunnels after the blockage of rubble and debris. Further, I find it most intéressant that not only Clyde Barnett, but you, aussi, know that Elroy could no longer play avec his blocks. The most fascinating question is, how did you know Elroy played with the blocks in that particular area of the tunnel where the stacks are located and that the blocks in that area emit a glow unless you had been there?" Pierre asked Sandy cagily. "And, if you know this, perhaps you also know of a certain explosion in Simon's basement...?"

While Dwight Sanders' face reddened and he stuttered guiltily with an unintelligible response Clyde looked down the tunnel from whence he had come.

"They are here!" exclaimed Clyde in panic. "I told ya. Every man for himself!" he yelled as he jumped behind Pierre thrusting him forward as a human sacrifice and Edith fainted in Dudley's arms.

CHAPTER 77

Matthew Flanderly, M.D. pulled the small vial of smelling salts from his ever present medical bag and waved it beneath Edith's nostrils.

"I am glad that someone else other than I must breathe in a sampling of Matthew's witches' potion." gloated Pierre with relief.

"Canna ye ne'er be quiet, ye selfish buffoon! This be yer own wife lyin' here in dire straits! But I still canna figure out why she fainted." Matthew puzzled aloud as he regarded his unresponsive patient with marked concern. "An' just who are these people?!!!" Matthew demanded bellowing petulantly in outrage, protective of his patient's right to privacy, as the unknown man knelt beside Pierre and gently transferred Edith's head and upper body from Pierre's arms to hold and cradle her within the fold of his own arms as the woman with him watched with concern and leant on Clyde's rifle.

"So, you are Edith's new husband?" the anonymous gentleman finally spoke disregarding Matt's belligerent query. "What happened to Norden?" he asked Pierre.

"Malhereusement, he passed on. Je suis Pierre Louis Dûçot." he announced proudly feeling a kindred spirit in this man who appeared to love Edith as much as he...well, maybe not <u>as</u> much.

"I am very pleased to meet you, Pierre. I am Brandon Chesterfield, Edith's older brother. And this," he nodded upwards towards a tall, blonde-haired lady with a heart-shaped face and blue eyes, "is my wife, Jeanette." he revealed as they both lowered their hoods.

This revelation was mind shattering. The bombshell momentarily stunned them all – except for Clyde.

"Who do ya think ya fooling with your hocus-pocus smoke and mirrors. Ya not pulling the wool over anyone's eyes with ya tear-jerker parable." Clyde jeered, sneering.

"Can it be true? Me old friends – yer alive!" cried Matthew joyously.

"Hold your horses, Matt. You haven't seen your friends for years. Let me handle this. Excuse me, I am Randmore McKinley." he introduced himself to the couple. "Can you tell us anything to confirm your identities? Do you have any children, for instance?"

"You are obviously my son-in-law." ascertained Brandon. "Carina has good taste. I would expect nothing less from her than to choose an astute man, such as yourself." he complimented Rand with a smile on hearing his loaded question.

"Hey, what about me? I'm Randy's cousin. Alex Caine, here. Pleased to meet you and your lovely wife, both!"

"Do you have a picture of your daughter – and what of your son?" Randmore impatiently interrupted Alex's preface to a flowery speech.

"Randy, you know that Cari doesn't-"

"Alex!" almost in tears, Randmore interrupted him to prevent Alex from inadvertently compromising and impeding his attempt at conducting a shrewd, pithy fact-finding investigation.

"I leave the picture carrying to my wife, Jeanette." Brandon said and laughed with a twinkle in his eyes as he appreciated Rand's frustrating predicament and took the picture of a little girl from his wife, who had just taken it out of her locket, to present to him. "We never were blessed with a son – but I am sure you already knew that." he added.

"That's why your daughter still keeps her maiden name as-"

"Alex!" Rand waved his cousin into silence as he took the

picture from Brandon and studied it closely.

"Cari was a cute kid." Alex volunteered his observation while looking at the picture over Randmore's shoulder.

"Excuse me? It may not be my place." broached Cyrus slowly while coveting the gaze of those who looked upon the photograph displaying the likeness of Cari as a young girl. "But I noticed that Cari has a birthmark. Could you tell us the shape of the mark and on what part of the body it can be found?"

"Well, well, well.... The monster speaks!" cried Jeanette.

"Now, Jeanette, dear. Since you are obviously <u>not</u> her husband, Cyrus, I would have to <u>assume</u> it was on an exposed body part. That is, if I did not already know that it was in the shape of a heart on the side of her neck. And, it is hard to notice unless you look quite closely. I can, therefore, ascertain that you have a huge crush on my daughter." Brandon said addressing Cyrus directly. "And that, in and of itself, should make you very mad at the man who held your in-laws prisoner, Randmore – son." concluded Brandon sentimentally as the impact of the fact that he had a son fully sunk in.

"That's all very nice but this sweet, sentimental moment means nothing! Those two tried to murder my boss man, the number one boss man, that is!" said Clyde accusingly. "And I caught them, red-handed, over his poor writhing body! He is in a coma, now, but before he went under he fingered the guy and said he did it. Ya can't dispute the facts!" Clyde expressed himself eloquently adamantly shaking his finger in blame and judgment. "The gun was right there by his side. I've got it in a safe place as evidence for just such a time as this. An' this poor boy's been looking after his father who is in a coma and wondering why his father tied those two up." said Clyde indicating Cyrus with a wave of a hand in his direction while striding purposefully to Cyrus's side to stand stalwartly next to him in order to lend the appearance of moral support with his steadfast presence. "I think that Roland knew that they was bad seeds and was about to call Cordell when they tricked <u>me</u> into letting 'em loose and went ta do him in!"

"You are wrong!" Elroy interjected. "I tied them up!"

"But I asked you then and you swore up and sideways that you hadn't done it!" protested Clyde reminding Elroy of his past denials of culpability.

"You misunderstood me, Clyde. As I recall, you had asked me if I had tied them up while playing cops and robbers or cowboys and indians. <u>This</u>, did not happen." he asserted firmly. "I did, however, tie them up playing a game with them of secret agent. They were spies against the state and I was interrogating them."

"Why, you.... I cannot believe...." Clyde said in vexed frustration unable to finish his sentences. "THEY WERE TELLING THE TRUTH ALL ALONG!!! But, that doesn't change the fact that he tried to murder Roland." he asserted to his audience stubbornly.

"We told you. There was a man in the barn and he was leaning over Roland choking him. Brandon fought with him – trying to pull him away. He heard your footsteps outside and ran away. After that we heard a shot and Brandon and I ran to Roland's side after having pulled away with the intention of chasing the culprit. It was then that Brandon saw that Roland was bleeding. He knelt beside him to feel the pulse in his neck-"

"I saw that he was still alive and attempted cardiopulmonary resuscitation to revive the victim." Brandon said authoritatively interrupting his wife.

"I taught him that." Matthew interjected modestly.

"We're telling you the truth!" Jeanette pleaded the case now addressing Cyrus and Clyde, both. "Roland was our friend – why would we want to harm him? He took Brandon and I – two complete strangers – into his own home and nursed us back to health. He stood by us even though we suffered from amnesia for years – even though he didn't know us. Who does that? We loved the man as if he were our own family."

"That's the voice!" Elvie cried victoriously alerting her now very tired, hungry and skeptical companions who had just made their way behind her into this section of the seemingly endless configuration of tunnels to her joyful discovery.

Startled by the gleefully trumpeted declaration, all eyes of the conversants looked forward to regard Elvie coming forth from the darkness.

"Edith is coming out of it!" Brandon shouted joyfully as Calvin, Alex and Randmore ran over to hug their wives and, on seeing her parents alive and well, Cari swooned in Randmore's arms.

CHAPTER 78

"So, you are Chris Colden's brother. I'm very pleased to meet you. I bet you are proud being related to a man of the cloth!" Detective Rafe Cordell articulated enthusiastically.

"I surely am, sir." Hank said emphatically scratching at his newly cultivated black beard. "We are all mighty praiseful of him, me and the folks back home."

'In your dreams!' Hank thought sourly again rubbing his itchy, new beard. The new facial hair was a pain in the neck but it was only a minor inconvenience. It helped to disguise his features, making him more difficult to recognize by the authorities and that is all that mattered. The less conspicuous he was the better. And it was obvious that he even had this backwoods police officer fooled. The important thing was that he achieve his goal. He had to talk Chris out of this nonsense of being a celibate minister before he took his final vows and it was too late! He had tried earlier on to talk him out of his foolishness but he had to cut out prematurely before he had convinced Chris because the law had been on his trail then. Jeepers! That had been a few years ago, more or less. Hank scratched his head. Well. You know what they say.... It was better late than never! Sure, the law was still looking for him. But the heat was on less, now, and they weren't being as vigilant in the police force hunting for him. Not to say that it was not still dangerous for him to be seen in plain sight, mind you. But it was worth risking capture if he could prevent his darn fool sibling from committing the most huge mistake of his life! Celibate.... It had taken him a while to figure out that it meant you could not have kids anymore. He did not know what they did to you.... But for all he knew, it might be permanent! His mama wanted grandkids and his jilted girlfriend, Velma, was waiting tearfully back at home – brokenhearted – but still eager to oblige! She would take him back if he would just give her some sort of a sign. What was that...? That bumpkin, Cordell, was speaking to him.

"I assume that you are here to visit your brother...." Rafe prompted the nonresponsive man who appeared to be in a daze quizzically.

"I am sorry. I was just so overcome with emotion.... Family pride, you know?" said Hank Colden hurriedly choking down the bile rising up and into his throat as he reflected upon his brother's stupidity and wondered where he got it from.

If he was able to head off Chris' dang craziness that would go a long way toward restoring the Colden family pride! A lunatic from around these parts had encouraged this lamebrained notion. They called him a mentor. Now, he didn't rightly mean to be sacrilegious or anything because maybe this celibacy thing was okay for some folks – but not for his brother!

"I have got to find him before it's too late!" Hank blurted out angrily to a startled Rafe Cordell who wondered at his angry sense of urgency. "That is, I don't want to be too late – I might miss the festivities!" he prefabricated his answer and happy expression on the fly as he noted Rafe's abruptly raised eyebrows and shocked facial expression. "I would be much obliged to you if you knew offhand where Chris was or could help me find him in a timely fashion." he said all the while ruminating on how at least that much was true – he did not wish to miss the festivities but not because of the reason Cordell likely thought!

"I am afraid that the ceremony has already taken place. But, the good news is that Chris is now a full-fledged man of the cloth! Let me take you to him. I believe that he is at the orphanage about one mile past Candlestick Manor. Let's get going!" Rafe said jovially as he clapped a friendly hand on the back of Hank Colden's shoulder and started to lead him outside of the exit with his guiding hand. "Jim! You're late." he called out to his tardy co-worker. "I am going to have to dock your pay!" Rafe threatened him jokingly with a solemn face which eventually cracked into a smile.

'Oh, no!' Hank silently exclaimed inwardly and his heart sank as he grimly realized that he was about to be found out and apprehended. Even though he now sported a beard, Lahy was no fool, well, not totally, anyway, and it would be no time before he recognized him as the guy who took Cari and Edith hostage after tying up the rest of their family and imprisoning them in their house. He pulled his cap down lower over his forehead and looked downward but it was only a matter of time....

"I am about to show this-" Rafe paused to pull the reluctant, escaping Hank back by the collar. "Why so, shy?" he asked Hank. "Now, Jim-"

"I have need of yer attention, right away – if I'm not bein' too pushy....Ye have te help me find my husband! PLEASE!?Ye have te help me!" pleaded the frantic lady in various shades of distress.

Hank heaved a huge inward sigh of relief. Some lady he had never seen before had brushed past him to take Jim Lahy by the elbow and usher him into the office which he and Cordell had just vacated. Whoever she was he silently thanked her for her divine intervention. He took it as a sign that he was doing right.

"Do not worry, Rafe. I know this young lady-"

"Go on, now! Ye always were a flatterer, Inspector!" the unknown lady said with a modest chuckle at being "mistaken" for a young lady while batting her eyelashes and looking at him imploringly.

'Whoever this anonymous woman was, he owed her one, big-time!' Hank thought gratefully. And, he always repaid his debts!

'Never let it be said that a Colden did not honor his debts!'

"Nice meeting you — whoever you are." Jim said to the newly hooded stranger who had just adjusted his jacket and pulled up the hood to cover his cap in preparation for exiting the building into the chilly afternoon air outside. "Go on wherever you're going without me, Rafe. I will take care of this matter personally." he said to Rafe slyly winking at Eleanor Flanderly. "Me and this hot tamale have some unfinished business to catch up on! Say, Rafe!" Jim called out after him as he was about to follow Hank out of the back door.

Rafe paused for what seemed like an eternity to Hank, holding back the door he was about to release to close behind him. Hank just held his breath waiting for the other shoe to drop. The inspector must have recognized him. He should surrender.... He should take his medicine like a man! After all, he had no gun...they had him dead to rights. He bowed his head and extended his hands waiting to feel the cuffs close around his wrists.

"There must've been some kind of explosion over at Candlestick Manor because the gazebo behind the house has a big, gaping hole at the side of it. In any event, whatever happened out there, the hole constitutes a hazard to the public. It is an attractive nuisance. We got kids playing out there in that area and one of them might fall into it. Or, worse, look to explore inside of the hole. Yes. An attractive nuisance is definitely what we have got here! Trespass is another issue which comes into play."

Hank breathed a huge sigh of relief, expelling air that he did not even realize that he had been holding in. He was safe for now. His identity still remained a secret.

"Don't worry, Jim. We will be going by that way. I'll check it out." Rafe assured him.

CHAPTER 79

"We suffered from amnesia for years, your father and I. We wandered as homeless people. Eating at soup kitchens or foraging in the trash behind restaurants for food. Living in cardboard boxes.... These things were all commonplace to us. It was not a very comfortable life, to say the very least, but we got by." Jeanette Chesterfield explained to her daughter and those listening as they walked along trying to find a way out of the catacombs.

"And then Roland found us and took us in. I remember that it was snowing. Jeanette and I had just finished a job we had found washing dishes at a restaurant during the Christmas rush. It was blistering cold outside-" Brandon Chesterfield continued before being interrupted by his wife.

"My fingers were turning blue...." Jeanette added. "The scenery was very pretty, though."

"It sure was." Brandon affirmed gazing into her eyes and holding her hand as if this were their first romantic interlude. "And then Roland saw us shivering in the cold outside as we were walking to the side doorway we sometimes took shelter under."

"He started walking alongside of us and asked where we lived and if we needed help and if he could help us. Of course, we said, no. We were too proud and we did not wish to bother anybody with our problems. But he persisted and eventually we succumbed to his charming personality and gentle persuasion. He opened his home up to us and treated us as if we were family." Jeanette concluded.

"And then ya turned traitor on him and shot out his lights.

That's how ya repaid him for saving your skins!" Clyde jeered at them in disgust and spit at Jeanette's feet.

"We told you-" began Brandon angrily as Jeanette turned into the crook of his arm to hide her face in his chest and sob.

"Yes. You told me!" Clyde said sardonically interrupting him. "There was a third person with ya in the room. Well, I didn't see anybody else. Except, I saw you kneeling over Roland's bleeding body with your hands around his neck and your gun ya used ta shoot him with smoking right by his side. The smell of gunpowder was still ripe in the air...." Clyde announced the damning facts eloquently denouncing their claim self-righteously with head held high, chin jutting forward and his right index finger pointing upward to accentuate his honesty in point.

"Your allegations against my brother and sister-in-law are preposterous! Chesterfields do not commit murder. It is not in their blood. Our lineage is spotless!" asserted Edith firmly. "And once we leave this place we will seek out Inspector James Lahy and he will clear up this whole distasteful matter!" she said matter-of-factly.

"Good idea, lady. Then, we can get them into the maximum security prison without delay!" Clyde rebutted with just as much certainty as Cari clung to the upper arm of her father and glared resentfully at the man threatening the liberty of her parents.

"I think it is time that you utilize your secret weapon, Matt." Rand said casually diverting the stream of the discussion as he perceived the fire snapping sparks in his wife's eyes and wished to forestall her potentially scathing rebuttal and having to deal with a fracas.

"Aye.... Maybe Charmer can find us the way te a proper exit." Matthew conceded reluctantly, very gingerly setting the sack of diamonds down on the cobblestones, as if they would break otherwise, so that he could unlatch the pet carrier door and swing it open to remove the cat.

After Matt set Charmer down the feline walked a few paces and then paused to stretch out her body luxuriously indulging in one long, unequivocally drawn-out yawn exposing her sharp, white teeth. Then, she sat down on her hind legs complacently and unconcernedly proceeded to clean her paws and face.

"Yeah. Maybe we could make it home before dinnertime – whenever that is." Alex said hopefully. "I'm hungry!" he griped so glumly that his voice garnered the cat's attention and she stopped preening herself to gaze up at him adoringly.

"Oui. Peut-être Alex can find for us another can of tuna which she can turn over." scoffed Pierre sarcastically.

"Ah, leave her alone! She saved our lives, Pierre! If it weren't for Charmer we wouldn't have known which staircase to take-"

"It was a…lucky guess." he responded interrupting Alex as he regarded the cat with an unspoken challenge in his demeanor which dared her to prove him wrong. "This cat could not find her way out of here with a compass!"

"Are you referring to the time Alex came limping up to the house in only one shoe?" asked Mary Jo. "Boy, that was a funny sight! If I hadn't been so worried about him, and you guys as well, I would have laughed right there! You fellas looked positively bedraggled when you are all usually so neatly dressed and clean!" she recalled with a chuckle as she remembered their incongruous appearances.

"Well, I, for one, think that it is a very sad testimonial of what we have degenerated to if we feel that we must resort to making jibes at one another at the expense of a helpless cat. The poor dear is probably just as apprehensive and confused as we are." Edith chided them waving all frivolity aside as she walked over to stand protectively by Charmer.

"Would all of you stop doggone playing around? We're in big trouble, here! We're lost down here! We have no food, water… we're all tired, and I don't know about you, but my feet hurt. So instead of blaming each other and complaining about things we can't change let's concentrate on finding a way out of this debacle!" Calvin lectured realistically.

"Simon told you. We were once trapped down here for days before we found our way out. If we ever find a way out of here, that is.... We may never leave here considering the way that these tunnels have degraded!" Trudy said pessimistically looking at the semi-crumbling walls about her and pulling her suit jacket more closely about her against the chill and damp in the dim, dank corridor.

"If you dang chickens would stop coming to roost we can find our way back to where these two murderers incorporated" Clyde said with a scowl as he pointed at Brandon and Jeanette, "had been secured before they chased me into this foggy unfamiliar neck of the tunnels. Then, we can shimmy into the house through the false window."

"I told you!" Pierre asserted jumping on Clyde's revelation which he considered somehow an admission of guilt. "I told you that I went through the looking glass and.... And I saw GRAND-MÈRE! We cannot faisons le promenade in that direction. I refuse." he declared defiantly his contrary declaration driven by his fear of meeting his deceased grandmother's spirit face to face.

"Dunna be so childish! I be certain tha' somewhere deep inside tha' pea-sized brain o' yours tha' ye know there be no Grand-mère Dûçot te be a-fearin'. Calvin and Dudley have admitted te us all tha' they were behind the whole Grand-mère escapade te begin with! They didna have te reveal this t'us. They coulda kept silent and avoided reprisal from ye. But they had enough compassion fer what ye've been goin' through and decency te be willin' te risk yer ire – and ours, too – te admit te their perfidy so ye wouldna have te suffer under the delusion any longer tha' yer deceased relation was out there lookin' te trap ye!" Matthew convincingly exhorted slowly and carefully as if he were explaining things to a young child.

"He saw his dead grandmother behind the fake window?" Dwight Sanders asked aghast at the unexpected revelation.

"Aye." confirmed Matthew regarding him oddly. "I know it be soundin' lunatic but this scatterbrained blowhard be sure she be chasin' after him."

"I believe him." Dwight concurred forcefully.

"Wha...t?! Then ye be just as daft as the Frenchman. I wash me hands o' ye both." Matt replied in confounded exasperation wiping off his hands one against the other in order to rid them of the dust of their imaginary essences.

"The townspeople think that the house is haunted – they won't come near the place. That's one of the reasons Cyrus wished to tear Candlestick Manor down. The staff thinks that whole section of the house where the false window is is cursed. That is why I was leading you away from it last time you were here.... But, then you... disappeared!" Dwight said exclusively to Pierre before continuing to speak to Matt.

Pierre stepped up a bit closer to listen to their exchange. 'Finally. Quelqu'un who believes me. Who knew that it would be this, Sandy, person?' he thought in astonishment. Dwight pointed the beam of his flashlight upwards from under his chin to highlight his face with its light accentuating his features starkly and lending a ghost-like aura to him and to those around him.

"Legend has it that the window takes you to the other world." began Dwight as Pierre's eyes widened to the size of saucers and he, therefore, drew even closer to Sandy. "It's like they say. The eyes are the mirrors of the soul. The window is like the eyes and anything you see through it is possible. They say that through the window is a whole other world and when you step through it... you are transported. Before Roland's father bought this place for his wife, Coreen, the house had been owned by a couple who were virtual recluses. Whenever they went to town to buy clothes, or shoes, or anything, they never spoke a word to anyone and then they just…disappeared. The cook, the housekeeper, the stableboy – the whole household staff – looked everywhere in the house for them and could not find hide nor hair…. The rumor was that they had gone through the false window in the corridor never to return! Of course, this was all talk. Idle gossip. Sometimes someone brings it up, though." Dwight finished mysteriously.

"So. You think that, perhaps, my Grand-mère Dûçot is maintenant in league with these lost people?" Pierre inquired earnestly having clearly been spellbound by Dwight's story.

"Malarkey!!! Are ye two peas in a pod out o' yer minds?!! I've never heard o' somethin' so utterly preposterous!"

"Matt's right, Pierre. You can't live your life based on superstitions, rumors and old wives tales!" Randmore told him.

"What Randmore be tellin' ye, Pierre, is te grow up!" translated the Irishman.

"Stop bickering!" yelled Dudley. "Charmer's on the move!"

They all ran to follow the feline. Down the corridor and twisting sharply to the left they followed Charmer. The high heels of the ladies clattered and clicked noisily against the cobblestone floor and the flat, rubber soled shoes of the gentlemen clapping on the floor in a different chord joined together with them to create a dizzying cacophony of sound which ended abruptly as they reached a cul-de-sac and skidded to a halt before it.

"Well, what do we do now, Miss. Secret Weapon?" Matt asked the cat between pants as he and the others sought to catch their breath and they all considered their predicament and puzzled over what to do next.

"In the wall…. Do you see it?" Elroy said excitedly as he pointed at the outline of a door in the stone wall.

"And look! There's a keyhole." said Alex noting the existence of an incongruously placed keyhole appearing strikingly out of place in the brick wall before him as he went up to the wall and bent down to peer through it. "I can't see a thing!" he remarked querulously.

"But who has a key?" asked Elvie perplexed.

"Charmer's collar! There MUST be a key on it that fits in the lock. Why else would she lead us here?" reasoned Mary Jo. "There are a lot of charms on her collar — we're just bound to find it. Eventually...." she said in vexation as she bent down to the cat's level and considered each charm on Charmer's collar respectively while Matt regarded her with disappointment.

"I expected more from ye than te have these outlandish ideas, lassie. Tryin' te suppose the application o' such complex thinkin' like that te the mind o' a cat!" Matthew stated with world-weary certainty.

"Got it, Matt! This one looks like it's just the right size!" Mary Jo said triumphantly as she rose with Charmer carrying the feline with one hand grasping her chest from beneath her front upper arms and fitting the key on her collar into the lock.

On turning the key there was a click in the lock as the door it was attached to swung open into the backyard of the manor to reveal the great outdoors beyond accompanied by a small rumbling sound in the tunnel that they had just vacated. The cat ran out into the fresh autumn air to disappear among the foliage beyond.

"We have te go back!" Matthew said suddenly with a stricken expression on his face. "We've got te go back!" he repeated the sentiment dolefully and more loudly on a rising note of hysteria as he turned around to reenter the glow of the tunnel's ghostly half-light to retrace their steps leading backwards.

"Are you bonkers, Matt?" Alex asked him. "We're practically out of here and you want to go back?"

"Yeah. What gives?" asked Calvin.

"I left it. I left it behind! I only set it down fer one moment!"

Matt practically wailed holding his head between his hands and closing his eyes in his shame-faced misery.

"Is this about the pet carrier?" asked Randmore. "We can buy
another one!"

"No! 'Tis not about the pet carrier." Matthew bemoaned casting
a tortured gaze in Randmore's direction.

"Well, then what…? Oh, Matt!!!" Rand said with compassion.

"What?" asked Dudley as he sought to connect the dots and
understand what they already seemed to know.

"Oh, no! Matt!" Mary Jo exclaimed as she looked into his glassy,
red-rimmed eyes speaking untold volumes on their own.

"You mean…? Oh, Matt!" Alex articulated stamping his foot.

"Say it isn't so!" cried Calvin, Elvie and Callie together to the
accompaniment of more rumblings throughout the catacombs.

"Would someone please clue all of us in?" Brandon queried.

"I have te go back te retrieve it. I only set it down fer a moment." whined the Irishman.

"The sack!!!" cried Pierre aghast.

"That's right…. I do recall you were carrying a sack, Matt. You
mean that you left it back there? I do hope it was nothing important." Jeanette said with concern coloring her voice.

"Would I be actin' this way if 'twere not of the utmost urgency?" Matt snapped peevishly and stalked off down the tunnel they
had just left.

"But, be reasonable, Matthew!" Trudy called out running after
him to lay a forestalling hand on his arm to halt his progress forward. "You will never be able to find your way back there to where
we were. We all followed the cat so quickly that we did not note
where we were going. And even if you did find your way back to
where you had set down the sack you would never be able to find
your way out again – at least not without the cat's help. Can't you
hear? The walls are already beginning to crumble down back there.

Simon told you how we were once lost in the catacombs for days and by some miracle of God we found our way out." said Trudy pleadingly trying to remind him of the potential dangers ahead if he persisted in pursuing his ill-advised, hastily conceived intentions. "You have a wife and two children. They should be your number one priority. Your life with them is what's important. DO NOT RISK THAT!!!"

"It was only a burlap sack. Who cares? We're out of the tunnels!" Brandon asserted rationally. "And apparently out of danger, as well." he noted as another rumble, louder this time, rippled through the tunnels behind them and above their heads. "But, what was so important about that brown burlap bag?"

"Because they say I blab I don't think I can tell you." Callie informed Brandon mischievously.

"Then I'll tell him." Cari said.

CHAPTER 80

"Let it go, Matt. There was nothing that you could have done." Randmore said comfortingly.

"Ye shouldna have stopped me. I know my direction. I'm not some kind o' scatterbrain like the Frenchman, over there!" he responded derisively.

"Pierre is not a scatterbrain." Randmore replied placing a restraining palm as a deterrent against Pierre's chest as, taking umbrage at his remark, he sought to jump on Matthew. "You are just letting your regret at forgetting the sack of diamonds make you lash out so that you can come to terms with what you consider to be your failure under the cloche of blaming someone else. But you have to realize that what happened to you could happen to anybody. We were all in a stressful situation lost down there in the catacombs. All of us were exhausted. We were probably walking around down there for days. I don't even know what day it is – none of us do! And when you are hungry and thirsty your mind starts to focus only on survival. Like I said. It could have happened to any of us. We also just discovered that Brandon and Jeanette were alive. Of course, it did not affect me to the extent it affected you because I had never met them before. But since you knew them from when Cari was a little girl, and they were your close friends, it was an emotional experience for you. Carrying all that baggage around with you can distract anybody." he lectured cajolingly and judiciously hoping that he sounded convincing enough to impart him with some courage.

"I will tell ye what distracted me." Matthew shared as they all walked to the sheriff's office. "It was those two booby hatches" he pointed to Dwight and Pierre, "who distracted me with all o' their mumbo jumbo of curses, an' spirits, an' lost souls. Bah!" Matthew expostulated adamantly somehow feeling much better after listening to Rand's enlightening and encouraging pep talk.

'I probably knew all o' these things tha' Randmore had pointed out te me locked in subconsciously.' Matthew thought relenting on his position of self-recrimination. But he had never considered them outright because he had been too busy focusing on blaming himself and concentrating on woulda, coulda and shoulda. The sting of not being able to boast a wealthy status, however, paled in comparison to what he could have done for his family. The money from cashing in the diamonds would have provided handsomely for Matthew Alexander and Megan's educations. And Eleanor and he could have gone on a second honeymoon. Their house was also in need of repair. Ah, well.... At least Alex had his handful of diamonds from the brick which he had found.

"We are the ones who should be <u>mad</u> <u>at</u> <u>you</u>." Pierre told Matthew poking his index finger against Matt's chest several times jolting him out of his reverie.

"He is right, you know, Outlander." Clyde said. "The Frenchie has got ya dead ta rights. Ye should have been watching that bag like a hawk. I know I would have been watching it with an eagle eye if it had been in my care!"

"Merci, Barnett – I think." articulated Pierre slowly taking exception at being called, Frenchie.

"Ya are quite welcome, Pete!"

"Look." Calvin interrupted tired of their pointless chitchat. "Me and Dudley are going home with our wives. You people can stay here and argue all you like. For me, I could use a hot bath, something to eat and a good night's sleep." Calvin said affirmatively stifling a yawn.

"But it's bright daylight out." Alex pointed out as they passed the gazebo and Calvin stared at him in annoyance on hearing his pastoral observation.

"So, I'll draw the shades." Calvin replied in exasperation.

"You know, Alex? You have an innate talent for stating the obvious. Hey! There's the barn. Is that the barn where Roland Sykes was assaulted, battered and put in a coma?" queried Mary Jo of no one in particular. "Let's have a look!" she declared heedless of her insensitive phraseology.

Stepping up her pace to approach the front door of the large, rustic red structure Mary Jo moved ahead of the rest. Pulling open the door of the imposing structure she quickly stepped inside.

"We gotta take those two felonious criminals ta the police station and get them under lock and key! We got no time for your namby-pamby parlor games!" Clyde shouted after her indignantly. "We got real perilous circumstances here."

"I, for one, am interested in whatever Mary Jo can find out that will shed some light on what really happened. I would not wish to have the wrong man locked up." Cyrus said breaking his guilty, long brooding silence.

"So says the man who kept us locked away for years! We could charge you with kidnapping!" Jeanette threatened Cyrus.

"Yes.... Cyrus's attempted murder charge does bespeak a bit of the pot calling the kettle black considering how he has treated us, my dear." Brandon admitted to his wife. "We have, in effect, already been serving a prison sentence."

"Don't let them scare ya off boss man. I know you are in the right!"

CHAPTER 81

Chris Colden stared down at the Good Book where it lay on his bed with regret. Hank had forgotten it. Or, what was more likely, considering his uncompromising negative attitude, had chosen to leave it. Chris had gifted it to him with the hope that on reading it and on digesting its message it would help him to see the light and know the error of his ways but he had been reluctant to receive it. A shame.... Hank and he had a discussion – argued really – regarding his choice of spirituality versus...alternative lifestyles and other assorted professions. He heaved a huge mournful sigh. Maybe there was still a chance to get through to him yet. He picked up the Holy Book and left his bed chamber. He walked to the nearest exit of the orphanage and stepped outside into the cool, crisp air. His searching eyes looked about him and fell upon his sought for subject.

"Detective Cordell!" Chris shouted in as genteel a voice and in as sedate a manner as he could muster under the current circumstances. "My brother forgot the Bible that I gave him in my room. I was hoping that in the name of the Lord and our church you could take it to him." he appealed to Rafe as he ran up to the After School Center which Rafe was exiting after visiting the orphaned children having fun inside.

As Rafe passed through the door while turning his head to wave good-bye and smile at a youngster he had been interacting with he turned to regard Chris in bewilderment. 'What a short visit.' Rafe thought. If it were his brother who had turned over a new leaf and just reached a milestone in his life he would be visiting with him for more than half an hour! Well…families! They all had their own ways of interacting. 'Maybe they had planned a private reunion later when Chris was not so busy encouraging the children and working with them.' he concluded self-satisfied, and pleased with his deduction. 'That must be it!'

"Of course. I would be delighted to do it. Any way at all that I can help."

Hank stalked angrily through the forest roughly pushing aside and brusquely barreling through bushes and overgrowth in his path before finally breaking through the foliage bordering the fringe of Candlestick Manor. Dang that stubborn, bullheaded brother of his. He insisted on following his goody-two-shoes routine. He had even tried to "turn" him around, as he put it, and had tried to pawn off a Bible on him! Thrust it right into his hands, he had. Well, he had none of it. He had left the Bible in Chris' room. And then, if that were not enough, he had followed him outside when he was leaving and pressed a string of prayer beads into his hand! Talk about adding insult to injury! He had just thrown that necklace to the ground when Chris had turned his head…. The audacity – giving his older brother prayer beads as if he needed to be reformed or do penance, or something. 'Dang those kids!' he thought cussing to himself as he tripped over a baseball bat hidden in the tall grass belonging to a boy who had obviously been playing in the area. 'Didn't those kids know that this was private property?' he fumed. He rose from where he had fallen on the ground, picked up the baseball bat and started swinging it. It was a great stress reliever. 'Such unbelievable ingratitude!' thought Hank. He had always tried to do right by his brother. Hank stopped short after having traversed halfway across the meadow. There was that French guy who helped put his brother in prison for a crime he had not committed with his cronies. And with them was the son of that mentor fellow who got his gullible sibling instituted in that ministering business in the first place! He had finished the job, too. Hank gnashed his teeth. It's too bad that he had not been able to finish him off the first time. And those two.... He knew them! They were the ones who came in the barn when he was finishing off Chris' mentor, Roland Sykes. That meddling busybody! Poisoning the mind of his naïve, innocent and impressionable younger brother! 'There should be a law against people like him.' Hank thought bitterly. Well, anyone who hurt a member of his family hurt him, too! 'It's funny how life worked sometimes.' Hank speculated. 'Fate has brought all of my enemies together in front of me in one place ripe for the picking....'

"So, you were standing there?" Mary Jo asked Clyde as he stood by the entrance to the barn.

"Yes, Miss. Quiz Kid. Now, let's get a move on afore all the good jail cells at the police station are taken!"

"As you well know, Clyde. JUSTICE does not take a holiday!" she proclaimed determinedly staring down the man who dared to argue with her into silence and tossing her blonde curls defiantly.

"When can I get up from here?"

"Oh, stop whining, Alex! I'm trying to recreate the scene of the crime!"

"You are wasting our time, Missy! This isn't any who-dun-it novel! You are just delaying the inevitable. We all know they are guilty. There ain't no doubt about it. I am a witness!" Clyde stated affirmatively to her and those listening.

"Not to the other man. You did not see him." Jeanette reminded him.

"I have the murder weapon under lock and key! Now, don't try ta deny your guilt. Confession is good for the soul. The truth shall set you free!" affirmed Clyde stubbornly as if he had not heard her with his hand over his heart.

"Barney doesn't lie. If he says that he saw them...." Dwight left his sentence unfinished and turned up his hands as if to ask, what else do you need for proof?

"Just humor me, okay? I don't know Cari's parents but I do know Cari. Her parents just couldn't have done such a horrible thing and I'm going to prove it!" Mary Jo asserted with utter conviction.

"And I back them one hundred percent. You are a good girl, Mary Jo!" Edith applauded her.

"Et, if my Edi croit que her family is innocent, so do I!!!" said Pierre gallantly stepping up to within only inches of Clyde's face to stare directly into his eyes defiantly.

"I be proud te say it tha', fer this time and this one time only, I agree with Pierre totally!" Matthew concurred unreservedly.

"Pierre Dûçot would not deign to align himself with a family of criminals. It is a situation que est highly implausible. C'est impossible."

"Can I take me previous statement back?" asked Matthew in exasperation taking exception to Pierre's vapid, shallow reasoning based solely on his own vaingloriousness rather than on any honest, steadfast or unwavering belief in Brandon and Jeanette's innocence of all criminal activity.

Cari turned tearfully away from everyone else. She could not emotionally tolerate their constant bickering conversation any longer and so she decided to do some investigating of her own. Cari caressed the railing of a ladder-like spiral staircase leading upwards to the second floor of the barn. She needed quiet – a distraction. Maybe she could find something in the loft above her. Some evidence, perhaps, on the upper floor of the edifice that would help explain everything. Climbing the stairs with a newfound alacrity, purposefulness and hopefulness in her heart, she stood upon the sawdust covered floor and gazed about her. Funny, a boy's baseball bat lay in one corner – how out of place it looked! There was also a large mound of hay before her, a bucket, a pile of grain from what appeared to be a miniature silo and....

"Oh, my!!!" Cari cried out from between quivering lips.

"Where is Cari?" Rand inquired of Edith as he glanced around the ground floor of the barn in search of his wife. "Is she still outside? I thought that she came in with us."

"I saw her go upstairs." interjected Trudy helpfully.

"She should not be roaming alone in an old building like this – not in her state of upset. I had better go upstairs after her." Rand stated worriedly already moving to the stairs.

"Clyde's accusations regarding her parents did disturb her greatly." she agreed.

"They were quite harsh." concurred Edith. "Let us go up there, as well." she suggested to her sister and nephew. "Trudy and I will also help to calm her down. The poor child must feel positively rattled!"

"Wait." said Trudy laying a hand on Edith's arm to forestall her. "I will tell Elroy where we are going."

Randmore reached the top of the spiral staircase of planks to lock eyes with an old nemesis. He hardly had the time to think, let alone prepare for an altercation, before being struck over the head with a baseball bat. Hank threw aside the bat and caught Randmore under his arms before he hit the floor and dragged him to a corner where a thick coil of sturdy rope hung on a hook. Tying up the unconscious man and stuffing his mouth with an oily rag from a catch-all wastebasket he then dragged him further down through a doorway to a back room and laid him beside his similarly bound and gagged wife. Hank returned to the front room and picking up the cast aside bat from where he had dropped it he waited for the other "visitors" he heard ascending the stairs.

CHAPTER 82

"Did Clyde say that Roland was pointing up there, Sandy?" Alex asked Dwight as he lay obediently on the spot on the floor as Mary Jo had bidden him to do and regarded the ceiling above him.

Dwight walked over to stand by Alex and spoke his piece candidly.

"Yep. Barney told me that Roland was writhing in the dust after being shot and the gun was sitting right by him. Roland pointed up heavenward and told him that the fellow, Brandon, done the shooting."

"I was just asking because there is a loft up there. There is a railing bordering the edge of a second floor up there. <u>And</u>, as I understand it, Roland did not mention either Brandon or Jeanette by name."

"The third person! The person Clyde didn't see. That person who really tried to kill Roland could have been hiding up there and that's why he pointed up instead of across directly at Brandon!" Mary Jo concluded vivaciously considering the supposition to be a major revelation and breakthrough in the case of the attempted murder of Roland Sykes.

"The man was flat on his back! O' course he's going ta be pointing upward and crooked. He was in the throes of death!" Clyde asserted in unequivocal exasperation.

"But Brandon and Jeanette had no motive for trying to kill Cyrus's father – how do you explain that?"

"Maybe they wanted his money. They were vagabonds. Sure.... They saw a fancy house. They wanted a piece of it. They'd gotten used to the cushy lifestyle!" he conjectured.

"And, maybe, if they had stayed in the house it would have frustrated your purpose and you couldn't have had it torn down, Clyde. Maybe that was your motive to make up your story blaming Cari's parents!"

"Are you accusing me, Missy?" he stutteringly responded in outraged disbelief.

"No. I am just pointing out that anyone can suppose a motive if he supposes hard enough – even if it's not true!"

"Well, I have the murder weapon!" Clyde asserted emphatically.

"Well, what's up there?" Mary Jo finally inquired mentally gritting her teeth and for the moment relinquishing her position as she realized the futility of bickering with Clyde and sought to get back on track with her initial investigation.

"It's a hayloft, my dear. Now, make something mysterious out of that, I dare ya." he proposed issuing the flat out challenge which he did not expect to be taken up.

"Where's everybody?" Mary Jo responded suddenly in surprise looking between the faces of Clyde and Dwight. "Listen.... It's as quiet as a tomb in here." she noted on realizing that the room was empty of all occupants save for themselves.

"Those two angels of death criminals have escaped custody! I told ya we shoulda gone straight ta the police station!" yelled Clyde in angry frustration as he stomped around in a circle. "Roland was the kindest, finest, fairest, sweetest, most giving man and ta let the people who tried ta murder him get away is sacrilege!"

"We are up here, Barnett. Do not blow a gasket." Brandon called down to him from the hayloft above as he put an arm about his wife's waist to cement their united front.

"Yes. Here we are!" added Jeanette tauntingly while glancing briefly at the stranger pressing a scalpel threateningly against Cari's throat.

"Let's get 'em, Barney." said Dwight moving toward the side stair leading to the loft purposefully only to be held back by his friend.

"Hold it, Sandy. You got any booby traps up there?" he asked Jeanette slyly. "You and ya husband come down here and surrender peaceably."

"Why would you be afraid of us, Mr. Barnett? You hold all the cards. You hold the rifle. And we found some telling evidence to present you with in any case up here." she answered quickly as Hank showed his displeasure at her inability to lure Clyde and his entourage up to the loft without delay by increasing the pressure of the scalpel slightly against Cari's neck so that a small drop of her red blood popped forth and trickled down to her collarbone.

"We are coming up ta get ya – and this time we are going right ta the police station. No more reprieve for ya." Clyde told her as, satisfied with her compliance and perceiving no imminent threat, he relaxed his guard and climbed the stairs followed by Dwight, Mary Jo and Alex.

When the foursome finished rattling up the stairs and stood with their feet planted firmly on the wooden plank floor of the roomy hayloft Clyde trained his rifle on the pair of escapees with their fearful, darting eyes and nervous ticks and tossed a coil of rope which was hanging from a hook on the wall to Dwight.

"Tie their wrists up good and tight, Sandy. We don't want them squirming out of this one. See how quiet and scared they got all of a sudden? That's the look of a trapped animal – the aspect of the wrongdoer! Remember it well, Sandy. Remember it WELL and be sure ta follow the straight and narrow route! So." Clyde said looking around the large section of the two room loft with its sawdust covered floor. "Where's your lovely, dutiful daughter?" he queried of Jeanette and Brandon.

"And where are the others? Did they go home?" Mary Jo chimed in to inquire curiously.

"No. They are here." replied a familiar voice from the not so distant past which chilled Mary Jo to the bone.

"HANK!!!" she exclaimed with dreaded fear as he stepped out of the shadows from the back room into the light.

"I see you remember me, sweet thing." he said chortling with glee at her terrified expression. "Married women do not appeal to me but all the ladies do find me hard to forget!"

"Hey! Sandy, look! It's Chrissy's brother!" Clyde blurted out good-naturedly rushing over to his side and slapping Hank affectionately on the shoulder in friendship. "How ya doing?" he continued stretching out a hand to shake his heartily. "Ya know, Sandy? This is Chrissy Colden's brother." he repeated amicably. "Roland mentored his brother Chris into a full-blown minister." he conveyed the information colloquially to his friend. "I'll bet you are right proud and tickled ta death at your brother's accomplishment of becoming a Holy Man of the Cloth and all. I will tell you, Henry. Chris is a shining example ta us all!"

"You think so?" Hank asked him slowly circling Clyde methodically as a snide expression barely masking his disgust overtook his features.

"Of course." said Clyde puzzled at Hank's response while swiveling in time with his movements to maintain eye contact with him. "I was mentioning ta Sandy just of...maybe last week...at the ceremony that it was a proud day for all of us who had watched him grow and bloom under Roland's tutelage ta watch all his accomplishments come ta fruition. Glory be! That day of the ceremony was most inspiring. I am so sorry that ya missed it." he expounded pulling a handkerchief from his pocket. "It brings a tear ta my eye thinking about it – it was that poignant!" he expressed soulfully dabbing at his eyes and blowing his nose loudly.

"Where are you going, Mary Jane?" Hank queried innocently with a mirthful tinge of humorous sarcasm coloring his tone of voice belying the banal aspect of his query while under the cloak of his exchange with Clyde, as unobtrusively as humanly possible, Mary Jo was in the process of backing up slowly and quietly to the stairwell where the ladder-like staircase descended in a contorted spiral to the ground floor exit of the barn. "Oh. I am sorry. It's Mary Jo, isn't it? I had a small lapse of memory. Why are you look-ing so fearful, Mary Jo?" he asked rhetorically as he approached the stricken woman and dragged her back to the center of the room by the wrist to throw her at Dwight's feet.

"Hey! You can't treat her like that!" Dwight sputtered with a surprised gasp.

"Tie her up, Sanders! And then tie up your friend over there!" Hank barked out angrily wresting Clyde's rifle from the relaxed grip of the bewildered man.

"But, ya got it all wrong, Henry! They are the two criminals who attempted ta murder Roland – not us!" demurred Clyde fran-tically pointing between himself and Mary Jo as he put out a hand to forestall Dwight when Hank cocked his rifle, pointed it and waved it threateningly toward Dwight Sanders.

"You said that they were the pair who attempted to murder your, Roland?" Hank asked indicating Brandon and Jeanette with a nod and a sneer on his face at the fondness in Clyde's voice when he mentioned Roland's name. "Well, if that were true, as far as I am concerned they would be heroes to me and would be free to go – if that were true. And my name is Hank – not, Henry!" he told Clyde irascibly before addressing Dwight curtly. "Now, Sanders, DO AS YOU WERE TOLD!"

CHAPTER 83

Alex ran as fast as he could out of the barn's back door. He had to get help. Since he had to push himself up off of the floor he had lagged a few paces behind the other three. He had been more than a few stair steps behind Mary Jo when she had reached the upper landing and been confronted by Hank. He would have known Hank's sneering, sarcastic voice anywhere and had stolen noiselessly back down the steps behind him and exited the barn. Regrettably, Alex failed to observe Rafe Cordell as he entered the barn from the opposite front entrance of the barn and so he could not warn him of Hank Colden's malicious rampage and vendetta. The police precinct was so far away — what was he to do? Where was he to go? SIMON'S! Simon would know the answer! Relieved that he had determined the most viable course of action to take — going to consult Simon — he changed direction only to collide with Chris Colden.

"What do you mean, IF that were true?" asked Clyde surreptitiously struggling against the ties of the bonds around his wrists while he watched Hank on the ground floor level below him pour liquid from a metal can on the baseboards along the surrounding inside perimeter of the barn. "What ya got me tied up for anyway? I've done nothing ta you."

"It made me sick hearing you gushing over Roland's virtues. How virtuous he is.... How pure and altruistic. Heck, I've been listening to it all morning long!"

"All morning long…? And what is that…STUFF? It smells funny." Clyde demanded sniffing the air noisily as Charmer entered the barn and walked around Hank meowing disapprovingly. "I am talking ta YOU, youngin'. What, were ya raised by wolves? Didn't your mother done teach ya ta show respect ta your elders?!" he asked rhetorically after not receiving an immediate response from Hank.

"Oui. I am complètement d'accord." agreed Pierre who had achieved consciousness only recently and despite a pounding mal à la tête could not resist weighing in with his opinion on the lack of proper behavior exercised by the younger generation of today.

"Dang young upstarts." Clyde observed. "Us sophisticates of society are the reason ya have gotten ta where ya are in life! Climbing ta prosperity on our backs and then crowing all high and mighty without conveying an ounce of appreciative humility – such ingratitude! It boggles the mind." he concluded as Pierre looked at him approvingly – although he did not know about this boggling.…

"My upbringing should be the least of your worries. But you needn't stress on that point. I was reared right and proper – it is called breeding. A pure sense of right and wrong. For instance. Was it right for Roland to take hold of an innocent young boy – my brother – and turn his head around by filling it with crazy notions that were against the future that was already planned for him? Of course not! That is why he had to die. To pay for his crime and do penance for his criminal behavior he had to die. My brother was just getting back on his feet after being incarcerated for a crime he'd never done. That Roland brainwashed him in all of Chris' vulnerability – that's why I had to kill him before he completed the job! Unfortunately, you came in before I could finish him off." Hank ended unfazed by the enormity of his confession.

"You are telling me that you are the one who tried to kill Roland?" gasped Clyde.

"Somebody had to do it!" he replied jovially with a smile on his lips. "He was ruining people's lives. I was doing a public service."

"He was the third man." Jeanette interjected as Clyde turned to her and Brandon mouth agape and stunned at the enormity of the revelation.

"And she recognized me right away, too – her and the French guy."

"Les éléphants n'oublient jamais." Pierre said haughtily as Charmer slipped behind him and he cringed as she clawed at his wrists. "Get away from me you crazy animal. Le chat, elle est dev-enue folle!" he exclaimed as Hank chortled at Pierre's discomfort and Matthew glared at him outright.

"Canna ye not stop yer foolish squeamishness fer once? We are all goin' te _die_ here!!!" Matthew chastised Pierre as Hank's laughter increased and seemed to ring throughout the barn.

"But, the gun…. The gun was sitting right next ta Roland's body, as plain as could be, and when I checked outside the back of the barn that night, not a soul was in sight!" argued Clyde reinsert-ing himself into the conversational mix.

"That, my clueless friend, is because I was hiding up in the hay-loft – I had never left the building! All I had to do was to shoot to kill and then drop the pistol down from up above. No one was the wiser and I was in the clear because you, Roland's best buddy, made the perfect witness!"

"That means" Clyde cogitated quickly, "that the gun has your fingerprints all over it proving your guilt!" he deduced covering his mouth in mortification that he had let the existence of such damn-ing evidence be known.

"Do not worry, Barnett." Hank said calmly with an innocuous wave of his hand. "It doesn't matter anyway. You won't be around to tell anyone about it." he concluded while searching in his pocket for a match book.

"That is correct, Hank. Clyde won't be telling me because you just told me yourself." stated Rafe Cordell as he stepped out of the shadow of the doorway's overhang and warily approached Hank to take the metal can from him and, putting its open spout to his nose, gave its contents a sniff.

After getting a whiff of the acrid odor of the liquid contents, which invaded and subsequently bloomed throughout his nostrils, Rafe pulled back coughing and wrinkled his nose in repugnance.

"We are preparing to commit arson, are we, Hank?" he queried keeping his pistol trained on him as he set down the can of kerosene and removed his handcuffs from his back pocket.

"Did you hear his confession, Detective?" Brandon called down to him in query.

"I heard it loud and clear." Rafe answered Brandon affirmatively. "And, I am so sadly disappointed in you, Hank. I thought that you were one of the good guys!" he added sadly as he approached Hank to cuff him and prepared to read him his rights.

Seeing a slick spot on the floor to the right side of Rafe, Hank raised his wrists in supposed acquiescence. Cunningly tripping forward in a calculated manner and stumbling awkwardly to Rafe Cordell's right in the process – while conveying the outward appearance of maintaining his balance – he surrendered. Seemingly, there was no more fight left in him. The jig was apparently up and, drained of all emotion, Hank spoke humbly.

"I surrender, Cordell. You have obviously outwitted me." he replied as Rafe regarded him suspiciously for a moment or two.

"Here." he said tossing him the handcuffs. "Put them on." Rafe directed moving sideways to stand facing him and slipping on the slick ooze of kerosene on the floor.

EUREKA! His well thought out positional orchestration had worked like a charm – just as he had hoped! Hank saw his opportunity and took it. He jumped toward Rafe and wrestled with him for the pistol in his grasp. As their arms flailed between them the sound of a shot rang out as a bullet issued forth from Rafe's pistol and both it and its owner fell to the floor. Concerned as to his own drama, Pierre shooed the cat away from him only to realize that his bonds were significantly loosened. The cat had cut them with her sharp claws...? But, how could the claws have sawed through the ropes? One would need a blade. He looked at Charmer in puzzlement. Could Charmer be harboring the spirit of...Grand-mère? 'Non! I must have loosened the ropes for her....' he thought. 'Mais, bien sûr. The superior strength of Pierre Dûçot could not be denied!' he presumed superciliously as he slipped the bonds from his wrists and then began to untie his bound together ankles.

"Hank!!! What have you done?" Chris asked appearing from out of nowhere and running to Detective Cordell's side and kneeling down beside him to take his pulse.

Meanwhile, Alex, who had reluctantly commandeered and accompanied Chris to the barn after he convinced him that he could talk Hank down and out of his diabolical intentions, snuck up the side stairs leading to the loft intent on helping the others to find Pierre and...Charmer(!!!?) untying Edith and Cari. Pierre looked up at him and spoke.

"We make a bonne team — vous savez?"

CHAPTER 84

"I am afraid that he is not here, Mrs. Eleanor Flanderly."

"Simon! It be so good te see you!!! Matthew told me ye were alive in his letters but there be nothing akin te seeing you in the flesh." affirmed Eleanor hugging him while Jim Lahy looked on in approval.

'It's good to see the close bond between friends and family.' Jim thought as he smiled at the happy reunion.

"I heard from Matthew that he liked your cooking so much that he married you!" Simon teased jokingly.

"We never would have met be it not fer you and Brandon securing me the job in the Chesterhollow kitchen." she stated warmly. "All those years that we believed you were passed on. Ye shouldna have kept us all at arms length an' in the dark pertaining te your whereabouts."

"It's a long story. I will tell you about it later. Now, about Matthew. His disappearance <u>had</u> gotten me a bit concerned as well. You see, he was supposed to rendezvous with me here – and, by the way, my wife was missing, too. You do not imagine that they ran off together, do you?" he inquired with a laugh at his attempt at whimsical humor. "But seriously. I should have, at that point in time, heard from him, Alex, Randmore and Pierre days ago. You see, we had a little project going on."

"The gold chunks?" Jim asked Simon.

"I see that Eleanor's been wagging her tongue! No. Not gold, per se. Indirectly, yes. But, let me explain. Actually, they are nuggets in various sizes. Some are shaped like bricks, some are misshapen blocks and some are offset nuggets which form different angles in multiple areas. A coloring resembling gold covers their exterior and an ochre-goldish dust clings to their outer coating. But what is <u>inside</u> of them is what's of value.... DIAMONDS." he pronounced dramatically.

"That is some find." Jim commented his interest piqued.

"Yes." he agreed. "But in any case, to continue with my story, I went to LaurelsHeath to inquire as to their whereabouts. I was told by Joan, the new assistant cook Edith summoned to help Trudy in the kitchen, that they had all left a few days ago – the night of Cyrus's cocktail party – and had never returned. Now, this I already knew. So, I had just been about to contact their friend at the police department, Inspector Lahy, that's you, Jim," Simon continued, nodding at Jim Lahy, "when Calvin and Dudley returned with Callie and Elvie. They informed me that they had all been lost in the catacombs for days and had only just found their way out. They had elected to return to LaurelsHeath while the others had chosen to remain on the grounds surrounding Candlestick Manor and investigate the barn behind the house. It seems that Mary Jo wished to re-enact the crime in which Roland Sykes was almost killed."

"Crime?" prodded Eleanor inquisitively in a questioning manner.

"Yes. Oh.... But you would not know of the happy news – although it is tainted with a bitter twist to it. Brandon and Jeanette are ALIVE!"

"I brought you your prayer beads, Hank. So, make good use of them and use them to pray. Please. Repent and turn yourself in. Let them all go. This man that you shot is not breathing. You have killed him." Chris said in a shocked voice as he looked up at his brother from where he knelt beside Detective Cordell.

"That is just another casualty of war, brother. Don't you see? They all have to pay for what they did to you. If you had never been put into prison in the first instance, you wouldn't be in the sorry state you are in now. It was all that McKinley's fault for calling the cops on you. And then, that Pierre went and told lies against you and got you convicted. If it weren't for them, you never would have met Roland Sykes who put the mind meld on you which took you away from the bosom of your family. Don't you see, Chris? They all have got to pay. It is just poetical justice at work. They took your family from you. Now, we take their family from them! That Cyrus Sykes will pay as well, for the sins of his father. You are supposed to be a preacher now thanks to Roland Sykes. You should know all about sinning!"

"Je pense que le cochon est fou." whispered Pierre squinting one eye and raising the eyebrow over the other.

"Me thinks tha' fer once in yer life ye be correct, mon ami." agreed Matthew in an aside to the Frenchman.

"It is so sad when a person's mind becomes as crippled as Henry Colden's." Jeanette observed in a hushed tone of voice.

"You are too Christian for your own good, my dear. The Colden fellow tried to frame us for Roland's attempted murder!" Brandon replied to his wife as he patted Charmer on the head with one of his recently freed hands.

"It is just that I knew him as a child. What a nice, well-mannered young boy he was then." she reminisced.

"His parents always held very strange moral values. The poor young chap could not help but have been influenced growing up...." he concluded ponderously.

"Now, who's being too Christian?" she asked Brandon with a smile.

"Touché, Jeanette. Touché." he replied.

"What's wrong with her?" Rand whispered to Brandon as the cat lay stretched out across the floor and meowed plaintively in moans.

"Would ye keep tha' animal quiet, begorra. She'll be givin' us away! Tha' maniac will be all over us an' here we are without a gun!" Matthew snapped keeping his voice as soft as he could.

"But, we have numbers. And we're not tied up anymore." Alex responded as he jumped to Charmer's side to stroke her comfortingly. "Something's bothering her." Alex observed as he noticed the feline favoring her right paw, continually flexing it and curling it up.

"We may have got the advantage o' numbers, laddie, but he be havin' the pistol!"

"Rifle." corrected Alex.

"Both." observed Rand. "Now that Hank has appropriated Detective Cordell's sidearm we are at a severe disadvantage."

"Aye." concurred Matt. "With the women with us anything could happen. Some person be bound te be shot!"

"Oh, pooh! What makes you men more special than the rest of us? Just what makes men more impervious to gunshots than women?" Edith asked on behalf of all womankind in a low, but nonetheless, snappish voice.

"Let us just be hopin' tha' Chris Colden who has turned te a peaceful religion can convince his fiendish brother te lay down his grievances as well as his arms." Matt expressed fervently to one and all in the hayloft.

"Got it!" proclaimed Alex who had been examining Charmer's paws. "Diamonds. She has diamonds in her paws. Between the pads on each paw is a super-sharp diamond — OW! That smarts!" he exclaimed as he attempted to remove one of them. "So that's how she cut through those ropes.... She SAWED at them! What a clever cat! Brave, too, because she must have also been in agony. What a smart cat!" he marveled a second time crooning to her and petting her head. "Pierre? Where are you going?" queried Alex in surprise as the Frenchman crept stealthily down the stairs without responding.

Pierre Dûçot was just as brave and willing to endure extreme pain in the interests of heroism as the next guy! As he descended the stairway he determined that he would show this resolve on his part to Alex. 'So much praise given for the accidental efforts of a cat.... Pah! Charmer was just, how you say, lucky bones.' Pierre thought. Pierre Dûçot was fearless and sans peur. He did not know how to do it yet, but he would teach Alex that he could snatch victory from the jaws of the cochon! Pierre abruptly halted as two new rogue elements entered the "mix".

"Drop your weapons, Colden!" Jim Lahy commanded brusquely on entering with Eleanor Flanderly while pushing Eleanor behind him, in order to shield her from harm, as well as pushing down the hammer on his pistol and advancing slowly toward Hank cautiously. "Put them on the floor nice and easy." he directed Hank who dropped his weapons and then stood frozen as if rooted to the spot.

"Me Ellie!!!" Matthew cried in fear for his wife's safety the knuckles of his hand swiftly flying to cover his mouth.

"It is better this way, Hank. You will see. This is the best thing that could ever have happened to you. You must needs pay for your crimes, of course, but when you leave prison you will have been rehabilitated and come out of prison a new man!" Chris assured him serenely in an effort to calm him and held out the prayer beads to his brother for him to accept.

The cajolingly serene tenor of Chris' voice momentarily distracted his brother as his message sunk in and Hank genuinely seemed to be considering Chris' words. However, the proffering of the said prayer beads appeared to break the spell of Chris' web of words and Hank bolted for the front door. Pierre collared him before he could exit the barn.

"Not so fast, Cochon!" warned the Frenchman as Inspector Jim Lahy relaxed his stance and advanced to where Hank now stood helplessly with his arms held pinned behind him by Pierre.

"You know." Hank admitted docilely, yet craftily, supposedly re-signed to his fate as captive. "All the <u>others</u>.... Aw! They were easy. Just hit 'em over the head and tie them up. Except the ladies, of course – NOT the ladies. You cannot hit a lady." he said firmly and shamefacedly that anyone should think to commit such a heinous act as he stood in front of Pierre.

Although still restraining them behind his back, Pierre uncon-sciously relaxed on hearing Hank's banter and held his arms less tautly in position behind his back. Peut-être this Hank Colden was not so très totally a bad seed, after all. Perhaps, there was some de-cent kernel of goodness within him still to be fostered.

"Oui. A gentilhomme must never lay a hand on the feminine la-dies." Pierre acceded cautiously, not wishing to be too friendly with the enemy, while smiling with triumphant glee at having appre-hended the slippery fiend singlehandedly and everyone descended from the hayloft above to the first floor.

"You know." Hank continued speaking conversationally. "You are the only one who ever put up half a struggle to resist me. I must admit that you were tough even for me to put down. You know, I was on the boxing team in school."

"So was I." said Pierre relaxing his grip on his prisoner even further and feeling a camaraderie toward him he could not help.

"Well, it shows. It took me two or three good whacks of the bat to your head to put you out."

"I sure'n te believe it. Pierre, here, has one o' the hardest heads I be knowin' of." Matthew stated unequivocally.

"Put out your wrists so I can cuff them." Jim Lahy commanded Hank.

"But, can I have one last request before I go to the station?" Hank asked him quickly before complying with his order. "C'mon. It's only for one cigarette." he pleaded as Lahy hesitated.

"Oui. It is just one little cigarette. Let him have it – c'est the civilized thing to do." Pierre pleaded on Hank's behalf – he was not an ogre!

"Does anybody have a light?" Hank queried after putting the cigarette given to him by Inspector Lahy between his lips and searching to no avail in his pockets for a match with which to ignite it.

"Allow me." said Pierre suavely, gallantly leaning toward him as he produced a silver-encased lighter from his blazer pocket and struck its flint so that a tiny flame materialized from its orifice.

On his extending the pocket lighter to light Hank's cigarette for him Pierre was astonished when Hank quickly grabbed it from his hand and threw it down into a deep puddle of kerosene behind him which he had been concealing with his body. Flames soared high up against the wall as the flaming wall of fire spread, continuing in a ring around the barn's inner perimeter where Hank had previously been busy pouring the kerosene from the now empty can. As Hank swooped to safety through the front exit of the edifice locking the aged barn door noisily behind him, with the sliding of an old bolt screeching and scraping audibly in its rusty lock, the other occupants of the barn scrambled to escape the uncontrollable, mounting flames through the back door.

CHAPTER 85

The flames crawled higher and higher as the smoke billowed gaseously throughout the structure of the barn. Charmer tripped the release mechanism of the grain silo inside the structure releasing the grain from the chute which extended outside to partially bury the escaping Hank Colden alive, trapping him in mid-stride. Everybody turned from the front door and scrambled in haste to the back door with Mary Jo out front leading the group. Behind her Pierre was a close second.

"Un moment." Pierre warned removing his blazer as Mary Jo reached out a hand to turn the seemingly inoffensive yet, in reality, red-hot doorknob before her. "Allow me." he said and turned the knob using his blazer as a potholder between his hand and the searing heat of the metal knob to absorb the chaleur as he pulled open the door. "Mary Josephine, Edi, Cari, Trudy, Eleanor…. All the ladies, prochaine, next, next, next, next!" Pierre shouted as he guided each of the girls with his hand at her back through the door with the flames on the wall less than two feet away from them and the hay in the loft above them igniting with an erupting "POOF" sound and raining down sparks upon their heads.

Fire engines could be heard in the distance and the collapse of a supporting beam falling right in front of the men wordlessly told the story of how especially detrimental in its destructive ferocity a kerosene fire was and how swiftly one could spread. A portion of the roof on their left caved in as the women escaped the burning building with their lives. In their last glimpses those at the doorway could do nothing but stare at their loved ones helplessly as part of the spiral staircase separated from the whole and fell crashing to the ground to block the entire doorway sealing off any access and totally obscuring their vision.

"The back door be completely engulfed in flames. The entire kit an' caboodle be comin' down around us. Our goose be cooked!" Matthew stated affirmatively holding his forearm across his nose to shield it, to some degree, from the overbearing, choking smoke.

"At least Mary Jo and the rest of the women are safe – and that is thanks to Pierre." Alex said gratefully and praisefully, proud of the feat of Pierre Dûçot.

"Pierre…." Matthew said resentfully. "Thanks to Pierre!" he stated bitterly contorting his voice into a ridiculous, exaggerated tone which did not sound like Alex's but came pretty darn close and was intended to imitate his tone of voice, none-the-less, in a mocking fashion. "Leave it te that brainless, pusillanimous simpleton te get out o' this without a scratch!" he concluded begrudgingly after recovering from a fit of coughing.

"You are wasting the air in here by arguing!" Randmore chastised him, yelling in a rare fit of anger. "Just be glad Pierre had the presence of mind to take control of the situation the way he did when the rest of us froze! Alex is right. At least the women got out."

"The boy is right, Doc. The welfare of the womenfolk is priority. And, Brandon, I truly am rightly sorry that, ya know, that I accused ya and Jeanette for trying ta kill Roland. All this time I was blaming you and your wife and you two were innocent all along of any wrongdoing. I jumped to conclusions and this may be belated in coming but I apologize."

"That is very good of you, Barnett. I accept your apology." Brandon said graciously.

"It seems fitting ta unburden your conscience before ya pass. And I apologize ta you, too, Elroy. I thought ya were a danger and

SHARON ELIZABETH SARKISIAN

convinced your own brother, Cyrus, ta ostracize ya without understanding all of the circumstances. I turned kin against kin. I am so ashamed of myself. I practically ruined your life." Clyde said hanging his head guiltily.

"This is all water under the bridge." Elroy noted judiciously.

"Hey, you guys! What are we doing here?! You all sound like you are giving up! We are not dead yet." Alex piped up optimistically in a strong, sure voice.

"Unfortunately, laddie, there is no chance fer us. Look around ye.... There are flames all about us. The fire not only be closin' in on us but the heat be unbearable! Nary o' us canna hardly take a breath." Matthew said ending with a bout of coughing and then continued. "I fear we are doomed. But, ye are right, as ye usually are. That backward – no, I be takin' tha' back. I shan't besmirch him. Pierre did do something good fer once. He saved our fair ladies and that be the important thing. We can all take comfort they be safe an' sound because of his quick, "gentilhomme" thinking. An' this be from the smoke." said Matthew pointing to and then fiercely wiping a tear falling from his eye.

"What are you doing over there, Chrissy? Dwight?" Clyde asked of the two men carrying Rafe's limp, yet upright, body between them as they approached him with Rafe's feet dragging across the floor.

"I was thinking about what Alex was saying – you know, that there must be a way out of here. He is right. I do not know why I did not remember it.... It was in the early days. Roland mentioned it to me, off the cuff, in the early days. He never thought it was important." responded Chris.

"I do not understand you, Chrissy. We are about ta say our prayers and expire right here and you are reminiscing about the old days! You are talking to me about something Roland told ya years ago which even he did not believe was important. Yer a doggone

Pip. Forgive me for saying so to a man of God, but you are out of this world! YOU are quite a character!"

"Oh, ye of little faith, Clyde. OH, YE OF LITTLE FAITH!!!" Chris said smiling while continuing to help Dwight Sanders drag Detective Cordell toward the center of the room.

"Would ye stop the blasted sermonizin', Colden, an' if there be something tha' yer tryin' te say, just say it!!!" Matthew said bombastically to the erstwhile criminal. "We all be chokin' te death in here!"

"And what are you doing with poor Rafe Cordell's dead body? Isn't it enough that we are all going to die that you cannot leave him to rest in peace?" Cyrus asked, finally speaking after maintaining a pensive silence.

"I fully concur with the scurrilous bloke. What ye be doing be downright gruesome!" Matthew asserted indignantly on behalf of the recently passed dead man.

"Rafe Cordell is alive. He is weak, though, and the smoke has overcome him but he has a strong pulse. I did not want my brother to fixate on Rafe and perhaps...finish him off, as they say. So.... I prefabricated a small fiction. A fib – which I pray I will be forgiven for – and proclaimed that he was dead. Rafe followed my lead and played possum. Unfortunately he passed out from the smoke and heat and has only now reached semi-consciousness." explained Chris.

"Well, why bring him all the way te here? Be it not enough that we are all goin' te suffer the fire? At least he would have passed on in his sleep!"

"I brought him here because he is coming with us. I brought him here because of what Roland said. He mentioned to me that there was a storm shelter under the center of this very floor. Whenever there was a twister he and his dad used to open up the trapdoor in the floor and weather out the storm in the shelter. So, who is to say that we cannot weather out this fire in the shelter? The handle in the floor that releases the trapdoor is right around the center of the barn!"

"What are ye waitin' fer then?!!!" Matthew yelled out joyously as he now saw a great bright, white light appear at the end of the dismal tunnel of hopelessness. "Let us be findin' tha' latch!!!"

"I'm ready." said Alex raring to get out of the barn and go home – right now the prospect of Mary Jo's biscuits did not seem so bad.

Producing a flashlight from his jacket and clicking it on in order to search on the floor for the storm shelter's handle in the foggy room clouded with smoke Alex's declaration rang out loud and clear:

"Always be prepared!" Alex said gloatingly quoting Pierre Dûçot.

Having been manhandled by Hank, smoke-smudged, tired to the bone and with clothes in tatters the women huddled together as they watched the lopsided structure which had once been a barn become totally consumed by the fire. Farther down from them, Pierre had not budged an inch. Rather, he looked on dumbfounded and appeared to be frozen in stone holding open the door of the burning barn as if he expected someone to walk through the blockage. Even as sparks of fire flew and rained down around him, and planks of fiery wood fell off of the edifice, Pierre waited patiently for his friends, Randmore McKinley, Alexander Caine, Matthew Flanderly, and the other men to materialize and walk out into the smoky afternoon air. Edith pulled away from the group of grieving survivors to approach him and lead him gently away from the burning structure. Without warning, however, Pierre suddenly broke free from her and began running toward a horse's water trough where the equine tethered to a nearby hitching post reared up and down issuing terrified whinnies and frantic snorts while viewing the raging blaze and the closeness of its proximity. Relieving the frightened creature of his horse blanket, heedless of the steed's flailing limbs compromising his own safety, he then submerged it in the water of the trough. Covering his head with the upper portion of the drenched blanket to form a hood and splaying the rest of it across his shoulders he ran to the window on the side of the barn and pushed it up and open without feeling the pain of the extreme heat to his skin. The blast of hot air released from inside of the structure with the opening of the window was equivalent to that of a blast furnace. Edith started to run forward frantically after him only to be pulled back and restrained by Cari and Mary Jo. The sound of timber crackling filled the air and charred burning beams still on fire fell to the ground as Pierre disappeared through the window. It took a few moments for his eyes to accustom themselves to the murky light and see through the fog of smoke before him and because of this he had to basically feel his way through the room with his arms stretched out in front of him. As he negotiated his way throughout the room searching for someone to rescue Pierre had to blink twice to clear his eyesight and maintain some semblance of reality as he saw the floor before him open up and the top of a person's head appear and form into the body of a complete human(?) being. He gasped in horror, paralyzed with fear, as the black clad figure floated toward him and, in the wink of an eye, yanked his unwilling personage to the space on the barn floor he had materialized from. The mysterious wraith then pulled him down after him – aided by the other grasping hands of his minions helping him – down into the deep depths of a dark abyss. Outside, the fire department could be heard drawing nearer and Simon rushed across the field of grass to stare in horror at the blaze embracing the barn....

CHAPTER 86

"We must be on, comment dit-on, Skid Row." Pierre said cringing backward from a malodorous blast of air, if you could call it air, as he observed a homeless man foraging through the contents of a trash can, presumably for food, in the alley with its crumbling brick walls before them. "Although, I do not know what this skidding and rowing have to do avec n'importe quoi." he noted raising a handkerchief to his nostrils to help mask the offensive smell around him.

"Aye...." Matthew concurred slowly, ignoring Pierre's last comment, as he looked at the squalor about him. "Who was te be knowin' tha' a downtrodden, oppressed place akin te this state be sittin' so close te the Laureltown train station."

"And behind the manor." added Cyrus meekly as he was still ashamed of himself for wrongfully blaming Brandon and Jeanette for attempting to murder his father and for holding them hostage without strong, substantial concrete evidence.

Whether real or imagined or unintentional, their silent snubs hurt. Cyrus felt that everyone was looking at him askance for having doubted Brandon and Jeanette's word to the contrary of his accusations – especially Cari. And he desired her approval most of all!

"What be wrong with that cat?" Matthew asked Alex who held the limp form of the moaning Charmer in his arms.

"Et, why did she lead us ici to this desolate area?" demanded Pierre. "This place is très unwholesome!" he added glancing about.

"Easy guys. You've been sick, too, Pierre! You didn't have to follow her." Alex said indignantly on the feline's behalf.

"By leading us out of those tunnels she <u>did</u> save our lives." Randmore said logically. "It was becoming very difficult to breathe down there in those close quarters of the shelter. If she had not showed us that escape chute leading to the tunnel we followed to the outside exit we would have eventually smothered to death – if the fire had not gotten to us first!"

"That's right." Alex agreed mollified by Randmore's cogent analysis of the situation. "Those other off-chute tunnels leading to other places were probably all blocked off, too. She had also freed us from those ropes. And, she had diamonds in her paws which I can't help but wonder if she picked up on purpose just for us from the floor in the catacombs when we were lost. I can say for sure that you'll be vying for those diamonds with Matthew once we get home, have gotten food into us and have had a good night's rest. But, she will probably still be sick!" he finished self-righteously, sniffing compassionately for the sick feline as Charmer meowed mournfully on cue as if in positive affirmation of all Alex said.

"Isna this trail leadin' te about the area where ye met Elvie in the buff an' scared her half te her death?" Matthew asked Pierre, turning from Alex to make the inquiry directly after conceding to himself that he could not prevail in an argument with him.

"I was just thinking that, too!" said Randmore. "When we were walking through the greenery about half a mile back I thought the place looked familiar. Remember, Pierre? It's the place you showed us where you had woke up in the nude and then Elvie had found you when she was on her way to LaurelsHeath from the train station and got lost."

"How could I ever oublier ça? Mes vêtements!" Pierre gasped in incredulous horror.

"We all are a bit unkempt. Truly." said Chris consolingly misinterpreting his concern. "When I reach the monastery I plan to take a nice hot bath and scrub off the grime."

"Non, non, non, brother of cochon. That.... That, how you say, bum." Pierre cried in outrage pointing his finger to indicate one of the vagrants inhabiting the area. "Il est portant mes vête-ments!" he elucidated stalking over to confront the offender where he slept with a cap pulled down low over his head in the alley as, prompted by curiosity, his companions followed in his wake. "Vois! Do you see?" asked Pierre accusingly. "Ma cravate! Edi m'a donné ce cadeau sûr mon anniversaire. Mon complet et my cufflinks – no-tice the monogramming...." he pointed out wrapping a hand in his handkerchief and then lifting the homeless person's wrist to more clearly show everyone the initials "P.D." engraved in bold letters. "Aussi...ces chaussures. Somehow they seem familiar. Those garish, pointed shoes are giving me a mal à la tête!"

"You were wearing those clothes the night of the soirée when the historical ladies came to the house. You know. That night I was supposed to escort you outside but I lost you in the house." Dwight recalled.

"By golly, you're right, Sanders. That is his suit!" Cyrus con-firmed with a laugh.

"That was the soir I saw Grand-mère Dûçot with one of her min-ions.... I then fell to unconsciousness. Just before I lost lucidity-"

"Which not be too hard o' a thing fer ye te accomplish." Matthew interjected impatiently only to briefly be regarded dismis-sively by Pierre who bestowed upon him a haughty glance before finishing his thought.

"Just before losing lucidity je souviens these garish shoes avec these pointed toe caps. Très ostentatious. And in very poor taste, I might add. Pierre Dûçot does not forget about such a fashion mis-step. Pardon the pun."

"You must have accidentally fallen into one of the sliding walls at Candlestick Manor that leads to the hidden tunnels. These old houses around here seem to be full of them. Then you must have seen Brandon and Jeanette tied up. You, being alone in the dark, and all, and in your fearful state of agitation, then believed Jeanette to be your grandmother and Brandon to be a companion spirit, or her…minion, as you put it." Randmore deduced as he faced a stone-faced Pierre who seemed reluctant to trade in his more fanciful interpretation of events for a more realistic one.

"It looks ta me like that there homeless fella is sometimes sleeping in that there section of the tunnels you was in and needed some warm clothes! He saw your fancy duds, brought ya out of the tunnels, stripped you down ta your birthday suit and left you high and dry!" Clyde said laughing outright.

"Stop, Pierre." Randmore forestalled him as the irate man bent down to shake the sleeping thief and reclaim his clothes. "Let him have them." he said indicating the fancy suit and accessories. "What would you do with the clothes once you had them? You would not wear them, anyway, after he wore them." he concluded, pitying the wretched waif while also knowing Pierre's germophobic idiosyncrasies and credo concerning cleanliness being next to godliness.

"C'est vrai. You are correct about the apparel, Randy. Tu as raison. Regrettably this is so. Even a thorough disinfecting would not make these clothes propres encore. I would have to burn them." proclaimed the Frenchman succinctly. "Mon mouchoir, aussi." he added distastefully with a grimace, as an afterthought, holding up for view the soiled square cloth handkerchief he had used to hold up the homeless man's wrist.

CHAPTER 87

"I just cannot understand how they let Hank get away." Mary Jo complained as she leaned with her back against the side of the fireplace in the living room at LaurelsHeath.

"Mary Jo, how can you be so cold and logical at a time like this?" Edith cried blowing her nose while Jeanette wept incessantly. "We have just lost our husbands and you are carrying on as if there was not a cloud in the sky and this were just another day!!!"

"Don't worry, Edith. I'm not worried and you shouldn't be worried either. Charmer is with them. And you know what they say about cats having nine lives. Anyway, Alex won't die. He'll find a way out – he always does. You've got to have faith! He finds a way out of everything. I don't know how he does it. I think there is an angel looking over his shoulder guarding him. Protecting him – you know? Because he can't look after himself – he never could. No, he'll be fine. He finds his way out of everything....You'll see. Mark my words, as Pierre says."

"How can you say that, Mary Jo? The whole barn is engulfed in flames! And my poor Pierre rushed in there to save your husband!" Edith choked out in grief-stricken accusation.

"Edith! Are you BLAMING me?" she asked incredulously.

"Well, I don't hear you giving thanks for Pierre's heroism or extolling his selfless virtues!"

"I would if I knew any EXISTED!" retorted Mary Jo.

"Oooh...! That is a low blow, Mary Jo. After all the times he put you on a pedestal. You...ingrate!"

"Would you stop it, you two! This isn't doing us any good at all!" Trudy scolded them. "Edith, Mary Jo is just obviously in denial! And there is no reason to cast stones. We all have someone we love in there. Parts of me are in there – my sons. Now, get a hold of yourselves. I believe Cari is in shock, as well. But instead of bemoaning the circumstances of the tragedy she's gone down to the fire station and is quizzing the fire chief to find out what can be done about the situation."

"I fear that nothing can be done." Edith responded dolefully on a hard sob as Cari approached them.

"They thought that Hank Colden was one of the victims of the catastrophe and so they freed him from a mound of ground wheat he had been trapped in outside when he was fleeing the scene. The grain had been released from the silo by a lever in the barn. In any case, they presumed that Hank was an innocent bystander and so they let him walk off scot-free. It was lucky for Hank that they had gotten to him when they did because just after they got him loose the whole silo fell down across that same spot where he had been and would have crushed him. You should see how it flattened the mound of grain. Anyway, when they'd rescued him, Hank played his part as a victim well. The firefighters said that he had pretended to be so utterly grateful at being liberated – he was after all an innocent bystander – and after expressing his untold gratitude he just nonchalantly walked off into the sunset." Cari explained evenly and a bit too eloquently as she tried to mask her sorrow with an outwardly calm attitude.

"Tsk, tsk, tsk! Such a state. Such a pretty state o' things, Officer Mahoney. It be a fine kettle o' fish when the homeless even start te robbin' the homeless!" lamented Officer O'Leary in irony to his fellow coworker as he stood over a guilty-looking Pierre Dûçot removing a gold tie clip from a sleeping hobo who repeatedly smacked his lips together and rolled over onto his side snoring somnolently after he had liberated it from the cravat of its wrongful wearer.

"Mais, officers, this tie clip was un cadeau – a gift – from my wife. I was not STEALING." Pierre explained with chagrin at being observed by an outsider in such an ambiguous situation. "I was merely retrieving it. Bien sûr, I shall have to soak it in alcohol for a few days...."

"Looks te be like we've got ourselves here a comedian." Shamus Mahoney remarked to his partner.

"An' be those baubles the property of yer wife, as well?" police officer O'Leary inquired indicating the gold cufflinks in Pierre's other palm with a nod of his head while pointing with his nightstick at the unsecured French cuffs encircling the sleeping hobo's wrists which lay open and missing their fasteners to hold their flapping ends together.

"Non. These are mine. You see?" Pierre asked ingenuously showing the cufflinks to Officer O'Leary helpfully. "They are engraved avec mes initials, P.D.. I am Pierre Dûçot. The fameux dance instructor. Peut-être you have heard of me?" Pierre asked after introducing himself and extending his hand in friendship. "Non?" he said, answering his own question and retracting his palm, as Officer O'Leary favored him with a blank, unresponsive stare and declined to shake his hand. "Perhaps, you would like my autograph?" he offered openhandedly as the two officers exchanged impatient glances and Shamus O'Leary began to tapping his foot to help ward off his increasing anger at what he deemed to be Pierre's avoidance of the issue at hand. "And I always carry tous les jours a press photo with me. Attendez, s'il vous plaît." added the Frenchman searching his blazer pockets. "Ah! Ici il est. It is a little wrinkled..." he warned unfolding the headshot and smoothing out its creases, "and it is not my best side. Mais, c'est certain that your wife will appreciate-"

"My wife has nothing te do with this! You and yer motley crew o' mismatched buddies are comin' down te the station with us. An' dunna ye be thinkin' about tryin' te resist arrest." advised Officer O'Leary taking in Elroy's oversized form and assessing his physical attributes through narrowed eyelids. "It'll go much easier on ye all if ye come along quietly."

"Officer. I am Inspector James Lahy. We have just escaped from a terrible fire and we have an injured man with us that we must get to a hospital. He may have a concussion."

"Oh, really, now?" said Officer O'Leary viewing the bent-over man who he assumed to be passed out from imbibing too much hard liquor. "I be knowin' o' no such Inspector Lahy on this side o' town." he concluded staring at Jim suspiciously. "What say you, Mahoney?"

"I say, show te us yer badge, Inspector Lahy."

"Ah, yes – of course! Well, you officers don't know me because I've just come into town to help a friend. I can't seem to find it... my badge." Jim said flustered checking his pockets. "It must have fallen out of my pocket during my attempted altercation with Hank – the arsonist who set the fire."

"An' which one o' ye be this, Hank, fellow?" Mahoney queried sarcastically as he shared a smile of skeptical amusement with Officer O'Leary who was rocking impatiently back and forth from the balls of his feet to his heels, marking time, with his thumbs threaded through his belt loops. "Ye know it be a crime te impersonate an officer o' the law." he scolded the inspector as he removed a spiral bound pad from his pocket and flipped it open with one hand so that its cardboard cover flew behind it while he searched for a pencil with the other, delving into another shirt pocket.

"Hey! Ya can't talk ta him that way – he outranks ya. And this, here, is Cyrus Sykes!" Clyde illuminated boastfully, proudly pointing at his boss and then pushing him forward.

"Delusional, O'Leary. I've seen it before with these drunkards. Too much alcohol – goes te their brains, ye know? Sad, it is. Just pitiful."

"I be knowin' what ye mean, Mahoney." he agreed while shaking his head with regret at the grievous circumstance. "OKAY. We're ALL o' us goin' te be takin' a nice trip downtown te the station. Ye can explain in entirety all o' yer fantasies there - LET'S GO!" Officer O'Leary harshly commanded in a louder, strident tone of voice.

"One moment, officers. I really am Cyrus Sykes. And when we do get downtown you both shall be in serious trouble!"

"Not as much trouble as you are in now fer threatening police officers!" Officer O'Leary informed him sternly. "I hope ye be writing all o' this down, Officer Mahoney. Cyrus Sykes.... That be a fresh one! De ye believe me an' me partner te be fools?" he queried stormily. "Claimin' to be an important man like that – ye dunna even look the part. Ye'll be lucky if he dunna sue ye fer maligning his identity. An' ye be doin' yer case no good, either. Yer only digging you and yer cohorts inte deeper trouble."

"Please, officers. I believe I may have a way to clear all of this up." Chris Colden informed the officers calmly. "You see, our injured friend, here, is Detective Rafe Cordell-"

"Ye hear this, now, Shamus Mahoney? We have got ourselves another one. Ye can write this one up, as well."

"He has a badge pinned to the shirt of his uniform. It most likely saved his life by deflecting a bullet that issued forth during his struggle with my brother and so it is a bit bent.... Well, never mind that."

"Yer brother.... Ye mean te tell me that he be the arsonist!?"

"But if you check the badge number it will confirm his identity." Chris quickly continued pretending that he had not heard Officer O'Leary's question.

"He is wearin' a badge, O'Leary." confirmed Officer Mahoney.

"An' how, Shamus Mahoney, do we know that they did not steal that, too?"

CHAPTER 88

"Kitty!" shouted Megan gleefully as Charmer crept into the living room limping and then plopped on the scatter rug in front of the fireplace moaning woefully.

Megan's joy-filled eyes rapidly glazed-over with concern. The warmth of greeting in her eyes evaporated and the happy giggles issuing forth from her mouth ceased as she rushed to Charmer and lay down alongside of her.

"What's wrong, Kitty?" Megan inquired of the feline as she hugged Charmer close to her and started to cry.

"Don't worry, honey. At least she survived the fire okay." Cari said soothingly to the upset child. "I know. I will get her a nice bowl of milk!" she said brightly, meanwhile, holding back her own tears for those surely lost in the fire as she left the room headed for the kitchen.

"Charmer is just constipated." Simon said to them as he entered the room in time to hear Megan's concerned query regarding the feline's welfare. "The front door was open and so we, Charmer and I, we just came in. We did not think you would mind."

"I did not even see the cat leave the barn." Edith noted mournfully. "She got out...but our loved ones...are gone."

"Hrumph. Well, she just showed up at the door of my house after I opened it to leave the cottage." Simon elucidated after clearing his throat uncomfortably.

"Wait a second, this is proof!" Callie stated triumphantly, entering the living area in time to hear Edith's somber observation, after passing Cari in the hallway. "I thought we could all use something to eat so I made some sandwiches. Elvie is bringing in some tea and coffee."

"I doubt that any of us could eat a bite. But, thank you, though, Callie, dear. That was very thoughtful of you and Elvie." Edith responded as Callie set the tray of small, crustless sandwiches on the coffee table.

"I figured as much, so I made these smaller <u>tea</u> sandwiches. All of this sitting vigil and morbidity isn't good for anybody. You have to keep up your strength. You should at least have a bite. Joan wanted to make this big dinner to honor everybody but I told her that no one had the heart to eat anything right now. When the time is appropriate, though, she does want to hold a eulogy dinner for Pierre. I think that he is her hero. She blames Chris Colden for everything, you know. His brother, Hank, may have started the blaze but that makes no difference to her. Despite everything, she lays the whole tragedy at Chris' doorstep. She says that Chris is at the root of all the trouble. Hank never would have come here if it weren't for him — and she's right. He may be a clergyman, now, but I don't think she'll ever forgive him for what he did to Jocelyn."

"Callie? Could you back up?" asked Mary Jo who had erstwhile sat wistfully silent, musing pensively, in one corner of the room regarding her cousin thoughtfully. "I think you may have hit upon something." she explained as Callie looked at her blankly. "You said to Edith that because she had not seen Charmer exit the barn with us that it was proof. Proof of what?" she prodded her impatiently for an answer.

"Oh. Well.... You know how you've always been telling us that Alex and the others are alive? Well, maybe you're right."

Mary Jo looked at Callie incredulously. Her cousin had the uncanny talent of being able to answer a question without really answering it. She shook her head from side to side in frustration, as if she were a canine shaking off excess water after a bath, hoping to nip her rising ill-temper in the bud with the quick repetitive movements. Sometimes Callie's logic could be frustrating to follow – maddeningly so. However, the hope that Alex and her friends might possibly be alive kept her from losing her temper and gave her the mental strength to pursue the matter.

"I found this on the lower shelf of a side table in my house, Mary Jo. It is the portfolio from the root cellar that Alex brought with him when they got out. I thought that you might want it." Simon interrupted them as he noticed from the extremely strained look on her face that Mary Jo was in the process of controlling her temper and needed some time to contain it and adjust.

"Thank you, Simon. I appreciate your kindness. I would like to have this." she replied, taking the structured portfolio from him as her eyes began to well up with tears. "It's like a part of him – you know?" Mary Jo said tearfully, referring to the case. "Alex always used to pick things up as souvenirs. The house back in Charlottesville has a whole shelf crammed with all sorts of useless paraphernalia that Alex has picked up from someplace or another. He always has an excuse for keeping them. He says the things might be useful someday.... Sometimes, you can't even sit on the couch without sitting on one of his discoveries that he hasn't put away. It's like picking up after a child to follow him around and put it back on that shelf.... Can you imagine if we ever were to have children?" she asked with a laugh as she rose from her chair to lean the portfolio against the side of the fireplace.

Simon looked at Mary Jo sadly and did not answer. Her eyes, as she spoke, had sort of a wild look to them as she struggled to keep hope alive and shut out the bleak alternative. Reality was slowly seeping through her wall of defense and Alex's loss was starting to hit her hard. He glanced at Megan following the cat to the litter box. He wondered if she fully understood why the grown-ups were so somber.

"Well…I better go and help Elvie with the tea-" Callie began, backing toward the door to leave the room and respect Mary Jo's sorrow-filled moment of privacy, only to be stayed by her voice.

"Why do you think that Edith not seeing Charmer come out of the burning barn is proof that Alex is alive?" Mary Jo asked her.

"Callie! Forgive my bluntness, but you are being a bit cruel to string Mary Jo along like this. Give her a chance to grieve!"

"That's all right, Simon. I'm fine. But I just have to know. Why, Callie, is it significant that Edith did not see Charmer leave the barn?"

"Well, did you see Charmer come out of the barn – did any of the others? If Charmer never came out of the barn through the door leading to the outside, clearly, there must be a way to exit the barn from the inside of the barn. That's why Edith, you and maybe Jeanette, Trudy, Eleanor and Cari didn't see her escape. And, if she got out, the chances are that the men followed her and they got out, too."

CHAPTER 89

"Ces officers sont tous fous." Pierre whispered to his companions. "They do not recognize who we are. And so, I say, let us – comment dit-on, make a break for it."

"Pierre!!! I am surprised to hear this from you, especially since you've always had such high standards regarding truth and justice, more than from any one of us here. You are talking about breaking the law!" Randmore berated him.

"Technically, we would not be breaking the law à cause we have committed no offense. Mais, sérieusement, je fais la plaisanterie. I did not really mean this, truly. My fans would surely hear of it and I would be disgraced! Ostracized – banned from polite société. They would be shocked if they were to learn that Pierre Dûçot was an escaped jailbird!"

"'Tis a shame ye didna mean it because I was under the misinterpretation that ye be growin' some backbone! I was actually beginnin' te develop a bit o' respect fer ye. Truthfully, it was almost scarin' me half te death!" Matthew said combatively. "An', it be your fault we be in this muddled mess te start with!"

"I was merely retrieving my legitimate personal belongings. Actually, if the press, peut-être accidentally, were to get wind of this faux imprisonment.... Then, the public would see that Pierre Dûçot is being unjustly accused. They, sans aucun doute, would then rally around their hero."

"So, ye've now decided te play the martyr in all o' this hullabaloo te gain sympathy – what a surprise."

"I am just tired of these jailhouses – I wish to see Edi! Aussi, j'ai très faim." whined Pierre rubbing his empty stomach which had just emitted a growl of hunger.

"Bah! Yer always lookin' fer te have food in yer belly even at the most inopportune moment. Canna ye not be thinkin' about anything else?" Matthew asked rhetorically while rubbing his own empty belly in irritation and realizing that, indeed, he was hungry, too.

"I confess that I'm glad you were kidding about making a break for it because I would have had an obligation to inform the officials." Inspector Jim Lahy informed Pierre.

"The officials...! De ye realize what yer saying man? These officers have turned their bloody <u>backs</u> on ye!" Matthew asserted emphatically.

"And, they called Pierre Dûçot a thief and a liar! Pierre Dûçot never tells des mensonges." Pierre said indignantly gathering himself up haughtily to stand at his full stature. "He...called us all liars." he amended when Matthew turned to fix him with a piercing stare and placed his hands on his hips with his arms akimbo.

"Stop fighting guys! We're upset, too." said Alex speaking on behalf of the others as well as for himself. "At least they took Rafe Cordell to the hospital and got Pierre's hands treated for burns and bandaged up in the Emergency Room while we were there. And I hurt my foot during the rockslide in the storm shelter. And, poor Charmer.... I was carrying her over the debris and I ended up dropping her. I don't know where she disappeared to after that. Luckily, the exit to the outside didn't get blocked off when the rocks tumbled down. Boy.... Candlestick Manor sure has a lot of tunnels underneath it and secret passages."

"They say that the old guy who used to own Candlestick Manor was pretty eccentric-" Dwight began to spin the tale only to be interrupted by Pierre's frightened gasp.

"The lost person?" Pierre queried breathlessly.

"Yup. The husband of the disappeared couple I told you about. He had a lot of idiosyncrasies. Well, the old guy was all out there and built all the tunnels...." Dwight said pleased at the rapt attention he and his story were receiving. "He would hire these contractors – all of them from places out of town – and swear them all to secrecy. He commissioned the architects, too, to design the catacombs. The workers were all questioned – but no one was talking...!"

Pierre and Alex both listened avidly: Alex with mouth agape and with Pierre biting the fingernails of his right hand. Officer Mahoney watched the ragtag bunch of misfits in the stark waiting area of the downtown police station suspiciously through narrowed eyelids.

"If yer conferrin' amongst yerselves plannin' yer escapes ye might as well ferget it. We currently be in the process o' securin' yer room an' board. Now, be quiet ye slippery rabble! Officer O'Leary be talking!"

"There be no more room in our jailhouse, officer, so I'd be personally beholden te ye if ye'd take these thievin' vagrants off o' me hands." said Officer O'Leary to the officer on duty who looked up bleary-eyed from the paperwork spread across his desk.

"I have a name, officer, and I'd appreciate it if ye'd be using it." Officer Patrick Jones informed him crisply while pointing to the placard engraved with his name on his desk. "And, can't you see that I am swamped with work, O'Leary? Come back tomorrow!" he retorted dismissively in a cranky voice.

"What are ye sayin' te me ye wet behind the ears whelp? I've got seniority over ye." snapped the red-faced officer who did not relish being dressed down by a newcomer on the police force in front of his partner and his prisoners.

"But you don't have the higher rank. AND, if you're looking for a resort to house your hard-core drunkard criminals..." Officer

Jones asserted authoritatively in an insulted tone of voice as he looked past Officer O'Leary to regard the motley crew behind him, "you can go elsewhere. This is a serious jailhouse for serious criminals and important matters."

"Ye have some nerve speakin' te me like that, officer JUNIOR!" bellowed Officer O'Leary intimidatingly.

"Officers. Please." Matthew Flanderly separated from his fellows to approach the front desk and address the officers who turned to stare at him in surprise. "Now that we are at a bona fide police station I believe that me and my companions are all entitled te one free telephone call each? Me wife, Eleanor, must be out o' her mind worrying on me behalf. Ye see, me friends an' I were in a great fire. But, unbeknownst te her, we managed te escape with our lives. She likely be thinkin' tha' I be dead as a doornail – burned te a mere crisp! Please have pity. Let us contact our loved ones!"

"DR. FLANDERY?!" Officer Jones queried in shocked astonishment while pushing back his chair and standing up.

"Dunna listen te any o' them – they're a tricky bunch o' reprobates!" warned Officer O'Leary, stepping in front of Matthew. "Full o' tall tales, they be, te turn yer head upside down. Ye canna trust a word that be comin' out o' their mouths!"

"Step aside, O'Leary!" snapped Officer Jones as he walked around him.

CHAPTER 90

"An' they be thinkin' we were inebriated criminals. 'Twas Pierre who was the actual culprit. He was takin' off the jewelry o' a vagrant in the alley."

"No! Pierre, how could you?" Edith chided him – although, the fact that she hugged him even closer to her with every spoken word belied her acerbic tone.

Edith was so ecstatic that he was alive. She loved him so much!

"They have all gone out to dinner and left me here tout seul in my agony." Pierre responded, deliberately ignoring her question, as he raised his bandaged hands for effect. "When you are infirm and lying in agony personne ne wants you any more!"

"Poor, Pierre!" said his wife comfortingly.

"SUCH INGRATITUDE. And after I risked my own life to save them."

"Bah! It be Chris who saved all o' our lives with his remembrance o' the storm shelter. An' I be with ye, now, babysittin' ye. An' who knows why I be doin' it either – I could be out with me Ellie celebratin' with the others. An' if ye tell this te anyone I'll deny that I said it, but ye did a brave thing comin' back te rescue us like ye did. It was a plain selfless act an' I must admit that I woulda done the same fer you, too. Yer me friend, Pierre, an' there are just some bonds of brotherhood tha' canna be broken." Matthew stressed emphatically. "-Now, dunna go te gettin' all high an' mighty on me an' lookin' like the cat eatin' the canary!" he added sharply on the heels of his remarks as a pompous look of self-importance overcame Pierre's countenance. "Now, remember, Pierre…. I'll deny it! The same goes fer you, as well, Edith."

"Of <u>course</u>, Matthew. You see, Pierre? You <u>are</u> loved and revered. We <u>all</u> appreciate you for the wonderful human being that you are. And, as a special treat, Joan will be preparing all of your favorite dishes for a banquet that will be held in your honor!"

"And reste calme, médecin. No one could <u>ever</u> mistake you pour mon frère." Pierre baited Matthew playfully.

"Are you inferrin'-" began the intemperate doctor about to erupt in anger.

"Daddy!" Megan cried as she approached Matthew eagerly. "I brought you a welcome-home present!"

"Now, the little lassie didna have te bring her rough an' tough old father a present! Seein' her be all o' the present tha' I need!" Matt responded indulgently to his little girl.

"Personne ne has brought me a present!" Pierre grumbled as Matthew favored him with a quelling glance.

"This isn't a present from <u>me</u>, Daddy. It's from Kitty. She thought you should have it. It's your most favorite thing!" Megan asserted giggling, holding forth her cupped palms expectantly.

"What on Earth be these…?" he wondered aloud.

"Ils ressemblent stones." Pierre said visually examining the contents of Megan's palms after setting aside the stranglehold of Edith's clinging arms and extricating himself from her cloying embrace to rise from the love seat and walk over to the armchair where Megan sat on Matthew's lap.

Matthew picked one of the "stones" for closer inspection. It was a very hard piece of rock which was about the size of a medium-sized pebble. It was encrusted with a dark coating which rubbed off as he manipulated it between his fingers exposing a dull sheen. He detected an odd odor to it and subsequently held the "pebble" to his nose momentarily to determine the origin of the putrid smell emanating from the stone. However, his attempted divination was to no avail. He could not fathom it. As the strange, dark substance was further polished away by the continued manipulation of his fingers, Matthew noted the emerging clarity of the pebble and how it sparkled and shined when he held it up to the light. Megan looked on with a mischievous glow lighting her juvenile countenance and a smile of anticipation.

"This be a diamond!" Matthew roared gleefully on full realization of the epiphany which struck him like a lightning bolt as Megan started to laugh because her father had finally ascertained what she already knew.

Matthew indiscriminately sorted through all the "pebbles" in Megan's palms, rubbing off each of their respective coatings in turn.

"These all be diamonds!" he proclaimed joyously as Matthew took his little girl by the shoulders and looked directly into her face. "Where did these come from, me girl?"

"I told you.... They're from Kitty."

"Well, where did the nice Kitty get them?" he asked trying to sound calm and only mildly interested while he attempted to extract the desired information from his daughter without spooking her into silence.

"I don't know." Megan said simply with a shrug of her small shoulders as Pierre looked on captivated by the hovering aura of drama in the air and even Edith's attention was captured.

"Now, Megan.... Meg. Listen te yer dear old dad very carefully. Are there any more of these?"

"Yes, Daddy – like in the brick."

"Aye." Matthew said with an avaricious glint in his eye – now he was getting somewhere. "So. They be in a brick, then?"

"No...." Megan answered. "Not exactly...."

Matthew wiped a hand across his mouth while Pierre and Edith remained silent, with bated breath, watching the ongoing drama unfold. 'I must be careful not te spook the fragile memory o' a capricious, spirited child. It be likely te flit an' turn te another direction o' thinking.' Matthew thought calculatingly. He decided to rephrase the question and try a more direct approach.

"Where are they?" Matthew asked coaxingly as he attempted to mask his eagerness at obtaining the information with a winning smile which said, I can keep a secret.

"In Kitty's litter box." she confided simply and ingenuously.

Matthew led her to the lavatory immediately where they both washed their hands – and the diamonds, too, of course.

CHAPTER 91

"It's good to have you back, Rafe." Inspector Lahy said boisterously in greeting to the returning detective.

"The weather sure is brisk outside." he responded, hanging his
jacket on the coatrack and then walking over to the window to
straighten out a bent slat of the venetian blind. "It's good to be back.
Everything's right where I left it. My old chair, the refrigerator, the
picture on the wall-"

"Your old desk...." Jim finished his sentence for him, picking up
the pile of overdue paperwork on his desk and dumping it on Rafe's.
"And, your old paperwork!"

"Oh, no! I walked right into that one, didn't I?" Rafe responded
with a chuckle at Jim's clever sally as he sat down and picked up one
of the sheets on top of the stack of forms. "I was wondering who
would be assigned to pick up the slack of my workload while I was
in the hospital and I can see that management chose you."

"It was a good thing that Officer Jones recognized Matthew
Flanderly as his old doctor in Charlottesville and let us go. If he had
not vouched for us I have got a feeling that officers O'Leary and
Mahoney would have kept us in the clink for as long as possible re-
gardless of whether or not they found us to be innocent!" Jim Lahy
stated with a chuckle.

"They sure were characters, those two. That O'Leary, especially, should've been a drill sergeant. I was wondering, at one point,
when he was going to ask you guys to get down and give him twenty
push-ups! By the by, speaking of the hospital, when I was being

discharged I met Cyrus Sykes at the front entrance of the hospital when I was leaving. The nurse was wheeling me out in a wheelchair and he was coming in. He told me that his father had come out of his coma and he had come to take him home. Now, I already knew that he had woken up but I did not realize that the doctors would release Roland from their care so soon. In fact, I had gone to Roland Sykes' room when he'd only just regained consciousness a few days ago. He was still a bit groggy but he remembers everything as clear as a bell as if it were yesterday. In fact, he thought it <u>was</u> yesterday. He confirmed Brandon and Jeanette's version of events that Hank had been present even before they had entered the barn. Hank was trying to convince him to talk Chris out of his intentions to join the clergy. They got into an argument when he refused and tried to convince Hank that Chris was following his destiny and he would not sway him from following his dream. That's when Hank went berserk and tried to throttle him. Enter Brandon and his wife witnessing the heinous act and so he disengaged himself from Roland and flew the coop! Or, so Roland thought. Hank saw Clyde approaching the barn through the side window on the way out and saw the perfect opportunity to take his revenge on Roland for destroying Chris' life and frame someone else for the murder at the same time. So, instead of leaving the barn, he climbed up the stairs to the hayloft and shot Roland from above knowing Clyde would hear the report of the gun. Then, during the confusion while Brandon was giving Roland cardiopulmonary resuscitation he just dropped the gun so that it fell nearby. That way Clyde would see Brandon and Jeanette next to his dead boss with the murder weapon right there by his side. Luckily, Clyde had the forethought to bag the firearm and put it in a safe place. I was just over there at Candlestick Manor. He was happy to surrender the pistol to me. The fingerprints on it are being checked as we speak and how much do you want to bet that they will match up with Hank Colden's?" Rafe challenged him.

"That is not a fair bet and you know it. The prints are not going to belong to Santa Claus! Oh, by the way. Were you invited to the party at LaurelsHeath?" asked Jim conversationally.

"I was. Are you going?" asked Rafe.

"Sure, I'm going. It'll be nice to talk with the others of the fire and compare notes. We sort of bonded in the tragedy, you know?"

"I met Joan Collins on the way over here. She was leaving town. She just got here and now she's going. When I asked her about it she said that she refused to stay in the same house as Chris Colden even if it were just for that one night of the upcoming party and so she was going home. She seemed scared to death of him. She told me that if I had been there and seen what he had done to her daughter, Jocelyn, then I would understand why she wouldn't be under the same roof as him, let alone in the same room! It's too bad. Chris Colden has just turned his life around and she won't give him a chance." Rafe said sadly.

"Chris saved us all so you would think that she would give him the benefit of the doubt. But, you know, it's a difficult situation to be in. You want to be all forgiving and flexible, but then, you just don't know. I gave Hank Colden a pass after Chris' prosecution because I figured that it was unfair that he was looked at poorly because of what his brother, Chris, had done. Since then," Jim continued, "I have thrice regretted that decision. I have regretted it twice in the past and this third time I almost paid for being forgiving with my life in the fire. I am sure that Joan is just doing what she has to to protect herself in, what to her is, an iffy situation. You do know that Hank Colden has attacked her twice in the past – don't you?" Jim inquired.

"Pardonnez-moi, officers."

Rafe and Jim turned to see an elegantly appointed man before them. His beringed fingers grasped a jewel encrusted walking stick. His gold brocade suit with its scarlet waistcoat and equally crimson necktie commanded their attention.

"Forgive my appearance. I am wearing my traveling clothes." explained the impressive stranger in the impeccably cut three-piece suit apologetically, noticing their obvious stares. "I am afraid they are a bit wrinkled – non? I apologize for this...disarray. Ces tailors – vous savez? You know? They can fit the vêtements to your form yet avec tous these modern conveniences they cannot keep a suit from wrinkling! And they call this progress!"

"I know you." said Jim. "You're Jan LaFitte!"

CHAPTER 92

"We were never formally introduced. But when he said that he was looking for Trudy LaFitte I remembered his regal form of dress and I knew it had to be Jan LaFitte!" Jim remarked eagerly.

"Ah.... Merci mille fois! I try toujours to make a statement avec my clothing." Jan responded graciously.

"We are all just happy to see you again, Jan." Cari told him handing him a glass of lemonade. "To what do we owe the pleasure of your visit?"

"Ah! Well. I came by to see my beautiful sister, Trudy, and handsome nephew, LeRoi – I named him, vous savez." he responded. "However, I could not find them at the Manor. This polite young man, about Alex's age, told me that Trudy had re-married and lived in a small cottage to the east. You can imagine I was curious about this new romance. Trudy usually tells her big brother everything. I was only glad that she had left that patriarchal, strict, Roland Sykes. He was NOT a bon choix for her. However, now that she is aligned with your uncle.... Alors, maintenant je respire!"

"When he could not find Simon at the cottage Jan came by the police station to inquire of his and Trudy's whereabouts. When I figured out who he was I immediately thought of you and your family, Cari. And now...here we are." said Jim expressively holding his palms upward to indicate his surroundings matter-of-factly.

"All I can say to you is that this pleasant surprise is the perfect end to a perfect day. Pierre and the others are home safe and sound after surviving that simply awful fire and now you are with us to share in our joy. And-" Edith continued expressively, joining in the conversation before Jan interrupted her.

"Please, Edith. Excusez-moi for interrupting a lady. But, what is this about the fire?" Jan asked as Pierre's mouth fell agape – Jan, somehow, always seemed to know everything!

"I thought that you knew everything, Jan." said Trudy teasingly.

"I saw Pierre leading people out of a fire. Are you telling me that he did not complete the task? L'Oile, I am surprised at you!" Jan scolded Pierre as he closed his mouth and hung his head in shame at his failure.

"Hank was the one who started the fire in the first place and Charmer sat on top of a storm shelter hatch, letting us know where it was, through which the rest of us all escaped. But, Pierre came back to save us. He couldn't help it that we were all in the storm shelter by then and he couldn't find us." explained Alex, introducing these telling facts into the conversation.

"Ah. Forgive my misinterpretation of the circonstances, Pierre. So, you apprehended this, Hank?" he asked the perspiring Frenchman who began to sit up straighter after Alex came to his defense and Jan offered his apology.

Pierre pulled at his collar to loosen it – it was beginning to constrict his breathing! He did not wish Jan to believe that he was less than competent and could not handle himself in the "sticky" situations. Jan's favorable opinion was very important to him. Pierre had just been about to relax when Jan asked about his capture of Hank. His mind now raced as he considered and rejected appropriate and plausible responses. Or, more to the point, excuses – because that is what they all sounded like to him! He was saved from embarrassment once more as Alex again spoke up in his defense.

"The firemen released Hank before Pierre had led us all out of the fire. They basically foiled any chance of apprehension." Alex explained. "Even the two policemen with us were unable to catch him. Pierre was so busy ensuring that the ladies got out safely and rushing back to save <u>our</u> lives he had no opportunity to catch Hank because then we were all trapped in the barn, Pierre included. Pierre suffered severe injury and serious burns trying to save everybody. The doctors said he could have permanent scars for life!"

"C'est très grave.... Are you all right, Pierre? Tu es en bonne santé?"

"I have...been better." Pierre said wearily, groaning for effect and holding up his bandaged hands for Jan to see. "Mais, anyone would have done what I did. Any gentilhomme, that is."

"Oui. You are correct, Pierre. The safety of the women, especially, is paramount. My cat.... He is in good health, aussi?" Jan quizzed Pierre.

"He escaped with us through the storm shelter in the barn."

"Alex. It appears that my network has some holes in it. The fire.... This, Hank.... The re-marriage of my sister.... Brandon, Jeanette.... This shooting of Roland Sykes you have just informed me of.... These are, how you say, just the very tips of the iceberg. I should know these things. My fabric of intelligence is falling apart! As I have heard – from the mouth of a little bird – it was you, Alex, who solved the mystery of the bricks with the diamonds inside and, aussi, divined the shooter of Roland Sykes. Alex, I need you as, how you say, my right arm. May I prevail upon you to ask you once more? Is there some way you could change your mind and join my network? I need the savvy of young men like yourself or else all I have worked for will be lost!" Jan pleaded.

"Mary Jo and I...." Alex glanced at his wife who looked at him with her eyeballs shifting back and forth in a negative fashion and then continued speaking. "I can't. I want to – but Mary Jo needs me at home. We want to start a family soon and our baby will need both of his or her parents. I simply can't go traveling around the world.

I just will not be able to devote the time and effort I would need to give the job the attention it deserves." he said apologetically.

"I am very sorry to hear this, for me, yet I am very happy for your family life. I reluctantly accept your decision. But, family comes first!" acceded Jan graciously in defeat.

"I am available for votre service, Jan!" Pierre volunteered eagerly for, what was to him, the coveted dream job.

"L'Oile, merci for your offer mais this inconvenience to you and your wife is not necessary. Ah! And who owns this impressive briefcase?" Jan inquired.

CHAPTER 93

Jan walked over to the fireplace in the living room to regard a structured portfolio which was propped up against one of its decorative inlaid borders. He picked up the briefcase and held it against his pant leg, noting how the contrasting colors complemented one another. Then, twirling the case around to face him frontally, he held it up to view the flap overlaying the front of it. The flap was secured to the case at the lower edge by a square metal latch, with a keyhole, holding it closed.

"It is locked!" Jan said in frustration to the occupants of the room as his attempt to release the latch and open the case failed. "And, here. The embossed initials, R.S., in the lower right-hand corner." he remarked, pointing to the faded gold-lettering.

"Roland Sykes." said Randmore hazarding a logical guess for what the letters might stand for. "That's the briefcase from the root cellar that Alex found." he added as well as he entered the living room from the doorway where he had been erstwhile standing to join them.

"Well, I wouldn't have even found it without Charmer's key." Alex commented humbly believing in giving credit where credit was due.

"So, he found it!" Jan said pointedly.

"Who found it?" Alex asked inquisitively.

"I taught my cat well. He knows how to navigate the catacombs and all of their secrets! Mais, bien sûr, I left clues…. Do you mind if I open this luggage?" Jan inquired politely. "I apologize that I did not ask before, but, I must confess that my curiosity overcame the better of me." he revealed sheepishly to Alex as he stared at the case. "May I?" he asked him tentatively.

"Sure you can open it. I was going to open it a long time ago but then all of these stories with the diamonds, Roland and Hank, happened."

"Ah...! LeRoi's, how you say, trust fund. The diamonds shall keep him living in comfort for many years — if he is careful and budgets it wisely! The blocks were a bonne hiding place — eh? And, I protected them from theft with my secret repelling agent!"

"The gold dust on the bricks!" deduced Alex.

"Oui. Before you can fly the chicken coop with them.... Well, just let us say that you will not get very far! Mais, I never anticipated LeRoi would play with them as a child.... But, it is a harmless re-pellent and its numbing effects quickly wear off." Jan expounded as he again pressed the release tabs on either side of the latch inward and yanking at it, pulling back on the latch extra hard this time, was met with the same resistance as when he had tried to detach it from the body of the case before. "It still will not open. It is stuck — locked! S'il te plaît, Alex. Où est la clef?"

"I don't have a key." Alex said crestfallen. "Golly. Now, we'll never know what is in that case."

"Do not despair, Alex.... Peut-être we can pick the lock." Pierre suggested. "Or, Alex can open it with the clef il est portant around his neck." he jeered sarcastically and laughed disparagingly.

"L'Oile, you are a genius. Alex. You told me, when we last met, that you retained the key from the tackle box that was given to Matthew Alexander for his birthday. May I have it, s'il te plaît?" Jan requested while Alex was already in the process of taking off the neck chain from which the key hung from around his neck.

"I knew that I had stashed my multipurpose key somewhere — but I could not remember where! When you become old the mind forgets the little things — tu sais? This key," Jan proudly claimed, "will open any and all locks!"

Jan smiled as Alex handed him the key and he inserted it into the lock. His smile faded, however, when he turned the key in the lock and nothing happened.

"This is impossible. It will not open!" Jan said mystified.

"Wait a second! Alex. Remember when we first met Simon?" asked Mary Jo as she snapped her fingers with the recollection.

"Aw, Mary Jo! What does that have to do with anything?" her husband pouted in frustration at what he believed was his wife's unwanted distracting interference wasting his and everyone else's time.

"He was looking for something...?" she persevered with her train of thought only to have Alex look at her blankly and impatiently. "Something that belonged to his son, Elroy...?" she pursued in prodding his memory, waiting for a glimmer of recognition.

"THE KEY!" Alex finally exclaimed as her prompts resonated with him and her meaning became crystal clear.

"The half key. The other half of the key that fits yours. Put them together, Jan, and they will open the portfolio."

"Mary Jo, you are brilliant. Why are not my operatives as sharp as you two?" Jan asked rhetorically as he took possession of the half-key his nephew, Elroy, had removed from his pocket, fit it together with Alex's half-key and inserted them both into the portfolio's lock.

On turning the key the lock opened with a clicking sound. Jan then opened the structured briefcase and delved a hand inside of it to remove a sheaf of papers.

"What is this?" Jan asked of no one in particular as he shuffled through five or six pages of what appeared to be blueprints of mazes and specific points of entry by which to gain access to them.

"What does that say?" Alex asked Jan, coming to look over his shoulder and noticing a single sheet of paper clinging to the inner wall of the portfolio that had obviously been left behind when he had removed the blueprints.

Jan placed the blueprints on the coffee table and pulled out the single sheet from the portfolio and scanned the document.

"This is a title deed to Candlestick Manor. It is in Roland Sykes' name. But it is signed over to the ownership of LeRoi and Cyrus Sykes. Who is this, Cyrus Sykes?"

"That is what I was about to tell you before you interrupted me, Jan. But, now I believe it is only proper that it come from Trudy, herself." Edith informed him mysteriously as, perplexed and concerned, Jan looked to Trudy for an explanation.

"Jan. I should have told you this years ago but, I was afraid of how you would react." began Trudy.

On hearing her ominous preamble Jan's expression became grave. On viewing her brother's taut facial muscles Trudy paused for a moment before speaking further and lowered her eyes. She struggled in her mind with the most appropriate way in which to reveal the long kept secret to her brother. It was clear to her that he had become deeply worried after her opening statement and she did not wish to inflame him further.

"You see, Jan...." Trudy said carefully. "I know that you never cared for Roland-"

"ROLAND SYKES.... I knew it! The scoundrel. What has he done to you?!!" Jan bellowed in anger as, taken aback by his explosive reaction, Trudy was shocked into silence.

In fact, all of the occupants in the room were rendered speechless. They had never seen Jan LaFitte so angry. A lion of the forest he had become, so protective of his sister, was he. Finally, Randmore spoke up succinctly breaking through the hard-core tension in the room.

"At Candlestick Manor you met what Roland did to her."

CHAPTER 94

The large living room which Callie had decorated in hues of bronze and tints of brown rang throughout with the melodies of classical compositions played by a symphony orchestra. Festooned with hothouse flowers of pink, magenta and yellow the room was the polar opposite of the dank and gloomy catacombs. A bar serving punch and cold drinks was set up at one side of the room and a banquet table of chafing dishes containing succulent meats, fricassees, vegetables and hors d'oeuvres graced the opposite wall. The survivors of the fire — including Chris Colden, the rescue team of the Laureltown Fire Department, Roland and even Officers O'Leary and Mahoney were there with their dates. Sadly, Joan Collins was not in attendance. She could not bear to be under the same roof as the reformed, Chris Colden. She still could not forgive him for what he had done to her favorite daughter or forget what he had done, either. Ah…well. Life continued and as couples danced, gliding across the floor in synchronized rhythm with the music and clusters of guests conversed with one another, Pierre spiked the punch.

"Pierre!" cried Edith. "What are you thinking of?!" she asked pulling the magnum of French champagne which he was emptying into the punch bowl from him.

"Je pense that I will make this party more lively. What is a celebration without excellent French champagne to begin with? And, adding it to the fruit drink is just spreading the festivities around — what can it hurt?"

"You have forgotten, my love, that some of the guests have brought their children with them. And, in addition, the firefighters have work tomorrow! They cannot fight fires while inebriated." she gently reminded him.

"Oui. They would misdirect their hoses. L'eau spraying every lieu." he commented with a foolish grin, already slightly tipsy himself.

"I can see that you have had too much to drink already. And you know that the police officers here should not be drinking alcohol, either."

"Alors, then they should not have come."

"Stop it, now! And, no more champagne for you!" Edith said commandingly, pulling the champagne flute that he was holding from his grasp. "Now, there is Roland Sykes speaking with Trudy, Jan and a few others. Let us go over and pay our respects!"

"I was always looking to protect my boys – and I am still. That is why I put the deed and blueprints in the safest place that I knew of – the storm shelter. I planned to tell them where the documents were but I never got around to it. I guess I never thought I'd be incapacitated so soon. I suppose that I thought I was indestructible."

"You always had the high opinion of yourself, Roland Sykes. Fortunately, my cat was with you and saw where you put them!" Jan said derisively sniffing in disdain at Roland's lack of forethought.

"But, he didn't see where I hid the key. And it is still in my desk drawer at the house. So how did he open the hidden wall safe?" Roland asked him challengingly with equal hauteur as he looked Jan squarely in the face.

"C'est simple – bohemian – I always believe in backup-"

"I do, too!" Pierre interjected ingratiatingly as Jan raised his eyebrows in surprise.

The eyes of the group turned toward the newcomers to recognize Pierre and Edith joining their circle. Jan frowned disapprovingly upon Pierre for interrupting him and then continued.

"As I was saying, I believe in, how you say, backup. I had LeLoup attach one of my all-purpose keys to Charmer's neck collar and put instructions to find the wall safe and to exit the root cellar in a place easily recognizable to Charmer-"

"The tuna fish can!" Alex deduced interrupting Jan in his excitement at being able to connect the dots.

"But, you were <u>not</u> supposed to <u>eat</u> the contents. You were only to discover the directions!" Jan stated satirically as he regarded the plate piled high with assorted hors d'oeuvres in Pierre's hand.

Standing on the outer fringe of this group discussion Rand smiled tolerantly while Cari and Mary Jo smirked slightly at Jan's remark. They all knew of Pierre's penchant for all things edible.

"I provided the can opener." Pierre added meekly perceiving the mildly sardonic looks on the visages of his friends.

"What's wrong with Kitty?!" asked an infantile voice plaintively as Megan and her parents entered the living room and made their way through the throng of dancers on the floor to join them. "Kitty isn't feeling well!" Megan whined a second time as she hugged the furry, white Charmer in her arms.

"It is probably from eating this substandard food! Joan did not prepare it and it is giving me a stomachache!" Pierre complained after swallowing a chicken croquette sans souci.

"Kitty doesn't eat people food." Megan said doubtfully.

"Do not correct your elders, Megan." Pierre reprimanded her.

"It likely be from ingesting all o' those diamonds." Matthew whispered exasperatedly in a low voice, lest he be heard by those out of the informational loop, to the others in the know.

"Wasn't Charmer such a smart kitty?" Alex asked rhetorically scratching the feline under the chin. "When she saw Matt had forgotten about the sack of diamonds, which he'd harvested from the bricks, and left it behind she gobbled up as many of the diamonds as she could that had fallen out of the sack onto the floor of the tunnel before they could get buried under the falling debris! That was a goo…ood kitty!"

"Little, Megan. Do not worry about Charmer. He is alright. He is just nervous — as all the expectant fathers are." Jan said to a confused Megan who looked from him to Charmer and then back again. "Maintenant, be a bonne jeune fille and bring to Uncle Jan some of those sweet, sweet cookies from the table across the dance floor, s'il te plaît?"

After Alex took Charmer from Megan's arms and she disappeared among the guests Jan turned to Matthew almost sputtering in his anger.

"I did not wish to lose my…COOL, as you say, and uncloak your act of perfidy and treacherous disloyalty in front of your bébé jeune fille. But, you are a thief! You dare to face me after you have just admitted to stealing my nephew's trust fund?!!!"

"Jan. S'il te plaît, forgive me, mais the police officers are près d'ici! They are très hot-tempered. Who knows how they will react at the very <u>sniff</u> of a crime!" said Pierre rushing to calm Jan down and contain the situation.

"Pierre definitely be correct, Jan. An' how be a person te know the diamonds belonged te yer nephew?" Matt said defensively trying to justify his actions.

"<u>Did</u> you or <u>did</u> you not see LeRoi's name on each gold block. And, did you or did you not have to gain access to the inside of each gold-dusted chunk with a key around Charmer's necklace which specifically denotes LeRoi as its owner?"

"Everyone be callin' yer nephew by the moniker of Elroy. It be no wonder I be a bit confused."

"C'est vrai, Jan. Aussi, the people who know Matthew well all know that he is un peu cuckoo." agreed Pierre backing up his friend and confirming his questionable state of mind.

"Excuse me. Jan?" Alex broached timidly. "I had found the first brick and I didn't know it belonged to Elroy. And, if Matt hadn't rescued at least some of the diamonds, they would all be buried back there in the collapsed catacombs."

"Oui.... Alex, tu as raison. You are correct. Always sensible, this one is." Jan declared clapping Alex soundly on the shoulder in approval. "Alright." he finally determined. "Si you return to me the diamonds you pilfered from LeRoi's trust fund to me all will be forgiven and forgotten, Matt. I will expect all of these diamonds at my hotel room tomorrow. I HAVE SPOKEN." Jan said regally fixing Matthew with a decisive stare which would brook no argument.

"Jan?"

"Yes, Alex?"

"Why do you keep referring to Charmer as "HE". And why did you call her an expectant father?" Alex asked Jan ponderously.

"You puzzle me, Alex. You do know about Jacklina and Charmer, don't you? Ah! The children have arrived." he said as Alex looked in bewilderment from Jan to follow the eyes of the rest to see Cyrus coming toward him with a basket emitting a cacophony of mewling sounds.

"Little kittens!" Megan squealed joyfully as the returning child handed the plate of cookies she had garnered to Uncle Jan before running to help Rand take the basket of newborn kittens and their mother from Cyrus.

"Cari? May I speak to you in private for a moment?" Cyrus asked confidentially leading her from the noisy living room as she looked backward at the room that she was loathe to leave while the band played on.

CHAPTER 95

"Just a little further down the hall...." Cyrus urged Cari as he led her by the elbow from the guests in the main living area to the empty sitting room opening off of the hall.

"Of course, Cyrus. But you sound so serious and this is supposed to be a celebration – not a time to mope."

"Well, it is not that.... It is just that there is something important that I wish to say to you and I hope that it will be equally as important to you, too. Please..." Cyrus pleaded as he moved to a love seat and patted its tufted back, "sit down."

After Cari complied with Cyrus's request and arranged the long, pleated, billowy skirt of her party dress accordingly she was surprised to find that he had sat down quite closely next to her.

"Goodness!" she exclaimed on noting his close proximity. "What you have to impart to me must certainly be of some gravity that you are being so formal and mysterious about it." she observed nervously as she moved away from him slightly, sliding along the seat of the small settee as far as she could without falling off of it.

"Cari – dear, Cari." he emphasized her name expressively deciding to be blunt and to take the bull by the horns, so to speak, before he lost his nerve. "The experience in the fire was an enlightening one for me. It showed me how fleeting life is by demonstrating how quickly it might be taken away from you. I do not want that to happen to...us."

"US?" Cari repeated the word with alarm as her heart began to pound slightly harder in her chest and she rose to her feet abruptly.

"Cyrus, what are you trying to say?"

"Surely, you know how I feel about you, Cari. I want to know if you feel the same way, too." Cyrus said fervently rising to his feet, as well, and regarding her hopefully.

"You have put me in a difficult situation, Cyrus." Cari said carefully. "You <u>know</u> that I do like you but I am a happily married woman-"

Engrossed with her attempt in finding just the right words to let the amorously tortured man down easy Cari was not prepared when Cyrus pulled her into his embrace and bestowed a deep, heartfelt kiss upon her partially parted pink lips, quelling her slow, deliberate speech.

"I love you, Cari. Is that plain enough talk for you? I have never met someone so beautiful and so kind. So loving and compassionate. No one is as wonderful and as sensitive as you are! You accept me with all of my faults and the mistakes that I have made.... Please, Cari, say that you love me, too. I will do anything. Come away with me. I will take you any way I can have you!" he pleaded ardently.

Cari looked away, obviously affected by his impassioned speech and the hot fervor of his kiss. She touched her lips thoughtfully, her mind racing, seeking a response to his transparent expression of selfless ardor but could not formulate a suitable reply.

"Is it the age difference? Don't you feel the chemistry between us?" Cyrus prodded her into speech on noting her hesitancy.

"You should not have done that." she finally said referring to his kiss.

"That is right!!!" said Elroy jealously as he watched their tender tryst from the sitting room entrance. "I saw her first!" he said possessively as he stalked over to them to take Cari into his own arms to plant a territorial kiss of proprietorial ownership upon her already moistened pink lips before she could move away.

"I saw her first!" Cyrus declared asserting his prior claim on her

SHARON ELIZABETH SARKISIAN

acquaintanceship and pulling Cari out of his arms and back into his own.

"She is mine!" Elroy asserted peevishly taking her arm and pulling her toward him while Cyrus held tightly onto Cari's other arm.

"Why, you ungentlemanly cur! I saw her first and she is mine!" Cyrus argued pulling her back from the grasping hands of his brother's appendages which sought to pull her away.

"I repeat, in the event that you are hard of hearing, I saw her first!" Elroy stubbornly maintained while he was in the process of yanking Cari in his direction.

"No, gentlemen." interjected a stern, icy voice, deathly quiet in all of its ferocity. "You are both incorrect. I saw her first and she is all mine!" Randmore stated affirmatively as he entered the sitting room and pulled his wife from the Sykes brothers by her waist, simultaneously tearing both of her arms from their two opposing grips. "And that is the way it is going to stay!"

CHAPTER 96

"Where <u>were</u> you yesterday? One minute you leave the room with Cyrus. The next minute you come back with Rand." Mary Jo inquired curiously.

"You will never believe this in a million years. What happened was that Cyrus took me to one of the side rooms off the hallway and, once there, declared his undying love for me. Rand discovered us there together and gave him a good dressing down for trying to steal his wife. Cyrus actually wanted to run away with me!" Cari told her friend.

"Oh, my gosh! I <u>told</u> you he had fallen hard for you!" said Mary Jo as she leaned toward her confidentially. "What happened? Did they come to blows?"

"No, but Randy told him in no uncertain terms that I was un-available and to stay away from me. You know, Cyrus actually <u>kissed</u> me?"

"NO! Rand must have just exploded! Are you holding out on me? Are you sure he didn't hit him?"

"Yes." answered Cari exasperatedly. "You know that Rand doesn't believe in violence. And, by the by, Elroy was there, too. He and Cyrus were actually fighting over me when Rand came into the room."

"No! Get out of town!" exclaimed Mary Jo in shocked surprise. "Two tall, handsome younger men fighting over you and a husband to boot. What do you <u>do</u> to men?"

"I don't <u>DO</u> anything – you've seen me with them. I am not a flirt! I have done absolutely nothing to lead them on. And…Elroy kissed me, too. However, Randy came in <u>after</u> the two Sykes brothers kissed me so do not tell him about it. After last night's incident I do not want, or need, any more drama or conflict on the subject. Let us just keep the issue closed." Cari confessed guiltily to a Mary Jo who was taken aback by her unexpected revelation and unorthodox request.

'Cari never kept secrets from Randy!' Mary Jo thought aghast.

"I will tell Randy about their kisses myself after we have left for Charlottesville." Cari continued speaking as Mary Jo nodded approvingly in agreement.

"Well, you're too friendly that's all I can say, Cari. Matthew!" Mary Jo called out in salutation as the doctor entered the room. "I am surprised to see you here. I thought you went to investigate that storm cellar further before we left this weekend."

"Me Ellie willna let me." he admitted sheepishly, embarrassed at succumbing to the dictum of his wife. "In any case, if Jan found out I be searchin' about on me own down there fer the diamonds he'd be bound te accuse me o' tryin' te steal Elroy's trust fund an' get me put in the pokey!"

"Isn't that what you'd be doing, though, going after Elroy's trust fund?" Mary Jo inquired earnestly.

"In the first fact o' the matter, it be <u>LeRoi's</u> trust fund." said Matthew assuming an offended tone of voice with a French accent and a slightly hoity-toity air as he mimicked Jan LaFitte.

"If you're trying to imitate Jan LaFitte you're not doing a very good job of it." Dwight said as he entered the room from the kitchen carrying a box with several holes cut out of its sides for ventilation and exited the house to the outside.

"Aussi, Jan LaFitte may hear you. I recommend that we do not anger him further." Pierre advised Matthew fearfully glancing about himself for any tell-tale "whiff" of Jan's presence.

MAISON LEGACY

"Aye. The way tha' the man be carryin' on ye'd think I be a major felon."

"Oui. Ces police officers, s'appelle O'Leary et Mahoney, could have heard him l'autre jour and arrested us again."

"It's fortunate that your friend, Patrick, recognized you or who knows how long they would have kept you in jail." Cari added.

"Aye. Patrick be a fine lad. I treated him when he be a tot. His parents were me first patients. Before they moved away they be some o' me dearest an' closest friends."

"Have you ever asked yourself, médecin, pourquoi qu'ils ne sont pas your patients any longer? Or, peut-être, considered <u>why</u> they moved away?" asked Pierre with a secret smile as he waited in anticipation for one of Matthew's temperamental responses.

Pierre was disappointed, however, as everyone's attention was diverted by the sound of the front door opening to admit visitors from the outside and then closing shut against its frame with an echo. Their eyes were drawn toward Alex entering the living room with Dwight striding past him carrying the same sturdy cardboard box vented with several air holes he had previously passed through the room with. Only this time the grocery box which he had obtained from the kitchen was not empty…Jacklina was inside.

"Alex, when did you go out? I thought you were in the house." Mary Jo exclaimed in surprise as her husband entered the room.

"I was at Candlestick Manor and at Simon's saying good-bye to Elroy and Cyrus. You do know that they are banned from coming here until we leave – or, at least, until <u>Cari</u> leaves!" elucidated Alex with a huge grin at the love quadrangle of Cari, Cyrus, Elroy and Rand.

"Oui. Randy, SOCKED, it to them good. I am proud of him for defending my niece's honor!" Pierre interjected unequivocally.

"So, there <u>was</u> blood! Come on, spill. Somebody, spill it – WHAT HAPPENED!" Mary Jo asked with a great curiosity lighting her eyes. "Tell me the juicy details!"

"Calm yourself, Mary Josephine. I am speaking figuratively seulement. You know that these Cyrus and Elroy made the, comment dit-on, MOVES on my niece." Pierre stated indignantly folding his arms across his chest and frowning disapprovingly.

"Be careful, Pierre. You're talking about Jan LaFitte's nephews!" she warned him precociously as he acknowledged her teasing reprimand with an unconcerned wave of his hand.

"Jan is very strict when it comes to preserving the family values." Pierre responded.

"That's why Cyrus sent me to pick up the last three kittens of the eight that none of the guests wanted from the shed out back. He didn't want to cause trouble in case Randmore was around." Dwight said disappearing through a door on his way to the back of the house where the kittens were being boarded.

"Daddy, can't we keep the kitties?" Megan begged on entering the room in time to hear Dwight.

"I be afraid not, me darlin'. Ye know how yer mum feels about cats!"

"Please…! I'll take care of them all by myself – I will, Daddy! I promise! They're so small. And they're such good girls."

"Ye know yer mum would throw a fit if I were te allow ye te keep even one o' those frisky felines. An' dunna be so quick te judge the kittens as being females. Ye see how Charmer turned out te be o' the manly persuasion."

"But, I want a kitty of my own – I do."

Megan started to cry, kicking the vertical column of mortared mosaic stones supporting the left side of the fireplace's upper shelf several times during her tantrum with her dainty foot.

"Now, yer gonna hurt yer foot by kickin' the rock o' the mantel, little lassie!" cautioned her concerned father.

"No, I'm not. This stone is spongy." she said tearfully. "Oh, the kitties!" she cried in delight.

Megan ran to Dwight as he entered back into the room with the blanket-lined box containing the three stridently mewling kittens.

"The kittens missed their mother, Jacklina. They were hungry!" said Dwight gazing down upon the newborns fondly.

"Oh, let me see." Megan begged Dwight as she pulled at his jacket.

Dwight looked into the pleading eyes of the little girl. It was so obvious that she wanted one of these kittens. He felt bad that her parents forbade her from having one. You had to have a heart of stone.... But, some people just didn't like animals. What could he do? He looked resentfully at Matthew. He couldn't help the resentment that he felt toward Matt and Eleanor Flanderly as he bent down so that Megan could see the newborns.

"They're so cute! You are good babies. Soft babies...." crooned Megan while Cari glanced at Edith and Edith returned her sympathetic regard vice versa while watching the little girl give her heart away to the tiny newly born kittens. "I like him!" Megan said with definite certainty holding up the scrawniest runt of the litter whose eyes were half-closed.

"You know, Pierre, we have a lot of mice at Chesterhollow." Edith said calculatedly.

"We do?" asked Pierre unaware of the method to her madness.

"YES, Pierre, we do! And these kittens might just be the solution to all of our problems. Mr. Sanders, would you consider letting me adopt those kittens?"

Dwight's face cracked into one big smile. He saw where she was going with this! And from the corner of his eye he could see the little girl's crestfallen face look up hopefully.

"And, Megan, you may visit them whenever you want to and have one very special kitten all your own that we will keep at the Chesterhollow house just for you. I can't take care of all three of the babies all by myself, after all. I'll need help feeding them and playing with them. Little kittens can be very frisky, you know. And, I will take that huge grin as a, yes, Mr. Sanders."

"Thank you, Aunt Edith!" squealed the child as she ran to her and threw her arms about her.

"But, that is only if your mother and father approve." Edith qualified sternly. "What do you think, Matthew?" she queried.

"Oh, Daddy, please say, yes. Mum will agree if you do!" Megan pleaded eagerly.

"Hmmm.... I dunna know about this." Matthew said ponderously stroking his chin. "Alright." he determined abruptly. "I agree. But yer goin' te be the one te tell yer mum – not I!"

"Tell her mum, what?" Eleanor asked with trepidation as she entered the room with the escort of Jim Lahy following behind.

"Mother...Aunt Edith gave me a kitten and she is keeping it at her house so it won't be any bother to you and I can visit him anytime." Megan said quickly in one breath, before she lost her nerve, ending with a gulp.

"Really.... And how did ya hoodwink her inte that one, young Miss?" she asked her without waiting for a reply and then she turned on her husband vigorously. "Matthew, ye know how I feel about cats – they are a breedin' ground fer disease!" she abjured fretfully.

"At the ranch we keep all the animals clean and well-groomed as a matter of course." Edith apprised her.

"Well, in that case it be all right, Megan – I'll not be insulting yer Aunt Edith. But, yer paying for the animal's boarding with yer allowance." Eleanor stipulated. "There'll be no freeloading in this family. Now, more te the point, I was at Simon's an' he told me he wouldna come with us when we go back te Charlottesville. He said that Trudy wants te be near her son, Cyrus, te try an' make up for not being a real mother te him all these years and so he'll be stayin' in Laureltown with her. Brandon wishes to stay put, too. He and

Jeanette want to stay here with Roland until he is fully rehabilitated an' up an' around. I tried te convince them te come with us but they would hear none of it. The good news is that the inspector, Jim, came along te say that everything be confirmed. The bullet which was fired inte Roland come from the same pistol Clyde collected at the time of the shooting and had that scurvy knave's, Hank Colden's, fingerprints be all over it." she elaborated.

"This is damning – excuse me, Megan. You should <u>never</u> use <u>that</u> kind of language. And, I apologize to you, Eleanor and Matthew, as well. But, to rephrase my sentence. The fingerprints on the murder weapon are proof positive of Hank's guilt. Otherwise, an attorney for Hank could argue that Roland – the eyewitness – was too foggy to know who shot him. And a barrister might also argue that Brandon and Jeanette were trying to cover their guilt in the crime by blaming someone else. And together with Clyde's testimony of what he saw that night there would be enough doubt to set Hank free, at least on the murder charge. Though we still could have arrested him on the arson charge as well as other criminal charges. Now, we just have to <u>find</u> Hank so that we can charge him officially." Jim expounded in detail.

CHAPTER 97

"Well, that be the last of it." Eleanor said entering the living room after having strapped the final piece of luggage to their conveyance. "Would ye pass me some of that iced tea on the coffee table, Mary Jo?" she asked as she plopped down, exhausted, onto the plumped-up cushions of the couch near the fireplace.

"What's the hold-up?" Mary Jo asked as she picked up the carafe, poured the amber liquid from the pitcher into a tall frosted glass and handed it to her.

"We be waitin' on Jim Lahy. He be returning with us te Charlottesville." explained Eleanor in reply.

"That's okay." piped up a childish voice. "We have to pack the babies, still." said Megan playing with the kittens while her mother, spreading apart the slats of a colorful paper fan, fanned herself and looked askance upon her daughter.

"Dunna remind me." her mother responded negatively.

"Gee, Megan." said Alex intentionally distracting the little girl's attention from her mother's disapproving glance and snidely-laced comment. "Which kitten do you want?" he asked walking to the spot where Dwight had previously set down the box of kittens to sit down on the floor next to her.

"I already told you. I want THIS one." she said firmly as her father approached to view the kitten of her choice.

"He be lookin' te be half-asleep. Wouldna ye rather have a more lively fellow?" asked Matthew gazing over Megan's shoulder at the kittens as his daughter shook her head negatively and lifted her chosen one out of the box to hold him up for all of the room's occupants to view.

With his eyes and small head slumped forward the kitten was truly a mere slip of a thing. His matted, tawny fur laying flat against his head showed him to be a sorry sight, indeed.

"What are you going to name your new kitten, Megan?" inquired Jim entering with Dwight whom Cyrus had sent to drive those departing Laureltown to the train station.

"Pierre." Megan replied promptly and adamantly in a voice that would brook no argument.

Matthew started laughing uncontrollably. Megan's disclosure was, to him, a breath of fresh air after all of the trying events which had taken place over the past few months.

"He surely does resemble our Pierre, o'er here!" Matthew affirmed between guffaws continuing to laugh heartily.

"The child obviously has superior taste! I wonder...who she gets it from?" asked the Frenchman ponderously in a defensive huff as he critically regarded the scrawny, lackadaisical newborn whose head Megan propped-up with one little palm.

"We can all call him Sweet Pete!" offered Dwight, trying to be helpful and stem any hurt feelings Pierre might harbor from being compared to the less than hearty kitten.

"Megan? What did you mean the other day when you said the fireplace was spongy?" Mary Jo asked suddenly, off-topic, with belated curiosity after fixatedly musing upon Megan's prior observation.

"Over here!" Megan pointed skipping to the fireplace and touching the stones in question.

Mary Jo rose from the brown living room chair, walked over to the fireplace and pushed the stones with her hands.

"They seem pretty solid to me." she noted aloud reflectively.

"Non, non, non, Mary Josephine! She kicked the stone here, comme ça." Pierre corrected her, demonstrating by striking his foot hard against the indicated stones in a similar fashion as Megan, almost losing his balance in the process as the stones moved inward.

"Now, ye <u>broke</u> the fireplace! Ho, ho, ho! I canna stand it! This be too precious!" Matthew said chortling uncontrollably as two of the stones recessed deeply, pulling backwards from the others, into the mantel column.

"Oh, la, la! I suppose that I do not know my own strength!" said Pierre momentarily flustered. "Cette construction was obviously <u>American</u> made. The French would not stand for such shoddy construction! <u>French</u> construction stands the test of the temps!"

Both Pierre and Matthew fell silent, their speech and laughter halting simultaneously, as the wall adjacent to the fireplace slid open to reveal a darkened room. Pierre's mouth fell open in astonishment as he looked at Mary Jo in speechless horror. His whole outward manner exuded fatalistic fear and seemed to project the thought of, "Oh, no! Not again!"

"This is the wall Elroy wouldn't let us touch!" Mary Jo said to Pierre. "Remember, Cari?" she asked turning to face her friend. "Remember, we wanted to wallpaper either side of this fireplace but Elroy wouldn't let us do it and he would not say why? I don't think he even remembered why, but it's like he knew this area should not be fooled with!"

"You know?" Dwight said slowly scratching his head as his thoughts reached backwards into the more distant past. "When he was a little, little child he liked to play around here. And, that couple I told you about, who used to own Candlestick Manor? They used to own this place, too – before disappearing. LaurelsHeath and Candlestick Manor used to be known as, what do you call, Sister Houses. Anyway. They would let Elroy play here in the house. They didn't have kids of their own and so they liked to have him around. Elroy was the only one they let in here – besides the contractors and architects, that is. He was probably the only one who wanted to come here, too. But then, he just stopped coming.... Anyway, he must have subconsciously remembered this hidden room without remembering he remembered it! So, he wanted to keep the entrance unhampered. That gold dust on those blocks probably addled his brain so much that it knocked it out of his memory! But the instinct to protect the accessibility to the sliding door in the wall remained."

"Well, I think we should investigate inside." Mary Jo said bravely.

"We are of a like mind, Mary Jo. I woulda liked te investigate the tunnels of the storm shelter if me Ellie hadna talked me out o' it. As she said, I have a family." Matthew elucidated.

"Me and Pierre aren't afraid, either!" boasted Megan cuddling her new pet.

"You stay put right where ye are and dunna move a muscle!" cried Eleanor shrilly in objection to more potential exploration. "Nobody be going anywhere! I dunna need any more excitement in me life!" she declared resolutely.

"Just turn on the light switch in that room and look inside!" Cari exclaimed in exasperation feeling around on the inner wall of the secreted room for a light switch and, on finding one, flicking it on.

"S'il te plaît.... Please!" Pierre frantically asserted, rattled by their discovery of yet another secreted enclosure. "Let us just – as you Americans say – let the snoring dogs lie down! Eleanor is speaking reason. We are about to leave this horrible, horrible place! I am sorry, Elvis-" Pierre started to apologize as she entered the room to wish them a safe trip home.

"It be, Elvie...!" Matthew corrected him.

"Oui, <u>EL-VEE</u> – are you heureux maintenant, médecin? I am sorry, Elvie. I am not unappreciative of, or disrespecting your generous hospitality. Mais cette place has only caused us malchance! I cannot wait to leave from here before un autre désastre strikes the fan...!"

"That is more than okay, Pierre. Believe you me, I wish I could go with you. This house is just plain...EERIE. That's what it is." Elvie said shuddering. "But Calvin is stubborn. He says LaurelsHeath is his legacy and he will not budge an inch. He's determined to stay and make a go of living here. I get the creeps just getting up in the morning and- OH!" she shrieked in fright. "What's that!" she queried after coming forth further into the room to see the gaping opening in the wall. "I think I am gonna faint, again." she disclosed swooning.

"Dunna do that, Elvie! I've packed me medical bag fer the trip!"

"Ye mean I've done the packing." Eleanor reminded him as Matthew looked away embarrassed at saddling her with the work. "And where are Cari and Mary Jo?"

"Ahhh!" screamed Cari and Mary Jo simultaneously from inside the newly discovered room.

Pierre and Edith grabbed onto Megan protectively. Jim Lahy automatically withdrew his weapon from his holster.

"You stay here with your Aunt Edith, Uncle Pierre and Dwight and protect Pierre, Megan. I am going in." Jim said somberly, pointing his sidearm ahead of him toward the entrance to the unexplored room as he marched forward – until Alex grabbed his arm.

"It's my wife in there. I'm coming, too!" asserted Alex firmly.

"I be right behind ye, laddie!" Matt seconded with Eleanor trailing right behind him.

"I sure wish Randy were here." Alex responded as he thought of Cari without her husband in various situations of untold peril.

"GOOD GRAVY!!!" gasped Jim loudly after disappearing through the sliding door ahead of the rest.

CHAPTER 98

"This is utterly surreal!" Cari said flush-faced, circling the table as she viewed the macabre sight from all angles and allowed her racing heartbeats to slow and return to normal rhythm.

"I have ne'er seen anythin' like it!" said Matthew haltingly after recovering from a wordless shock the like of which he had never before experienced. "How can this be?" he queried in amazement of no one in particular.

"Matthew? I be needin' ye te hold onte me about now!" exclaimed Eleanor as she glommed onto her husband.

Mary Jo and Alex stared awestruck along with the others as all of them speculated on the skeletal structures of two people they assumed to be a man and a woman seated across from each other at a square dining table. They both held champagne glasses in their bony hands, the taller skeleton with his arm raised as if in a festive toast. An uncorked bottle of what appeared to be champagne in a silver cooling vessel resting between them in the center of the table lent an added eeriness to the ghoulish scene. Velvet burgundy-colored draperies hung from the walls at various junctures alluding to the presence of windows overlooking the outside world where there were none. Gold wallpaper decorated with sprays of purple and red blossoms papered the walls while a burgundy-upholstered couch and settee, facing a coffee table topped with a white marble slab, resided in one corner of the space. Across from the sitting area was a large king size bed with a coverlet, also of burgundy, upon which rested various plump, fringed pillows of different shapes and sizes.

The ceiling above the sleeping area was painted with blossoms like to those on the wallpaper and was framed on all four sides with cyan scrollwork, delineating the resplendent area from the rest of the plain gold-colored portion of the ceiling.

"WOW.... What a love nest." Alex exclaimed as he, along with the others, drank in the entire sight. "But, why would these people," he asked pointing to the skeletons, "choose to stay in here and just die?"

"Perhaps they had no choice." responded Mary Jo, speaking from the entrance to the room where she was examining a frail, decorative handle and the release device of the sliding door.

"We were looking for a lamp, or something, with which to further illuminate the room and we found this...." stated Cari, manipulating back and forth, opened and closed, a locking mechanism which connected to the back of the fireplace stones Pierre had kicked in.

"It seems that the catch to open and close this sliding door is poorly constructed-"

"Or, as Pierre would say disdainfully: American made – Pah." Cari interrupted her laughing.

"Well, it was not very funny for them, Cari. You see, the sliding door is open now and so the two stones Pierre kicked are jutting out toward us - inside the room. But. When the door to the chamber is closed these two stones of the fireplace mantel slide back to their normal position to lay flush with the other stones in the mantel. Therefore, no one on the outside of the chamber suspects that there is a room on the other side." she illuminated shedding some light on the matter. "I guess they" Mary Jo said indicating the two skeletons somberly, "felt that this kind of secret hideaway was romantic. However," she continued, "something went wrong. This handle – which I shall call Exhibit A – which was used to pull back the spring mechanism which released the lock, allowing the door in the wall to slide open so you could exit this room, broke off when they tried to leave. Thus, the lovers were trapped! For aesthetic purposes it seems that the handle was crafted very delicately. The locksmiths must have used a cheap metal, too, because as you can see from the worn ends on the handle and the worn off ends of the lock release mechanism it was connected to, it broke off. There wasn't even a contingency plan in the eventuality this were to happen. So, with no way to solder or to reconnect the handle to the ends of the main mechanism, the two lovers had no way to pull back the bolt and open the door!" she elaborated at length belaboring the point a bit in her dogged pursuit of the truth and her excited satisfaction at having solved the case. "So, whatever you do DO NOT CLOSE THE DOOR!" she warned them nervously.

"Ye be meanin' te tell me tha' we can get in here but if we close the door we canna get out?" Matthew asked rhetorically.

"Gad! Those poor people! Te die in such a manner. Trapped and all alone.... With no one te miss them or te say a prayer o'er them." Eleanor said courageously looking at the two seated skeletons.

"Aye.... 'Tis a gruesome fate, te be sure." Matthew concurred. "I be glad tha' Matthew Alexander be back home with the babysitter an' Megan be with Edith an' Pierre outside. This be not a sight fer a child te see!"

"Well, at least they left this world with smiles on their faces." Alex commented boldly quipping into the somber atmosphere, approaching the skeletons seated at the table and examining their bony faces. "They're in such good condition. I guess with the door closed there was kind of a vacuum effect which preserved the remains of the poor souls in the exact positions they were in when they died."

"I don't know about that, Alex, but I think that the couple probably realized that there was no way out for them and accepted their fates. They decided to make the best of it and engaged in some revelry. At least they had each other." said Cari.

"Edith wants to know what's taking you people so long in here. Holy Moley!" exclaimed Dwight on passing fully through the chamber door and then taking one step back as if the force of an ill-wind had initiated his backward momentum.

"THE LOST PEOPLE!" Pierre shouted in fright as he, too, entered the room with Edith, Elvie, Megan and Sweet Pete not far behind and looked upon the bizarre scene.

"I am definitely going to faint!" declared Elvie before collapsing, unconscious, into Dwight's arms.

"You're scaring, Sweet Pete!" Megan cried as the kitten jumped from Megan's arms and made a beeline for the exit.

"Wait, Megan. I will stop him." declared Pierre referring to the kitten gone wild who had suddenly developed a mind of his own and, deciding to assert himself, was making a mad dash toward freedom.

Pierre pushed the sliding door closed just in time to prevent Sweet Pete from escaping through it. He then turned to face everyone triumphantly wiping his hands off, one against the other, with a huge smile of satisfaction decorating his visage. He had, en effet, saved the day. But, then, why did the original occupants of the chamber stare at him horrified. And why did Matthew approach him with a look of fury on his face and arms extended as if he wished to throttle him while Cari sought to pull him back? Pierre pondered for a moment upon this puzzling conundrum. Jealousy…? C'est cela! That was it! How seedy. Well. It was just good à savoir who your friends really were!

CHAPTER 99

"What is taking them so long?" Randmore asked Calvin as he came over to him from across the train platform after speaking with the conductor.

"They'll get here on time with the tickets – don't worry! You know that Elvie is over at the house saying her farewells to everybody – don't you? I bet she's talking to Edith and crying and indulging in all kinds of sentimental stuff. WOMEN! And why aren't you just travelling back home the way you came?" inquired Calvin.

"We could. But the roads leading home aren't that well-traveled and so they're kind of bumpy and rocky. We had a pretty uncomfortable ride coming here. I don't want to put the girls through that, again. Especially after all they've been through already. On top of that, it would also be slow going and I have an emergency at the Homestead. In addition, thanks to that avalanche, the main road is blocked off and we would have to take the long route to Charlottesville which would mean even more hours on the road. It is much more efficient and easier for us to return home by train."

"Hey! What are you two doing around here? You better not be going where I <u>think</u> you are going!" Calvin said threateningly as he moved in front of them, followed by Randmore, blocking their path.

"Enough is enough. You two are behaving childishly. We have a right to bid our newly found relatives, good-bye. I met my new sibling on his way to LaurelsHeath, as well, and we realized that we had both come to the same conclusion: we shall see our relatives before they leave. It is clear that great minds think alike. Now, STEP ASIDE, Calvin Maison, if that is your true name, and allow my brother and I to pass." Elroy commanded regally as he stood, bending over, nose to nose and toe to toe with Calvin.

"You have to get through me first and foremost. I will not have you and Cyrus foisting your unwanted attentions on my wife." asserted Randmore.

"If you had not entered when you did who is to say they were not wanted...? However, you may relax on that score. You need not concern yourself regarding our intentions, Randmore. Cari made it quite apparent that her heart and her loyalties, lie with you. Though, do not ask me why this is so because we have so much more to offer her in contrast. You, are not much!" Elroy stated profoundly glaring at Rand and speaking in an insulting tone of voice meant to belittle him.

"Hey! You can't talk to him like that!" Calvin said with bellicose fervor. "You want me to clobber him now, Randy?" he asked while sizing the much taller man up.

"Never mind, Cal. They're turning around and going back to wherever it is that they came from!" he suggested to Elroy and Cyrus strongly although his speech was directed toward Calvin.

"You cannot stop us!" Elroy stated challengingly.

"Mr. McKinley. We are leaving in two hours whether your party is here or not. I spoke to the scheduling department at the office and we cannot hold the train for you any longer than that!" said the conductor of the train interrupting their argumentative conversation, taking Randmore and Calvin unawares and, thus, diverting their attention from Elroy and Cyrus.

"That's not right. They paid for their tickets fair and square!" Calvin argued on Randmore's behalf.

"I am sorry. We cannot wait any longer than that."

"But-" Randmore began to object.

"I apologize profusely, Mr. McKinley, but there are no more, buts, about it. In point of fact I believe that the station master was being overly generous in extending to your party the two additional hours. We always try to be accommodating to the traveler but we have a schedule to keep. Our other passengers are also counting on us to reach their destinations in a timely manner. I know of you and your ranch, Mr. McKinley, and so we have stretched the limits of our time limitations and have extended to you these extra two hours. But, our other passengers are busy people, as well. I can only suggest that you, corral – a little ranching humor, there – your group together and get back here in two hours because after that the train will have, to coin a phrase, left the station." the conductor said and then left to reassume his post inside the train.

"Where did they go?" Rand asked Calvin as he gazed about searchingly for Elroy and Cyrus.

"Why, those low-down, sneaky little so-and-sos! Those malodorous skunks. They skulked away while we were talking!" Calvin answered.

CHAPTER 100

"Hello? Is anybody here?" Cyrus called out through the partial-ly open door and listened to his voice echoing throughout the large entryway.

"They must still be inside packing." urged Elroy, prodding Cyrus to move forward.

Cyrus pushed the ajar door fully open and stepped inside. A loud creaking sound echoed through the main entryway.

"I do not see a soul about." Cyrus noted aloud, puzzled.

"The living room, Cy. Check the LIVING ROOM!" Elroy said persistently pointing toward the spacious room opening off of the hall on the right side of them and across from the sitting room.

"I do not feel right about this, Elroy. Going into someone else's house without having been invited does not sit well with me. I feel like a thief." Cyrus divulged to the man dogging his heels.

"Do not <u>feel</u> that way. The door was open. There is absolutely nothing to feel guilty about!"

"Then, why are you tiptoeing? And <u>why</u> are you whispering?!" he queried stopping abruptly to face an Elroy who barreled into him, unprepared for his unexpected cessation of movement.

"You are being too picky." Elroy retorted striding ahead of him boldly into the living room. "Where is everybody?" he asked taken aback on viewing the plates of half-consumed food and half-filled glasses of drink.

A child's toy lay on the rug next to an open pet carrier. 'A child's toy....' Elroy reflected staring with a frown thoughtfully at the small wind-up toy.

"It looks to me like they were in the midst of eating and then just…disappeared into thin air!" Cyrus observed walking over to the coffee table to pick up the bitten end of a breadstick off of a plate and a cup of coffee to examine them. "OW! This coffee is still hot!" he complained in a sharp voice dropping the cup back onto its saucer with a clatter and watching it accusingly as it rattled back into place. "What's that?" he asked distractedly cocking his head while intermittently blowing on his hot hand to cool the coffee burn.

"I did not hear anything." Elroy responded coming out of his reverie to address the present.

"It must have been Trudy working in the kitchen." he surmised.

"I just left our mother at home with Simon. It could not have been her."

"Maybe, they left already." Cyrus replied sitting on the couch and watching Elroy wipe at some scuff marks on the fireplace mantel.

"These marks…. They were not here before when I assisted Cari and Mary Jo in painting this wall next to the mantel. I…. I remember now. I used to play here as a small boy. I forgot that I would sit right here and play with my little tin soldiers. I would wind them up and they would march into the adjacent room."

"You mean that they would march all of the way into the kitchen?"

"NO! Of course not! That would be ridiculous. Tin soldiers do not cook! They marched into the…next room." he corrected Cyrus, pointing to the fireplace wall with a perplexed look on his face. "There was a room here!!!!" Elroy summarily exclaimed in excitement at his sudden epiphany. "At least, I <u>think</u> that there was a room here…."

"How would you ever know that?"

"I <u>told</u> you. I played here when I was a toddler! I <u>think</u> I used to play here when I was a toddler...."

"Well, make up your mind, Elroy! Did you, or didn't you?"

"What <u>was</u> that noise?"

"I thought we would find you here!" Calvin cried out in anger, charging forward into the room. "You could not miss just one last chance to sniff around his wife! I told you, Randy." he stated single-mindedly in a grim tone of voice as he stared at the two interlopers. "No respect for the sanctity of marriage. You tell them to stay away for five minutes but they just move right on in anyway!" he concluded, sweeping his hands in a wave-like gesture across his body.

"You watch your mouth, Mr. House. We have every right to bid farewell to our relatives!" Elroy retorted.

"That's right. We just discovered who they are and now they are leaving and we may never see them again!" added Cyrus, shoring up his brother's point of view.

"Okay." Calvin said levelly, pacing up to face Cyrus, as if he were seriously considering the weight of Cyrus's excuse for being in the forbidden house off-limits to him and his brother, and gave him a hefty, obviously loud sniff. "Then, what's that chintzy, overpowering cologne you're wearing and how about your fancy schmancy suit?" he asked with ingenuous sarcasm grasping the lapel of his jacket in order to feel the quality of the fabric it was made of and then releasing it contemptuously.

"It appears that they both have gotten haircuts for this "sentimental" occasion, as well." Randmore noted, observing Cyrus's and Elroy's freshly-clipped locks.

"Oh! And my, oh my! The gloss on those shoes!" remarked Calvin shielding his eyes with a hand and glancing away theatrically. "I cannot stand the glare — you two must have just got them polished and shined. You should warn a person. I've got to get out my shades."

"I find your tomfoolery not in the least humorous. It is not a crime to look nice for your relatives!" Elroy replied, fudging the issue, with a look of disdain. "Your juvenile, territorial display is not only beneath you, but it also says much about just WHO is, sniffing, as you yourself put it, around WHOM."

"Stop fencing with us, Elroy! Just tell us where everyone is, including Cari, so we can leave. The train is about to depart the station." Randmore said in concern.

"Well. I do not know, Cy. Should we let them know where we...stashed the others?"

"I don't know...." Cyrus said pretending to consider the idea as he stepped in front of Elroy.

"Quit the games, you big palooka, and tell the man where everyone went to!" Calvin said angrily to Elroy as he stepped around Cyrus to glare at him threateningly.

Cyrus relaxed his stance. He was concerned about the others, as well. His concern overshadowed his animosity.

"To tell you the truth. Elroy and I were wondering the same thing when you and Randmore entered the room." Cyrus confessed. "The door to the house was ajar and when we called out no one answered so we let ourselves in. We looked in this room and saw all the uneaten food.... The hot coffee.... Elroy was just telling me how he remembered another room in here. He used to play in it when he was little."

"What does that have to do with anything?!" Calvin asked belligerently as Charmer trotted swiftly into the room and started to meow incessantly and paw at the wall to the side of the fireplace mantel. "Would you shut that cat up! I can't think!" he yelled stridently.

"Calm down, Cal. Getting upset won't tell us where Elvie is, or, where my wife is. What is that echo?! The cat's voice seems to be repeating on the heels of every one of his mews." Randmore noted.

Calvin cocked his head to one side to listen more closely.

"You are right." he replied. "But...the echo doesn't <u>sound</u> like him. It sounds like a younger cat is answering him back. Like a kitten! There are two kittens sound asleep in this box." Calvin noted.

"A kitten?" queried Randmore rhetorically. "Didn't Jacklina just have kittens...? And they are Charmer's kittens! Charmer <u>knows</u> something! Charmer?" Rand asked him, feeling foolish for addressing a cat. "Is that your kitten?"

No one in the room was more surprised than Randmore when Charmer ceased his mewing and pawing at the wall to turn and render a loud screech. Then, the feline returned to his previous occupation – this time scratching at the wall. Possessed by various stages of surprise none of the men said a word until Calvin finally broke the silence.

"It was almost as if Charmer said, YES. But, that's impossible! He is just a cat!"

"MEE – OW. RR...!" Charmer ceased meowing momentarily to growl stridently in protest.

"These are footprints!" Elroy stated, rising up off of his bended knee from the area of the floor next to the fireplace mantel where he had been examining the scuff marks on the stones. "There are people behind there! That is where they are!" he stated as Cyrus left the room.

"Are you bonkers, or something? Why would they be behind there? And, if they were behind there, why aren't they coming out?" Calvin asked challengingly.

"I <u>KNEW</u> I remembered a room near the fireplace." Elroy said ignoring him. "There are so many tunnels in this area that it makes perfect sense. They must be trapped behind the wall and cannot get out! Charmer must know of this room, as well, and that is the reason he indicates to us the wall!"

"Elroy. You are – excuse me for saying so, but you are probably still mesmerized by the effects of that gold dust. Remember. You were under the influence of those fumes for a long time. We have to put this all in perspective!" Rand said reasonably in a logical manner.

"I got the sledgehammer from the shed out back." Cyrus informed them on reentering the room and hefting the implement above his shoulder. "Stand back." he warned preparing to strike the wall.

"Hey!" Calvin shouted inserting himself between Cyrus and the wall. "We just fixed up this place!"

"Would ye make tha' animal keep quiet so I can hear what be transpiring out there!" Matthew said in frustration. "This could be our one and only chance te get out o' this place."

"Sweet Pete is scared. He wants to go out!" Megan complained between sobs.

"Dunna cry, Megan! Yer father only be a trifle upset!" said Eleanor softly trying to console the child.

"Ye are correct I be upset! If it werena fer that blasted animal and his evil twin o'er there," he answered indicating Pierre with an index finger, "we wouldna be in this mess! We would be nice an' comfortable in our seats on the train – perhaps in the dining car enjoying a bit o' sustenance about now!" he ranted.

"It's too bad these walls are soundproof. The way the Doc is exercising his lungs there is no doubt they would know we were back here." Dwight remarked glumly.

"It is no use. We are doomed!" Matthew lamented plopping down on the couch next to Alex and burying his face in his hands.

"Wait." shouted Mary Jo. "I think the two stones of the locking mechanism are moving!" she said excitedly.

"The sliding door is opening." said Jim.

All eyes turned toward the glaring bright light slowly being revealed as the sliding door in the wall gradually rolled back. And, on uncovering his eyes, Matthew stood up praising the Lord.

"Alleluia. Saints be praised." exclaimed Matt gratefully, raising his shaking palms and staring up above in thanks.

"Elroy!" shouted Cari tearfully as he appeared with an aureole of light behind him. "You saved our lives!!!! You are a hero!"

"My name is, LeRoi, Carina, and you could be my reine." he responded with a crooked smile as she threw herself into his arms, wrapping her arms about his lowered neck.

"Hey! That's my wife!" said Randmore coming up behind him with Calvin and prying her arms from about his neck.

CHAPTER 101

"Aye.... Tha' Elroy be a fine, strapping lad!"

"If you overlook the fact that he overtly flirts with Cari!" Randmore responded uncomfortably.

"Matthew be correct. 'Twere it not for him we would still be trapped in that ghastly place with those dead people!" said Eleanor with a shudder.

"At least now they will get a proper burial in the cemetery." said Cari solemnly.

"Oui. That is where they belong! Si they had not choisi to consort avec Grand-mère in the premier lieu, peut-être they would have found their eternal peace sooner!"

"What a terrible thing to say, Pierre!" Edith scolded him.

"I thought that we had established that there was no link between your deceased grandmother and any current state of events!" Randmore chastised him in exasperation.

"You have gotten very quiet, Matthew." observed Jim as he watched him return the piece of a half-eaten chicken drumstick to his plate and wipe his hands with a cloth napkin.

"I have learned not te argue with the convoluted logic o' an imbecile. I have tried te talk reason te Pierre before — we all have — an' it not be doin' none o' us a bit o' use. Even after Calvin an' Dudley confessed tha' they had configured this Grand-mère character out o' thin air, Pierre still will not see reason. So, if he be willin' te believe in spooks and hobgoblins, I say, let him! I wash me hands o' the whole matter." the doctor concluded raising his water glass so that the waiter in the dining car could refill it with fresh water from his pitcher.

After all, Matthew considered as he sat back and admired the clear liquid and ice flow into his glass with languid satisfaction, after all he had been through he deserved a wee bit o' pampering!

"If you wish to incur the wrath of Grand-mère Dûçot, so be it! Mais. Do not say I did not warn you!" stated Pierre with hauteur.

"Bahhh!" retorted Matthew in response.

"C'mon, guys! Can't we just agree to disagree? We are going home – finally. And no disrespect to your relatives, Mary Jo, or to yours either, Cari, but I never want to visit Laureltown, again. It's just too plain creepy a place!"

"Don't worry, Alex." said Mary Jo as she exchanged a nod of agreement with Cari. "We know how you feel. After all we've been through over there I don't think any of us want to go back there any time soon."

"Even poor Megan is exhausted and children are supposed to have boundless amounts of energy and resilience." Cari added.

"I know! The poor thing was just terrified to be trapped in that gaudily decorated room with those two skeletons." Mary Jo replied.

"I agree, Mary Jo. The way she was holding on so tightly to Sweet Pete for dear life spoke volumes."

"I wonder what led Elroy to the conclusion that we were trapped behind the wall."

"I asked him about that. The FIRST clue was the scuff marks. When he saw the scuff marks Pierre had made on the bricks, you know, the ones that he had made when he was trying to imitate how Megan had kicked them? Well, when he saw the footprints of Pierre's shoes it jogged his memory to recall that as a toddler he would sometimes come to play at LaurelsHeath in that very room. He remembered that at that long ago time another room had existed near the fireplace mantel. SECOND, he thought that he heard things – sounds – from behind the wall so-"

"So, the room wasn't as completely soundproof as we thought it was!" said Mary Jo.

"Right. And, <u>THIRD</u>, Charmer came running in, as if he were on a mission, headed straight for the wall and started pawing at it. Charmer, with his extrasensory cat hearing, must have heard Sweet Pete mewing for help and was trying to scratch through the wall to let him out!"

"Talk about a father's instinct! His intuition must have brought him there. And to think that Matthew, here, was getting peeved at all of Sweet Pete's mewing. So, our bacon was saved and it appears that three times was the Charm-er, eh, Cari?"

"Yes, Mary Jo." Cari responded laughing indulgently. "3X the Charm!"

As the circle of friends and family in the dining car laughed heartily at Cari and Mary Jo's witty repartee, from somewhere within the bowels of the train chugging its way inexorably toward Charlottesville, Sweet Pete was heard to meow vociferously in agreement.

*X*X*X*T H E E N D *X*X*X*

www.ingramcontent.com/pod-product-compliance
Lightning Source LLC
Chambersburg PA
CBHW030746030726
47497CB00001B/159